Praise for Melissa Hill

'Delightfully, deliciously enjoyable'
Patricia Scanlan

'The perfect escapist romance'
That's Life

'All the ingredients for an irresistible tale'
Roisin Meaney

'Its beautiful descriptions of the gorgeous settings make this novel the escapism we all need now'
Woman's Weekly

'Thoroughly enjoyable . . . sparkling with glamour, romance and suspense'
Anna McPartlin

'If you need some escapism, this lovely read . . . is the ideal pick'
Good Housekeeping

'A delicious setting for this perfect holiday read . . . irresistible'
Rachel Hore

'Another great read from the bestselling Irish author'
Hello!

'Plenty of twists and turns'
Sheila O'Flanagan

'I was completely gripped'
Sarah Morgan

'Addictive!'
Grazia

Melissa Hill is a *USA Today*, No. 1 *Irish Times* and international bestselling author living in County Wicklow, Ireland. Her page-turning contemporary novels of family, friendship and romance are published worldwide and translated into twenty-six languages, with many adapted for film and TV.

Follow her on Facebook and Instagram: @melissahillbooks

Also by Melissa Hill and published by HQ:

Keep You Safe
The Summer Villa
Only in New York
A Taste of Paradise

The Apple Cider Orchard

MELISSA HILL

HQ

ONE PLACE. MANY STORIES

HQ
An imprint of HarperCollins*Publishers* Ltd
1 London Bridge Street
London SE1 9GF

www.harpercollins.co.uk

HarperCollins*Publishers*
Macken House, 39/40 Mayor Street Upper
Dublin 1, D01 C9W8, Ireland
This edition 2026

1
First published in Great Britain by HQ,
an imprint of HarperCollins*Publishers* Ltd 2026

A catalogue record for this book is available from the British Library.

ISBN: 9780008831851

Set in Minion Pro by HarperCollins*Publishers* India

Printed and bound in the UK using 100%
Renewable Electricity at CPI Group (UK) Ltd

FSC
www.fsc.org
MIX
Paper | Supporting responsible forestry
FSC® C013604

The Apple Cider Orchard

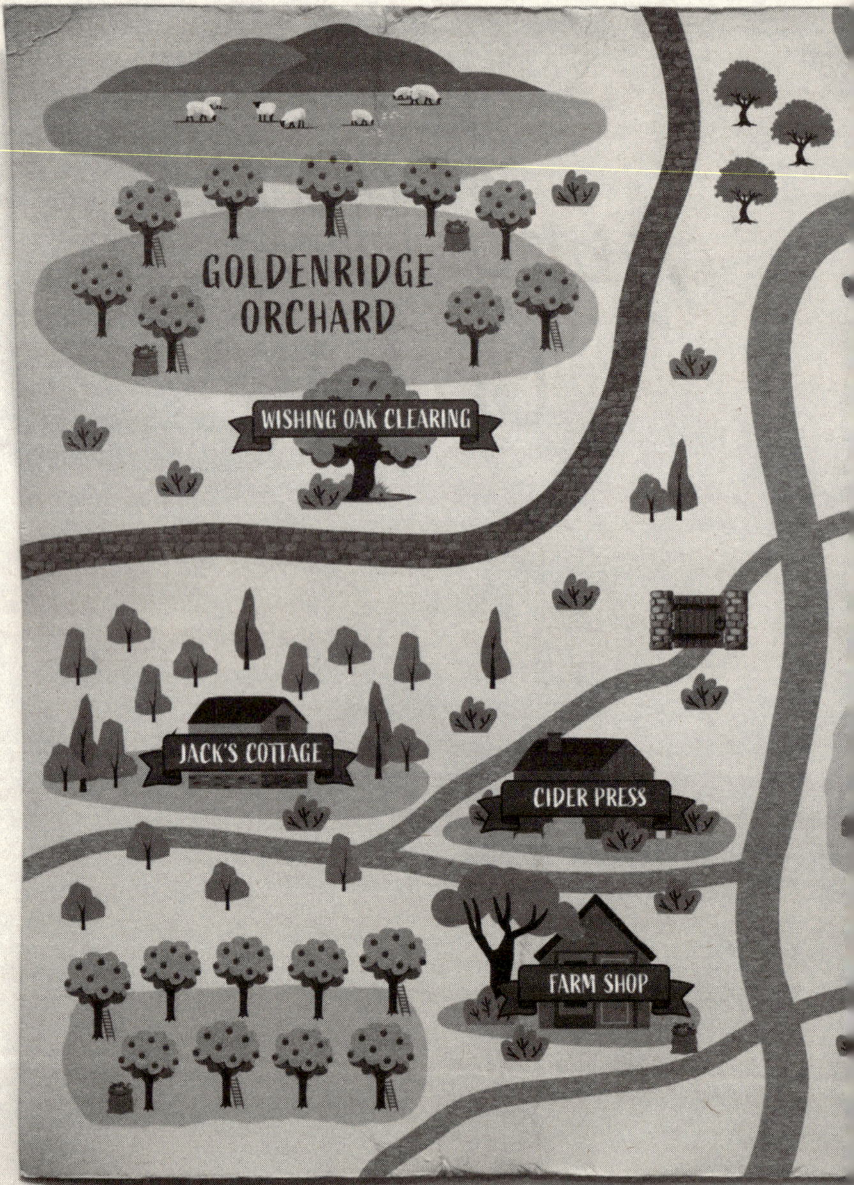
GOLDENRIDGE ORCHARD
WISHING OAK CLEARING
JACK'S COTTAGE
CIDER PRESS
FARM SHOP

LOUGH CORRIN
LAKESHORE WALKING PATH
CHERRY BLOSSOM CAFÉ
WILDFLOWER BOOKS
CARVED OAK BUTCHERS
THE GLEN REMEDY
THE SQUARE
THE ORCHARD PUB
GOLDEN VALLEY VILLAGE
THE GLEN ARMS HOTEL
POST

Chapter 1

Molly Harris hadn't cried at her own grandmother's funeral, but she very nearly did over a broken conference call.

The screen froze just as the client's face sharpened into interest – not exactly enthusiasm, but close enough that she felt the shift like a change in air pressure – until the damn spinning wheel appeared. Buffering. Silence.

'Molly?' Her boss frowned from the far end of the boardroom table.

She didn't look away from her laptop. 'One sec,' she said crisply, fingers already flying, toggling between tabs, rerouting the call through her phone hotspot. Her pulse thudded in her ears, but her voice stayed level.

Calm was her currency.

The Manhattan skyline stretched behind them in plate-glass perfection, the late afternoon sun slanting between steel towers. Forty-two floors up, the city hummed – traffic horns muted, helicopters slicing the air like clockwork – but inside the conference room there was only the low buzz of impatience and the faint, traitorous wheeze of Molly's own breath.

She fixed the situation in less than twenty seconds.

'I'm back,' she purred seamlessly to the client. 'As I was

saying . . . we're not just selling a product. We're selling a feeling. Belonging. Trust.'

Out of the corner of her eye she saw her boss lean back, arms crossed, watching her the way one might observe a high-wire act: impressed but alert to the possibility of a fall.

Molly clicked to the next slide, her reflection briefly ghosting across the glossy screen; dark hair pulled into a ponytail, tailored blazer, lipstick just bold enough to mean business, pale skin that hadn't seen the sun in some time.

She talked them through the campaign with practiced ease: market data, emotional hooks, storytelling arcs. She spoke about warmth and connection as if she hadn't spent the last six nights leaving the office after nine, eating takeaway salads at her desk while the cleaning crew worked around her.

When it was over, there was a beat of silence. Then applause; polite, corporate, but real.

'Well done,' the client said. 'This feels . . . human.'

Molly smiled. She always smiled at that line.

By the time the meeting ended, her adrenaline had nowhere to go. It pooled in her chest, sharp and restless, even as her colleagues filed out with murmured congratulations. Her assistant hovered in the doorway.

'You okay?' Jenna asked, lowering her voice.

'I'm great,' Molly chirped automatically, already packing up her laptop. 'Could you send the revised deck to legal and schedule a follow-up for early next week?'

Jenna hesitated. 'Molly . . . it's five p.m. On Friday.'

She blinked, genuinely surprised. 'Right,' she said after a moment. 'Of course.'

Molly returned to her office; glass walls, minimalist desk, a single framed photo on the credenza behind her. In it, her beloved grandmother, the woman who'd raised her, sat in a messy kitchen, flour on her hands, laughing at something just out of frame.

Her phone buzzed.

Cole.

She ignored it. It buzzed again. Molly sighed and picked up. 'Hey,' she said, already scrolling through emails with her free hand.

'Do you know what day it is?' her brother asked.

'Yes,' she said. 'A disaster, unless I get three more approvals before close of business.'

'It's been a year, Mol.'

Her fingers stilled. She leaned back in her chair, the city sprawling below her like a map she knew by heart.

'I know,' she said quietly.

Though she'd been trying her utmost to forget.

There was a pause on the line – the kind that meant her brother was choosing his next words carefully, which always unnerved her more than his usual bluntness.

'You promised,' he said.

Molly closed her eyes. 'I haven't forgotten,' she assured him.

'Yet you haven't done anything to make it happen.'

'I've been busy.'

'Busy isn't a reason,' Cole said gently. 'It's an excuse.'

She stood abruptly, crossing to the window. The sun was dipping now, gilding the city in gold. It was beautiful. It always was. And yet today, it failed to move her.

'I'll get to it,' Molly said, sharper than she meant to. 'I have a lot on right now.'

'Like what?' her brother asked. 'You barely take weekends off anymore.'

She didn't answer.

When the call ended, the silence pressed in. Molly returned to her desk, reached for her coffee, cold now, but she took a sip anyway. Her hand shook slightly.

Her boss, Bruno, appeared in the doorway not ten minutes later.

'Harris,' he said, tone carefully neutral. 'Walk with me.'

They didn't make it far; just to the quiet seating area by the windows, but she felt the shift immediately. This wasn't praise. This was concern.

'You're one of the best we have, Molly,' he said. 'But you're running on fumes.'

'I'm fine,' she said, a reflex.

'No vacation this year, no time off, nothing.' Bruno shook his head. 'You're exhausted, pushing yourself to oblivion since your grandmother's passing. And if I can see it, so can everyone else.'

She swallowed.

'I'm mandating a sabbatical,' he continued. 'Holiday campaigns are all locked-in, so the pressure's off. A month. Starting now.'

'What?' Her composure cracked. 'I can't—'

'You can,' he said firmly. 'And you will.'

The city blurred beyond the glass. A whole month. No meetings. No seasonal campaigns. No carefully curated urgency.

Just . . . space. Time to think. But worse, to grieve.

When she finally left the office that evening, the lobby lights were dimmed and the security guard nodded sympathetically. Outside, the city breathed; warm pavements and food carts, laughter drifting from bars. Life happening regardless.

Molly stood on the sidewalk, laptop case in hand and for the first time in longer than she could remember, she had nowhere she needed to be.

Four weeks' leave. The thought was both terrifying and, somewhere in a corner of her mind she rarely acknowledged, faintly appealing too. A month without deadlines, without the constant pressure to perform, to exceed. To . . . forget.

Across the street, a man was selling roasted chestnuts from a steel cart, the air threaded with smoke and sweetness. Somewhere nearby, a saxophone street-performer was playing slow, deliberate notes that echoed off the buildings.

Molly exhaled.

She hadn't noticed autumn arriving. In her line of work, it

appeared in spring in the form of advanced branding decks, pumpkin-spiced product tie-ins and color palettes approved months in advance. Fall, to her, was a concept. A campaign.

But this was the real thing. She bent and picked up a leaf, its surface dry and fragile, veins standing out like a map. She turned it between her fingers, vaguely embarrassed by the gesture, as if doing something indulgent.

And all of a sudden her grandmother's voice appeared in her head.

'Nature never rushes,' Aoife had told her in the small backyard behind their Brooklyn house, hands buried in the soil. 'Yet everything still gets done.'

Molly closed her eyes. She could see it as clearly as if she were there again: her beloved nan planting a rosebush in their backyard, apron smudged with dirt, hair escaping its pins.

Molly had been so young then, impatient, tapping her foot while waiting to be driven somewhere, a practice or lesson, she couldn't recall. 'But it's so tiny,' she'd commented. 'How long will it take to grow?'

Her grandmother had smiled at her then, that knowing, sideways smile. 'Anything that matters always takes time.'

Chapter 2

Molly's apartment sat fourteen floors above the street, all gleaming surfaces and sharp angles. Floor-to-ceiling windows displayed the glittering cityscape like expensive wallpaper, the kind of view that featured in luxury real-estate brochures.

She'd been proud of it once, this sleek Soho rental she'd secured after a promotion five years ago. Tonight, as she paced the hardwood floors in bare feet, it felt like an overpriced hotel room; somewhere she stayed, as opposed to lived.

Molly changed into yoga pants and an oversized NYU sweatshirt, her work clothes hanging with precise spacing in a closet full of similar pieces.

Sabbatical. The word still sent a flutter of anxiety through her chest. Projects would advance without her input. The marketing world would continue spinning without Molly Harris at its center.

She pressed her forehead against the cool glass of the window. Below, the city moved in its ceaseless rhythm, headlights and taillights flowing like blood cells through concrete arteries. A whole month stretched before her, empty and unstructured. The thought made her palms sweat.

But today, at least, there was still one more thing on the agenda.

Her grandfather answered on the second ring, his voice warm and slightly gruff. 'There's my girl. I was just thinking about you.' Eddie always said that and Molly never had any idea if it was true.

'Hey, Pop,' she said, tension automatically releasing from her shoulders at the familiar sound of his voice. 'How are you feeling today?'

'Old,' he replied with a chuckle. 'But I finished that bookshelf for Mrs Wilson, so I can't be too decrepit yet.'

'You should be taking it easy, not building furniture for the neighbors,' Molly chided, settling onto her couch.

'Pot, kettle, black,' he said, the smile evident in his voice. 'Your brother called earlier. Says you're working yourself into the ground as usual.'

Molly rolled her eyes. 'You know Cole's flair for drama.'

'Maybe so, but he's not stupid either.' Eddie's tone shifted, losing its teasing edge.

The concern in his voice loosened something in her chest. She curled her feet beneath her and leaned into the phone as if her grandfather was sitting beside her instead of in the Brooklyn home in which Molly was raised. 'Pop, really, I'm fine,' she insisted. 'Just been pushing a bit too hard lately. The boss wants me to take some time off.'

'Well, I'll be. And are you going to listen to the guy, or is he just another person you're going to steamroll?'

Molly couldn't help smiling. For all his gentle manner, Eddie Harris had never pulled punches. 'I'm taking the time,' she said.

His surprise was audible in his sharp intake of breath. 'Damn, there might be hope for you yet.'

'Don't sound so shocked.'

'Sweetheart, you've been running full tilt since you were ten years old. Even as a kid, you had to be the best at everything – best grades, best at piano, best at helping Nan in the kitchen. Taking it easy isn't exactly in your DNA.'

The mention of her grandmother – the real reason for her call – sent a familiar pang through Molly's chest. 'She would be giving me the eyebrow right now, wouldn't she?'

Eddie laughed softly. 'Your nan could say more with one raised eyebrow than most people manage in a full conversation. And yes, she'd be telling you to slow down, breathe deep, and remember that life is for living, not just achieving.'

Molly closed her eyes, still able to picture her grandmother's face so clearly – the fine lines around bright eyes that matched her own, the silver-streaked dark hair always neatly pinned, the hands that moved with grace whether kneading dough or mending clothes. Impossible to believe a whole year without her had passed already.

'I miss her,' she said quietly. 'Today especially.'

'Every day,' Eddie mumbled, his voice thick with emotion. 'She'd want you to take care of yourself, you know. I always said you were too much like her – all fire and not enough chill.'

They sat in comfortable silence for a moment, the phone connection bridging the physical distance between Manhattan and Brooklyn, between sleek modernity and the weathered brownstone where she had grown up, raised by Eddie and Aoife after their daughter, Tara – Molly and Cole's mother – had died prematurely.

They'd never known their dad, who'd disappeared when she and her brother were just toddlers.

'So what will you do with the time?' Eddie asked now. 'A vacation, maybe? Just ensure that whatever it is involves actual rest, and not just working from a different location.'

Molly's gaze drifted to the window, to the night sky barely visible behind the city's glow.

'I think,' she said suddenly, 'I might head to Ireland.'

The words hung in the air, weighted with everything unsaid. A half-formed plan that had been far too long in the making.

'Ireland,' he repeated, his voice careful. 'You sure?'

'I've been putting it off for long enough. This might be the perfect opportunity to kill two birds with one stone – get some rest and . . .' Molly trailed off, unable to fully articulate the other.

'She'd love that,' Eddie said gently, understanding everything she couldn't say. 'That you're finally going, I mean.'

'I promised her I would,' she said, throat tightening. 'And Cole's right, I've just been making excuses.'

'You just weren't ready before, is all,' her grandfather said, the absolution in his voice a balm to Molly's lingering guilt. 'Some things can't be rushed.'

She nodded, tears beginning to form in the corner of her eyes. 'But first, I should come and spend some time with you, make sure you're looking after yourself.'

'I'm not the one who needs looking after, kiddo,' Eddie said with a hint of his typical gruffness. 'Cole checks in every other day, and I've still got more casseroles in my freezer than I can eat in a month, courtesy of Mrs Wilson and her book club ladies. I'm doing just fine, and don't need anyone cramping my style.'

'Still,' Molly persisted, 'I should visit more often too, I know that.'

'You've been building your life,' he corrected. 'That's what you're supposed to do. Your grandmother and I didn't work so hard to give you and your brother opportunities, so you could sit around keeping old folks company.'

The knot in Molly's chest loosened further. 'Love you, Pop.'

'Love you too, kiddo. Now, about Ireland – do you want me to dig out your grandmother's old address book? Maybe find some cousins from those parts.'

'Nan told me where I need to go,' Molly assured him. 'She talked about Golden Valley so much, I feel like I've already been there.'

'You and me both,' Eddie joked.

'The lake,' Aoife had told them. 'Not large or dramatic. Just wide and calm. On still days it looks like glass, the sky laid down on the earth. You could stand there and feel as though the world had paused for a moment just to let you breathe.'

Molly pictured it now in her mind – water stretching into the distance, the horizon softened by mist.

'And the orchard . . . rows and rows of apple trees on the hills leading down to the shore,' her grandmother would say. 'Gnarled trunks and low branches that caught at your sleeves if you weren't paying attention. In spring, the blossoms; pale pink, almost white even – it was the most beautiful thing. In summer, the leaves grew thick and green, but autumn . . . autumn was magical. Apples heavy on the branches, the ground scattered with them, bruised but perfect all the same. The air sharp with cider and earth and rain.'

Molly could almost smell it.

'And town,' Aoife went on. 'Stone buildings, close together. Doors painted bright, as if to make up for the gray days. Everyone knew who belonged and who didn't, though they'd never say it aloud.' Her grandmother had chuckled faintly. 'In the mornings, you could smell bread long before you saw the bakery. And the apples would roll loose along the lanes when the carts were full. As kids, we all loved that.'

Molly's throat tightened. 'I just . . . wish she could be there to see it all with me.'

'She will be,' Eddie said gently. 'And you'll see it exactly the way she would have.'

They talked a few minutes longer about more practical matters; the more preferable Irish airport (Shannon), the weather in Ireland this time of year (unpredictable), the rental car situation (drive on the left, remember) and Pop's insistence that she bring proper clothing and practical footwear (not those ridiculous heels you wear to the office).

'I'll call while I'm there,' Molly promised. 'And send pictures.'

'Good girl,' he said. 'And, Mol?'

'Yes?'

'I'm proud of you for doing this, sweetheart. Nan would be too.'

The words settled around her like a warm blanket. 'Thanks, Pop.'

After hanging up, she sat still for a moment, phone cradled in her palm. The low-level anxiety that had been her constant companion to the carefully contained grief of last year seemed to have retreated a little. In its place was a sense of purpose that had nothing to do with client presentations, marketing strategies or determination not to cry.

Molly opened her laptop and navigated to the airline website with practiced efficiency. The ticket prices were higher than she'd like; last-minute bookings always were – but for once, she didn't hesitate over the cost.

When the confirmation email arrived, she forwarded it to her grandfather, then hesitated before sending a text to Cole:

Listened to you earlier (don't gloat). Flying to Ireland next week.

His response came almost immediately: Wonders will never cease!

Molly smiled, typing back: Take care of Pop. Will keep you posted.

I always do. And you better do more than that. Daily check-ins or I'll assume you've been kidnapped by fairy folk or something. Seriously though, you've got this. :)

Next, Molly moved to her bedroom closet. Unlike the rest of her minimalist apartment, her wardrobe was a testament to careful curation; rows of tailored blazers, pencil skirts, and silk blouses in a palette of neutrals with occasional jewel tones. Business armor, arranged by color and season.

She pushed these aside, reaching instead to the rear corner where rarely worn casual clothes hung with department store tags still attached. A soft cashmere sweater in forest green and another in red, jeans that hadn't seen daylight in months, hiking boots she'd bought for a team-building thing that had been canceled when a client emergency arose.

'Practical,' she muttered, pulling items from hangers and laying them on the bed. 'Layers, and rain gear. Obviously.'

'The seasons are different back home,' her grandmother used to say. 'You feel them long before the calendar. Spring comes slowly; blossoms appearing one by one, pink and white against the gray. Summer is just a warmer extension of sunlight really, not hot like it gets here. And autumn is when the land earns its keep.'

As she worked, memories continued to surface like bubbles in still water. Aoife showing her how to fold a sweater properly, small hands guided by weathered ones.

'Treat your things with respect,' she'd said in her lilting Tipperary accent, 'and they'll serve you for a long time.'

Those same hands teaching Molly to knead dough, weave daisy chains in spring, or press wildflowers between the pages of heavy books. Hands that had written letters to dwindling family members in Ireland, still maintaining connections across the ocean over decades.

She paused, looking at her own hands – smooth and manicured. She hadn't written a letter in years. Hadn't baked bread since college. When had efficiency replaced these rituals?

Main packing complete, Molly returned to her closet and stood on tiptoe, reaching for the highest shelf, until her fingers found what they sought; a small parcel wrapped in midnight-blue velvet embroidered with a swirling Celtic symbol, secured with a silver ribbon frayed slightly at the edges.

She brought it down carefully, cradling it in both hands as she carried it to her bed. The velvet was soft against her palms, not heavy in the physical sense, but weighted with significance that made her movements deliberate, reverent.

Molly didn't need to open it to know what it contained. Had known since the day her grandmother had asked her the favor with uncharacteristic solemnity.

'When the time is right,' Aoife had whispered, her voice weakened by age and illness, 'you'll know.'

It's been a year, Mol.

And now it seemed – Cole's scolding ringing in her ears, and the ache of exhaustion settled deep in her bones – that time had finally arrived.

Molly brought the parcel to her lips, pressing a soft kiss against the velvet before carefully rewrapping it, making sure the ribbon was secure. With deliberate movements, she placed it in her suitcase, nestled between layers of clothes like something precious and breakable.

Aoife would surely have approved of the timing too – autumn in the golden vale, when the light turned amber and the apples ripened. *When the veil between worlds grew thin*, her grandmother used to say with a wink and a smile that suggested she both believed and didn't believe the old folklore.

As she prepared for bed, moving through her nightly routine with automatic precision, Molly felt a peculiar sense of lightness. The knot between her shoulder blades had loosened. The constant inner refrain to hold back tears had for once, quieted to a manageable whisper.

'Sleep well, *mo chroí*,' Nan seemed to whisper as Molly drifted off. 'The journey begins.'

Chapter 3

The JFK check-in agent's smile never wavered, but her eyes hardened as she placed Molly's suitcase back on the scale for the third time.

'Sorry, but you're still three pounds over the weight limit. You'll need to remove some items or pay the excess baggage fee.'

The woman's badge read 'Cheryl' with a golden star beside it, marking her as some kind of supervisor. Even at this late in the evening, her lipstick was perfect, her airline scarf knotted with geometric precision.

'How much is the fee?' Molly asked, already reaching for her wallet. Time was money and right now, the line forming behind her was ticking like a meter.

'A hundred and fifty dollars.'

Molly's hand stilled. The rational part of her brain – the part that managed marketing budgets in the millions – knew this was a trivial expense. The stubborn part, the one that sounded suspiciously like her grandmother, balked at the principle of it.

'I'll repack,' she said, hefting her suitcase off the scale with a grunt.

'There's an area over there.' Cheryl gestured vaguely toward the terminal's center, where the fluorescent lighting seemed particularly harsh against the darkness outside.

Molly dragged her suitcase to an open spot on the floor. She knelt on the hard tile, her cream blouse and tailored black pants – chosen for comfort but still unmistakably business attire – already collecting dust. With quick, efficient movements, she unzipped her meticulously packed luggage.

She began removing items, mentally calculating their weight. She could swap the ballet flats she was wearing now for the considerably heftier suede boots she'd packed, and maybe take out her cardigan and bulkier coat as carry-on along with her laptop case (old habits . . .).

As she made the footwear switch and tucked away the flats, her fingers brushed against something soft – the velvet parcel – as she realized she'd forgotten to take this out to pack in her carry-on. So maybe the luggage snafu was a blessing in disguise. Molly tucked the pouch protectively alongside her travel documents in her laptop case, then continued sorting the suitcase with renewed determination.

Ten minutes later, she approached the counter again, hair escaping her neat bun of earlier, a fine sheen of sweat on her forehead despite the terminal's aggressive air conditioning.

'Let's try again,' Cheryl said, lifting the suitcase onto the scale. The digital display flashed: 49.8 pounds.

Molly exhaled. 'Thank you,' she said, though she wasn't sure what she was thanking the woman for.

The agent handed over her boarding pass with that same professional smile. 'Gate 42B. Boarding to Shannon begins in an hour.'

Security was its own special form of torment. Molly joined the snaking line, shuffling forward in socked feet, her boots and coat in one plastic bin, electronics in another. Ahead of her, a harried mother struggled with a toddler who'd decided that the checkpoint was the perfect place for an impromptu dance recital.

Molly checked her watch; forty minutes till boarding. Her

stomach growled, reminding her that coffee and perhaps actual food should be a priority. The line inched forward.

When she finally cleared security, she made a beeline for the nearest refreshment kiosk. The line there was mercifully short, just one person ahead of her – a man in a rumpled suit jabbing at his phone while he waited. His agitation was palpable, radiating from him in waves that pushed against Molly's own frayed nerves.

'Coffee, splash of milk please,' she told the barista when her turn came. And a sesame seed bagel. Simple, efficient, enough to power through until she ate on the plane.

Drink secured with a plastic lid, she turned to head toward her gate – only to collide with the rumpled suit, who had decided to backtrack at precisely the wrong moment. The lid went flying and hot liquid sloshed over the rim of her cup, splashing across her cream blouse in an impressive display of physics.

The brown stain spread instantly across the silk, a Rorschach test of her misfortune.

'Jeez, sorry,' the man said, jumping back. 'I didn't see—'

'It's fine,' Molly cut him off, though it was anything but. It wasn't his fault, really.

The restroom mirror reflected a woman she barely recognized. Her hair was mussed, dark circles shadowed her green eyes, the left one smudged where her mascara had started to migrate. The coffee stain on her blouse formed an irregular continent across her abdomen. She dabbed at it with thin paper towels that disintegrated on contact, leaving tiny white pieces across the silk.

'Perfect,' she muttered to her reflection. 'Just perfect for a seven-hour flight.'

She did her best to clean it with what was available, then pulled on the cardigan, and buttoned it over the damage. The temperature in the terminal was somewhere between refrigerator and meat locker, so at least the extra layer wouldn't seem out of place.

The gate agent's voice crackled over the intercom, announcing priority boarding for her flight and Molly looked up, startled by how quickly the time had passed.

Only when she'd settled into her window seat, belt fastened across her lap, did she finally switch her phone to airplane mode. The small act of digital disconnection felt both terrifying and liberating – like stepping off a ledge, unsure if she'd fall or fly and she fidgeted a little.

'First time to Ireland?'

Molly turned to find her seat mate – a silver-haired woman with kind eyes and an Irish accent – watching her with interest.

'Is it that obvious?' she asked, smoothing her hair self-consciously.

The woman smiled. 'You have the look. Part excitement, part terror.'

'My grandmother was from there,' Molly found herself saying. 'County Tipperary.'

'Ah, lovely part of the country. What brings you over? Looking for your ancestors, I suppose.'

Molly hesitated. 'A promise,' she said, uncertain where that had come from.

The woman nodded, as if this explained everything. She introduced herself – Nora or Noreen, Molly couldn't quite catch it over the noise of the engines – then mercifully lapsed into silence as the plane taxied toward the runway.

Take-off pressed Molly back into her seat, the force a physical manifestation of momentum she couldn't control. Below, New York receded, buildings shrinking to miniatures, then toys, then nothing as they pushed through cloud cover into the blue-white emptiness above.

Her eyelids grew heavy as the travel chaos ebbed. The steady hum of the engines wrapped around her like white noise. Her neck settled awkwardly against the window, but she was too tired to care.

Sleep claimed her in fragments – five minutes here, ten there, never deep enough to truly rest. A patch of turbulence jolted her awake just as she'd finally sunk into something resembling real sleep. The plane dipped and swayed, passengers gasping as their stomachs floated momentarily. The seatbelt sign pinged on.

'Just a bit of a tumble,' the captain's voice announced in a comforting Irish lilt. 'Should be through it in no time.'

Molly's neck screamed in protest as she straightened. Her right hand had instinctively moved to her laptop case, tucked securely under the seat in front of her.

The turbulence smoothed out eventually, but sleep remained elusive. Molly watched a movie without absorbing it, picked at the rubbery airline meal and paced the narrow aisle to stretch her cramping legs. Her body ached with fatigue, but her mind buzzed with alertness.

When the captain eventually announced their initial descent into Shannon, the windows showed nothing but darkness.

It was the early hours of the morning in Ireland, of course, still a while before dawn would reveal the landscape below. Molly felt a pang of disappointment – she'd imagined her first glimpse of her grandmother's homeland would be those famous forty shades of green, not this impenetrable blackness.

Shannon Airport at 5.30 a.m. was a peculiar limbo – half-asleep yet fully operational, albeit sparsely populated with bleary-eyed travelers and airport staff moving with the deliberate slowness of the pre-dawn hours. Molly followed signs to passport control, joined a short queue and was processed with surprising efficiency by an officer whose brogue was so thick she had to ask him to repeat himself twice.

'Business?' he asked, eyeing her more formal attire as he stamped her passport.

'Personal actually,' she replied, and he gave her a surprised glance.

The baggage claim area was empty, passengers from her flight circling the carousel like planets around an absent sun. Molly waited, checking her watch, then checking it again as the minutes stretched until the bags appeared. One by one, other passengers claimed their luggage and departed, until she stood alone beside the slowly rotating belt.

'Excuse me,' she said, approaching the service counter where a young man was tapping at a computer. 'I'm still waiting for my suitcase from the JFK flight.'

He glanced up, nodded and checked his watch. 'Sometimes stragglers come through on the next one if the lads stopped for their morning cuppa in-between. Give it a few more minutes.'

Molly's eyes widened at this, but sure enough, some fifteen minutes later, her suitcase surfaced – it had evidently been a casualty of the inexplicable tea break.

'Told ya,' the baggage handler said, with a relaxed smile that suggested this was a common occurrence.

Her luggage finally secured, Molly made her way to the transportation desk, where a cheerful woman with dark hair greeted her, smiling when she told her where she was headed. 'Golden Valley? Lovely spot.'

Molly nodded, pushing the small talk aside for now. 'What's the fastest way?'

'Taxi would be quickest, but it'll cost you a fortune, to be honest – a hundred and fifty euro or thereabouts.'

Molly winced. Between airline tickets, excess baggage palaver and overpriced airport food, the hits just kept on coming. 'Any other options? Besides a rental car.' She had already decided she wasn't going to risk that, since she'd never driven on the left side of the road in the darkness, nor indeed anywhere other than within the US. Heck, as it was, she barely drove in New York.

'Yeah, the bus goes down that way. A longer spin, but only twenty euro.'

Molly hesitated, weighing time against money, her natural inclination to efficiency battling with the more practical voice in her head. Aoife would have taken the bus without question, would have chatted with fellow passengers and arrived at her destination with three new friends and an invitation to dinner.

'That'll work,' she replied decisively.

With timing, instructions and a ticket in hand, Molly found a café and ordered a tea this time – warm, rich and strong, and infinitely better than the tepid varieties back home. She claimed a small table by the window while waiting for the bus departure time, watching as the first hint of dawn lightened the sky outside.

Despite the discomforts of the journey, despite her exhaustion, the sticky stain and rebellious luggage, a sense of rightness settled over her. She was actually here, in Ireland. About to fulfill a promise a long time in the making.

Whatever came next, she had finally taken the first step. Then, suddenly overcome by the significance of it all, to say nothing of the grief burden she'd been successfully holding back all year, tears finally brewed in Molly's eyes.

If only her grandmother could see her now.

Chapter 4

The bus was practically empty at this early hour – just Molly, an elderly man dozing in the back corner and a young woman with headphones who stared intently at her phone.

Molly claimed a window seat a couple of rows down, setting her laptop case carefully on the seat beside her. The driver, an older guy with salt-and-pepper stubble, eyed her luggage with good-natured suspicion before hefting it into the storage compartment beneath.

'American?' he asked, the question more statement than inquiry. When she nodded, he smiled. 'Visiting the 'oul sod, I suppose.'

But when Molly mentioned that she was headed to Golden Valley and he told her she'd been facing the best part of two hours' journey further, her mood deflated afresh.

That long?

The bus seats were narrower than she expected, upholstered in a scratchy blue fabric patterned with what might have been shamrocks or maybe just abstract squiggles – it was hard to tell in the dim interior lighting.

She shifted, trying to find a comfortable position for her travel-weary body. Her neck still ached from her awkward airplane sleep, and her lower back protested after hours of sitting in cramped quarters.

The engine rumbled to life, vibrating through the floorboards and up into her bones. As they pulled away from the airport, she pressed her forehead against the cool window glass, watching the airport service roads give way to a bigger highway.

Dawn was breaking now, the sky transitioning from charcoal to gray, revealing glimpses of the landscape beyond. Molly's eyelids felt weighted, but she fought against sleep. She didn't want to miss this – her first real view of Ireland, the homeland her grandmother had described in such vivid detail that Molly sometimes felt she'd already visited.

'You'll know it when you see it,' Aoife had said once, describing the particular green of Irish fields after rain. 'Like God took all the emeralds he could and crushed them into dust to paint the land.'

The memory made Molly smile despite her exhaustion. Her grandmother had never been one for understatement.

After about an hour, the highway narrowed, becoming a two-lane road that twisted between hedgerows so tall and dense they formed green walls on either side.

Molly's breathing gradually slowed to match the rhythm of the passing scenery. Her shoulders, which had been hunched nearly to her ears since the airport check-in in JFK, began to lower incrementally.

She hadn't truly realized how tightly she'd been holding herself until the tension started to unwind. Then the bus hit a pothole, jolting her forward. Her hands instinctively went to her laptop case, steadying it on the seat beside her. Her fingers lingered on the zipper, confirming it was securely closed, protecting what lay within.

Occasionally the bus would round a corner and the landscape would open suddenly – fields stretching to the horizon, patch-worked in various shades of green and gold beneath the gradually lightening sky.

‘First time to Ireland?’

Molly turned to find the bus driver watching her in the rear-view mirror, his eyes crinkling at the corners with what might have been amusement, or simple curiosity.

‘Yes,’ she replied, straightening in her seat. ‘My grandmother was from Tipperary.’

He nodded as if this explained everything. And it did.

‘Tipp people can be stubborn as the day is long, but sound out to be fair.’

Molly couldn’t help but smile. Stubborn was certainly a word that applied to her grandmother.

The sky continued to brighten further, clouds breaking apart to reveal patches of pale blue. Rain had fallen the night before – the road glistened with puddles that reflected the emerging sunlight and drops sparkled on the hedgerows. Molly found herself leaning closer to the window, taking in details.

The hedgerows were a universe unto themselves. Not just green, but a hundred variations of it – dark ivy intertwined with lighter hawthorn, golden lichen crusting the occasional stone wall that interrupted the living barrier. And there, nestled among the green, were clusters of blackberries – a deep purple-black that gleamed in the morning light.

‘We used to pick those wild when I was a young fella,’ the driver commented, noticing her gaze. ‘Make jam that puts shop-bought shite to shame.’

Molly nodded, remembering her grandmother’s preserves, made from berries they’d picked in Prospect Park – a poor substitute for Golden Valley’s crop, Aoife had claimed, but better than nothing.

‘My grandmother made jam too,’ she told him, the words emerging without conscious thought. ‘She said Irish blackberries tasted of sunshine and secrets.’

The driver laughed, a rich sound that filled the small bus. ‘Your granny obviously had a way with words.’

The road curved again, and suddenly they were passing through open countryside. Fields of barley stretched on one side, the grain golden . . . almost amber in the strengthening morning light. The stalks rippled in the breeze like waves, moving across the surface in hypnotic patterns. On the other side, a scattering of sheep dotted a hillside, their white forms stark against the green grass like miniature clouds.

Molly shifted her laptop case onto her lap, cradling it there as the bus navigated another rough patch of road. The familiar weight was comforting, a tether to her purpose here amid the unexpected beauty that threatened to distract her.

They passed a small farm where a man in a flat cap waved at the bus, a young border collie circling his ankles with barely contained energy. The driver returned the wave with a friendly honk and Molly glimpsed a smile beneath the cap before they rounded another bend.

The road wound higher now, offering glimpses of the wider landscape through gaps in the hedgerows, which began to appear more frequently, sectioning the land into irregular parcels that were far more organic than the precise grids of US farmland. Some were mere suggestions – tumbled stone half-reclaimed by moss and wild grass.

'Nearly there,' the driver announced. 'Golden Valley's just over this rise.'

Molly straightened in her seat, suddenly alert despite her fatigue. This was it – the place her grandmother had spoken of with such longing, such precise detail that Molly now worried whether Aoife's memories had been polished into something brighter than reality could possibly match. Then the bus crested a hill, and her breath caught in her throat at her first glimpse of the Golden Vale.

Lough Corrin spread below, just as her grandmother had described, like a mirror laid on the landscape, its surface a shifting palette of slate-blue and silver where the emerging sun caught ripples. The lake curved gracefully between undulating hills that almost seemed to breathe, their green slopes dotted with sheep. At the near end, nestled against the water's edge, lay Golden Valley village itself – a cluster of buildings with slate roofs, smoke rising from chimneys in the morning air.

Surrounding the township on three sides was woodland – different to the dense, impenetrable forests of wilderness, and something far older. Native trees, their massive trunks testifying to centuries of slow, steady expansion, their branches spreading to create dappled shadows across the ground beneath. Even from this distance, Molly could see that the leaves were beginning to turn, hints of gold and copper among the green.

'Oh my . . .' she whispered, the words escaping without her permission.

The driver chuckled. 'Told ya.' There was pride in his voice, as if he personally owned the countryside they were about to traverse.

Molly couldn't tear her eyes away. This was it – *exactly* as Aoife had described, down to the particular way the light caught the water, the specific curve of the shoreline where the lake embraced the village. She blinked hard, surprised to find her eyes damp again. She'd been so focused on the physical journey, on the logistics of flights and buses, that she hadn't prepared herself for the emotional impact of seeing the place her grandmother had loved so fiercely.

The bus began its descent toward the village, winding down a narrow road that offered changing perspectives of the lake and woods with each curve. No wonder Aoife had never seemed quite at home in Brooklyn, despite building a full life there with Eddie and Molly's late mom. No wonder her stories always returned to this place, these hills, this particular quality of light that seemed to gild everything it touched.

The road straightened as they approached the village outskirts. Modest contemporary houses and smaller thatched holiday-cottages appeared, set back from the road behind low walls or fences, their gardens still vibrant with late-summer blooms, despite the cooling weather. A dog barked, the sound carrying clearly in the morning air. Through gaps between buildings, Molly caught various glimpses of the lake, now closer, its surface textured with tiny ripples from the growing breeze.

Something about the quality of the light changed then and she glanced up to see clouds gathering from the west – deep gray harbingers of rain.

As if on cue, the first drops appeared on the window glass, small translucent pearls that caught the light before streaming downward in irregular paths.

'And here's your Irish welcome . . .' the driver announced cheerfully.

Molly watched as the raindrops multiplied, quickly blurring the landscape she'd been admiring. The perfection of the moment fractured slightly, reality intruding on what had begun to feel like a dream. Yet there was beauty in this too – the way the rain softened edges, the fresh scent that seeped in through the bus's ventilation system, earthy and green and alive.

Her grandmother had spoken of this also, of course – the Irish weather's quick-changing moods and how rain could sweep across the lake like a curtain being drawn. 'We're all ruled by the weather,' she'd say watching a Brooklyn thunderstorm from their front window, while Cole complained about a missed hockey game. 'Learn to live alongside it, not against it.'

The bus slowed as they entered Golden Valley village proper, passing a row of buildings, one with a hand-painted sign that read The Orchard Pub in faded lettering.

Next, a row of charming shopfronts – a bookstore with a display of colorful volumes in the window called Wildflower Books, a cozy café Molly didn't catch the name of, and a small convenience store, butcher and pharmacy side by side.

'This is the square coming up now,' the driver said, helpfully announcing Molly's stop.

She nodded, gathering her things, suddenly nervous. The rain streaked down the window glass now, transforming the village into an impressionist painting of blurred colors and shapes. Yet even through this watery lens, Golden Valley was unmistakably real, solid and present in a way that even Aoife's most vivid description failed to capture.

The bus pulled into a quaint area paved with cobblestones, stopping beneath a tired-looking bus shelter that offered minimal protection from the elements. 'Watch your step getting off now – cobbles can be slippery when wet.'

Molly rose on stiff legs as she slung her case over her shoulder with careful movements. The velvet parcel within seemed to almost pulse with its own energy now.

Her first step off the bus sent a shock of cold through her suede ankle boots – not the wisest choice as it turned out, but still better than the flimsier flats.

Rain pelted her head and shoulders, instantly transforming her makeup into something more abstract. She tugged the case strap higher on her shoulder and waited as the bus driver hefted her suitcase from the luggage compartment underneath. It emerged already glistening with rain despite its brief exposure to the elements.

'The Glen Arms Hotel is right at the top of the square,' he said, pointing through the downpour. 'Can't miss it.'

'Thank you,' she said. 'For all the advice, I mean. It was nice to hear about the place.'

He smiled, the creases around his eyes deepening. 'Ah, sure, we all love the chats around here, as you'll soon find out. Enjoy your visit. Despite the wet welcome,' he added, rolling his eyes at the rain.

As the bus pulled away with a hiss of tires on wet stone, leaving Molly alone in the increasing downpour, she gripped the handle of her suitcase with determination.

The first tug sent water spraying from a puddle onto her already dampening pants. The second revealed a more pressing problem – the suitcase wheels, perfectly adequate for the smooth floors of JFK and Shannon airports, were completely unsuited to old cobblestones slick with rain.

The wheels caught between stones, jammed against uneven edges, and skidded sideways when they hit particularly smooth, worn patches. Each step required a calculated readjustment, a fresh battle of will against physics and architecture. Another tug. Another spray of water, higher this time, splashing the hem of her jacket.

The rain intensified, as if taking Molly's determination as a personal challenge. She could barely see through the water streaming down her face, her hair now plastered to her scalp in dripping tendrils.

Through rain-blurred vision, the village revealed itself further in glimpses and fragments. The famed square was smaller than she'd imagined – more intimate than grand, enclosed by buildings that huddled together like old friends. In the middle stood a curious ornate stone fountain, water streaming down its carved surface and pooling around the base.

All around the square, not-yet-open shop fronts glowed with warm interior light. The bookstore on one side, its bay window displaying volumes arranged by color rather than genre, creating a rainbow effect visible even through the rain.

Only the doors of the café stood ajar, the scent of early baking wafting out to mingle with the rain-soaked air. A wooden sign swung in the wind above it, The Cherry Blossom Café. Alongside it, a butcher shop, the sign lettering barely legible from where Molly stood: Carved Oak Butchers – Est. 1847.

Her marketing brain activated involuntarily, assessing the place as if it were a potential client. The color scheme was inconsistent – duck-egg blue beside forest green, alongside weathered stone – yet somehow harmonious. The hand-painted signs displayed craftsmanship and the overall aesthetic was hotch-potch but authentic, giving the impression of a place that had evolved organically rather than being designed for appeal.

A woman hurried past, dressed in a waxed jacket, a small dog trotting at her heels. She nodded with casual friendliness, seemingly unbothered by the weather. 'Howya,' she called out, as if Molly was a familiar neighbor rather than a bedraggled stranger fighting a losing battle with luggage and elements.

'Hello,' Molly replied automatically, the word half-swallowed by a gust of wind.

The woman and dog continued across the square without breaking stride, disappearing into the café. Moments later, an older man on a bicycle pedaled past, completely unbothered by the rain or the wind, his lack of rain gear suggesting either extraordinary optimism or complete surrender.

Molly felt acutely foreign suddenly – not just American, but urban. A creature of climate-controlled offices and ride-share apps, thrust into a world where rain wasn't an inconvenience; just a condition of existence.

Her jacket, designed more for style than function, had surrendered completely. Water trickled down her neck and between her shoulder blades, cold fingers tracing her spine. Her pants, increasingly sodden, clung to her legs with clammy insistence. The suitcase, as if sensing her moment of distraction, chose that precise moment to tip sideways, landing in a puddle with a decisive splash.

'Perfect . . .' Molly muttered, yanking it upright.

She stood still for a moment, rain streaming down her face, as she checked her phone, trying to get her bearings. The driver had said the hotel was at the top of the square, but which way was considered the top or the bottom? In the downpour, both looked equally possible and equally uninviting. Her eyes stung with a mixture of rain and exhaustion-fueled emotion.

This was *not* how she'd imagined her arrival. In the countless times she'd pictured this journey – initially when Nan had made the request, and more recently when Molly'd made the decision to come – she'd somehow always envisioned sunshine. Golden light catching on the lake's surface, the village warm and welcoming, perhaps someone from her grandmother's past recognizing her immediately ('those Brennan eyes!').

A Hollywood version of an Irish homecoming.

Instead Molly stood lost, drenched and shivering in a unfamiliar place, her expensive luggage proving useless, her carefully planned wardrobe increasingly waterlogged, with no clear direction and definitely no welcoming committee.

She felt a laugh bubble up from somewhere deep inside her.

Of course it would rain. Of course her suitcase wheels would catch on every cobblestone. Of *course* she would look like a drowned rat within minutes of arrival.

Aoife would have loved this moment – would have thrown her head back and laughed at the sky, arms spread wide to embrace the chaos. Molly's grandmother had never met a situation she couldn't find humor in, even when that humor had a sharp edge of irony.

'You're overthinking it, *mo chroí*,' she seemed to whisper now through the rain. 'The path only reveals itself to those who start walking.'

Chapter 5

Jack Flynn's steel-toe boots splashed through puddles with indifferent ease as he unloaded crates from the back of his mud-spattered pickup. Raindrops sneaked beneath the collar of his worn leather jacket, but he barely noticed it anymore – this time of year meant accepting you'd be damp more often than dry.

The weight of each crate felt right in his hands, the familiar burn across his shoulders a testament to years spent hauling the fruits of his labor from orchard to village and beyond. He set another crate beside The Orchard Pub's service entrance, nodding at the proprietor through the half-open door. 'Last one.'

'Good man yourself,' Seamus O'Shea called back. 'Though who'll be drinking it in this weather is beyond me.'

Jack glanced up at the sky, gray as slate and just as unyielding. 'Ah, that'll clear by noon.'

'Let me guess, the apple trees told you.'

Jack's mouth quirked into the closest thing he had to a smile. 'West orchard never fails.'

Seamus guffawed. 'I'll take your word over the apps any day, to be fair.'

Jack turned back to his truck, delivery complete. He didn't mind the rain at all. If anything, it kept the nuisance day-trippers away, leaving the village to those who respected its rhythms and peculiarities. September rain meant the apples would be plump and sweet, the cider rich with tannins.

The square was quiet at this hour, only a few business owners setting up behind rain-streaked windows before opening.

Jack liked it best this way too – before the day fully assembled, when you could still see the bones of the place beneath its daily bustle. The fountain stood sentinel in the square as it had forever, water collecting in the shallow basin at its foot. Apple blossoms carved into its base seemed to soften in the wet, as if the stone itself was mourning better days.

The village had changed little in Jack's lifetime, which suited him perfectly. New coat of paint on the pharmacy, a few modernizations up at the hotel, and the occasional tourist-crap shop that rarely lasted more than a season – these were surface changes that never quite penetrated to the heart of Golden Valley.

The essence remained constant: a place where you knew the names of your neighbors' dogs, where the lake's moods dictated daily plans, and where generations of Flynns had coaxed Goldenridge apple harvests from stubborn soil.

The rumble of an engine drew Jack's attention as he loaded his now-empty crates back onto the truck bed. The first bus of the day rolled into the square, windshield wipers fighting a losing battle against the downpour. It groaned to a stop outside the bus stop, exhaust mingling with the mist.

Only one passenger disembarked – a woman clutching a laptop case to her chest like a shield.

Tourist. Everything about her broadcasted it: the nonsensical footwear, the expression of dismay as rain plastered dark hair to her face, the way she stood momentarily frozen, as if waiting for the weather to reconsider.

Jack shook his head, allowing himself a private smile. American probably. They always seemed surprised that rain in Ireland actually got you wet. The English and most Europeans were used to it of course, but the Yanks . . . they always seemed to expect fairies and rainbows. Well, the ones he'd encountered at least.

He pulled another crate from the truck – this one filled with eating apples, destined for the Glen Arms kitchen. The Ryans insisted on local produce for their hotel breakfasts and Goldenridge apples were the pride of Tipp. After the hurling team of course, he admitted with a wry smile.

The newcomer was moving now, struggling across the cobblestones with a suitcase that clearly wasn't designed for anything rougher than airport terminals. She stopped every few steps to check her phone, holding it at awkward angles to shield the screen from raindrops. Her free hand wiped repeatedly at her face, a futile gesture against the persistent drizzle.

'Where the heck is this hotel?' he heard her mutter as a gust of wind carried her voice across the square.

Yup. And not just city, but Big City.

Jack's shoulders tensed slightly, an instinctive reaction he couldn't quite control. The village had seen an increasing number of tourists lately, to say nothing of a concerning increase in property developers and estate agents with smiles as polished as their shoes, all talking about 'authentic Irish experiences' and 'untapped real-estate potential.' The last one had offered to buy half his orchard to build holiday cottages overlooking the lake. Jack had shown him the door with more restraint than the fecker deserved.

This one looked like that corporate type too, with the laptop and everything. Even her posture seemed at odds with the village – too rigid, too purposeful, as if she could bend the world to her schedule through sheer determination.

Jack arranged the apples in the hand-wheeled cart he used for smaller deliveries with limited parking options, stacking them in neat pyramids – classic Goldens at the center, surrounded by the deep red Bloody Butchers and a few early Winter Pearmains. The cart rested beside his truck, wheels safely locked against the cobblestones' uneven surface.

The woman was heading in his direction now, pulling her suitcase with increasing frustration. Each time the wheels caught between stones, she tugged with more force, her shoulders hunching against both rain and aggravation. She'd given up on the phone, shoving it into a pocket to focus on the physical battle with luggage and elements.

Jack watched amused from the corner of his eye as he worked. It was like watching a salmon fighting upstream, admirable in its wrongheaded persistence. She was closer now, close enough that he could see that her cheeks were flushed with cold and effort, lips pressed into a thin line of concentration as she navigated another treacherous patch of cobblestones.

Pretty, though.

'Excuse me,' she called, American twang carrying loudly through the rain. 'Can you tell me where—' Her suitcase wheel caught in a deep groove between stones and she yanked reflexively with the impatient strength of someone at the end of their tether.

The wheel came free with unexpected speed, sending the suitcase careening sideways – directly into the side of Jack's apple cart.

He lunged forward, one hand outstretched toward his carefully arranged display, but he was too late. The cart teetered for a heart-stopping moment, then tipped with deliberate grace.

The pyramid of fruit collapsed, spilling in all directions like billiard balls after a perfect break. Dozens of shiny, perfect apples – each handpicked, polished and arranged with care only this morning – bounced across the cobblestones. They rolled down the gentle slope of the square, gathering speed, some disappearing beneath parked cars while others headed straight for the gutter beneath the fountain where the rain had formed a miniature river.

Jack watched, momentarily transfixed as a particularly fine Golden rolled in a perfect line toward the fountain, circling its base like a satellite finding orbit, then disappeared down a drain with a final, unceremonious plop.

The woman stood frozen, her hand still gripping the suitcase handle, horror etched across her features. Her mouth formed a perfect 'O' of dismay, eyes wide as she watched quite literally the fruit of Jack's labor scatter across the wet square.

'Oh gosh! I'm so sorry . . .' she gasped, green eyes wide, releasing the suitcase to reach for an apple that had stopped right by her foot. 'I didn't see the— I was just trying to . . .'

Her hair had long-escaped whatever style she'd attempted, dark strands plastered against her cheeks and neck, which made her look like a bedraggled urchin.

Rainwater dripped from her chin as she bent to retrieve the apple, her movements suddenly careful, as if handling something precious.

Jack assessed the damage with a quick glance. The cart hadn't broken, just tipped. Most of the apples could be recovered, though they'd need washing of course. The real casualty was time – time he didn't have to spare, with three more deliveries still to make before nine.

He blinked, droplets catching on his eyelashes. Time to salvage what he could of this situation – and his apples. And maybe give the poor woman a hand.

He bent to right the fallen cart, already calculating which deliveries would have to be delayed or topped up, to accommodate this unexpected detour in his morning routine.

She remained frozen, rainwater dripping from her chin, her ruined blouse, her expensive suede boots.

Looking for all the world like someone who had just realized they truly weren't in Kansas anymore.

Chapter 6

Before Molly could even form an apology, the guy was in motion. He strode toward the scattered fruit with purpose, scooping up apples with quick, efficient movements. Rain darkened the leather jacket across his broad shoulders as he knelt to retrieve three gleaming apples from a puddle, his large hands gentle despite their obvious strength. She stood frozen, mortification washing over her in waves hotter than her rain-chilled skin.

'Oh gosh! I'm so sorry,' she finally managed, her voice thin against the drum of rain. He didn't respond, already moving to capture another apple that was making a slow escape toward a drain. His silence amplified her embarrassment. 'I didn't see the— I was just trying to . . .'

'Set them free?' he called, his voice rich with mirth and an accent that turned the simple question into something musical. He lunged sideways, hand shooting out to catch an apple mid-bounce off a cobblestone. In one fluid motion, he straightened and tossed it to her.

The apple arced through the rain and Molly caught it reflexively, the fruit cool and smooth against her palm. 'Nice catch. You'd make a great camogie player.'

She laughed, the sound surprising her. 'I have no idea what that this,' she replied, her smile feeling a bit rusty, but real. 'But if it's a compliment, I'll take it.'

Something shifted in the man's expression – a slight softening around his eyes, a quirk at the corner of his mouth that wasn't quite a smile but suggested the possibility of one. 'Just in from the airport?'

She nodded, suddenly acutely aware of water trickling down her neck, of her drenched pants clinging uncomfortably to her legs, of her hair hanging in rattails around her face. 'Shannon.'

'Long journey to make in this weather,' he observed.

'I didn't exactly plan the weather part,' she replied, another smile tugging at her lips despite her discomfort.

His expression lightened, the severe lines of his face rearranging into something altogether more appealing.

'Nobody plans the weather,' he grunted. 'It does what it pleases, when it pleases.' He glanced up at the sky. 'This should pass soon enough, though. These autumn squalls never last long.'

As if in direct contradiction, thunder rumbled overhead and the rain, if possible, intensified on cue. Molly couldn't help it – a laugh bubbled up. 'You were saying?' she teased, gesturing at the deluge.

He shook his head, those almost-smile lines deepening around his dark eyes. 'My own fault. Never try to predict anything in Golden Valley,' he said. 'This place has a mind of its own.'

Molly moved closer, gathering two more apples. They were smaller than the ones she was used to seeing in markets back home – more delicate somehow, their skin a watercolor blend of yellow and blushing pink.

'They're beautiful,' she commented, turning one in her hand before placing it back in the cart. 'But I don't think I've ever seen one this small.'

'Well, no one's ever told me *that* before.' He winked and Molly reddened automatically at the blatant double-entendre. Then he chuckled, reaching beneath a parked bicycle for another fugitive. 'Katy variety. Early season. They don't travel well, so you wouldn't find them in your American supermarkets.'

She raised an eyebrow, pausing in her retrieval. 'That obvious?'

Now his mouth did curve into an actual smile, revealing a dimple in his right cheek that did unreasonable things to Molly's pulse rate. He gestured vaguely at her entire person. 'You're wearing "lost tourist" like a sign around your neck.'

Instead of feeling insulted, she found herself smiling back. 'Oh really?'

'Let's just say first-time visitors to Ireland are easy enough to spot.' He moved toward the fountain at the center of the square, where more apples had come to rest against the ancient stonework. 'Like cats caught in the rain – offended by the very existence of weather,' he added, eyes twinkling mischievously.

'I'll have you know I was fully prepared for the rain,' Molly protested, following him. 'Just not for . . . amphibious transportation across medieval cobblestones.'

He guffawed, the sound warm against the cold morning. 'They've been here since 1772, actually. Not quite medieval.'

'My mistake. Merely antique, then,' Molly quipped, thoroughly enjoying the exchange.

They worked in tandem, moving around the square in a widening circle. She found herself matching his rhythm – bend, retrieve, return to the cart – falling into a dance with a stranger whose name she didn't even know.

Their hands brushed as they both reached for the same apple, his fingers warm against her rain-chilled skin. Molly felt the contact like a current, surprisingly intense for such a brief touch. She glanced up, finding his eyes – brown with flecks of gold– already on hers.

'Sorry,' they said simultaneously, then both smiled awkwardly.

'Ladies first,' he said, withdrawing his hand.

Molly picked up the apple – larger than the others, with a

deeper red blush across its skin. 'This one's different,' she observed, turning it in her palm.

'Yep, that's a Honeycrisp – sweeter, crisper.' He was beside her now, close enough that she could smell apples and rain and something warmer on him, like cedar. 'Show-offs, these. Always trying to stand out from the crowd.'

'You seem to know a lot about apple . . . personalities,' she teased.

He took the fruit from her, his fingers lingering against hers a moment longer than necessary. 'I read apples like some read tea leaves. People too, by the kind of apples they favor,' he added mischievously.

Molly's smile reappeared – he was unashamedly flirting now. 'So what does this one say about me?' she challenged, nodding at the fruit in her hand.

He studied it with exaggerated seriousness. 'Well, now, this one tells me that you're a woman of great character. Even though you're tired and soaked to the bone, you're the kind who still helps a stranger when you could've just apologized and hurried away.'

'All that from a piece of fruit,' Molly said, suddenly aware of how close they were standing, how the rain had plastered her clothes to her skin, how his eyes crinkled so attractively when he smiled. 'You must be very good at your job.'

He winked. '*Very* good.'

Molly swallowed, suddenly finding it difficult to remember that she was drenched, jet-lagged and completely out of her element.

They continued their apple-gathering, but something had shifted. Molly found herself increasingly aware of his physicality – the breadth of his shoulders beneath the battered leather jacket, the graceful economy of his movements, the way raindrops clung to his dark eyelashes.

'So what brings you to our neck of the woods?' he asked then. 'Business or pleasure?'

'Neither, exactly,' she replied, focusing on corralling two apples that seemed determined to roll down the slight incline of the street. 'More . . . obligation.'

His eyes widened. 'Bit ominous.'

She laughed. 'Not really. Just long overdue.'

He nodded, accepting her vague answer without pressing further. 'These parts have a way of making people keep their promises.'

Something in his tone made her look up then. For an instant, she glimpsed something deeper behind his easy manner – a shadow of something else. Then it was gone, his expression open once more as he straightened up.

'You're good at this yourself,' he said, nodding toward the three meandering apples she'd managed to trap against a wall with her foot. 'Ever considered a career in fruit wrangling?'

'I missed my calling,' Molly replied, scooping them up. 'Currently stuck in the corporate treadmill, but I'll add it to my resume for emergencies.'

His laugh was unexpected and genuine, transforming his face completely. The dimple reappeared, deeper this time, and she found herself wishing she could capture the sound somehow, bottle it.

'Let me guess – big city, corner office with a view?'

She raised an eyebrow. 'You psychic too, or just showing off?'

'Neither. You just have that look.'

'There's a look?'

'Absolutely. Efficient, precise, probably terrifying in a meeting.' His eyes traveled over her with open appreciation that should have felt inappropriate but somehow didn't. 'Though at the moment, more "drowned efficiency" than "corporate terror".'

Molly glanced down at herself – soaked, stained blouse, rain-drenched pants and sodden suede boots – with a rueful smile. 'Not exactly the look I was going for.'

'Working for you all the same,' he said, his voice dropping slightly, the words landing with obvious weight.

Heat bloomed in her cheeks despite the chill air. Molly couldn't remember the last time she'd openly flirted with a stranger – or indeed when any flirting had felt this natural, this effortless. Her previous relationships (what few there were) had been brief sparks that usually fizzled out in no time.

This . . . this was a goddamn bonfire.

They were down to the last few apples now. Molly spotted another nestled against the base of the fountain and moved toward it, aware of him doing the same.

'I think this is the last one,' she said, her voice softer than intended.

Neither moved to pick it up though. Rain pattered around them, a sound that seemed to create a private space in the otherwise empty square.

'You should probably claim it,' he said, his breath warm against her cheek. 'Since you started the great escape in the first place.'

'Seems only fair.' She picked up the apple, cradling it in her palm.

'That's it then,' he said as she placed the final apple back on the cart. 'Crisis averted.'

Molly became aware again of her soaked clothes, her exhaustion, the hotel she still needed to find. Yet she found herself reluctant to end this unexpected interlude. 'Again, I really am sorry about crashing into your cart.'

'No harm done,' he said, running a hand through his wet hair in a gesture that seemed unconscious, but drew her attention to the strong line of his forearm where his sleeve had pushed up. 'Apples are tough, and they've definitely survived worse.' He glanced toward his truck, then back at her, his expression shifting toward something more practical. 'You're looking for the Glen Arms, is it? It's that way. Can't miss it – big stone building with ivy all over the front.'

Faintly disappointed at the dismissal, Molly nodded and

gripped her suitcase handle. But before she moved away, he reached into his cart and selected a fresh apple, its skin still gleaming with raindrops like tiny jewels.

'Here,' he said, extending it toward her. 'Fresh from Goldenridge this morning.'

Molly's head snapped up, eyes suddenly intent on his face. 'As in Goldenridge Orchard?'

'You've heard of it?' he asked, surprised.

'Yes, I—' She paused, something shifting in her memory. 'A local landmark, isn't it?'

He studied her more carefully now, his gaze landing on her laptop case, previous warmth cooling slightly. 'Not especially. Small operation. Family-run.'

'Do you work there?'

'You could say that.' He began repositioning his cart, checking that the wheels were properly aligned on the uneven cobblestones.

'With the old cider press and the row of ancient trees along the western border?' Molly continued speaking, her voice tinged with wonder.

Aoife's old stories had painted such a vivid picture of the orchard that Molly felt as if she'd walked its rows of apple trees herself, could almost smell the sweet-tart scent of fruit ripening in the sun, could nearly taste the crisp cider that her grandmother had claimed was like drinking autumn itself.

He looked up sharply, dark eyes narrowing suddenly. 'How do you know that?'

'Well, it's quite famous around here, isn't it?'

He studied her face with newfound intensity. 'Not really,' he said shortly. 'Unless you're in the apple business.'

His posture had changed, the easy camaraderie of moments ago replaced by something far more guarded.

'I'm not.' Molly laughed lightly. 'My grandmother used to talk about it.'

'Your grandmother's from around here?'

'Yes,' Molly confirmed.

'What's her name?' he asked, his tone carefully casual, but his eyes watchful.

Molly hesitated. She wasn't ready to share her reasons for being here with a complete stranger, or anyone as yet. Not until she'd had time to settle, get the lay of the land, as it were. 'Brennan,' she said simply.

Something flickered across his face – recognition, perhaps, or calculation maybe? 'Very few Brennans around here,' he said neutrally. He moved to the front of his cart, though his movements had lost their earlier ease, becoming more deliberate, more contained.

'Do they still make that cider?' Molly asked, genuinely curious. 'The one aged in oak barrels? Sun something . . .'

He paused, his back to her. 'Sunrise,' he stated flatly, turning then.

Molly could immediately tell that for some reason this, in particular, bothered him. 'Like I said, my grandmother—'

'Must know our orchard very well indeed,' he interrupted, his expression hardening. 'Well enough to know about a cider we haven't produced commercially in over thirty years.'

When he turned back, his expression had closed completely. The man who had just flirted with her, who had tossed her an apple with that devilish half-smile, had vanished. In his place, stood someone wary and remote, regarding her with the careful assessment of a man who'd been proven right about something unpleasant.

What had just happened? One moment they'd been bantering in the rain, the next he was treating Molly like she'd come to steal the village silver.

He shook his head, and now looked for all the world as if he was about to wrench back the apple he'd given her, then seemed to reconsider, his hand falling back to his side. 'Keep it,' he barked stiffly. 'Our specialty, but you probably know that already.'

Molly was completely bewildered by the sudden change in demeanor, but before she could ask outright what she'd done wrong, he gestured to the top of the square.

'Like I said, hotel's that way.'

Through the rain, Molly could now make out the imposing facade of the Glen Arms Hotel at the top of the square. Stone walls softened by climbing ivy, windows glowing with warm light that promised comfort within. The sight lifted her spirits slightly. Soon she could shed her wet clothes, wrap herself in whatever the Irish equivalent of a hotel bathrobe might be, and finally, finally rest.

Yet first she felt the need to rescue whatever had gone awry with this guy. But before she could gather her thoughts, he'd grabbed the handles of his cart and with one last look – part suspicion, part something that might have been disappointment – turned and began pushing it down the street, the cart's wheels rattling over the uneven cobblestones.

'Wait—' Molly called after him, but to her disbelief he didn't even give her the courtesy of a goodbye.

What the heck . . .? Her grandmother's stories had painted Golden Valley as warm and welcoming, a place where strangers were treated with respectful curiosity, rather than outright suspicion.

Or hostility even.

'Huh. So much for a thousand welcomes,' Molly muttered confused, as the apple guy finally disappeared around a corner, the fruit he'd thrust at her now heavy in her palm.

Chapter 7

The Glen Arms Hotel's mullioned windows glowed amber in the gray morning light, sprawling ivy vines framing the Georgian facade with picture-perfect charm. A solid oak entrance door stood as imposing as a cathedral's, its carved apple tree motif seeming to mock Molly after what had just happened.

She pushed against it with her shoulder, expecting resistance, but it swung open with surprising ease, sending her stumbling slightly into a reception area that momentarily stole her breath.

Oak-beamed ceilings arched overhead, their aged wood glowing with the patina of centuries. A massive stone fireplace dominated one wall, stacked with what looked like peat, flames dancing merrily as if in deliberate contrast to the morning's gloom. An old grandfather clock stood at the end of the hallway and the walls bore black and white photographs documenting history – faces gazing across time with solemn dignity and a few unexpected smiles.

The effect should have been welcoming, magical even. But all Molly felt was the squelch of her socks, the chill that had since come right through her sodden clothes and settled deep in her bones, and the weight of travel exhaustion threatening to drag her to the polished wooden floor.

A woman in her fifties appeared from a doorway behind the reception desk, her dark hair pulled into a neat chignon. She wore a tailored navy dress that managed to be both professional and welcoming, and her smile was practiced but genuine.

'Good morning,' she said, her lilting accent softening the greeting. 'Welcome to the Glen Arms. I'm Anna Ryan.'

Molly mustered what she hoped was a passable smile while the woman's eyes assessed her with swift efficiency, taking in her bedraggled state with a flash of sympathy that was quickly professional again.

'Thanks. Molly Harris. I have a reservation.'

'Harris, yes, I have you here.' She looked up at the grandfather clock as by reflex, apology already forming in her expression. 'But I'm afraid check-in isn't until two.'

Molly's heart sank as she checked the time. *Six* more hours to wait before a hot shower and dry clothes? She glanced down at herself – sodden, bedraggled, looking for all the world more like something that had been fished from the lake, than a visitor on a mission.

And kicked herself for not making the reservation to start a night earlier.

'Is there any chance of an earlier check-in?' she asked, desperation edging her voice. 'I've literally traveled across the ocean and as you can see . . .' She gestured pointedly at her waterlogged state.

Anna's expression softened with genuine regret. 'I truly wish I could accommodate you, but we had a big wedding party over a long weekend and they only left yesterday. Housekeeping staff are working as quickly as possible, but . . .' The woman seemed to make a decision then, her posture shifting slightly. 'What we can offer is somewhere warm to wait in our lounge. The fire's well-stoked and I'd be happy to bring you tea and some breakfast if you're up to it? You look like you could use something warm in any case.'

The kindness, so unexpected, made Molly's throat tighten unexpectedly. 'That would be amazing, thank you.'

'Come with me, so.' Anna stepped around the counter, her movements fluid and graceful. 'You can leave your luggage here and we'll take it up when your room is ready. Meanwhile I'll ask housekeeping to make it a priority.'

Molly followed her through an archway into a smaller room that somehow managed to be even more inviting than the reception area. Deep brocade armchairs and a worn leather sofa surrounded a second fireplace, this one with a fire already crackling behind a brass guard. Bookshelves lined one wall, filled with well-thumbed volumes in mismatched bindings. Rain-speckled windows offered views of what must be the hotel's garden, though the weather rendered it a watercolor blur of greens, and a distant gray-blue from windows on the other side that was surely the lake.

'Make yourself comfortable,' Anna soothed, gesturing toward an armchair nearest the fire. 'I'll bring tea and arrange a full Irish. Any dietary restrictions?'

'None, thank you.' Molly shook her head, already drawn toward the warmth like the proverbial moth.

Left alone, she sank into an armchair that seemed designed to accommodate weariness. The upholstery was worn in places, but clean and soft. The fire's heat reached toward her, promising to chase the damp from her bones if she let it.

She slipped off her ruined boots and set them before the hearth, hoping the suede might be some way salvageable once dried. Her socks followed, and she curled her bare toes toward the flames, a small sigh escaping as warmth began to seep back into her extremities. The laptop case with its precious contents sat safely beside her, never far from reach.

Only then, in the quiet comfort of the empty lounge, did Molly allow herself to fully process the morning's strange encounter.

The apple guy had seemed so genuine at first, openly flirtatious as they'd gathered the scattered fruit. And then, as quickly as the connection had formed, it had vanished. One moment they'd been engaged in easy banter, the next he'd been looking at her with suspicion bordering on hostility.

What had triggered the change?

Molly had expressed a casual interest in his work, nothing more, but it seemed like that was off boundaries, or a cultural misstep maybe? Was that somehow offensive in rural Ireland? Too invasive for casual conversation?

She reached into her pocket and withdrew the apple he'd given her, turning it over in her fingers again. It was perfectly formed, its skin a blend of red and gold that caught the firelight like a small jewel.

Goldenridge Orchard. The name had sparked recognition instantly – how could it not? Nan had mentioned it countless times, describing the fruit that Molly had mentioned to the bus driver earlier as 'tasting like sunshine.'

The memory sent a fresh pang through her chest. This was supposed to be so different. In Aoife's stories, this place had been a haven of warmth and welcome, of community so tight-knit you apparently couldn't walk ten steps without someone offering tea or conversation.

The Golden Valley of her grandmother's youth sounded almost magical – a place where the light fell differently across the lake, where music spilled from pub doorways on summer evenings, where even strangers were treated as old friends.

Instead, Molly was met with rain that soaked to the skin, cobblestones that fought her every step, and a handsome orchardist whose initial warmth had suddenly frozen into hostility without explanation. Even this hotel, nice as it was, couldn't offer her a room on arrival.

Molly closed her eyes, exhaustion washing over her in waves. This had been a mistake. Her boss had prescribed rest after all, not a wild goose chase through a rainy Irish village where she knew no one, and apparently couldn't avoid offending locals within minutes of arrival.

She should just get the job done quickly – fulfill her promise to her grandmother, and then head onwards for sightseeing in Dublin for the remainder of her stay. At least in the capital, she'd have anonymity, modern conveniences and city people too busy with their own lives to judge her for asking innocent questions.

The soft clink of china roused Molly from her thoughts and she opened her eyes to find Anna setting a tray on the small table beside her chair.

'Traditional Irish,' she said, arranging the contents with practiced efficiency. 'Tea, brown bread, and honey from hives kept just up the hill. The eggs and bacon are from McCarthy's farm, not two miles from here.'

The food smelled wonderful, rich and hearty and nothing like the protein bars and tasteless airline crap that had sustained Molly for the past twenty-four hours. She murmured her thanks as Anna poured tea into a delicate china cup, the amber liquid steaming fragrantly.

'Business or pleasure bringing you to our little corner of Tipp?' The question was polite, but Molly caught the genuine curiosity beneath it.

'Just a personal thing,' she replied, having well and truly learned her lesson earlier.

Though if Anna was insulted or disappointed by the lack of specifics, she didn't show it. 'Well, be sure to let me know if there's anything else I can do to make your stay more welcoming. I've checked again on your room and there really shouldn't be too long of a wait.'

The sentiment was kind, but Molly couldn't deny the irony. *More* welcoming? Some welcome this was; soaked to the skin, homeless till this afternoon and already on the wrong side of at least one local. She managed a smile nonetheless. 'Thanks. I appreciate that.'

Left alone again with her breakfast, Molly forced herself to eat despite her exhaustion. The food was undeniably excellent – eggs with yolks the color of marigolds, delicious bacon that bore no resemblance to its American counterpart, bread that tasted of something deeper than the mass-produced versions she usually grabbed from the corner deli.

As she ate, she gazed out the rain-spattered window at what she could make out of the hotel grounds. A flagstone path wound through to a rear walled garden that must be glorious in better weather, leading to what appeared to be a small gate in a distant wall. On the other side, she caught glimpses of Lough Corrin itself, pewter in the morning light, its surface textured by raindrops.

Her grandmother had described swimming in that lake as a girl, claimed the water was sweet and cold and cleansing. Had spoken of picnics on its shore, of starlight reflected on still water in the darkness.

Again, Molly tried to reconcile those stories with the rain-blurred reality before her, but the gap felt insurmountable. Perhaps time had gilded her grandmother's recollections? Transformed ordinary experiences into something magical through nostalgia and distance.

Or perhaps Golden Valley had simply changed in the decades since Aoife Brennan had left its shores, becoming just another rural village struggling to maintain its identity in a rapidly changing world.

Either way, Molly couldn't escape the feeling that she'd made a bad decision.

In her current state – exhausted, uncomfortable and smarting from her encounter with the grumpy local – she truly wasn't sensing whatever magic her grandmother had been talking about.

Chapter 8

The following morning, sunlight streamed through the windows of the hotel breakfast room, casting honeyed patterns across the tiled floor.

Molly sat at a corner table, cradling a steaming mug of tea between her palms. After a hot shower and almost eighteen hours of near-comatose sleep, she felt human again, a marked improvement over yesterday's rain-soaked arrival.

Her hair, now freshly washed and smoothed into a neat ponytail, caught the morning light as she surveyed the room – dark beams and whitewashed walls, decorated with watercolor landscapes of the surrounding countryside. The air smelled of freshly baked bread and bacon.

She'd exchanged yesterday's sodden travel attire for jeans and a forest-green cashmere sweater; casual clothes she rarely wore in Manhattan, but which felt somehow right for this cozy space. Aoife's velvet-wrapped parcel was tucked away safely in the closet in her hotel room, but its presence lingered in her thoughts like gentle pressure.

'Morning,' came a greeting. 'And how did we sleep?'

Molly looked up to find an elegant older woman approaching her table. Silver-streaked hair framed a knowing face lined with what looked like equal parts humor and determination. She wore a tailored skirt in deep plum and a matching cardigan, with a vintage brooch pinned at her throat that glinted beneath the overhead lights.

'Better than I have in months actually,' Molly admitted, setting down her tea. 'I don't think I moved once after my head hit the pillow.'

'That's the Tipperary air for you,' the woman said with a knowing smile. 'I'm Brid. My daughter told me you were half-drowned yesterday when she checked you in. Welcome to the Glen Arms – run by my family for as long as I can remember.'

Molly extended a hand. 'I must thank Anna for the room upgrade. It wasn't necessary, but very appreciated.'

Brid waved her away, her bracelets jangling musically alongside her accent. 'Sure, we're not full and the corner rooms have the best views of the lake.' She tilted her head slightly, studying Molly with shrewd eyes. 'Now, what'll I get you for breakfast? The full Irish might be a bit much if you're still on American time, but our porridge is famous throughout the four provinces.'

'Porridge sounds perfect, actually.' Molly smiled. 'And maybe some brown bread, if you have it?'

'If we have it,' Brid echoed, her expression suggesting gentle mockery. 'Like asking if we've air to breathe.' She lifted the teapot from Molly's table. 'I'll bring you a fresh pot as well. This one's gone cold while you were daydreaming.'

As Brid moved away toward the kitchen Molly found herself smiling. Her accent and brisk efficiency immediately reminded her of Aoife, who had navigated life with the same no-nonsense approach, softened by unexpected kindness. And much like Brid, had also been quite youthful and light on her feet, despite her age.

The Glen Arms breakfast room had only three other occupied tables – an older couple poring over a map, a solo businessman typing furiously on a laptop, and a family with two teenagers who seemed to be communicating exclusively through grunts and eye rolls. Morning light filled the space, highlighting the rich sheen of the oak tables and the intricate pattern of the vintage tile floor.

Brid returned momentarily with a tray balanced expertly on one arm. She set down a bowl of steaming porridge topped with berries and honey, and a plate of thickly cut brown bread beside a butter dish and a fresh pot of tea.

'Here you go,' she said, pouring the tea with practiced precision. 'Proper fuel for an autumn day.'

The oatmeal was creamy with an almost velvety texture, sweetened just enough by the honey drizzled across the top. The berries burst with tartness that balanced it all perfectly. Molly spread butter on a slice of bread, watching it melt into the dense, seed-flecked loaf. The first bite transported her instantly back to their Brooklyn kitchen growing up; that same nutty flavor, same chewy crust.

'This is incredible,' she murmured, taking another bite. 'It tastes just like . . .' She trailed off, suddenly wary of revealing anything too personal after yesterday's baffling interaction with the orchard guy.

Brid paused in the act of refilling Molly's water glass. 'Just like what, pet?'

'Just like what I imagined Irish bread would taste like,' Molly amended, focusing on buttering another slice. 'Everything here is so . . . authentic.'

'Mm.' The older woman's noncommittal response suggested she wasn't impressed by such overt flattery. She moved to Molly's side, straightening condiments with determined precision. 'Have you been to Golden Valley before?' she asked, her shrewd eyes betraying little, but it was obvious she was fishing.

Molly tensed a little as she carefully crafted her response, keeping it friendly but vague. 'First time in Ireland, actually,' she said.

'Is that so?' Brid leaned slightly on the back of the chair opposite. 'Funny thing, but I was only thinking earlier that you looked a bit familiar. The eyes, maybe.'

The butter knife stilled in Molly's hand. 'I have one of those faces,' she offered with a lightness. 'People are always thinking they've met me before.'

'Probably.' Brid straightened, smoothing her skirt. 'Well, if you're exploring today, you should know the forecast is dry until this afternoon. Take advantage of any break in weather while it lasts – September here can be fickle as a cat's affection.'

'I will, thank you.' Molly turned her attention back to her breakfast, keenly aware of Brid's lingering gaze.

'The walking path around the lake is lovely this time of year,' the older woman continued, seemingly reluctant to end the conversation. 'The ancient oaks along the western shore are just starting to turn too. Golden light on golden leaves –'tis something to behold.'

At this, Molly looked up sharply. 'Are there many ancient oaks around here?'

'Oh yes, lots – some hundreds of years old.' Brid seemed about to say more, when another diner nearby signaling for something caught her attention. She straightened, professional smile returning. 'Enjoy your breakfast, and be sure to let me know if you need anything else.' As she moved away to attend to the other guest, Molly returned to her porridge, mind churning with this new information.

Lots of oak trees.

So how was she supposed to know which was the right one?

When the last crumb of bread was gone and the tea reduced to dregs, Molly gathered her lightweight jacket and headed out on her quest.

Outside, the air carried a crisp edge that hadn't been present yesterday morning. Church bells rang out from somewhere, their tones clear and resonant in the stillness. She paused on the hotel's stone steps out front, breathing deeply. No traffic sounds, no city hum – just birdsong, faint voices and the distant lapping of lake water against the shore.

The village looked completely different in daylight. Buildings that had been gray smudges through yesterday's rain, now revealed themselves as a charming collection of stone structures, a few whitewashed, others showing their natural limestone.

Window boxes overflowed with late-season wildflowers in shades of purple and gold. Carved wooden signs hung from wrought-iron brackets, identifying shops with names that could easily have been plucked from Aoife's stories.

Molly descended the steps and stepped out on to the village square. Those cobblestones, so goddamn treacherous in yesterday's rain, now formed a picturesque path that guided her between buildings standing shoulder to shoulder, their fronts adorned with ivy and climbing roses. The space opened up before her, a broad expanse of ancient stones surrounding the central ornate fountain she'd glimpsed yesterday.

Now in full daylight, she could clearly see the detailed carvings on its base – apple blossoms and Celtic knots intertwined in a pattern. Water trickled from the mouths of stone fish, the sound a gentle counterpoint to the fading church bells. Molly circled the fountain slowly, taking in the shops that lined the square.

The Cherry Blossom Café with its duck-egg blue door stood directly opposite, windows steamed slightly from the heat of ovens within. Beside it, the bookstore with the rainbow display she'd seen yesterday, the traditional butcher shop, a pharmacy called The Glen Remedy – and what appeared to be a combination post office and newsagent – made up the majority of the square's commercial offerings.

A few locals moved about, nodding politely to Molly as they passed. Unlike the city where eye contact was often avoided, here it seemed expected – a brief acknowledgment of shared space that was oddly comforting.

She headed for the bookstore first, drawn immediately by the cheerful display. A bell tinkled as she pushed open the door, releasing a waft of that distinctive oh-so-comforting bookstore smell. Shelves rose from floor to ceiling, packed with volumes ranging from brand-new releases to well-loved classics with cracked spines.

A woman in her fifties with short steel-gray hair looked up from behind a counter cluttered with bookmarks. Pencils and various utensils. 'Good morning,' she called. 'Just browsing, or looking for something specific?'

'Just browsing,' Molly replied, running her fingers along the spines of nearby books. 'You have a beautiful shop.'

'Thank you. Been here twenty years next spring.' The woman smiled and returned to the paperwork she'd been checking, leaving Molly to explore at her own pace.

She wandered deeper into the shop, discovering a section dedicated to local history and folklore. Her fingers quickly found a slim volume titled; *Trees of Tipperary: Myths and Legend*s, and she flipped through it, pausing at a chapter about ancient oaks and their significance in Irish culture. There was no mention of the specific tree she sought, but the book felt like a sign nonetheless.

At the counter, the bookseller looked up from her work as Molly approached. 'Found something of interest?'

'I think so,' she said, placing the book beside the register. 'Do you happen to know much about the old oak trees around here? I've heard there's a famous one in particular.'

'The Wishing Oak, I expect,' the woman said, ringing up the purchase. 'Been standing longer than any building in this village.' She chuckled. 'Some say it remembers the old gods.'

Molly's heart quickened. 'Can visitors access it?'

The bookseller hesitated, placing the book in a brown paper bag with practiced movements. 'It's on private land and the owners tend to be a bit particular about people wandering around, especially during harvest season.' She pushed it across the counter. 'They do open the gates for the Harvest Festival though, so you could catch it then.'

On private land.

Her grandmother hadn't mentioned anything about that when she'd made her request.

Uncertain how to proceed, Molly said goodbye to the woman

and continued her exploration, stopping next at The Glen Remedy to purchase a few toiletries she'd forgotten to pack. The pharmacist, a jovial man with ruddy cheeks, engaged her in conversation about the weather while ringing up her purchases.

'Perfect day for a walk along the lakeshore,' he suggested, bagging her items. 'Path goes all around the western edge, gives you a nice view of the vale from across the water.'

With each step through the village, Molly found herself comparing reality to Aoife's descriptions – the way sunlight caught on the weathervane atop the church steeple, the particular shade of the lake in morning light, the smell of peat smoke that occasionally drifted from chimneys. Yet there were differences too – contemporary houses on the outskirts, modern cars parked alongside centuries-old stone walls and, of course, people with smartphones.

Eventually, Molly's steps led her down toward the lakeshore, where a well-maintained gravel path wound along the water's edge. She followed it, watching sunlight dance across the surface of Lough Corrin, creating patterns of light and shadow that shifted with each passing cloud. Beyond, rolling hills gave way to orchards – neat rows of fruit trees that must be the Goldenridge place, though from this distance they appeared as orderly brushstrokes against the landscape.

Molly paused at a wooden bench facing the water, sitting for a moment to absorb the view. From here, she could see further across the lake to the far shore, where older native trees grew thick and tall.

Her eyes scanned the treeline, searching for anything that might resemble the ancient oak her grandmother had described so vividly. 'Wider than three men could span with their arms, with branches that reach for the sky like fingers toward heaven.'

The Wishing Oak, the bookstore owner had called it. But from here, the distance was too great, the details too indistinct. The tree remained hidden from this perspective, still keeping its secrets. Would Molly be able to persuade the landowner to allow her access?

She sighed, frustration bubbling beneath her calm exterior. Aoife's request had seemed pretty straightforward when Molly had made her promise. Now, faced with the reality of gaining access to private property and who knew what else entailed, the task felt somewhat more complicated.

She stood, brushing invisible dust from her jeans, and continued along the trail. The rising sun warmed her shoulders now as she walked, its heat a pleasant contrast to the cool breeze coming off the lake. All around, the community went about their morning business – people flitting here and there on errands, a pair of joggers on the trail, a young mother pushing a stroller while chatting on her phone.

Ordinary life in an extraordinary setting.

Molly could see why her grandmother had loved it all the same, why its memory had sustained her through decades of exile. There was a timelessness to Golden Valley, a sense that while the surface might change, the essence remained constant – like the lake itself, reflecting different skies but fundamentally unaltered.

As she rounded a bend in the path, the village itself came into view again, its stone buildings clustered protectively around the square, the church steeple rising above them like a sentinel.

Molly squared her shoulders, determination settling over her like a familiar coat. She hadn't clawed her way up Manhattan's corporate ladder by shying away from obstacles.

If direct access to The Wishing Oak was blocked, she'd just find another route. After all, she was Aoife Brennan's granddaughter – and if there was one overall lesson Nan had taught her, it was persistence.

In a village this size, information surely flowed like the water in that fountain – all Molly needed to do was find the right channel.

Chapter 9

Jack had woken a full sixteen minutes before his alarm was set to sound, roused by some internal clock that had regulated his life since boyhood.

He lay still for a moment, listening to the calming silence of the land before the birds fully woke, his body already preparing for the day ahead, muscles remembering the previous one's work.

The wooden floorboards creaked beneath his bare feet as he padded to the window. The first hint of peach-gold light was just beginning to illuminate the eastern edge of the orchard. Morning mist hung between the rows of trees, transforming the familiar landscape into something almost ethereal.

Jack rubbed the sleep from his eyes, the rough callouses on his palms scraping against his stubbled face.

The cottage was small but sufficient – a two-bed stone structure that had housed generations of Flynns before him. The walls were thick, the ceilings low, everything built to withstand the elements rather than impress visitors. The few furnishings were practical and well worn: an oak table his great-grandfather had apparently crafted from an ancient tree felled in a long-ago storm; the leather armchair by the hearth, its arms polished smooth by decades of use; the dresser stacked with neatly folded work clothes, nothing fancy.

Family photographs lined the mantelpiece in simple frames – his parents on their wedding day, a much younger one of his father, Tom, grinning with one arm slung over his mam's shoulder. Another solo shot of his mother, Margaret, in her nursing uniform. The most prominent was a faded color snapshot of Jack himself at age ten, outside their old house, standing proudly beside his father with a bushel of apples between them. In the photo, Jack's smile revealed a missing front tooth, and Tom's eyes crinkled with pride.

The cottage kitchen was compact and utilitarian. Jack filled the kettle and flicked it on with the practiced movements of daily ritual. While the water heated, he pulled back the curtains to let in the strengthening dawn light.

On a peg by the sink hung his father's chipped mug – white ceramic with an old Liverpool FC logo in faded letters, the handle repaired with epoxy after a drop years ago. Jack reached for it without hesitation, as he did every morning. The ritual was so ingrained he scarcely thought about it anymore – three Barry's tea bags into the pot, two minutes of steeping, then pour and the splash of milk added last. The comforting scent filled the kitchen as he poured, and wolfed down two slices of buttered toast.

Tom Flynn's battered leather jacket hung by the door, its brown surface cracked and softened by years of work in all weather. Jack ran his fingers over the still-damp collar as he pulled it on. Outside, his work boots waited on the stone step, mud from yesterday's labor and heavy rain still drying on them. He tugged them on without sitting, balancing on each foot in turn with the ease of long practice. As he straightened, he pulled his phone from the pocket of his flannel shirt and checked the weather app – clear morning, showers by afternoon.

Jack scoffed. *We'll see about that.* Though he scrolled through the extended forecast with a frown, noting the projected overnight temps in particular. Early frost was always a concern this time of year all the same.

The door hinges protested with a metallic groan as he stepped outside, mug still in hand. The orchard stretched before him in neat rows, trees planted with mathematical precision decades before his birth. Morning mist lingered between them, curling around trunks and softening the edges of leaves and fruit. Dew glittered on the grass beneath his feet as he walked, each step releasing the sharp scent of crushed blades. The rising sun caught the eastern edges of the land, painting the uppermost branches in gold while the ground remained in cool shadow.

Jack cradled his tea in both hands, letting its warmth seep into his palms as he walked the first row of trees. These were Cavan Russets, one of the oldest varieties, their fruit just beginning to develop the characteristic brownish patches that gave them their name. He stopped at the third tree, setting his mug on the ground before running his hands along a low-hanging branch, fingers gentle but knowing.

'Morning, old girl,' he murmured, voice rough.

His fingertips traced the junction where branch met trunk, checking for the slight swelling that might indicate disease. Finding nothing concerning, he moved to inspect the leaves; deep green and firm, healthy despite the dry spell they'd had in August. The fruit was sizing up nicely, each apple already displaying the distinctive flattened shape that marked the variety.

He continued along the row, his inspection both systematic and intimate. To an outsider, the trees might look identical, but Jack knew each one's quirks and tendencies, could tell you which had suffered storm damage three seasons back, which had struggled with aphids last spring.

The eastern section held the Kilkenny Pearmains, their slightly conical fruit still predominantly green with just a hint of the crimson blush that would deepen as harvest approached. Jack gave particular attention to a tree near the center of the block, which had shown signs of stress the previous season.

'Better,' he said quietly, tracing a calloused thumb over new growth that signaled recovery. 'But we'll keep an eye on you.'

Birds called from the trees, their dawn chorus in full voice. A robin watched him with bright, curious eyes from a nearby branch, head tilted as if evaluating Jack's work. In the distance, he could hear the occasional vehicle passing on the lane that connected Goldenridge to the village – the world beyond the orchard boundaries slowly coming to life.

By the time Jack reached the cider press house, morning had fully arrived. The building stood at the western edge of the main orchard by the main gate, its limestone walls and slate roof weathered by more than a century of Irish seasons. Ivy climbed one corner, its glossy leaves contrasting with the rough-textured stone. The heavy wooden door creaked as Jack pushed it open, releasing the layered scents of apple wood, fermentation, and the faint metallic tang of the old press machinery.

Inside, sunlight streamed through high windows, illuminating the press itself at the center of the space – a massive copper structure reinforced with iron bands, its wooden slats darkened by decades of use. Along one wall, stainless steel fermentation tanks gleamed, their modern efficiency a stark contrast to the traditional equipment beside them.

Jack crossed to the small office tucked in the corner, where a battered old desk held the orchard's ledgers and paperwork. He pulled out the chair – the same one his grandfather had used – and sat heavily, the wood groaning beneath his weight. The previous season's production records lay open where he'd left them, pages filled with neat columns of figures in his precise handwriting.

He pulled a more recent ledger from the drawer and flipped it open, comparing the numbers with furrowed brow. The story they told wasn't encouraging – costs rising steadily each year while wholesale prices remained stubbornly fixed. Energy bills, equipment maintenance, extra labor during the harvest – everything demanded a higher spend while customers balked at even modest price increases.

Jack's fingers tightened around his pen as he jotted calculations in the margin. Goldenridge cider line was holding its own, winning awards and commanding higher prices from specialty shops and select pubs. But the retail apple business – once the orchard's reliable backbone – was being squeezed by massive commercial operations and imported fruit.

His knuckles whitened as he flipped to the next page, where projected expenses for the coming quarter were listed. The irrigation system needed repairs, the cold storage facility was operating at reduced efficiency, and the small tractor they used for hauling bins during harvest was becoming increasingly temperamental with age. Each item represented an expense they could ill afford.

The business wasn't failing – not yet – but the trend lines pointed toward a future that made Jack's jaw clench and his shoulders tighten with tension. Four generations of Flynns had weathered agricultural hardships on this land, adapting and persevering through changing markets and challenging seasons.

He closed the ledger with a decisive snap, unable to stare at the troubling figures any longer. The press house suddenly felt confining despite its spacious interior, the weight of responsibility pressing down like a physical force. Jack stood, pushing the chair back perhaps more forcefully than necessary, and moved to the doorway.

He drew a deep breath, straightening his shoulders. The figures in the ledger told one story, but the orchard before him told another – one of persistence, resilience, and the steady rhythms of a life measured in seasons rather than quarterly reports.

His mind drifted back to earlier this year when three men had appeared at his gate unannounced. The memory still burned like acid – their gleaming rental car raising dust on the gravel drive, their aftershave detectable before they'd even stepped from the vehicle. Three identical suits in varying shades of gray, with identical smiles that assessed the orchard in terms of square footage and profit potential rather than the living heritage it represented.

'Flynn? Jack Flynn?' The leader had extended his hand without hesitation, seemingly unbothered by Jack's soil-stained palms. 'Martin Walsh, Director of Acquisitions for Crest Beverages. These are my colleagues, Stephen Doyle and Richard Murphy.'

They'd smiled with teeth too white and even, their handshakes firm but somehow soft, uncalloused. Jack remembered noticing their shoes first – posh leather, polished to a high shine, already gathering dust from the orchard paths. Utterly impractical, like they'd dressed for a boardroom rather than a working farm.

'We've been admirers of Goldenridge for some time,' Walsh had continued, his Dublin accent polished smooth by education and corporate training. 'We'd love to take a look at your press house.'

Jack had led them toward the main barn with reluctance, every instinct telling him these men spelled trouble. But his great-uncle Patrick had raised him with manners, and anyway it was sometimes useful to know what the competition was thinking.

'You've stuck to traditional craft methods in an age of industrialization,' Doyle had observed, notepad already in hand, eyes darting from the copper press to the fermentation tanks. 'Commendable dedication to craft.'

'It's not dedication,' Jack had replied, bristling at the reduction of generations of knowledge to a marketing buzzword. 'It's how you make proper cider. Always has been.'

The men had exchanged glances – a quick, practiced communication that sent unease crawling up Jack's spine. He'd seen that look before, at agricultural conferences and industry meetings. The look of men who saw tradition as an obstacle to efficiency.

'Of course,' Walsh said smoothly. 'And that approach is precisely what makes Goldenridge so valuable in today's market.'

They'd walked the orchard rows then, with Walsh casually

narrating a vision of the business's future that made Jack's stomach clench tighter with each sentence. Words like 'streamlining production,' 'maximizing yield potential,' and 'vertical integration' peppered his speech.

'These older heritage varieties are certainly . . . interesting,' Murphy had commented, examining a Cavan Russet with the detached curiosity one might show a museum artifact. 'Though the yield ratio must be challenging. Our agronomists have had tremendous success with high-density plantings of more commercially viable cultivars.'

Jack had stopped walking then, turning to face the three men directly. 'These trees produce exactly what they're meant to; apples with character, complexity, and history that personifies Goldenridge. Not the waxy, tasteless crap they sell in supermarkets.'

If his bluntness had offended them, they hadn't shown it. Instead, Walsh had smiled wider, his eyes calculating. 'Absolutely right. And that's precisely why Crest is interested in honoring that legacy by bringing such traditional methods to a wider audience.'

Beads of sweat had since formed on the executives' foreheads, their suit jackets long since removed and draped over arms. Yet they'd persisted, seemingly oblivious to their discomfort in their determination to make their pitch.

When they'd finally settled in the shade of a sycamore, Walsh had pulled out glossy presentation materials from his leather briefcase. 'We're prepared to offer what we believe is more than fair market value for the land and the business,' he said, sliding a document across the rough wooden table. 'Crest recognizes the unique value proposition Goldenridge represents.'

Jack remembered staring at the figure, the string of numbers momentarily disorienting. It was more money than he'd ever seen, far more than the orchard could generate in years of perfect harvests. For one dizzying moment, he'd allowed himself to imagine what accepting might mean – freedom from constant financial worry, from the physical toll of maintaining the orchard pretty much single-handedly, from the endless battle against cheaper competitors.

But most of all, a chance to see what the world outside of Golden Valley might offer.

Until Murphy had started outlining their 'vision'.

'We'd maintain the Goldenridge name, of course – the brand equity is substantial, nationally at least. The cider line would be incorporated into our Crest Heritage Collection.' He'd flipped through a sleek brochure pointing out other small Irish brands they'd acquired. 'As for the orchards themselves, we'd likely maintain a showcase section of the heritage varieties for tours and marketing materials, while transitioning the bulk of acreage to more viable cultivars.'

The momentary temptation had evaporated instantly. 'You'd rip out trees that have been producing for generations, you mean,' Jack had stated.

Walsh had smiled his corporate smile. 'We prefer to think of it as . . . evolution, Mr Flynn. The market demands consistency and scale. Authenticity is valuable, but it must be balanced with commercial reality.'

'And the cider press? The traditional methods?' Jack had asked, already knowing the answer.

'We'd preserve the antique equipment for demonstration purposes,' Doyle had answered smoothly. 'For production volumes, we'd naturally integrate Goldenridge into our main facility in Dublin. State-of-the-art stainless steel, temperature-controlled fermentation, fully automated.'

They'd continued talking, outlining how Goldenridge's heritage would be preserved even as they dismantled everything that made it what it was. Jack had barely heard them, rage building behind his sternum with each word. When they'd finally paused, clearly expecting his gratitude for their generous offer, he'd stood abruptly.

'I'm not interested. The orchard isn't for sale.'

Their expressions had shifted then, polished enthusiasm giving way to something harder, more calculating.

Walsh had closed his presentation folder with deliberate slowness. 'I understand this must seem sudden. Take some time to consider. But I should mention . . . the market for traditional cider is volatile these days. Large producers like Crest can weather those fluctuations. Small operations . . .' He'd let the implication hang in the air.

'I know my business,' Jack had replied, his voice tight with suppressed anger. 'And I know what you've done to the others you've acquired. How many heritage varieties did Green Valley in Kilkenny have before Crest Beverages bought them? How many now? And how many of their employees still have jobs?'

The question had hung in the air, unanswered.

'This conversation is over,' Jack had said finally.

They'd left behind their business cards and the offer document, Walsh calling a final reminder that the offer 'wouldn't remain open indefinitely' as their car had disappeared down the lane.

'Jack?'

The sound of his name pulled him back to the present. Patrick stood in the doorway of the press house, two steaming mugs in his weathered hands.

At almost seventy-eight, his great-uncle moved more carefully than he once had, but his eyes remained sharp beneath silver brows. He crossed to where Jack sat and placed one mug on the desk.

'Staring at those numbers won't change them,' Patrick observed, settling into the chair opposite with a soft grunt.

Jack pushed the ledger aside and accepted the fresh brew with a nod of thanks. 'Just trying to make sense of it all.'

The older man's gaze was knowing. 'You're thinking about those Crest lads again.'

A humorless laugh escaped. 'Hard not to. Every agricultural magazine I open has another story about a family business being swallowed by corporations. Did you see that the O'Neill's in Waterford sold last month? Fifth generation, gone just like that.'

'Times change,' Patrick said simply, blowing on his tea.

'That's the problem, isn't it? We're endangered – small orchards, traditional methods, varieties that don't meet the supermarket standard of perfect shiny sameness.' Jack's voice roughened with emotion he rarely displayed. 'Every year, more disappear.'

Patrick nodded slowly, his expression thoughtful. 'Been happening since before I was born, lad. My own father worried about the very same things.'

'But it's accelerating,' Jack insisted. 'And the pressure's getting worse. It's not just Crest. That developer in the summer, talking about "luxury holiday cottages with orchard views".' He shook his head in disgust. 'People might want to look at an orchard, but not actually have one functioning nearby. God forbid they smell fermentation or hear a tractor before noon.'

A comfortable silence fell between them as they sipped their coffee.

The older man set his mug down and leaned forward, resting his elbows on his knees. His hands; gnarled now with arthritis but still strong, clasped together as he considered him.

'Goldenridge has weathered far worse than business sharks and property developers,' he said finally. 'Blight that nearly wiped out whole sections. The storm of '86 that took down thirty mature trees in a single night. Markets collapsing, wars, economic crashes.' His eyes, the same deep brown as Jack's own, held steady. 'And yet, here we are, still growing, still pressing cider the way we've always done.' He reached across and tapped the ledger. 'Numbers are just one part of the story, Jack. They don't measure what matters most.'

'They matter when the bills roll in,' Jack countered, though the tightness in his chest had eased slightly at his great-uncle's words.

Patrick smiled, the creases around his eyes deepening. 'Fair enough. But this land has provided through harder times than these. It's not just soil and trees, Jack. It's something in the blood.' He gestured out the window toward the ancient oak, visible in the distance, above the orderly rows of apple trees. 'Something that can't be bought or sold, no matter what numbers they put on their offers.'

Jack followed his gaze, feeling the truth in the words. The orchard wasn't simply land or trees or a business – it was identity, heritage, purpose. The thought of surrendering it to men who saw only profit margins and market share was physically painful.

'Besides,' Patrick added, his voice lightening, 'Nellie Flynn would haunt us both if we let Dublin fellas get their hands on her apple trees. Your great-great-granny could hold a hell of a grudge, from beyond the grave even.'

Despite himself, Jack laughed, the sound loosening something that had been wound too tight inside him.

Patrick drained his mug and stood, placing a hand briefly on Jack's shoulder – a rare physical gesture from a man who expressed affection through action rather than words. 'Come on now. Rain's on the way.'

As they walked together from the press house back into the sunlit orchard, Jack felt his resolve strengthen.

Whatever challenges lay ahead, this land was worth fighting for – not just for himself, but for Patrick and every Flynn who had tended these trees before him, and those who might come after.

Some things mattered more than balance sheets and profit margins.

Some things were beyond price.

Chapter 10

Mid-morning found Molly battling the disorientation of jet lag, her body convinced it was the middle of the night across the Atlantic, while her mind raced forward to the problem at hand.

The village square had grown busier, locals going about their daily routines with an unhurried pace. Her feet carried her almost instinctively toward The Cherry Blossom Café, drawn by both the need for a caffeine hit, and the inviting display of pastries visible through the steamed windows. The duck-egg blue door stood slightly ajar as if in casual invitation, and the weathered wooden sign swung gently in the breeze, its painted blossoms faded to a gentle watercolor wash by years of sun and rain. She pushed the door open, another small brass bell announcing her arrival with a bright, cheerful tinkle.

Obviously a thing around here.

Inside, the café enveloped her in immediate comfort; low wooden beams, darkened by decades of wood smoke and conversation, crossed the ceiling. Worn floorboards creaked pleasantly beneath her feet, their surface polished to a honeyed glow by countless footsteps. The rich aromas of cinnamon, vanilla, and freshly baked bread wrapped around Molly like a familiar embrace, triggering a memory so powerful it momentarily took her breath away. Growing up, *this* was how the kitchen in her childhood home had smelled on Saturday afternoons.

Behind the counter, a pretty woman who Molly guessed to be in her early thirties, about the same as herself, was arranging an assortment of pastries on tiered stands. Her auburn hair was tucked beneath a colorful bandana, the rest escaping in curls around her face, which was flushed from the heat of nearby ovens. Flour dusted her forearms and spotted her apron, which proclaimed *Life is Short, Eat Cake* in cheerful embroidery.

The café was half-full, the lull between breakfast and lunch. Several tables were occupied by locals; Molly could tell by their relaxed postures and the way the woman behind the counter called them by name as she delivered steaming mugs and plates.

A pair of older men played cards further down the back, their game punctuated by good-natured bickering, while a woman with a laptop sat in the opposite corner, typing between bites of something flaky and golden. At a round table right in the center, three older women leaned close, their conversation dropping to whispers as Molly entered. All eyes turned briefly toward the newcomer – not hostile, but curious, assessing. A few nodded politely before returning to their conversations, though she still felt the weight of sidelong glances as she approached the counter.

The proprietor looked up, wiping her hands on her apron. 'Morning!' Her smile was wide and genuine, crinkling the corners of her eyes. 'Welcome. I'm Eva O'Sullivan, and this is my floury little kingdom.' She gestured around the café. 'What can I get ya?'

Molly glanced at the display case, where fruit scones the size of her fist sat next to delicate pastries and sturdier slices of cake. 'Tea would be great, thanks. And one of those scones, if they're as good as they look.'

'Better,' Eva said with a wink, reaching for a plate. 'Plain, fruit, or cheese even?'

'Fruit, please.'

'Wise woman. Just pulled 'em from the oven five minutes ago.'

Eva bustled about, preparing a tray with efficiency that reminded Molly of her own morning routine – a series of movements so practiced they required no conscious thought. 'Take a seat wherever you like and I'll bring everything over.'

Molly chose a small table by the window, where sunlight streamed through lace curtains to create patterns on the wooden surface. She positioned herself with her back to the wall – an unconscious habit from years of business lunches where situational awareness was as important as the conversation. From this vantage point, she could see the square outside while still observing the café's interior.

The jet lag hit her in waves, a peculiar floating sensation followed by sudden, intense clarity. She'd experienced it before on international business trips, but this time it came without the buffer of immediate work demands. She pressed her fingertips against her temples, trying to ground herself in the moment.

Within minutes, Eva appeared beside her table, setting down a tray with practiced grace. 'Here you go – breakfast tea, steeped exactly three and a half minutes. Any longer and it gets bitter, any shorter and sure you might as well be drinking dishwater.' She placed a large mug in front of Molly, followed by a small jug of milk and a bowl of sugar. 'And your scone.' The treat sat on a blue willow plate, golden-brown and studded with plump raisins and currants. Beside it, two small ramekins held cream so thick it formed ridges, and glossy jam the color of wine. A sprig of herbs and small purple flowers in a tiny vase completed the presentation.

'You've got meadowsweet and marjoram around here?' Molly murmured in surprise, touching the delicate white flowers beside deeper purple blooms.

Eva arched a brow. 'Not many visitors recognize local wildflowers,' she said, studying Molly with renewed interest.

'My Irish grandmother was a gardener,' she explained, which was true enough. 'She grew all sorts of herbs.'

'Mine too,' Eva said fondly. 'Taught me everything I know about which plants heal and which flavor.' She nodded toward the herbs. 'Meadowsweet's good for headaches, which you look like you might have brewing yourself.'

'Jet lag,' Molly admitted. 'Everything feels slightly off-kilter.'

'The tea will help. And sugar – no better cure for travel fatigue.' Eva pushed the plate closer. 'Go on then, before it cools too much.'

The scone broke apart with gentle pressure, revealing a still-warm interior. Molly spread a generous dollop of clotted cream followed by a spoonful of jam. The first bite melted on her tongue – buttery, sweet, with a hint of cinnamon and the bright burst of berries.

'Oh,' she moaned, eyes closing briefly. 'That's incredible.'

Eva beamed with genuine pleasure. 'Family recipe. My grandmother started this place with nothing but a cast-iron stove and these scones. Said good food creates loyalty faster than anything else.'

'She wasn't wrong.' Molly took another bite, savoring the contrasting textures. 'These are like crack.'

'I'll take that as a compliment so.' Eva glanced around the café, gauging whether her other customers needed attention. Apparently satisfied, she remained by the table. 'So, what brings you to our little corner of nowhere if you don't mind my asking? Most Americans who make it this far are either looking for their ancestors, or filming travel vlogs.'

The question was direct but not intrusive, asked with the casual interest of someone used to engaging with strangers. Still, Molly felt herself tense slightly, once again remembering the apple farmer's suspicious turnabout yesterday.

'A bit of both, maybe,' she answered carefully. 'My grandmother was from this area. She always talked about how beautiful it was.'

'Ah, ancestors so. We get a lotta those all right.' Eva nodded knowingly. 'Looking up old family records, visiting the church where great-great-someone was baptized and all that jazz?'

'Kind of.' Molly sipped her tea; perfectly brewed, as promised. 'Though more just . . . getting a feel for the place she loved so much.'

Eva's expression softened. 'That's lovely, actually. Most just want the certificate or the gravestone photo to put online.' She leaned forward slightly. 'What was her family name, your grandmother's? Might have a few relatives still knocking around.'

This time, the directness of the question caught Molly off guard. She hesitated, cup halfway to her lips. 'Brennan,' she said finally. 'Though I don't expect anyone to remember her. She left half a century ago.'

'Brennan,' Eva mused, tapping a flour-dusted finger against her chin. 'There's a few around. Pat Brennan runs the hardware shop in the next town over– cranky as they come but decent with his prices. And the Brennan sisters out past the old mill, though they're from the Protestant side, if that matters.'

'It doesn't,' Molly assured her. 'And I'm not looking to connect with distant relatives really. Just wanted to see the place for myself.'

Eva seemed to accept this, though her eyes remained curious. 'Well, you picked an ideal time to visit. The leaves are just starting to turn, and we've had a dry August, which means the walking trails aren't mud pits yet. Have you been out to the lake path? Views are stunning.'

'I walked part of it this morning,' Molly said, relaxing slightly as the conversation shifted to safer territory. 'It's beautiful. So peaceful compared to back home, Manhattan especially.'

'You're from New York?' Eva's eyes widened with interest. 'With the skyscrapers and yellow taxis and all that *Sex and the City* glam?'

She nodded, smiling at her enthusiasm. 'Yep. Though I promise it's less glamorous when you're just trying to get to work in the rain and traffic.'

'Still,' Eva sighed, 'must be exciting. The most excitement we get here is when someone orders apple tart with cream instead of custard.'

They both laughed, and Molly felt some of her guardedness slip away. There was something genuinely likable about Eva – an openness that invited confidence without demanding it.

As they talked, the proprietor's hands remained in constant motion – adjusting the flower vase, brushing invisible crumbs from the table, tucking escaped curls back beneath her scarf. Her stories were punctuated with expressive gestures, her entire body involved in the telling. She described village life with affectionate humor, pointing out the café's regulars with subtle nods and whispered asides.

'That's Dr Murphy there by the window – retired now but still expects everyone to call him "Doctor". Comes in every day at half-eleven for tea and a fruit slice, leaves exactly forty-five minutes later.' She leaned closer, voice dropping confidentially. 'And the three 'oul wans who were whispering when you came in? Tidy Towns committee. Currently debating whether the Christmas lights should extend to the blow-in houses on the lake road. Three meetings so far with no resolution.'

Molly found herself charmed by these glimpses into the village's inner workings, Eva's animated storytelling making even the most mundane local politics seem fascinating. The warmth of the café wrapped around her like a blanket, easing the disorientation of jetlag.

'Oh, and see yer man just coming in now?' Eva nodded toward the door as it opened with another musical chime. 'That's Father Dolan. Youngest priest we've had in twenty years, and half the 'oul wans lining up for daily mass since he arrived.' She winked conspiratorially. 'Though he's more interested in his fishing rod than their plamausing to be fair.' The young priest nodded politely to Eva as he passed, claiming a small table, and taking out a well-thumbed book. His white collar stood stark against his dark shirt, but his weathered hands and sun-browned face suggested time spent outdoors rather than in cloistered study.

'Been running this place long?' Molly asked, taking another sip of her perfectly brewed tea.

'Took over from Mam about five years ago,' Eva said, absently rearranging the herbs in the tiny vase. 'She ran it for twenty before that, and her mother for thirty before her.' Her fingers stilled on the delicate white meadowsweet blooms. 'Could have been a chef in Dublin – that's what I trained for. But Dad got sick, god rest his soul, so I came home to help Mam and then . . .' A shadow crossed her face, quickly replaced by her usual brightness. 'Wasn't the plan, but turned out to be the right thing. There's something about being around people you've known all your life.'

'You never wanted to leave again? After your father . . .' Molly let the question hang, suddenly worried she was overstepping again.

Eva shrugged, the movement sending a loose curl bouncing against her cheek. 'Thought about it. But by then I'd put my stamp on this place, started changing things up a bit – brought in some fancy techniques from my training, modernized Gran's recipes just enough to keep them interesting.' Pride colored her voice. 'Turns out you can make a difference even in a tiny spot on the map.' A timer dinged from behind the counter, and she glanced over her shoulder. 'That'll be the soda bread. Back in a sec.'

As Eva moved away between the tables, Molly found herself studying the café with renewed interest. What had seemed simply charming at first glance now revealed itself as a careful balance of tradition and innovation. The blue willow plates were classic, but they sat alongside modern, hand-thrown pottery. The menu board listed traditional Irish fare alongside items with a contemporary twist – Whiskey-glazed Bacon Tarts and Wild Nettle and Goat's Cheese brioche.

Eva returned moments later, the scent of fresh bread following her like a fragrant shadow. 'Sorry about that. Can't let it go even a minute too long or the bottom burns.'

'This building must be standing a long time,' Molly asked, genuinely curious. 'The stonework and everything . . .'

'Yep, old as the village itself, nearly,' Eva confirmed. 'Used to be the milliner's shop back when hats were a thing. Then it was a cobbler's for a while. My great-grandmother bought it in the forties, when the old cobbler died without an heir.' Her eyes crinkled with amusement. 'They say she won it in a card game, but that might just be family legend.'

'This whole village feels like it's full of them,' Molly enthused, glancing out the window at the square, where a pair of older men were engaged in what appeared to be a spirited debate beside the fountain.

'Oh, if these walls could talk!' Eva laughed. 'Every corner of Golden Valley has seen something worth telling, to be fair. Like that fountain out there – it was a gift from a local lad who went off to make his fortune in Boston during the famine years. Came back rich as Croesus and built it as a thank-you to the village that raised him.' She leaned forward slightly. 'They say the love of his life waited fifteen years for him, never even looked at another fella the whole time he was gone. And hadn't he gone off and married an American one in the meantime.' She rolled her eyes. 'Sure, that's men for you.'

Molly smiled.

'But it's not all romance and homecomings either,' Eva continued, her voice dropping conspiratorially. 'We had our fair share of scandal too. Back in the sixties, there was this huge falling out between two of the oldest families. Something about land boundaries and a disputed orchard. Half the village wouldn't speak to the other half for nearly a decade.'

Molly's attention sharpened at the mention of the orchard, but she kept her expression neutral. 'Sounds serious.'

'Ancient history now.' Eva waved dismissively. 'Though some

of the oldies never forget. That's village life – long memories.' She gestured to Molly's now-empty plate. 'Another scone? Or maybe a slice of apple tart? Made fresh this morning with Goldenridge apples from up the road.' Again, the mention sent a small jolt through Molly, but she managed a casual smile. 'I couldn't possibly. Another tea would be lovely though.'

She was keen to continue listening to the proprietor's chatter. But more, she genuinely liked the woman. There was something irresistibly disarming about Eva's openness, a quality that invited reciprocity despite Molly's carefully maintained guardedness.

Having sorted the priest's order, Eva returned moments later with a fresh brew. As she set it down, her gaze lingered on Molly's face with open curiosity. 'So, New York. Do you work in one of those glass skyscrapers then?'

'I do,' Molly admitted. 'Thirty-fourth street. Marketing executive.'

'So cool . . .' Eva said dreamily.

Molly laughed, the sound surprising her with its genuineness. 'Not really. Mostly endless meetings and too many emails. Not nearly as exciting as deciding the fate of the Christmas lights.'

Eva grinned, acknowledging the gentle tease. 'Well now, don't underestimate the gravity of festive illumination. Last year, Maureen Flynn – no relation to the orchard Flynns – hung those icicle lights upside down so they pointed to the sky instead of the ground. Caused such a tizzy you'd think she'd painted the church purple.'

The image made Molly laugh again, and she felt some of the tension she'd been carrying since her first local encounter begin to ease. She nodded. 'My grandmother used to talk about the local celebrations around here actually. Summer festivals, that sort of thing.'

Eva's face lit up. 'Yep, we're mad for celebrations in Golden Valley. Actually now that you say it, The Harvest Festival is coming up weekend after next – whole village turns out for it. We hang fairy lights in all the trees around the square, every shop puts out specially themed stuff, The Orchard Pub serves harvest cider that's only brewed once a year.' She gestured enthusiastically, nearly knocking over the tiny vase of herbs. 'There's a band and dancing in the square and everything, a market too.'

'Sounds amazing,' Molly said wistfully.

'How long are you staying? You might still be here for it.'

She hesitated. 'I'm . . . not entirely sure to be honest. I haven't made any definite travel plans.'

Her intention was to come here, do the necessary and then head to Dublin for a bit. But that was before she realized she might have a hurdle to overcome to reach Aoife's special tree.

'Well, if you're around, you have to come. I do special autumn-themed creations just for the festival.' The door chimed again, admitting a rush of newcomers – a group of hikers, their faces flushed with exertion and crisp autumn air. Eva glanced over. 'Duty calls again,' she said, rising reluctantly. 'Sure, I'll leave you to it.'

Left alone with her thoughts and her tea, Molly gazed back out the window at the square with some satisfaction.

This was more like the Ireland her grandmother had described – not just the physical landscape, but the easy hospitality, the weaving of past and present in everyday conversation. She watched as the elderly men by the fountain concluded their debate with handshakes and parted ways, one heading toward the newsagent, the other toward the pharmacy. A woman passed with a basket of fresh flowers, pausing to chat with the doctor as he emerged from the café. Each interaction seemed meaningful, unhurried, part of a complex web of relationships that had evolved over time.

Molly sipped her tea slowly, savoring both the rich flavor and the moment of connection she'd just experienced. Aoife had always told her too that in Ireland, a cup of tea was never just a beverage – it was an invitation, a shared ritual.

For the first time, she felt a genuine sense of possibility. Eva's café was like a bridge between the Golden Valley of her grandmother's stories, and the real village before her.

And if Molly could find her way here, perhaps she could also find her way to the oak tree her grandmother had spoken of with such reverence.

Chapter 11

The café had since grown busier, with Eva moving efficiently between tables, yet still finding time for a quick joke or personal question with each customer. It was the kind of place where everyone was treated as a regular, even on their first visit.

As the café owner returned to clear her cup, Molly decided to brave it with a casual mention of yesterday's encounter.

'I met someone from that orchard you mentioned, I think,' she said, aiming for nonchalance. 'When I arrived off the bus yesterday morning, I accidentally knocked over some guy's cart of apples with my suitcase.'

Eva's eyebrows shot up, then a knowing smile spread across her face. 'Ah, you've had the pleasure of Jack Flynn's acquaintance so. Tall, dark and grumpy?'

Jack Flynn.

Molly nodded. 'That's him, I think. He seemed . . . very protective of his apples.'

'Ha! Protective is one way of putting it,' Eva tittered and put a hand on her hip. 'Flynns have been growing apples in these parts since before anyone can remember and Jack treats those trees like they're his children.' She leaned her hip against Molly's table, in no hurry despite the café's increasing busyness. 'Was he short with you? He can be with strangers, especially if his precious fruit is involved.' She rolled her eyes.

'A little,' Molly admitted, carefully editing the encounter. 'But I could hardly blame him, given the damage I'd caused. He was nice enough at first, but I got the impression he doesn't warm to outsiders.'

Eva snorted, the sound unexpectedly unrefined against her otherwise gentle demeanor. 'That's putting it mildly. But look, don't take it personally – Jack's bark is worse than his bite.' She glanced around, then lowered her voice a little. 'Been through the ringer, to be fair. Lost both of his parents young – when he was only twelve, I think. His great-uncle Patrick raised him – distant relative from another town over but the only Flynn left until Jack was old enough to take over at Goldenridge.'

Something in Eva's tone suggested a deeper history, and Molly found herself genuinely curious. 'You know him well then?'

'Sure, everyone knows everyone here,' she replied with a small shrug. 'But yeah, we were in school together. Jack was two years ahead of me, mind – quiet, always had dirt under his fingernails from helping Patrick at the orchard after classes.' A fond smile softened her features. 'Smart though – could have gone to university, had the points for it and everything. But he never wanted anything but those feckin' apple trees.'

She shifted, adjusting her colorful bandana. 'I remember once in school, our science class was supposed to track the growth of bean plants. Everyone else's died within a week, but Jack's not only lived – it produced actual beans. A real-life Jack and the Beanstalk! Ah, he just has this way with growing stuff, always has.'

Molly could almost picture him as a solemn-faced kid carefully tending a plant while other children lost interest. It humanized further the man she'd encountered in the rain.

'His uncle must be proud of him, carrying on the family business,' Molly prompted, hoping to learn more.

'Great-uncle. Like I said, they're barely blood relations

really – Patrick is second cousin once-removed to Jack's grandfather or something . . . but he's Jack's biggest champion. Though of course they're both way too Irish to show it.' Eva smiled fondly. 'Patrick Flynn's a living legend around here though – knows every secret of apple growing, could predict the harvest down to the bushel just by studying the spring blossoms. Handed over the reins to Jack about ten years ago, though he still runs a small farm shop there at weekends.'

Eva reached out absently to straighten the tiny vase of herbs. 'It was a big deal when Patrick stepped back – everyone wondered if Jack would modernize or maybe sell the place to one of the bigger commercial outfits. Lot of pressure for a young lad in his twenties.'

'But he kept it going?' Molly observed thoughtfully.

'More than that – he's preserved ways that other orchards abandoned decades ago. Still presses cider the traditional way, still grafts his own trees.' Pride colored Eva's voice, as if Jack's achievements somehow reflected on the entire community. 'Won awards three years running at the apple fair in Clonmel.'

A timer dinged from behind the counter, and Eva glanced over her shoulder. 'Hold that thought,' she said, hurrying to retrieve what turned out to be a tray of miniature apple tarts, their crusts golden and glistening with sugar. The rich scent of cinnamon and caramelized fruit wafted through the café, prompting appreciative murmurs from nearby tables.

When she returned, she carried a small plate with one of the tarts. 'On the house,' she said, placing it before Molly. 'Just out of the oven – be careful though, it's hot.'

The tart was a work of art in miniature – a perfect circle of buttery pastry cradling slices of apple arranged in a pinwheel pattern, their edges caramelized to a deep amber. A dusting of cinnamon and what might have been nutmeg completed the simple yet elegant presentation.

'That's very kind, but I couldn't possibly . . .' Molly began.

'Consider it cultural education,' Eva insisted with a wink. 'You can't come to apple country without trying an authentic Tipperary apple tart.'

Molly relented, taking a cautious bite of the still-steaming pastry. The flavors were a revelation – apple mellowed by caramelization, buttery pastry with a hint of salt that perfectly balanced the sweetness, and an elusive spice note that lingered pleasantly after each bite.

'This is . . . incredible,' she said honestly. 'The apples taste so different from the ones back home.'

'Jack would tell you it's the limestone soil and the particular angle of the hillside where his orchard sits. Plus those trees have history – some varieties he grows you can't find anywhere else.' As Eva spoke, her expression became more serious. 'That's part of why he's so protective of the place. Been getting pressure from developers the last few years from England and America wanting to build holiday homes with "authentic orchard views". As if you can have an authentic orchard once you've cut down half the trees for scenic overlooks.'

'Sounds . . . challenging,' Molly said, suddenly better understanding the suspicion in Jack's eyes. Perhaps when she'd started asking questions he'd assumed she was yet another corporate scout?

Eva nodded vigorously. 'Goldenridge is prime land – sits on a rise overlooking the lake, old trees, historic stone cottages and what-have-you. But it's more than that to the village. That orchard employs half a dozen locals during harvest, supplies fruit for three counties, and the cider press is part of our heritage.' She leaned closer, her voice dropping conspiratorially. 'Between you and me, I think the constant pressure is part of what's made Jack so . . .' She waved a hand, searching for the right word.

'Prickly?' Molly suggested with a small smile.

'Very diplomatic!' Eva laughed. 'I was going to say "like a hedgehog with a rotten tooth". But he's a good one underneath it all. Just . . .' she hesitated, 'lonely, maybe. The orchard's demanding – doesn't leave much room for a social life.'

A thoughtful silence fell between them, interrupted when a hiker at the counter called over, asking about walking maps. Eva excused herself with an apologetic smile, leaving Molly to finish her tart and contemplate this new information.

When Eva returned, Molly carefully steered the conversation in a new direction. 'Speaking of trees, I heard there might be some interesting ancient oaks up by the lake. The woman in the bookshop mentioned something about a famous one?'

Eva's face brightened immediately. 'The Wishing Oak. Beautiful, hundreds of years old. It's actually on Goldenridge property, at the far end of the orchard.' She brushed crumbs from the table into her palm with practiced movements. 'Legend says it was already ancient when the first Flynn started growing apples there. Some folktale about fairies and lovers and magic – you know how those old stories go.'

On Goldenridge property.

Molly's heart sank, but she kept her expression merely interested. 'Sounds wonderful. Can you give me directions maybe?'

'Well . . .' Eva drew out the word, her expression turning apologetic. 'It's in the back acreage, away from the main orchards. The Flynns don't like people wandering around there, especially during harvest season.' She brightened. 'You can see it from a distance on the lake trail, but like I said, festival's coming up and they always open the gates for that – it's tradition.'

Eva briefly gave directions to a good vantage point on the trail, but was soon caught up in the lunchtime rush. So Molly thanked her, leaving enough euros on the table to cover the food plus a generous tip – even though she figured they didn't really do that in Ireland – promising to return again tomorrow.

The brass bell tinkled cheerfully as she stepped back into the sunshine, her mind whirring with this new information. The square was fully alive now– shoppers carrying bags, children chasing each other around the fountain, tourists consulting maps and taking photos of the quaint storefronts. Molly moved through it all in a slight daze, her weariness returning in a gentle wave as the stimulation of Eva's company faded.

To say nothing of the implications of what she'd just learned.

The oak tree – the object of her mission – stood on private land. Goldenridge land.

Of course it had to belong to the apple guy. Jack Flynn. Upon whom Molly'd already made a poor first impression.

A breeze rippled across the lake, carrying the faint scent of fruit from the distant orchard.

'I'll find a way, Nan,' she murmured. 'Always do.'

Jack Flynn might be the obstacle between her and her grandmother's final wish, but Molly Harris had never backed away from a challenge.

One way or another, she would get to that oak.

Chapter 12

Jack grabbed his pruning shears from the small shed by the cottage, the familiar weight of the tool settling into his palm like an extension of his arm.

There was comfort in physical work, in tasks that demanded complete attention and left no room for brooding over corporate threats or dwindling margins. Pruning required precision, judgment, an understanding of how a cut made today would shape growth for seasons to come. It was the perfect antidote to the anxiety that had knotted his stomach since reviewing the ledgers that morning.

He headed toward the northwest section, where a block of younger trees needed corrective pruning. These five-year-old Bloody Butchers, a heritage variety he'd rescued from near extinction, were still establishing their shape. Their branches reached in all directions with youthful enthusiasm, prioritizing growth over fruit production. Jack's job was to channel that energy, to create the open-center form that would allow light to reach all parts of the tree.

The first cut released a sharp, clean scent of fresh wood. Jack worked methodically, moving from tree to tree with easy efficiency. Each required individual assessment – this one needed its vigorous central leader removed to encourage lateral growth; that one had crossing branches that would rub against each other, creating wounds vulnerable to disease. His hands moved with decisive confidence, shears snipping through young wood with crisp precision.

Patrick had taught him this skill when he was barely tall enough to reach the lower branches, explaining how each cut was a conversation with the tree.

'You're not forcing it,' his great-uncle had said. 'You're suggesting. Showing it the way to grow strong.'

As Jack worked, the sun progressed in the autumn sky, warming his shoulders through his flannel shirt. Sweat began to bead on his forehead, and he paused to wipe it away with his sleeve. Around him, the orchard hummed with subtle life – bees investigating the wildflowers that grew between rows, birds calling from the windbreak trees along the property's edge, the occasional rustle of field mice in the groundcover.

The repetitive nature of the task allowed his thoughts to settle, his breathing to synchronize with the rhythm of his work. Cut, step back, assess. Move to the next branch, position the shears at precisely the right angle, apply pressure. The tension that had gathered between his shoulder blades began to ease, muscles loosening as they warmed with use.

By the time he finished the pruning section, the knot of anxiety in his chest had loosened considerably. Jack gathered the larger pruned branches into a tidy pile for later chipping – nothing was wasted at Goldenridge, not even trimmings that would return to the soil as mulch.

Next came the irrigation lines. Several sections had shown reduced flow during the last watering cycle, likely due to clogs or breaks in the old system.

Walking the rows, he scanned for wet spots that might indicate leaks. The work was methodical, requiring patience and close observation. Jack moved slowly, eyes trained on the black irrigation tubes that snaked along the base of each tree row. Halfway through the third row, he found it – a small but steady spray of water from a cracked connection.

The repair was straightforward but finicky. Jack shut off the water flow, then knelt in the cool soil to cut out the damaged section and splice in a new connector. There was satisfaction in these simple fixes – immediate problems with clear solutions, unlike the larger, more nebulous threats to the orchard's future. When he restored water flow and saw a properly functioning line, the sense of accomplishment was immediate and tangible.

One small thing set right in a world where so much felt beyond his control.

He straightened, stretching his back with a satisfied groan, and realized he'd worked straight through lunch. The sun had passed its zenith and now cast longer shadows across the orchard rows. In the distance, the lake's surface glittered with afternoon light, visible through gaps in the trees at the property's southern edge.

Physical labor had always been his most effective remedy for mental unrest – a fact his great-uncle understood perfectly well, which was probably why Patrick had suggested the irrigation repairs in the first place.

Instead of heading back to the cottage Jack found himself wandering toward the opposite side, where the ancient oak stood sentinel. The tree predated the orchard itself, was already mature when the first Flynn had planted crops on this hillside. Its massive trunk and spreading canopy dwarfed everything around it, creating a cathedral-like space beneath its branches.

Jack approached, his pace slowing as he neared the oak. Some deep-rooted instinct always made him move more deliberately in the presence of this tree, as if approaching an elder deserving of respect. The ground beneath it was covered in fallen acorns that crunched softly underfoot. Dappled sunlight filtered through the leaves above, creating shifting patterns on the grass.

He reached out and placed his palm against the rough bark,

feeling the subtle warmth of life beneath the weathered exterior. The trunk was wider than three or four people could span with their arms, the bark deeply furrowed with age. Jack's eyes traced the countless initials carved into its surface – generations of local couples who had commemorated their relationships here. Some carvings were fresh and sharp-edged, others worn to mere suggestions by decades of weather.

Near eye level, partially obscured by newer markings, were his own parents' initials enclosed in a rough heart. Jack traced the carving with his fingertips, the connection to them momentarily overwhelming. His parents had stood in this same spot, young and in love, never imagining that their time together would be cut short, or that their only son would one day stand here alone.

Not alone, he corrected himself. Standing in a line of Flynns stretching back through time and hopefully, forward into a future he couldn't yet see. The tree had witnessed it all – courtships and marriages, births and deaths, the natural cycles of growth and decline that put human concerns into perspective. Jack leaned his forehead against the bark, closing his eyes briefly. 'I won't be the last,' he murmured, the words half promise, half prayer. 'This land stays with us Flynns.'

He wasn't typically given to dramatic declarations, but something about this ancient living thing invited honesty, as if its roots reached deep enough to anchor his words in reality.

With renewed resolve, Jack turned back toward the orchard. The afternoon was advancing, and there was still the cider press to check before day's end.

As he headed along the boundary, movement near the lakeshore path caught his eye. A solitary figure walked slowly along the water's edge, pausing occasionally to look out across the lake. Even at this distance, Jack recognized her immediately – the American newcomer from yesterday's rain shower, the one who'd known far too much about Goldenridge for a casual tourist.

He slowed. She'd exchanged her rain-soaked attire for jeans and a green sweater that caught the afternoon light. Her dark hair was pulled back, revealing the clean line of her profile as she gazed across the water toward the orchard.

Something tightened in Jack's chest – an instinctive wariness mingled with reluctant attraction. She was cute as a button, as his mother used to say, with those striking green eyes and the determined set of her chin.

Under different circumstances . . .

But those circumstances couldn't be ignored. Her knowledge of Goldenridge's heritage varieties and a product discontinued decades ago, suggested research beyond casual interest.

The American tourist season pretty much finished by August, so Jack wasn't convinced by her explanation yesterday. And what tourist brought a laptop on their holiday? Was she from Crest Beverages, gathering intelligence before yet another acquisition attempt? Or perhaps working for one of the international developers who'd been circling the land like vultures.

Whatever her purpose, her presence by the lake now – clearly studying his land – couldn't be coincidence either.

He turned back toward the cider press, his earlier calm giving way to renewed vigilance. If she represented some corporate interest, she'd soon discover that the Flynns weren't easily uprooted. This land, these trees, the legacy they represented – they weren't for sale, not at any price. Yet he found himself glancing back once more. The woman remained by the lake shore, seemingly lost in thought as she gazed across the water.

For a fleeting moment, Jack allowed his mind to wander away from the reason that might have brought her to Golden Valley, and onto why the sight of her there, backlit by afternoon sun, stirred something beyond suspicion in his carefully guarded heart.

Chapter 13

Molly followed the narrow trail that curved along the lake's eastern shore, her feet crunching on the carpet of fallen leaves. The crisp afternoon air carried the scent of water and earth, of things growing and things dying back for winter. Perfect walking weather, though her purpose wasn't merely recreational.

The lake stretched beside her like polished pewter, its surface rippled by an occasional breeze that sent wavelets lapping against the rocky shore. Ducks paddled in the shallows, leaving V-shaped wakes behind them. On the opposite shore, the village looked like a watercolor painting; stone buildings with smoke curling from chimneys, the church spire rising above them all. Molly paused to take a photo with her phone, then thought better of it. Some moments demanded to simply be experienced.

She continued walking, the path narrowing as it wound between the water and a rising slope dotted with rowan trees. Their berries hung in bright-red clusters, drawing eye and hand alike. Molly resisted the urge to pick some, then paused as she remembered some old Irish superstition about it being bad luck.

She smiled, feeling silly.

A gust of wind swept across the lake, stronger than before, sending a shower of golden leaves spiraling down around her.

One landed on her shoulder, and Molly plucked it off, examining its perfect star shape before letting it flutter from her fingers.

The trail curved again, leading away from the shore and up a gentle incline. She followed it, her breathing quickening slightly with the climb. At the crest of the small hill, the path divided; one fork continuing along the lakeshore, the other cutting inland between mature sycamores whose peeling bark revealed patches of cream and olive beneath.

Eva's directions from earlier echoed in her memory: 'Take the inland path when you reach the sycamores. The oak is in a clearing further beyond, though you'll see it well before you reach it.'

Molly took the path, ducking beneath low-hanging branches. Sunlight filtered through the canopy above, dappling the ground with shifting patterns of light and shadow. The sounds of the lake receded, replaced by the rustle of leaves overhead and the distant tap-tap-tap of a woodpecker. The trees thinned ahead, allowing more light to penetrate.

And then, suddenly, she saw it.

A ginormous oak tree rose from the landscape like something from another age, impossibly massive against the backdrop of smaller trees surrounding it. Its trunk was wider than Molly had imagined possible, gnarled and textured with centuries of growth. Branches spread in all directions, some as thick as normal trees themselves, creating a canopy that must have spanned fifty feet or more. Even now in autumn, it retained many of its leaves – deep green at the center, burnished gold at the outer edges. It stood quite a way behind a low stone wall that marked the boundary of the neighboring property, but even from this distance, its presence was commanding.

She paused, her breath catching. This was no ordinary tree. This was a living monument, a bridge between past and present, exactly as her grandmother had described. She could almost hear Aoife's voice: 'The kind of thing that makes you believe in magic.'

A strange feeling washed over her – part déjà vu, part homecoming.

Though she'd never stood in this spot before, had never seen this tree except through her grandmother's words, something about it resonated in Molly's blood. Recognition without memory.

She approached the boundary wall slowly, her footsteps hushed by the carpet of leaves and moss. The stone barrier was low enough to step over; roughly waist-high and weathered by centuries of damp. Lichen painted its surface in patches of silver-gray and pale green. In places, the mortar had crumbled away, leaving gaps between stones where ferns had taken root.

She reached the wall and placed a hand on its rough, cool surface, leaning slightly to peer at the tree beyond. The velvet parcel back in her hotel room seemed to call to her across the distance, urging completion of the task she'd traveled so far to fulfill.

'This is private land.'

The voice cut through the stillness, startling her.

Molly spun sideways, heart hammering, to find the apple guy from yesterday, Jack Flynn, standing several paces away on the other side of the wall. He'd approached silently, his footsteps masked by the rustle of leaves and her own absorption.

He stood with arms crossed over his chest, legs planted firmly apart in a stance that claimed his territory. The afternoon sun caught in his dark hair, highlighting strands of chestnut among the deeper brown. Combined with his rugged handsomeness, the effect would ordinarily have been arresting, only for his expression, which was guarded, suspicious.

'I . . .' Molly began, but couldn't quite find the words. Caught red-handed at the boundary of his property, she had no ready explanation.

'I said, this is private land.' He gestured toward the wall. 'Goldenridge property starts here. No trespassing.'

'I wasn't trespassing,' Molly said, finding her voice. 'I was just . . . looking.'

Jack's eyes narrowed, skepticism evident in the downward turn of his mouth. 'Looking pretty intently. At an area that's not visible from a public path unless you go looking for it.' He took a step closer, his gaze harder now. 'Crest doesn't quit easily, eh?'

Molly's brow furrowed in confusion. 'I don't even know who that is.' She glanced back at the oak, then to Jack again. 'I heard about an ancient oak tree from Eva at the café. I like old trees.' The explanation sounded weak even to her own ears.

'Right,' Jack said, the single word dripping with disbelief. 'You rolled into town only yesterday, someone happened to mention a specific tree on private land, and you happened to find your way here, and you happened to be now admiring it with such . . . casual interest.' He gestured toward her phone, which she'd unconsciously pulled out with the intention of photographing the tree to show to Cole.

Molly slipped the device back into her pocket, realizing that this confrontation was heading in the wrong direction again. This guy had already formed his opinion of her as a potential enemy to his land, so antagonizing him further wouldn't help. She needed a different approach.

She softened her posture, letting her shoulders relax and allowing a small smile to curve her lips.

'You caught me,' she chuckled. 'I'm a bit of a tree enthusiast. Back home, I volunteer with the parks department in my spare time.' The lie came easily, a small one – just until she got back enough on his good side to explain her true interest in the oak, and ask permission to access it. 'When Eva mentioned a tree older than the village itself, well . . . I couldn't resist coming to see it.' Molly stepped away from the wall, moving slightly closer to Jack instead. 'I'm not from any company or corporation, I assure you. Just someone with a weakness for impressive oaks.' She extended her hand. 'Let's start over. Molly Harris, a tourist. Absolutely not affiliated with Crest, whoever that might be.'

Jack looked at her outstretched hand as if it might bite, making no move to take it. His eyes, deep brown and flecked with amber in the afternoon light, held hers with unwavering intensity.

Again, Molly felt a flutter of something that had nothing to do with the confrontation – an awareness of him as more than an obstacle. The stubborn set of his jaw, the way his battered leather jacket stretched across broad shoulders, the strength evident in his weathered hands.

'Right,' he said finally, ignoring her attempted handshake. 'Look, I don't know what your game is, but I've seen your type before. The friendly approach, the casual questions, the interest in my land.' His voice hardened. 'Then comes the offer, always presented as some great opportunity that I'd be a fool to refuse.'

She let her hand fall back to her side, the flutter of attraction quickly overshadowed by embarrassment.

'I'm not interested in buying your orchard,' Molly assured him. 'I'm here on personal business that has nothing to do with you or your land.' Not entirely true, but close enough. She tried once more, letting her smile widen just enough to create the dimple in her left cheek that her colleagues called her 'secret weapon' in difficult client meetings. 'In fact, I was hoping to try some of your famous cider while I'm in the village. Eva tells me it's worth crossing the Atlantic for.' The flirtation in her tone was subtle but unmistakable – a tactic she'd rarely needed to employ in her professional life, but in this case, was worth a shot. Especially when he'd been perfectly fine with it yesterday.

Jack's posture became, if possible, even more rigid. 'The Orchard Pub serves our cider. Edge of the main square. Can't miss it.' Each word was clipped short, while his face was a mask of cold resistance. 'Now, if you're finished "admiring" my oak, I have work to do.'

His emphasis on 'my oak' carried a clear message: whatever Molly's interest in the tree, he considered it off-limits. Boundaries were being drawn, not just in the physical space but in the interaction between them.

She'd miscalculated, Molly knew, a little ashamed now. The charm that disarmed corporate boardrooms had only deepened his suspicion. Worse, after their flirtatious encounter yesterday, she found herself genuinely disappointed by his response – or lack thereof. There was something about this guy – his directness, perhaps, or the evident passion he had for his land – that sparked unexpected interest.

Interest that was clearly not reciprocated.

'Fine,' she said, stepping back from the wall. 'So sorry to have bothered you.' Molly turned to go, frustration and disappointment mingling uncomfortably in her chest.

A few steps down the path, she paused and looked back.

Jack Flynn stood where she'd left him, silhouetted against the afternoon sky, the ancient oak rising majestically behind him. For a moment, they looked like parts of the same picture – the man and the tree, equally rooted, equally stubborn.

Noticing her pause, he gestured toward the village again. 'Pub's that way,' he reiterated. 'Enjoy.'

The dismissal was unmistakable. She turned away, trying to ignore the sting of his rejection – both of her interest in the tree and her subtle overtures, and headed back along the path, autumn leaves crunching beneath her feet, the sound no longer pleasant but percussive with frustration.

The worst part wasn't Jack Flynn's suspicion or his brusque manner. It was the fact that despite all that, despite his entirely unreasonable hostility, Molly still found herself drawn to him.

The intensity in his eyes when he spoke of his land, the evident pride he took in his heritage, even the protectiveness that manifested as rudeness – all hinted at a depth of character that intrigued her far more than it should.

'Ridiculous,' she muttered to herself as the path curved back toward the lake. She was here for her grandmother, for a promise made at Aoife's bedside.

Not to develop an inconvenient attraction to a grumpy apple farmer who clearly wanted nothing to do with her.

Chapter 14

On Saturday afternoon, Molly stood this time at the official entrance to Goldenridge Orchard. Outside the gate, a makeshift sign hung gently: Goldenridge Farm Shop.

After another fruitless (hah!) encounter with Jack Flynn, she'd retreated to the hotel to lick her wounds and reconsider her approach. Eva had mentioned something about a weekend farm shop at the orchard, and so she'd asked the older woman, Brid, at the Glen Arms about it.

'Sign at the main gate, can't miss it, open Saturday and Sunday afternoons. Tell Patrick I said hello.'

Though 'shop' was an overstatement, Molly thought now. A small outbuilding sat nestled against a larger structure that must be the cider press. The main building appeared much older, with thick stone walls and small, latticed windows that reflected the light. Roses climbed one wall, their late blooms adding splashes of pink against the weathered white paint.

The orchard seemed peaceful today, with only the distant sound of a tractor's engine in the background. Hoping that Jack Flynn was safely out of the way this time, Molly approached the outhouse and pushed open the door.

The interior enveloped her in a symphony of sensations. Light streamed through the small windows in golden shafts, and the room smelled of polished wood, ripe fruit, and the sweet-sharp tang of fermentation from the cider press next door. Beneath these dominant scents lingered subtler notes: beeswax, hay, and the earthy scent of fresh apples.

Wooden shelves lined the walls, laden with Goldenridge products arranged in meticulous displays. Bottles of cider in varying shades of amber stood in orderly rows, their labels embossed with the orchard's logo; an oak tree with roots that transformed into flowing script.

Jam jars filled with apple butter, preserves and chutneys caught the light, their contents glowing like jewels. A small refrigerator held wedges of cheese, small tubs of cream, and what appeared to be homemade ice cream.

At the center of the shop, a large oak table displayed the star attractions – apples arranged by variety in shallow wooden bowls. Each bore a handwritten card identifying the type and best uses: Cox's Orange Pippin – Dessert, Great for Fresh Eating; Bloody Butcher – Cooking, Holds Shape; Kilkenny Pearmain – Cider, Complex Flavor.

Behind the table sat a tall, lean man with a shock of silver hair. He stood up as Molly entered, his weathered face composed and watchful. Despite his evident age – seventy-something at least – he stood straight, with only a slight stoop to his shoulders. A thick sweater in oatmeal wool hung loosely on his frame, and his hands resting on the counter bore the callouses and slight tremor of someone who'd worked the land for decades.

This must be the great-uncle, Patrick.

'Afternoon,' he greeted, his voice carrying the melodic lilt of rural Ireland softened by age into a gentle burr. 'Welcome.'

'Hey there,' Molly replied, trying to mask her nervousness with a bright smile. 'Your shop is lovely.'

The man nodded acknowledgment but offered nothing more,

his brown eyes watching her with careful assessment. Unlike Jack's outright suspicion, his gaze held more measured curiosity.

Molly moved to the table of apples, giving herself time to gather her thoughts. She picked up a small, golden-russet fruit, its skin rough against her palm. 'Is this the Pippin? I've read about them but never had the chance to try one.'

'Heritage variety, those don't travel well now,' Patrick said, his voice warming slightly at the question. 'Most commercial growers won't touch 'em – too finicky, too fragile for supply chains. But there's nothing that matches their flavor all the same.' He moved from behind the table with careful steps, coming to stand opposite her. 'Try it,' he suggested, gesturing to the fruit. 'Best way to understand an apple is to taste it.'

Molly bit into it, surprised by the resistance of its skin before it yielded with a satisfying crunch. The flesh was dense and aromatic, with a complexity she'd never experienced in supermarket varieties – sweet honey notes followed by a sharp, refreshing acidity, finishing with something almost nutty.

'Oh,' she said, eyes widening involuntarily. 'That's incredible.'

A smile flickered across Patrick's face, softening the weathered contours. 'That's what real apples taste like. Not those waxy yokes they grow for looks.'

Molly took another bite, savoring the flavors. 'I can see why you keep growing them, even if they're challenging.'

'Some things are worth the extra trouble,' Patrick said, his eyes never leaving her face. There was an assessor's quality to his gaze, as if he were cataloging her reactions against some internal standard.

Molly moved around the table, examining the other varieties. 'Do you have many trees of these heritage types?'

'More than most orchards these days to be fair,' Patrick replied. 'The boss is stubborn about keeping the old varieties going, even when it would be easier to switch to modern stuff.' There was unmistakable pride in his voice. 'Says the world doesn't need another Pink Lady, but might just need the last remaining Cavan Russets.'

'He sounds . . . passionate about preserving tradition,' Molly said carefully, testing the waters.

Patrick nodded, reaching out to rearrange a display of small honey jars. 'The boy was born with apple sap in his veins, I swear it. Could tell varieties apart by the blossom alone by the time he was seven.'

Molly moved toward the shelves of bottled cider, running her fingers over the embossed labels. 'Eva at the café in town mentioned your harvest special cider is something special,' she said, changing the subject to safer ground. 'Will you be selling it at the festival next week?'

'Indeed we will.' Patrick followed her, his movements deliberate but graceful for a man his age. 'Special batch just for the occasion – only released once a year.'

'Sounds amazing,' Molly said honestly. 'Eva described the festival as magical – lights in the trees, music, the whole village celebrating.'

'Been that way for generations,' Patrick confirmed, leaning slightly against the shelf. 'Tipp knows how to honor the harvest. Always has.' He studied her for a moment. 'Your first time in these parts, is it?'

'First time to Golden Valley, yes,' Molly answered carefully. 'My grandmother was from around here, though she left a long time ago. Didn't talk much about any relatives,' she added quickly. 'But she always spoke of Golden Valley with fondness. Especially during autumn – said there was nowhere on earth more beautiful when the leaves were turning.'

Patrick nodded approvingly. 'Your grandmother knew her stuff, so. Autumn's indeed when the Golden Vale shows its true colors.'

Molly moved toward a display of jars labeled Apple Blossom Honey. She picked one up, examining the contents.

'Wild honeybees have lived in the hollow trees at the eastern edge for as long as anyone can remember,' he told her. 'We just leave them to their work.'

As they talked, Molly found herself genuinely interested in the orchard's operations. Patrick's initial reserve continued to warm as he explained how certain tree varieties were grafted to preserve their lineage, how the honey's flavor changed depending on which blossoms the bees favored in a given year, how the cider press still used methods that had remained essentially unchanged for centuries.

'The festival must be a great opportunity to showcase all of this,' she observed, gesturing to the products surrounding them. 'Do you get lots of visitors to the farm usually?'

'Just at weekends,' Patrick said, a note of ambivalence in his voice. 'My great-nephew worries about commercializing too much. Says he doesn't want the place to become a "tourist attraction".' The quotation marks were audible in his tone.

'There's a big difference between commercializing and sharing heritage,' Molly mused thoughtfully. 'In my work – marketing – I often help traditional businesses highlight what makes them special without compromising their values.'

Patrick's head tilted slightly, interest piqued. 'How so?'

'Well,' Molly said, warming to the subject, 'for instance, these heritage varieties have stories behind them. If it were me, I'd create small cards with each apple's history – where it originated, how long Goldenridge has grown it, what makes it unique. People connect with stories.' She gestured toward the cider bottles. 'Or maybe offering guided tastings that explain the traditional pressing methods, why they matter, how they affect flavor.'

She moved back to the central table, automatically rearranging a few apples in their display bowls. 'You're not just selling fruit or cider after all; you're selling centuries of knowledge, a connection to something authentic in a world where that's increasingly rare.'

Patrick watched her with intensifying interest as Molly

continued, unable to help herself. This wasn't any kind of play to get him on side, she was genuinely passionate about this stuff.

'The key is to educate visitors rather than simply sell to them. Help them understand why preserving these varieties matters, why traditional methods produce superior results. People pay more for something when they understand its true value.' Her professional instincts had well and truly taken over, as she found herself imagining how Goldenridge might better tell its story. 'You could even—'

Her words were interrupted by the sound of the door opening and Molly turned, instinctively knowing who she would see even before the tall foreboding figure filled the doorway.

Chapter 15

Patrick Flynn had seen his great-nephew angry plenty of times before, but rarely with the particular intensity that now darkened Jack's face as he caught sight of the tourist. The lad's shoulders went rigid beneath his jacket, jaw clenching tight enough that Patrick could almost hear teeth grinding.

Outside, clouds scudded across the sun, momentarily dimming the golden light that had filled the shop seconds before. The timing wasn't lost on Patrick – nature itself seeming to acknowledge the sudden shift in atmosphere.

'What the hell are you doing here?' Jack demanded, his voice low and hard as he stepped fully into the shop. Soil clung to his boots, leaving small clumps on the worn wooden floor. His hands – capable hands that could graft a sapling with surgical precision – clenched and unclenched at his sides.

The woman straightened her spine, those green eyes flashing with defiance. 'I'm shopping,' she replied coolly, holding up a jar of apple butter. 'That's what shops are for, isn't it?'

Jack took another step forward. 'I thought I made myself clear before. This is private property.'

'The sign outside says "Open",' the American girl countered, setting the jar down with deliberate care. 'And your uncle has been kind enough to answer my questions about your products.'

Patrick watched the exchange with curiosity. Jack's hostility seemed disproportionate, even accounting for his usual wariness of strangers. The lad practically vibrated with tension, though Patrick couldn't help noticing how his gaze kept returning to the woman's face, despite his evident desire to dismiss her.

'Jack,' Patrick said mildly, moving from behind the table with unhurried steps, 'this lady has been expressing interest in our heritage varieties. Good eye for quality, she has.'

Jack's head snapped toward him, betrayal flashing across his features. 'She's been asking about more than apples too, I'd wager.' He turned back to her. 'What was it this time? Production volumes? Property boundaries? Or straight to the land valuation?'

Patrick felt his eyebrows rise. He thought she was from one of those corporate outfits, then. That explained the heightened reaction, though not the intensity of it.

The woman set down the jar she'd been examining, her movements controlled but her cheeks flushing. 'For the last time, I'm not interested in buying your orchard. I'm a tourist visiting my grandmother's homeland, nothing more.'

'A tourist who just happens to know about discontinued Sunrise cider? A tourist who just happens to find her way through the lake trail to our boundary? A tourist who conveniently appears right when Crest is making another push to acquire us?' Jack's voice rose with each question, filling the small shop.

'I told you I don't know who or what Crest is,' she insisted, matching his intensity. 'And I've already explained how I knew about the oak – Eva told me.'

Patrick cleared his throat, drawing both their attention. 'Perhaps,' he suggested, his voice cutting through the tension, 'we might all take a breath.' He turned to Jack. 'Whatever you think this young woman's intentions are, she's still a customer in our shop. We've never turned away anyone wanting to buy our apples, not in four generations.'

Jack's expression hardened further. 'Times change. And we've never had so many corporate vultures circling.' He gestured toward her. 'They send them in looking friendly, asking innocent questions, getting the lay of the land before the men in suits show up with their threats about "market realities".'

'I'm not—' the woman began, but Jack cut her off.

'I want you off my land,' he said flatly. 'Now.'

Patrick felt a flare of irritation. The lad had good reason to be suspicious after the Crest Beverages business, but this was different. There was something genuine about the woman, something Jack was too blinded by his fears to see.

'That's enough, Jack,' Patrick said, his voice firmer now. His age and the legacy of raising the boy gave weight to his words, stopping Jack short. 'This lady is a guest, and she'll leave when she's ready. If she wants to purchase something before she goes, all the better for our accounts.'

The silence that followed was thick enough to slice. Jack stared at him, disbelief and embarrassment warring in his expression. She looked between them, clearly uncomfortable at being the cause of family friction.

'I should go,' she said quietly, heading for the door. 'Thank you for your time, Mr Flynn.' The formality was clearly meant for Patrick alone.

'Take this with you,' he said, reaching for a bottle of their premium reserve cider. 'Consider it an apology for the . . . misunderstanding.' He met Jack's glare with calm certainty, daring the younger man to contradict him.

She hesitated, then accepted the bottle with a small smile that transformed her face in a way that made Patrick's heart constrict for some reason.

'Thank you. That's very kind.'

'A poor substitute for proper hospitality,' Patrick said, walking her toward the door. 'Perhaps you'll give us another chance at the festival if you're still here.'

Jack made a sound that might have been protest, but Patrick silenced him with a look honed over decades of authority. Some battles weren't worth fighting in front of strangers, and the lad knew it.

The woman paused at the threshold, the bottle cradled against her chest like something precious. 'I'd like that,' she said softly, then added with a glance toward Jack, 'though not everyone seems to share the sentiment.'

'Don't mind him,' Patrick said, lowering his voice though he knew Jack could still hear. 'Bark's worse than his bite.'

A smile flickered across her face. 'So I've heard.' With a final nod of thanks, she stepped outside, the door closing behind her with a soft thud.

Patrick turned to find Jack radiating silent fury, arms crossed tight across his chest. Beyond him, through the shop window, the woman's figure receded down the path toward the main gate, autumn sunlight catching in her dark hair.

'What are you playing at?' Jack demanded once she was out of earshot. 'Inviting that one to the festival? Giving away our reserve stock?'

Patrick moved back behind the counter, taking his time to gather his thoughts. Age had its privileges, including the right to make others wait for answers. He adjusted a display of honey jars before replying.

'I don't share your conviction that the girl's here with ill intent,' he said finally. 'She asked good questions. Showed genuine interest in our methods, our history.'

'That's their technique,' Jack insisted, stalking closer to the counter. 'They research you, figure out what you're proud of, then use it to soften you up before the kill. I've seen it before.'

The Crest affair had left deeper scars than he'd realized. Patrick studied his great-nephew's face – the stubborn set of his jaw, the defensive posture, the almost desperate need to protect. All admirable qualities in their way, but sometimes a man's strengths could blind him to opportunities.

'She understands modern sales better than you or me,' Patrick continued. 'Said some interesting things about how we could better show what makes Goldenridge special without compromising our values.'

'We don't need marketing advice from some Yank blow-in who doesn't know the first thing about apple growing,' Jack muttered, but with less conviction than before.

Patrick hid a smile. The lad's defenses were cracking, just a little. 'Knew enough to appreciate the Pippin at first bite.' He paused, then added casually, 'Pretty thing, isn't she? Even when she's angry.'

The color that rose to Jack's cheeks confirmed what Patrick had suspected since the moment his great-nephew had burst through the door – the lad's intense reaction wasn't solely about business concerns.

'That's got nothing to do with anything,' Jack said stiffly. He pushed away from the counter, clearly eager to escape the conversation. 'I need to get back to the irrigation lines in the east section. Those new couplings are leaking again.'

Patrick nodded, recognizing the retreat for what it was. 'Clean those boots before you track half the orchard through the place. Brid's coming up with the hotel order later, and you know how she notices dirt.'

With a grunt of acknowledgment, Jack headed for the door. He paused with his hand on the latch, looking back with a frown still creasing his brow. 'Don't go inviting her to anything else,' he said, an attempt at firmness undermined by uncertainty. 'The American one. I don't trust her.'

The door banged as he left, leaving Patrick alone in the quiet shop. Outside, the clouds had parted, allowing sunlight to stream once more through the small windows.

He moved back to the table, his old joints protesting the day's exertions. Jack's suspicion was understandable but misplaced. The girl wasn't a threat – of that, Patrick was certain. Whether she might be a blessing remained to be seen, but he'd lived long enough to recognize possibility when it appeared on his doorstep.

As for Jack's reaction to her – that fierce, immediate intensity that went beyond mere suspicion – Patrick had recognized that too. The lad might insist he distrusted the woman, but his face told a different story.

The way his eyes followed her movements, the heightened color in his face when she challenged him, the tension that crackled between them like static before a storm – Patrick had seen it all before in various guises.

Maybe inviting the woman to the festival might have been a brainwave? God knew Jack needed more in his life besides apples. Patrick worried enough as it was that the lad didn't seem to live for anything else but the orchard.

Much as he too loved Goldenridge, that really wasn't a life at all. Something Patrick himself understood all too well.

Chapter 16

Molly strode along the lakeshore, each step punctuated with frustration.

The bottle of premium cider the older man had gifted her swung in its paper bag, the glass clinking against her leg with every determined stride. She hadn't come halfway across the world for her mission to be thwarted by a stubborn apple farmer who couldn't see past his own suspicions.

'Corporate vultures,' she muttered, mimicking Jack's accusatory tone. 'As if I care about his precious apples.'

But even as the words left her lips, she knew they weren't entirely true. The brief encounter with Patrick had revealed something special – an operation that valued tradition and quality over commercial efficiency, a place where apple varieties with history and character still thrived.

In another context, she might even have admired Jack Flynn's dedication.

The lake stretched beside her, its surface rippling under a gentle breeze that carried the scent of water and soil. Sunlight danced across the small waves, creating shimmering patterns that shifted with each gust.

Molly paused, her irritation momentarily forgotten as she

watched a heron glide low over the water, its reflection a perfect mirror image before it disappeared into the reeds.

The vibration of her phone broke the moment. She pulled it from her pocket to see Cole's face filling the screen, her brother's familiar grin distorted slightly by the wide-angle lens of the video-calling app. She swiped to answer.

'There she is . . .' Cole's voice boomed, slightly tinny through the phone's speakers. Behind him, a locker room bustled with activity – bare-chested hockey teammates in various stages of dress, equipment bags being unzipped, voices echoing off tiled walls. 'How's my favorite sister enjoying the old country?'

'I'm your only sister, smartass,' Molly replied automatically, a small smile breaking through her foul mood. 'Gimme a second.' She spotted a weathered wooden bench facing the lake and sat down, adjusting her position until she found the perfect angle that showed her face without catching the afternoon glare. 'That's better,' she said. 'Now I can properly see your smug mug.'

Cole's laugh was as warm and familiar as a childhood blanket. 'Uh oh. Not having the idyllic Irish vacation you imagined?'

Molly sighed, her shoulders slumping. 'It's beautiful here, don't get me wrong. The village is exactly like Nan described it. But I'm hitting a wall with accessing the oak tree.' She lowered her voice, though there was no one within earshot. 'It's on private land – an apple orchard called Goldenridge – and the owner is . . . difficult.'

'Difficult how?' Cole leaned closer to the screen.

'He thinks I'm a corporate spy trying to buy his orchard,' she grumbled. 'He practically called me a Yank and ordered me off his property just now.' Molly ran a hand through her hair, disheveling it further. 'It was like something out of that movie Nan used to make us watch – *The Field*. I half-expected him to start ranting about his father's father's land.'

Cole burst out laughing. 'Only you, Molls. Only you could travel to the land of a thousand welcomes and immediately make an enemy.'

'It's not funny,' she protested, though a reluctant smile tugged at her lips. 'I need to get to that tree, Cole. I promised Nan.'

'And when has Molly Harris ever failed to keep a promise?' His voice softened. 'Remember when you were eleven and promised Mrs Abramowitz you'd shovel her walk all winter? Pop said it was too much, but you did it anyway – even during that massive storm when the snow was up to your waist.'

'I had to stand on a bucket to reach her doorbell,' Molly remembered, the image clear as yesterday.

'Or what about the time you were determined to get Nan's recipe for soda bread exactly right? Fourteen batches, Molls. The apartment smelled like flour for a month.'

'Fifteen,' she corrected. 'And I still didn't manage it.'

Cole's expression grew more serious, his voice dropping. 'My point is, you don't give up. Ever. It's your superpower and your curse. If anyone can break down this farmer's defenses, it's you.'

The reminder of her own tenacity straightened Molly's spine a little. 'Thanks for the pep talk, Coach.'

'Anytime.' His grin returned. 'So tell me more about this difficult farmer. Is he all rugged and handsome too?'

Heat rushed to Molly's cheeks. 'Irrelevant.'

Cole's eyebrows shot up. 'Oh-ho, he is! This just got interesting.'

'Shut up,' she chided, but she was smiling. 'How's Pop doing?'

The abrupt subject change didn't fool Cole for a second, but he allowed it. 'He's great. Still refusing to use the pill organizer I bought him, insisting he can remember which medications to take when. But I check the bottles every few days, and he's keeping up with them.' Cole shifted, and the camera angle wobbled. 'Speaking of, he told me to check that you're eating OK.'

The familiar worry in their grandfather's question made Molly smile. 'Tell him I'm being force-fed Irish fry-ups and apple tarts. The food here is amazing, actually.'

A voice called Cole's name from off-camera. Her brother turned and nodded before facing her again. 'Gotta go – team huddle.

But hey, you're supposed to be relaxing too, remember? Not just mission-focused. Enjoy the downtime.'

'I am,' Molly assured him. 'The village is beautiful. The people are friendly. Well, most of them.'

'Except your Hot Farmer Nemesis,' he teased.

'He's not hot,' Molly lied. 'And he's not mine.'

'Yet.' Cole's grin widened.

'Goodbye, brother! Go break a leg or whatever.'

The screen went dark, and Molly stared at her own reflection for a moment before pocketing the phone. Cole's confidence in her was heartening, but he didn't understand the full complexity of the situation. This wasn't a matter of pure determination. Jack Flynn was proving a helluva tough nut to crack.

The breeze picked up, rustling the leaves of nearby trees and sending ripples across the lake's surface. Molly shivered slightly, realizing the evening had advanced and the air had cooled. Her stomach growled, reminding her that anger and frustration burned calories.

She stood, stretching muscles stiff from sitting, and headed back toward the village, her feet carrying her almost automatically back to The Cherry Blossom Café. The blue door stood invitingly ajar, and the rich aroma of Eva's baked goods wafted onto the street. Her mouth watered in Pavlovian response.

Inside, the café embraced her once again with warmth; both physical from the ovens and emotional from the cozy atmosphere. Late afternoon light streamed through the windows, casting long golden rectangles across the worn wooden floor.

Eva stood behind the counter, her curly auburn hair escaping from beneath yet another colorful bandana. Flour dusted her forearms and speckled her apron as she poured tea into mismatched mugs; a blue willow pattern for one customer, a hand-painted ceramic for another. She looked up, her face brightening with recognition as she spotted Molly.

'There she is! I was beginning to think you'd abandoned us

already.' The proprietor's smile was wide and genuine. 'Perfect timing too, I just pulled a batch of gingerbread from the oven. Crisp edges, soft center, like the best men. If we could only find them,' she added wistfully.

Molly perched onto a stool by the counter, her frustrations settling heavily on her shoulders. 'I'll take *all* the gingerbread, thanks. And the strongest tea you can legally serve.'

Eva laughed, already reaching for an oversized mug painted with tiny rabbits. 'That bad, eh? What happened? Did you get lost on the lake path? Told you some of those trails can be tricky.'

'I didn't get lost,' Molly said, unwinding her scarf. 'I've just been up to the Goldenridge farm shop.'

'Ah.' Eva's expression became knowing as she set the steaming mug before Molly. 'Jack charming as ever, I take it?'

'If by "charming" you mean "accused me of being a corporate landgrabber and ordered me off the property", then yes, absolutely.' Molly wrapped her hands around the warm mug, inhaling the fragrant steam. 'He seems utterly convinced I'm there to . . . what was it? Make an "insulting offer" for his precious orchard. Why the heck would I do that?'

Eva winced sympathetically as she slid a plate with a generous square of dark gingerbread across the counter.

Molly bit off a corner. The gingerbread was still warm, the spices releasing their aroma as she brought it to her lips. The first bite was a perfect balance of sweetness – ginger, cinnamon and something else she couldn't quite identify, all wrapped in molasses depth.

'Oh man,' she murmured, momentarily distracted from her frustration. 'This is incredible.'

'The secret is fresh ginger and a splash of stout. Guinness to you,' Eva added, winking.

'OK, I finally get the attraction.' Molly swallowed and took a fortifying sip of tea. 'So who or what is Crest? Jack Flynn keeps throwing the name around.'

Eva lowered her voice and look around, even though the café was practically empty. 'A big multinational drinks company that's been buying up smaller operators all over the country. Once they get a place, they gut it – rip out old trees and crops on the land, replace them with more commercial varieties, let go most of the staff.' Her expression darkened. 'They've had their eye on Goldenridge for a while now. Aggressively pressuring Jack to sell up.'

Understanding dawned on Molly's face. 'And he thinks *I'm* their latest tactic?'

'Sounds like it.' Eva straightened. 'One of their executives was sniffing around town in the summer and Jack sent yer man packing with the kind of language you'd only hear in The Orchard Pub. So you showing up now asking questions straight off the bus about the orchard? I can see why his suspicions were raised.'

'But that doesn't explain why he's so . . . hostile,' Molly protested. 'I have no interest in his stupid land.'

Eva's expression softened with something like sympathy. 'It's not just about the land for Jack though. Goldenridge is his identity, his purpose. The Flynn family has worked that soil for generations. When his parents died, the orchard became even more significant to Jack – his last connection to family, I suppose.' She refilled Molly's mug. 'For Jack, selling would be like cutting off a limb.'

Molly absorbed this, feeling a twinge of guilt for her anger. She understood legacy and promises all too well. Wasn't her own mission here driven by largely similar forces?

'His uncle seemed more personable at least,' she offered. 'He actually gave me a bottle of cider as an apology for Jack's behavior.'

'Ah, Patrick's a gem,' Eva agreed fondly. 'If anyone can make Jack see reason, it's him.' She paused, studying Molly with newfound curiosity. 'Though I'm surprised he took to you so quickly all the same. Usually just as wary of outsiders, just a bit more polite about it.'

Molly shrugged, focusing intently on her gingerbread. 'Maybe he recognized that I'm not a threat.'

'Or maybe he saw something else entirely . . .' Eva suggested, a hint of mischief in her tone.

Molly looked up, caught off guard. 'What do you mean?'

The other woman wiped her hands on her apron, a smile playing at the corners of her mouth. 'Just that amongst other things, Patrick Flynn has always had a great eye for matchmaking. Claims he can spot a good match the way he spots the right weather for harvest.'

Heat rushed to Molly's cheeks. 'That's ridiculous. Jack Flynn can barely stand to be in the same room with me.'

'Mmm,' Eva hummed noncommittally. 'Strong reactions often mask even stronger emotions.'

Molly rolled her eyes, though the thought sent a traitorous flutter through her stomach. Despite herself, she found she wanted to know more. She tried for casual interest, keeping her tone light. 'Has Jack always been so . . .' she searched for a diplomatic term, '. . . intense?'

'Since I've known him, yeah,' Eva said, her voice warm with obvious fondness. 'Even as a boy, he took everything so seriously. While the rest of us were passing notes in school, he was off studying grafting techniques and soil compositions.'

'I'm surprised someone hasn't managed to . . . soften him up by now. Young farmer with his own land? Must be quite the catch in these parts.'

Eva's eyes twinkled knowingly. 'Oh, there have been attempts. Maura Delaney chased him all through secondary school, and more recently a blow-in from one of the new houses tried her luck.' She leaned in, voice dropping confidentially. 'There was a summer romance with a Dublin girl who was here on holiday one time – serious enough by all accounts, until he made it clear he wasn't interested in a move to the city, so that was the end of—'

The bell above the door jingled, and Molly glanced over her shoulder, then froze, a piece of gingerbread halfway to her mouth.

Jack Flynn himself stood in the doorway, a box of apples

balanced against his hip, his tall frame blocking most of the evening light. His dark hair was windswept, his expression guarded as he spotted Molly again at the counter. For a heartbeat, their eyes locked – his narrowing slightly, hers widening in surprise.

Eva straightened, smile broadening with what looked suspiciously like delight. 'Speak of the devil!' she sang, and Molly glanced at her, horrified. 'I was just talking to Molly here about the festival.' The impressively smooth transition held not a hint of their actual conversation.

Jack's gaze flicked between them, clearly not believing this for a second.

He stepped fully into the café, the floorboards creaking beneath his heavy boots. Molly turned resolutely back to her gingerbread, determined not to acknowledge him, though every nerve ending in her body seemed suddenly, traitorously aware of his presence.

Was there no escaping this man?

Chapter 17

Jack set the crate down on the counter with a deliberate thud, the box landing harder than he'd intended. He nodded curtly, hating the immediate jolt of awareness that shot through him again at the sight of the newcomer – Molly – perched on Eva's barstool, those green eyes stubbornly fixed on her plate.

The woman was trouble – and yet he couldn't seem to stop noticing things about her: the slight flush on her cheeks, the determined set of her jaw, the way her dark hair caught the evening light streaming through the windows.

'Your delivery,' he said to Eva, his voice gruffer than intended. 'Twenty pounds, picked this morning.'

Eva circled the counter, inspecting the apples with a professional eye. She ran a gentle finger over the skin of one fruit, checking for bruising and smiled with satisfaction. Jack shifted his weight, acutely conscious of Molly's deliberate non-acknowledgment. The woman was as stiff as new grafting tape, her attention fixed on a piece of gingerbread as if it contained the secrets of the universe.

He remained at the counter, standing uncomfortably as Eva disappeared into a small office out back, returning moments later with an envelope. 'Here you go. Though I'll need a bit more next week. The russets for a special I'm doing for the festival.'

Jack pocketed the payment. 'Tuesday, OK? I've to check the east orchard irrigation system first thing, but I could pop over after.'

'Perfect.'

The café hummed with energy – a couple sharing scones by the window, the soft clinking of teacups against saucers providing a gentle backdrop to their conversation. The warmth from the ovens had fogged the windows slightly, creating a cozy bubble that seemed separate from the world outside. Jack found himself reluctantly settling into the familiar comfort of the space, despite the prickling awareness of Molly's presence.

'Like I said,' Eva continued, her innocent tone setting off warning bells in Jack's mind, 'I was just telling Molly about the festival and how your cider is always the first to sell out. People start lining up at your stall even before ye've finished setting up.'

Jack grunted noncommittally. He knew Eva too well to miss the mischief dancing behind her eyes. Whatever game she was playing, he wanted no part of it.

Her smile widened. 'Even won gold at the nationals last year. Not that he bothered to attend the ceremony to receive it.'

He shifted uncomfortably. 'Had plenty of trees that needed attention.'

'Sure, you always do,' Eva said with a fond eyeroll. She turned to Molly, who was watching their exchange with cautious interest. 'Jack's talent is wasted on us locals who've known forever how great he is. What he really needs is someone to bring that talent to a wider audience.' Her eyes twinkled. 'Did you know Molly works in marketing? No better woman to help boost your sales – or anything else,' she added suggestively.

Heat rushed to Jack's face, his collar suddenly feeling too tight. Beside him, Molly's eyes widened, a similar flush spreading across her cheeks.

'Eva,' she protested, 'I'm sure Jack doesn't need—'

'I've managed perfectly fine without—' he spluttered simultaneously.

'Of course, of course,' Eva interrupted blithely waving away their objections with flour-dusted hands. 'Just thinking out loud, really. Though it would be a shame not to take advantage of such professional expertise when it drops right into our little village. Especially with the big boys still sniffing around?'

The reminder of Crest Beverage's continued interest in his land tightened Jack's jaw. 'I'm not interested in "boosting" anything, thanks. I'm interested in preserving what my ancestors built.'

'And wouldn't the best preservation be ensuring its success?' Eva challenged, her tone gentler now. 'All I'm saying is that Molly might have a few insights worth considering. Outside perspective and all that.'

Molly appeared as uncomfortable with this conversation as Jack felt. Her fingers traced the rim of her mug, and she seemed to be studying its contents with unusual intensity.

'I really wouldn't want to—' she began.

'You wouldn't be interfering if that's what you're going to say,' Eva interjected. 'Jack's just too proud to ask for help. Always has been.' She patted his arm with maternal affection. 'Remember when you broke your ankle falling off that tree at sixteen? Crawled all the way back to Goldenridge rather than call for someone to give you a lift home.'

'Eva,' he growled, warning in his tone.

A group entered, momentarily distracting his friend from her efforts. With one last meaningful look at him, she moved to greet the newcomers, leaving Jack and Molly in awkward silence.

So she *was* a marketing executive, then. *Not* a corporate spy.

He trusted Eva's judgment; no better woman to sniff out a fraud. But the absence of her cheerful buffer only made him more acutely aware of Molly's proximity. She smelled faintly of something floral – different to the heavy perfume he associated with city women, subtler, fresher. The distance between them suddenly seemed both too wide and not wide enough.

'I'm . . . sorry about earlier,' he muttered suddenly. 'I genuinely thought you were one of Crest's flying monkeys.'

When she raised a small smile, he relaxed somewhat. 'No, I'm from New York, Wicked Witch of the *East*.'

Jack smiled, even though he didn't quite get the joke. 'My great-uncle mentioned some of your ideas actually,' he said then, the words emerging more abruptly than he'd intended. She looked up and he shifted his weight, discomfort warring with his inherent honesty. 'They were . . . decent. The cards explaining each variety's history, the cider tasting tours.' The admission cost him something, but fairness demanded it. 'He was quite taken with the concept.'

'Oh,' Molly said again, this time with a hint of pleased surprise. 'I was just thinking out loud, really. I didn't expect him to take me seriously.'

'Patrick doesn't miss much.' Jack's fingers traced a knot in the wooden countertop, avoiding her direct gaze. 'He says your suggestions might help people understand why we do things the way we do. Why it matters so much.' He looked up then, meeting her eyes directly for the first time since entering the café. Up close, they were even greener than he'd remembered, flecked with gold in the evening light. 'He was even talking about implementing some of them.'

Molly set down her mug, her expression shifting to professional interest. 'That's great. Simple, educational, authentic to who you are.' She hesitated, then added, 'I could help him with the wording of the cards, if you'd like.'

Jack studied her, trying to reconcile this seemingly earnest offer with his lingering suspicions. Could he have misjudged her? Or was this simply a more sophisticated approach to gaining his trust?

'Why would you do that?' he asked bluntly.

She shrugged, the gesture elegant despite its casualness. 'I liked your great-uncle, it's what I do. And . . .' she hesitated, something vulnerable flickering across her features, 'I actually admire what you're trying to preserve at Goldenridge. Traditional methods, heritage varieties – those things do matter.'

The sincerity in her voice caught him off guard completely, chipping away at the defensive wall he'd built. Jack found himself nodding slowly. 'They do.'

Another silence fell, but this one felt different – less charged with tension, more contemplative. In the background, Eva laughed at something one of her customers said, the sound bright and infectious in the warm café air.

'Again, I apologize,' Jack reiterated, the words coming easier now. 'For my behavior at the shop earlier. And by the lake the other day too.' He met her gaze directly, owning his mistake. 'I was . . . out of order.'

Molly's eyebrows rose, genuine surprise evident in her expression.

'Patrick pointed out that I might have jumped to conclusions,' Jack admitted. 'He usually knows what he's talking about.'

A small smile curved her lips, transforming her face from merely pretty to something that made Jack's breath catch. 'Apology accepted. And I understand better now why you were suspicious. Eva told me about Crest Beverages.'

He felt something tight in his chest ease slightly. 'They've been relentless,' he conceded. 'Three approaches this year alone, each more aggressive than the last.'

'Must be exhausting,' she said, and she sounded like she meant it.

'It is.' The admission slipped out before he could stop it. He rarely acknowledged the toll the constant pressure took on him, not even to Patrick. Yet somehow, sitting in Eva's warm café with golden light pooling around them, it felt possible to speak the truth.

'For what it's worth,' Molly said, breaking off another piece of gingerbread, 'I really am just a tourist. No hidden corporate agenda.' Jack found himself believing her, though caution still remained at the edges of his thoughts. He couldn't help it. 'My grandmother used to talk about the ancient trees of Ireland. Said they were like living history books, if you knew how to read them.' She smiled faintly. 'Maybe I was hoping to see a few pages of that history for myself.'

The answer wasn't fully satisfying, but Jack sensed pushing further would only rebuild the walls that had just begun to come down between them. Instead, he nodded, accepting her explanation for what it was.

'The big oak is special all right,' he admitted. 'Been standing since before any Flynn planted the first apple tree. Some mornings, in the right light . . .' He trailed off, suddenly self-conscious about sharing something so personal.

'What?' Molly prompted, her voice soft with genuine curiosity.

Jack hesitated, then continued. 'Some mornings it looks almost like it's breathing. Sounds fanciful, I know.'

'Not at all,' she replied, her eyes shining with understanding. 'The best things often look that way in the right light.'

Their gazes held for a moment too long to be casual, something unspoken passing between them. Jack felt a peculiar lightening in his chest, as if a burden he'd carried for miles had suddenly shifted to a more comfortable position.

Eva returned then, her eyes darting between them with undisguised interest and he straightened, the moment evaporating. 'I should get going.'

Yet Jack found himself oddly reluctant to leave the warmth of The Cherry Blossom Café and the unexpected connection that had begun to form across Eva's counter.

Chapter 18

'Ah stay for a cuppa, Jack,' Eva ordered, already pouring without waiting for an answer. She set down the fresh mug of tea in front of him, purposefully lingering as she arranged it just so, her lips curved in a smile. 'Sit yourself down there.'

He cleared his throat, shifting his weight from one foot to the other. 'I should really get back to—'

'The orchard, yeah, yeah, we know.' Eva thrust the steaming cup at him anyway. 'Ten more minutes won't kill you. And it's Saturday.' Her tone was light but brooked no argument, the same voice she'd likely used on him since they were children.

Molly sensed a trap closing, though she couldn't deny that Eva, having now ensured Jack knew that Molly wasn't the enemy, was very deftly smoothing the path for her to properly broach him about access to the oak tree.

The café had grown busier now, people trickling in for late coffees and treats, so Jack had no choice but to take the stool beside hers at the counter.

'So,' Eva declared then, as if a sudden thought had just occurred to her. 'Maybe what Goldenridge needs to fight off all these corporate feckers once and for all, is to fight back.' She looked at Jack, eyes bright with growing enthusiasm.

'What do you mean?' he asked.

But Eva simply turned to Molly and topped up her mug. 'You know more about this stuff than the rest of us combined . . .' The proprietor leaned forward, lowering her voice conspiratorially though her words remained perfectly audible. 'Think about it – authentic local cider, ancient apple varieties that corporate giants have abandoned, all made by hand using methods unchanged for generations. Under threat from the big bad corporation. Sure, the story practically writes itself.' Eva gestured back toward Jack. 'Plus, it doesn't hurt that the cider-maker himself looks like he stepped out of one of those Hot Farmer calendars, does it?'

Jack choked on his tea, a flush creeping up his neck. 'Eva, for God's sake.'

Molly bit the inside of her cheek to keep from smiling at his discomfort, though her own cheeks felt suspiciously warm. 'I'm sure Jack doesn't need anyone interfering . . .'

'Interfering?' Eva exclaimed, loud enough that several nearby customers turned to look. 'It's not interfering to help show the world what Goldenridge is truly about, make sure it gets the recognition it deserves. You should see the awards Jack's won – only they're all sitting in a box in the press because he can't be bothered to display them.'

A local appeared alongside them at the counter as if out of nowhere, abandoning any pretense of not eavesdropping. Molly recognized her as one of the committee women Eva had pointed out the other day.

'I'm always saying that Goldenridge really should be doing more to attract the tour buses from Dublin. They all go to bloody Bulmers instead.'

Eva beamed at the unexpected support. 'Exactly, Josie. And here we have a secret weapon, a high-flying marketer from New York to raise our profile.'

'New York?' The older woman's eyebrows shot up with

newfound respect. 'Isn't that the ticket. What about one of those big billboards like in the films?'

Before Molly could answer, a familiar voice joined the conversation. 'Well now, I had no idea we had such talent in our midst. It's always the quiet ones.' Brid from the hotel had just come in, a wicker shopping basket over one arm, her elegant figure again perfectly tailored in a rich purple dress, despite the casual setting. Her shrewd eyes took in Molly with fresh interest. 'Very good of you to agree to help us out.'

'I haven't actually agreed to anything,' she spluttered, glancing at Jack who looked as trapped as she felt.

'But you could?' Brid pressed, her tone suggesting refusal wasn't an option.

'Well, yes, technically,' Molly admitted. 'That's part of what I do, but—'

'Oh, that's brilliant!' A short-haired woman she recognized as the bookshop owner also appeared as if out of nowhere, carrying a cardboard box. 'Brid and I have just come away from a committee meeting and we were desperate for fresh ideas for next year's tourist season instead of more miserable flyers.' She set down her box with a thump. 'We've been trying for years to put Golden Valley on the map. Cork and Kerry get all the tourism while we're just as picturesque here in Tipp – friendlier too. And Goldenridge is the jewel in our crown.'

Jack, who had been watching this snowball of enthusiasm with growing alarm, finally found his voice. 'Hold on now, Maeve. Everyone's running away with themselves here.' He turned to Molly, his expression a complex mixture of embarrassment and curiosity. 'She's here on holiday remember. I'm sure she has better things to be doing.'

'It . . . wouldn't be a problem, really,' she heard herself saying, professional instincts kicking in despite her better judgment. 'I'd be happy to help. Even a simple online campaign showcasing the heritage offerings could be effective.' She hesitated, seeing Jack's face tighten. 'If you wanted to be involved, of course.' But by the look on his face, Molly could tell that he was intrigued by the prospect all the same.

Plus she really did need to get him on side.

'"If you wanted . . ."' Eva mimicked with a laugh. 'Jack, when was the last time a high-flying marketing expert offered advice? A gift horse if I ever saw one, and you're examining its dental work like it's going to bite you.'

'Exactly,' Brid agreed, her bracelets jangling as she gestured emphatically.

Jack ran a hand through his hair, further disheveling it in a way that Molly found inexplicably charming. 'It's not that I don't appreciate the offer,' he said, his voice strained. 'But Goldenridge isn't about flashy online promotion and what-have-you. It's about heritage and . . .'

'Tradition, yeah, yeah, we know,' Eva repeated drolly.

'But who says those things can't coexist with modern marketing?' Molly challenged. 'The best promotion doesn't change what a business is – it merely amplifies what already makes it special.'

A murmur of agreement rippled through the group.

'I can see it already,' Eva said, warming to the theme. 'Beautiful shots of the orchard amidst the autumn leaves.' She gestured her arms dramatically in the air. 'Short clips explaining the pressing process. Maybe even a series highlighting the history behind each variety.' She turned to Jack, her expression suddenly more serious. 'The kind of thing that might even make the likes of Crest Beverages appreciate that you can't just swallow up what makes Goldenridge special.'

At the mention of Crest, Jack's expression shifted subtly. Molly watched as something more calculated and considering entered his eyes, replacing the knee-jerk resistance.

Quick as you like, Brid seized on this crack in his defenses. 'And more awareness means more understanding of what those types want to destroy.' She turned to Molly. 'The hotel would benefit too, of course. You'd include a mention of the Glen Arms in your plans?'

'And Wildflower Books,' Maeve added quickly, not to be outdone. 'We've a few local history authors that would only love to be part of it. Landscape artists too.'

The requests continued to pile up as others drifted into the conversation, each suggesting how their business might be included in this hypothetical awareness campaign. Molly watched with a mixture of amusement and alarm as the scope expanded with every passing second.

'Wait,' she said finally, raising her hand to stem the flood of suggestions. 'I'm not planning anything yet.'

The little group fell silent, all eyes turning to her with expressions ranging from surprise to dismay.

'But you will, won't you?' Eva asked, her voice softer now, genuine. 'It would mean so much to the village. And to Jack, even though he's too stubborn to admit it.'

Molly looked at him, finding his dark eyes already fixed on her face, studying her with that intense focus she was beginning to recognize. Despite his evident reluctance, there was something else there too – uncertain optimism, even?

She thought of Aoife's stories about Golden Valley, about the orchard, about the ancient oak tree that remained her ultimate goal. From a purely selfish perspective, agreeing to help would allow her legitimate access to the land, the oak, and the man who was now watching her with such complex emotions behind his guarded expression.

Though it also meant she'd need to stay around here longer than she'd planned.

'I could look at maybe putting together something simple alongside the festival,' she conceded. 'A good opportunity to showcase what makes Goldenridge and Golden Valley unique?'

'Good woman!' Eva clapped her flour-dusted hands. 'Jack,

you'll cooperate now, won't you? Show Molly around the orchard properly, show her the trees, explain the process, give her access to everything?'

If Molly didn't know better, she'd swear Eva could read her mind and was actively trying to get her closer to the oak tree.

But the café owner's face was all innocence.

For his part, Jack's jaw worked as he visibly struggled with his conflicting instincts. Molly could almost see the internal battle taking place, his ingrained suspicion of outsiders warring with practical business sense.

'Fine,' he said finally. 'But nothing too . . . fancy. Nothing that makes it look like we're changing what Goldenridge stands for.'

'Authenticity,' Molly assured him, meaning it. 'That's always what resonates.'

Their eyes met briefly and, for a moment, the café and its chattering occupants seemed to fade into the background. Jack's expression softened almost imperceptibly, the tension in his shoulders easing by the slightest degree.

Molly felt something shift between them – not quite trust, but a tentative bridge spanning the gap of their initial misunderstanding.

'Right, so,' Jack said, breaking the moment as he turned to gather his empty crate. 'Come out on Monday maybe. Eight o'clock. I've a lot to do and you can tag along for a bit in the morning.'

'I'll be there,' Molly promised, slightly dazed by his change of heart. In more ways than one.

Jack nodded once, then turned to leave, his tall frame silhouetted briefly in the doorway before he stepped out into the evening. Through the window, she watched as he paused on the cobblestones, momentarily frozen as the clouds parted and golden sunlight spilled across the square, illuminating his figure against the backdrop of the village. Then he was moving again, striding away with long, purposeful steps, the empty apple crate tucked under one arm.

Eva sidled up beside her, following her gaze with a knowing smile. 'Well now, that went very well, I'd say.'

'You set us up,' Molly accused, though she couldn't muster any real indignation.

'Me?' Eva pressed a hand to her chest in mock offense. 'I merely provided an opportunity for two people to recognize their mutual interests.'

'Professional interests,' Molly clarified, trying to ignore the flutter in her stomach that suggested otherwise.

'Of course,' her new friend agreed with exaggerated sincerity. 'Purely professional.' She patted Molly's arm and winked. 'Now, you'll need sustenance for all this planning. Another piece of gingerbread, I think. On the house, since you've just become Golden Valley's honorary marketing director.'

As Eva bustled away, Molly found herself surrounded by Brid, Maeve and the other woman Josie – who it turned out ran the newsagents – the committee members eager to share their thoughts on what should be included in the campaign to put Golden Valley 'on the map'.

She nodded and smiled, making mental notes, but part of her mind was already racing ahead to Monday morning.

To Goldenridge. To Jack Flynn and his ancient oak tree.

Molly definitely hadn't planned on becoming so entangled in village affairs when she'd arrived in Golden Valley. Her mission had been singular and specific: fulfill her grandmother's final wish. Yet somehow, within days, she'd committed to help save a suspicious apple farmer's business and, by extension, promote an entire Irish village.

As she eventually left the café and ambled back towards the hotel through the square now bathed in the golden light of approaching sunset, Molly's marketing mind automatically filled with campaign concepts. Heritage varieties photographed against ancient stone walls. Jack's hands – strong, capable – demonstrating the grafting techniques passed down through generations. The cider press in operation, capturing the rich amber liquid as it flowed from apples to barrel.

And perhaps, if she played her cards right, the ancient oak tree in all its glory, standing watch over the orchard as it had for centuries. The tree that had called her across an ocean, and still waited for her to fulfill a promise made at her grandmother's bedside.

Well, if there was one thing the Harris family knew how to do, it was adapt to changing circumstances. Jack Flynn and his oak tree might have started as obstacles, but now they were becoming something else entirely – something she wasn't quite ready to name, but couldn't deny feeling.

Monday morning at eight, he'd said.

The thought sent an unexpected shiver of anticipation down Molly's spine that had nothing at all to do with marketing plans, and everything to do with dark eyes that softened when speaking of ancient trees in morning light.

Chapter 19

Jack was at the orchard gate twenty minutes early on Monday, the morning dew still clinging to the grass as he paced the gravel path. The sun had barely cleared the eastern hills, painting the apple trees in soft gold light that caught on fruit-laden branches and turned ordinary leaves into stained glass.

He'd slept poorly all weekend, his mind churning with conflicted thoughts about Molly Harris and this madcap marketing scheme the entire village seemed determined to thrust upon him.

The route was already mapped out in his head, but the prospect of showing a stranger – particularly this stranger, with her too-observant eyes – around his family's legacy left his stomach tight with something that wasn't quite dread but wasn't comfort either.

He checked his watch again. Seven-fifty. She'd be here soon, if she kept her word. Part of him half-expected her not to show, to have second thoughts about the entire arrangement or make excuses since she'd been so expertly strong-armed into it all when she was supposed to be here on holiday.

Personal obligation, he'd remembered her saying that first morning in the rain and his curiosity pricked. Wasn't this yet another obligation?

A flash of movement at the lane's end caught his attention.

Molly appeared, walking briskly up the path from the front entrance gates, her dark hair pulled back in a practical ponytail. He straightened, watching her approach with reluctant curiosity. Long gone was that city polish of their first meeting; today she wore jeans, sturdy hiking boots, and a red sweater that brought out the color of her eyes even more. She carried a small leather notebook tucked under one arm.

'Morning,' she called as she drew closer. 'Hope I'm not late.'

'Right on time,' Jack replied, his tone carefully neutral despite the unexpected leap in his pulse at the sight of her. She looked . . . right, somehow, against the backdrop of the orchard's autumn colors. Less the corporate threat he'd first imagined and more like someone who might actually understand what this place was all about.

'OK if I do a bit of filming?' she asked gesturing unnecessarily with her phone. 'For social media stuff. Nothing too intrusive, I promise.'

'OK. Just don't expect me to start yapping into the camera like an eejit,' he warned, and was gratified to see her smile a little.

'Not a problem. So, Mr Flynn,' she said jauntily, 'maybe start by telling me all there is to know about apples.'

He nodded, turning toward the orchard entrance to hide the flush creeping up his neck. 'We'll start with the heritage varieties, then work our way to the newer sections.'

He held the gate open, the metal hinges creaking softly as Molly passed through. She moved carefully, eyes already scanning the neat rows of trees that stretched across the hillside in geometrically perfect lines. Jack followed, hyperaware of her presence as they walked side by side down the central path.

'Orchard's divided into seven sections,' he explained, falling into the familiar rhythm of describing his life's work. 'Each with different varieties suited to the particular soil and exposure of that area.'

'How many types do you grow?' she asked.

'Twenty-three total. Fifteen heritage varieties that date back generations, five modern cultivars for commercial viability, and three experimental crosses that we're still evaluating.'

She nodded, taking brief notes.

Jack gestured toward the nearest row of trees. 'These are Cavan Russets. They've been in Irish orchards since the 1800s, maybe earlier. Not much to look at –' he plucked one from a low-hanging branch and handed it to her – 'but the flavor is complex. Honey notes with a sharp finish.'

Molly accepted the fruit, turning it in her hands. The russet apple was mottled brown-gold, with none of the polished perfection of supermarket varieties. She raised it to her nose, inhaling deeply, and Jack found himself watching her face, oddly invested in her reaction.

'Smells amazing,' she said softly, the genuine appreciation in her voice loosening something tight in Jack's chest. 'Like . . . honey and cloves.'

'Good nose,' he said, surprised. 'Most people miss the spice notes.'

They continued down the row, Jack pointing out different trees, explaining the challenges and rewards of each variety. To his surprise, (and still lingering suspicion) Molly asked intelligent questions – about pollination patterns, disease resistance, and the relationship between soil composition and flavor development. Not surface-level questions but ones that suggested genuine interest in the science behind his work.

He truly hoped he wasn't making a mistake here and giving away all his secrets. It was true what they said about fools and women.

'The commercial orchards focus purely on appearance and shelf life,' he explained as they paused beside a gnarled tree whose branches bowed under the weight of small, misshapen fruit. 'Perfect red spheres that look good under supermarket lights but taste like nothing.' He couldn't keep the disdain from his voice. 'These won't win any beauty contests, but they've got character.'

She snapped some photos, then crouched to capture footage of fallen fruit nestled in the grass beneath. 'Character sells, you know. Especially these days. People are tired of perfection – they want authenticity.'

Jack watched her work, the morning light catching in her hair as she shifted angles. 'That's what Patrick said.'

She glanced up, a smile quirking one corner of her mouth. 'Great minds.'

They moved deeper into the orchard, the morning sun warming the air and releasing the complex perfume of ripe apples. Fallen leaves crunched beneath their boots, and somewhere in the distance a pheasant called, its harsh cry cutting through the stillness. Jack found himself relaxing despite his lingering reservations, the familiar surroundings and the rhythm of explanation soothing his wariness.

At a junction between two sections, he paused before a tree that stood apart from the orderly rows. 'This is one of our oldest,' he said, resting his palm against the gnarled trunk. 'Planted by my great-great-grandfather. The variety is nearly extinct now – Bloody Butcher, named for the deep red flesh. But modern consumers don't want an apple that bleeds when you bite it.'

'May I?' Molly asked, raising her phone to take some footage.

Jack nodded, stepping back to give her room. She circled the tree slowly, capturing it from different angles, her movements deliberate and respectful. Not like the Crest goons who'd strode through his orchard with measuring eyes, seeing only acreage and potential profit margins.

'The tree needs careful handling,' he continued, surprising himself with how much he wanted to share. 'We've grafted from it several times to preserve the line, but there's something about this original stock – the apples have a depth the younger trees don't match.'

'Like wine from older grape vines,' she suggested, lowering her camera.

'Exactly like that.' Jack studied her face, finding unexpected pleasure in her understanding.

'My grandfather likes wine,' she explained. 'Always talking about terroir and stuff. I guess the same principles apply across different fruits.'

Jack led her toward the grafting shed then, a small structure nestled between orchard sections where the delicate work of propagation took place. Inside, benches lined the walls, tools hung in precise arrangements, and bundles of carefully labeled scions sat in dampened cloth, waiting for spring's work.

'This is where the real magic happens,' he said, unable to keep pride from his voice as he explained the process of joining different apple varieties to rootstock. 'Patrick says it's a bit like matchmaking – you need to understand the characteristics of each partner, the strengths and weaknesses they'll bring to the union.'

Molly leaned against the workbench, occasionally filming but mostly listening as Jack demonstrated how a small section of one variety could be skillfully attached to another, creating a tree that combined the best attributes of both. His hands moved with practiced grace as he described the technique, fingers tracing the paths where cambium layers must meet to create a successful graft.

'It's incredible,' she said when he finished. 'All that knowledge, passed down through generations. You can't get that from a textbook.'

'No,' Jack agreed, surprisingly pleased by her appreciation. 'Patrick taught me, just as his ancestors taught him. There's a feel to it you develop over time.'

They stepped back outside, the cooler autumn air a relief after the close warmth of the shed. Jack checked his watch – they'd spent longer there than he'd intended, drawn out by Molly's interested questions and his own unexpected enthusiasm for sharing his craft. As they walked the path between orchard sections, a flash of white caught Jack's eye. A hawthorn tree grew at the junction between two apple rows, its gnarled branches dotted with the last of the season's berries, bright red against dark leaves.

'Better not cut that one down,' Molly commented, a light smile playing at her lips. 'Fairies won't be happy.'

Jack blinked, studying her. 'That's . . . not something tourists usually know.'

She shrugged, her eyes darting away momentarily. 'Another tip from my grandmother.'

He nodded, satisfied. 'Well, true enough, most farmers would have removed it long ago,' Jack admitted. 'Takes water and nutrients from the productive trees. But my great-great-grandfather refused to touch it, and Patrick after him.' He hesitated, then added, 'Some superstitions make sense.'

They continued walking, but Jack found himself watching Molly more closely now. There was something about her casual reference to the hawthorn – not delivered like a fact learned from a guidebook, but with the offhand familiarity of someone raised on such stories.

Another small piece of the puzzle that was Molly Harris.

A breeze stirred the trees around them, sending a shower of golden leaves spiraling down. One landed in her hair, and before he could think better of it, Jack reached out to pluck it away. His fingers brushed against the dark strands, and he was startled by their softness.

'Sorry,' he muttered, withdrawing his hand as if burned. 'You had a—' He gestured vaguely.

'Oh.' Her cheeks flushed slightly. 'Thank you.'

An awkward silence fell between them, the easy rhythm of their conversation suddenly disrupted. Jack cleared his throat, pointing toward a particularly fine specimen of Cox's Orange Pippin.

'This one's at peak ripeness now,' he said, his voice rougher than intended. 'The perfect balance of sugar and acid.'

He reached up to carefully twist a fruit from its stem, the motion practiced and gentle to avoid damaging the tree. As he handed the apple to Molly, their fingers touched, and Jack felt a jolt of awareness that had nothing to do with apples or marketing campaigns.

'The skin should have slight resistance,' he found himself saying, his voice dropping lower as she took the fruit. 'Then give way to dense, aromatic flesh.'

Molly's eyes met his, something unspoken passing between them. The orchard seemed to fall away, leaving only this moment, this connection humming in the space between their bodies.

He was suddenly acutely aware of how alone they were among the trees, how the dappled sunlight caught in her dark hair, how her green eyes sparkled in the light. His gaze dropped to her mouth, and for one disorienting moment, he imagined closing the distance between them, tasting the sweetness he somehow knew would be there.

The thought jolted him back to reality. This was madness. She was here on holiday – carrying out a silly volunteer project before returning to her real job in New York. And he was what? Mooning over her like some lovesick teenager because she'd asked good questions about apple varieties and known an old superstition about hawthorn trees?

Jack stepped back abruptly, his boot crushing a fallen apple with a wet sound that broke the spell. 'We should move on,' he said, his voice deliberately brisk.

Confusion flickered across Molly's face, quickly replaced by a neutral professionalism that made him feel both relieved and oddly bereft. 'Of course,' she agreed, tucking the apple he'd given her into her pocket. 'Lead the way.'

The comfortable ease they'd developed had vanished, replaced by a prickling awareness that made the back of Jack's neck burn. He strode ahead, shoulders rigid with embarrassment at his momentary lapse in judgment.

Behind him, Molly followed in silence, the only sound the

continued crunch of leaves beneath their feet and the whisper of the breeze through the apple-laden branches.

The morning wasn't yet half over, and already Jack was struggling to remember why he'd agreed to this nonsensical arrangement in the first place.

Chapter 20

Molly followed Jack's stiff-shouldered figure through the orchard rows, the warmth of their earlier connection rapidly cooling in the autumn air.

Something had shifted between them among the apple trees just now – a moment of unexpected intimacy that had clearly rattled him. Now he moved with deliberate haste, putting physical distance between them as if to compensate for that brief, electric moment when his fingers had brushed against her hair.

'Time for a break,' he muttered, not quite meeting her eyes. 'Tea OK for you?'

She nodded, not trusting herself to speak just yet. The moment had affected her too, more than she cared to admit, leaving her pulse fluttering in a way that complicated her already complex reasons for being in Golden Valley. This wasn't part of the plan – this deepening awareness of Jack Flynn as more than an obstacle.

They walked in silence along a narrow path that curved away from the main orchard, winding between a row of native trees whose massive trunks dwarfed the apple varieties they'd been examining. The path opened onto a small clearing where a small cottage stood, nestled against the hillside as if it had grown from the earth itself.

The cottage was smaller than she'd imagined, built of weathered gray stone with a slate roof turned silvery with age. Climbing roses, now past their prime but still bearing the occasional late bloom, framed the doorway in a tangle of woody stems. The front garden was a study in practical beauty – no manicured lawns or fussy ornamentals, but neat beds of herbs interspersed with late-blooming wildflowers in shades of purple and gold.

Apple trees, unsurprisingly, dominated one side of the clearing, their branches extending protectively over the cottage roof. What struck Molly most was how seamlessly the dwelling fit its surroundings. Unlike the jarring newness of tourist cottages she'd seen just outside the village, with their too-perfect thatching and chocolate-box charm, this home bore the patina of genuine history.

It belonged here, as did he.

'I'll put the kettle on,' Jack said, moving toward the entrance. 'Won't be long.'

He disappeared inside, the door closing behind him with a soft thud that made it clear she wasn't being invited to follow. The exclusion stung slightly, though Molly understood it. His home represented another boundary, another level of intimacy he wasn't prepared to cross. She was still trying to figure out how she should broach the subject of the oak tree and why she needed access to it. Maybe over the shared warm drink?

Molly approached a small workbench that stood against one wall of the cottage. Tools hung in neat rows – pruning shears in graduated sizes, grafting knives with worn handles, coils of wire and twine. Each implement had its designated place, speaking to Jack's methodical nature. Yet there was artistry here too – a half-carved piece of wood sat on the bench beside a whittling knife, the wood grain exposed in gentle curves that captured the fruit's essence.

'Good likeness, isn't it?'

The voice startled her. Molly turned to find Patrick emerging from around the corner of a nearby barn, his weathered face creasing into a smile. He moved toward her with unhurried steps, his gait betraying the slight stiffness of age managed with dignity. One hand rested lightly on a walking stick – not leaning heavily, but using it for balance as he navigated the uneven ground.

'Your great-nephew is talented,' she replied, gesturing toward the carving. 'In more ways than one.'

'That he is.' Patrick's eyes, bright and alert in his time-worn face, studied her again with undisguised interest. 'Though he'd never admit to it. Especially not the artistic bit.'

He reached her side, his movements deliberate but not frail. Yet there was nothing diminished about Patrick Flynn. His handshake was firm, his gaze clear and perceptive. He stood straight despite the subtle curve of age in his shoulders, and when he smiled, years fell away from his face.

'I hear you've been drafted into service by our Tidy Towns committee,' he said, his voice carrying the melodic lilt of rural Ireland softened by age into a gentle burr. 'The village is buzzing about this New York marketing whizz who's going to put us on the map.'

Molly laughed softly, tucking her hair behind her ear. 'We were both basically strong-armed into it,' she admitted. 'Your nephew more than I.'

Patrick's eyes twinkled knowingly as he replied, 'Some things are meant to be.'

There was something in his tone that made Molly wonder if he was referring to more than just the marketing arrangement. A hint of mischief, perhaps, or deeper knowledge. His gaze, still sharp despite the years that had faded his hair color to silver, seemed to look right through her oh-so-casual persona.

'Jack's gone to make tea,' she mumbled, changing the subject slightly. 'Hope he has enough for three.'

'Oh, he'll have seen me coming up the path. Eyes like a hawk, that fella.' Patrick gestured toward the wooden bench beneath the older tree. 'Shall we sit while we wait? These old bones appreciate a rest more than they used to.' He moved toward the bench with careful steps, one hand still lightly holding the walking stick. 'Join me,' he said then, patting the space beside him. 'Best view of the orchard from this spot. My 'oul fella claimed you could see all the way to the lake on a clear day, though my eyes haven't been able to confirm that for some years now.'

Molly settled beside him, the wood smooth and sun-warmed beneath her. From this vantage point, the orchard spread before them in orderly rows, the trees heavy with fruit in varying shades of green, gold, and red.

'How long have you lived here?' she asked, genuinely curious about this man whose lined face held so much history. And figuring for the first time that he might even have known her grandmother. Should she ask?

Patrick leaned back, his weathered hands coming to rest on his knees. 'All my life,' he said simply. 'Born in the back bedroom of that cottage seventy-eight years ago come December.'

Molly studied him as he spoke, noting how his hands – those gnarled, capable hands that had tended apple trees for decades – moved expressively despite the swollen joints. His forearms, exposed where he'd rolled up his sleeve, were corded with muscle developed through a lifetime of physical labor and maintained through continued use.

'The place gets in your blood,' Patrick continued, his gaze roaming the neat rows with evident pride. 'My father used to say Flynns had apple sap instead of plain blood in our veins. Some mornings I think he might have been right.' He shifted slightly, adjusting his position with the careful movements of someone who had learned to manage chronic discomfort without complaint. 'Jack tells me you've a keen interest in our story,' he said, those sharp eyes returning to her face. 'Not many visitors look beyond the pretty red apples in the shop.'

'Like I told you last time, this place has true character,' Molly replied honestly. 'And history. That's worth preserving.'

Something like approval flickered across Patrick's features. 'Indeed it is. Though the preserving gets harder each year, with the big commercial outfits pushing their bland, tasteless stuff.'

They fell silent for a moment, watching a pair of blackbirds dart between the trees in a flash of glossy wings. The orchard hummed with subtle wildlife, and Molly felt that time seemed to move differently here, measured in seasons rather than minutes.

The cottage door creaked, and they both turned to see Jack emerging with a tray of steaming mugs. He paused when he spotted them together, an unreadable expression crossing his face before he resumed his approach, boots crunching on the gravel path.

'I see you've found one other again,' he said, his tone careful, neutral.

Patrick smiled, the expression transforming his weathered face. 'Just telling Molly here about the view. Whether you can really see the lake from here, or if that was just another of Paddy senior's tall tales.'

Jack's shoulders relaxed slightly at his great-uncle's easy manner. He set the tray on a small table beside the bench – a weathered piece that looked as if it had served this purpose for generations of tea drinkers before them.

Molly accepted a mug with murmured thanks, wrapping her fingers around the warm ceramic. Steam rose in fragrant curls, carrying the scent of strong black tea and something else – apple blossoms? She wondered if it was her imagination or if everything here was infused with the essence of the orchard, even down to the tea they drank.

She sipped carefully, watching over the rim as Jack and Patrick exchanged glances, some unspoken communication passing between them that indicated years of shared understanding.

'The Spartans in the west section need attention before the

frost,' Patrick said, picking up what was clearly an ongoing conversation between them. 'Saw signs of collar rot starting on two trees near the stone wall.'

Jack nodded, his earlier discomfort seemingly forgotten as they slipped into the familiar territory of orchard management. 'Noticed it last week. Already treated them with copper paste, but we should probably plan for replacement next season.'

'Shame,' Patrick sighed. 'Those were good producers.'

Molly subtly opened her notebook, inputting observations – not just about the orchard's needs, which were hardly relevant to her marketing task, but about the men themselves. The way Jack's face softened when discussing the trees, the respect with which he addressed his great-uncle despite clearly being the one in charge now. These were the human elements that would make Goldenridge's story resonate.

'The irrigation system needs more work before we shut it down for winter,' Jack continued, his hands wrapped around his mug in a gesture that mirrored Molly's own. 'Some of those connectors are from the 1970s installation.'

'Parts still in the shed?' Patrick asked, his weathered fingers tapping thoughtfully against his knee.

'Some. We'll need to order more though.' Jack took a long sip of his tea. 'And the press roof has that leak over the storage area. Needs patching before the heavy rains come.'

Molly found herself unexpectedly fascinated by this glimpse into the year-round commitment an orchard required. Her grandmother had spoken of farming as a calling rather than just a profession, and now she understood why. The crop demanded constant attention, each season bringing its own challenges and tasks.

The conversation flowed easily between them, technical details interspersed with observations about weather patterns and reminiscences of past challenges. She found herself drawn into their world, the rhythm of their discussion as soothing as the play of sunlight through leaves and the distant hum of bees still working the late-blooming flowers in the flower bed.

Utterly relaxed, she found herself humming softly under her breath as she wrote.

The older man froze mid-sentence, his weathered hand tightening on his mug. 'Where'd you learn that?' Patrick asked, voice suddenly sharp with interest.

Molly looked up, startled by his tone, her fingers stilling on the notebook. The humming had been unconscious, a habit she'd picked up from years of hearing Nan sing while working. The melody had risen unbidden; an old Irish ballad Aoife often hummed while kneading bread or hanging washing.

Too late, she realized her mistake – this wasn't some universally known Irish folk tune, but perhaps something specific to this region, or maybe even to her grandmother's generation?

'Not sure, really,' she answered, her voice deliberately casual despite the sudden racing of her pulse. 'My grandmother used to sing it, I think.' Patrick's gaze didn't waver, those keen eyes studying her face with new intensity. If they started asking questions, maintaining her cover story that she was just an innocent tourist here to help would become trickier.

She'd been careless, letting her guard down too easily in the comfortable atmosphere, allowing muscle memory to betray her.

'So like I was saying the other day . . . you really should think about running orchard-to-bottle tours in summer,' she said brightly, changing the subject. 'People love seeing the process; from blossom to fruit to finished cider. Educational tourism is huge right now, especially with sustainability-minded travelers.'

The abrupt pivot wasn't subtle, but Molly pressed on, professional expertise providing a shield. She turned to Jack. 'I'd love to see the press house next if we have the time.' She looked up, finding his face stilled, suspicion returning to his expression.

Her stomach dropped. She'd overcompensated, the marketing talk too forced after the natural flow of their earlier conversation.

Jack was too perceptive not to notice, his earlier doubts about her clearly resurfacing.

While Patrick studied her too, his lined face was unreadable. Unlike his great-nephew's open wariness, the older man's expression held something more complex – curiosity, certainly, but also a thoughtfulness that suggested he was trying to fit pieces together in his mind.

Damn.

Molly kept her expression composed, years of corporate presentations helping her maintain a calm facade despite the turmoil beneath.

'Most tours stick to the straightforward stuff,' Jack observed. 'Cider varieties, apple picking, pretty views for their photos. Whereas you seem particularly drawn to the older elements. The heritage varieties. The local songs. The old oak.' He emphasized the last words slightly, the implication clear.

Molly felt heat rise in her cheeks despite her efforts to remain composed. She'd spent years in boardrooms facing down skeptical executives, but something about Jack Flynn's direct gaze always made her usual poise falter.

Perhaps because with the others, she'd been representing clients, companies, products. Here, the deception was more personal, wrapped up in her promise to her grandmother and her own unexpected emotional response to this place and its people.

'I'm always drawn to authenticity,' she answered, meeting his gaze directly. 'Especially in a world full of mass-produced experiences and corporate homogeneity.' She hesitated, then added softly, 'My grandmother valued that too.'

It wasn't a lie, though it skirted the deeper truth she couldn't yet reveal – not when she was supposed to be here to help them with marketing, as opposed to furthering her own agenda in getting access to the land. Hopefully if she played her cards right, that would come later. And Aoife had indeed valued authenticity, had instilled in Molly a respect for traditions and connections that ran deeper than commerce or convenience.

'Your grandmother sounds like she had good taste,' Patrick said finally, his voice gentler than before. 'In songs and values.'

'She did,' Molly agreed simply.

The conversation had shifted into uncertain territory, the easy flow of earlier replaced by fresh caution.

Jack cleared his throat. 'Time to call it a day, I think. I've a lot to get through.' Much to her dismay, Molly realized she was being dismissed.

'What about the cider barn? I'd really like to . . .'

'Another day maybe.'

As he gathered their empty mugs, she couldn't shake the feeling that her careless humming had changed something fundamental in how both men perceived her.

As Molly stood up, she caught Patrick studying her with particular intensity. Something in his expression – a flash of doubt, disappointment, even? – sent a flutter of apprehension through her.

The question was whether he would share those doubts with Jack, and whether Molly's remaining fragile access to Goldenridge orchard – and the ancient oak that stood as its sentinel – would survive if he did.

Chapter 21

Much to Molly's relief, Jack had arranged to meet her back at Goldenridge the following afternoon to continue the cider-making element of her tour. She'd been filming some of the eastern orchard rows for her campaign, when the first raindrops fell – initially tentative, then a sudden deluge.

'This way,' Jack called out over the heavy spattering of water on the leaves. They made a mad dash through the muddy lanes, arriving at the cider barn breathless and drenched despite the short distance.

Now, as raindrops drummed against the roof, Molly stood dripping on ancient floorboards, surrounded by the rich, tangy perfume of fermenting apples and centuries of Flynn family history.

'Sorry about your hair,' he said, looking rather unapologetic as he struck a match. The small flame illuminated his face from below, catching on stubble that had darkened his jaw since yesterday. He touched the fire to a lantern wick, and warm amber light bloomed outward, pushing back the shadows of the building's cavernous interior.

Molly winced. 'Seems like it's kind of a theme around here.' She ran her fingers through her sodden ponytail, freeing her hair from its elastic to help dry it easier. The barn air was cool and heavy with fermentation scents that reminded her of sourdough, wine cellars and something distinctly apple-sweet. But her damp clothing in the colder air made her shiver involuntarily.

'Here.' Jack shrugged out of his leather jacket – miraculously barely damp – and offered it with an awkward thrust of his arm. The gesture surprised her more than the rain had.

'Thanks.' She slipped it over her shoulders, immediately enveloped in a warmth that carried subtle notes of woodsmoke and male skin. The sleeves hung past her fingertips and she rolled them back, feeling oddly small within the leather cocoon. 'So this is where the magic happens . . .'

Jack glanced around the barn as if seeing it through her eyes – the rows of oak barrels lining the walls, the gleaming copper of the press catching the lantern light. 'Not magic,' he corrected. 'Just patience and time.'

Now *that* was truly ad-worthy Molly thought, swooning a little.

He moved deeper into the space, his footsteps echoing slightly in the vast room. The rain's rhythm intensified, creating a natural percussion overhead that somehow made the space feel smaller, more intimate. Water slipped through a crack in one corner, dropping with precision into a strategically placed bucket.

'I started making cider here when I was sixteen,' he said, running a hand along a barrel's curved side with the casual intimacy of long acquaintanceship. 'Patrick showed me how to judge when the fermentation was complete by sound alone. Said a good cider-maker's ears were as important as his taste buds.'

'How do you tell when it's ready?' Molly asked, genuinely curious. She followed him past rows of barrels marked with chalk notations – dates, variety names, cryptic symbols that must hold meaning to the initiated.

'The bubbling changes pitch.' His voice had dropped to match the hushed atmosphere of the barn. 'Gets slower, more deliberate. If you're paying attention, the cider tells *you* when it's ready.'

A fleeting smile softened his features. 'It's like listening to the apples' final song.'

The poetry of the phrase surprised her. Jack Flynn, with his gruff exterior and suspicious nature, hadn't struck her as a man who thought in metaphors. Yet here, surrounded by the fruits of his labor, something in him always loosened.

'Sounds like your marketing campaign just wrote itself,' she said, smiling.

He chuckled. 'Maybe I should get you to come with me to the bank then.'

'The bank?'

He nodded. 'Another meeting on Friday; the regional manager from town visits only once a month. I've been trying to get them to approve a loan. It's not looking great, to be honest.' She knew it was killing him to admit this. 'The previous manager knew me since we were boys,' Jack continued, his voice low. 'His father and mine played football together. But for the latest guy, business is business and the numbers just don't . . .' He trailed off, jaw tightening. 'The numbers don't support the kind of leverage we need.'

Molly remained quiet, sensing he needed to let it out, more than seek advice.

'The irrigation system needs a complete overhaul,' he told her, pacing a short line between barrels. 'Three tractors need major repairs. The processing equipment has parts so old they need to be custom-made now.' His hand raked through his hair, leaving it standing in damp spikes. 'And that's before we even talk about the roof on this place, or the new planting we need to do in the south section.'

Molly's professional mind immediately began calculating, assessing possibilities. 'Could you phase the repairs somehow? Prioritize what's absolutely critical for this season's harvest and next year's—'

'We've been "phasing" for three years,' he interrupted,

frustration edging his voice. 'Patching instead of fixing or postponing and making do. There's a point where that approach costs more than doing it properly would have in the first place.' He exhaled sharply. 'We're well past that point now. And I'm all out of ideas.'

He turned away, but not before Molly caught the flash of pain in his eyes. This wasn't just business concern; this was deeply personal anguish. Jack Flynn wasn't merely worried about profits or production; he was terrified of failing the legacy he'd been entrusted to protect.

'What about Patrick? Surely he has some ideas?' she asked gently.

Jack shook his head. 'He doesn't know how bad it is. I've kept the worst of it from him.' His voice dropped even lower. 'He'd offer his retirement savings in a heartbeat, but I can't – I won't take that from him. The man's earned his peace.'

Molly leaned against a sturdy wooden post, watching him move among his barrels with ease until he grabbed two glasses from a small shelf; sturdy, hand-blown specimens with gently curved sides.

'Fancy a taste?' He arranged the glasses on top of an upturned barrel that served as a makeshift table, then selected a long copper instrument that reminded Molly of an oversized turkey baster. 'The thief,' he explained, catching her curious glance. 'For extracting samples without disturbing it.'

Jack approached a barrel marked with a white chalk X, inserted the narrow end of the thief through a small bunghole, and drew up a column of liquid. With practiced precision, he dispensed amber fluid into two glasses, the cider catching the lantern light as it flowed.

'First pressing of the season,' he said, offering her one. 'Still young, but promising.'

Molly accepted the glass, noting how the cider's color shifted with the changing angle of light – honey to amber to deep gold.

She raised it to her nose first, inhaling the complex bouquet. Apple, certainly, but layered with notes of caramel, vanilla, something almost spicy that reminded her of cloves.

'I always smell before I taste,' she said, aware of his eyes on her. 'Pops, my grandfather, says ninety percent of what we think is taste actually comes through the nose.'

Jack nodded. 'Sounds like a man who knows his gargle.'

Molly took a careful sip, letting the liquid linger on her tongue. The cider was alive with flavor – crisp apple undercut by earthy tannins, a pleasant acidity balanced by subtle sweetness, and a finish that evolved even as she swallowed. Her brow furrowed slightly as she considered the complexity.

'What do you think?' he asked, his voice quieter now, almost intimate in the rain-muffled space.

'It's like . . . drinking autumn itself,' Molly answered honestly. 'But . . .' she hesitated, unsure of whether her observation would be welcome.

'But?' His eyebrows lifted slightly, more curious than offended.

She took another thoughtful sip. 'I wonder if it might benefit from a touch more sweetness. Not sugar,' she added quickly, seeing his expression. 'Maybe honey? Sweetness into the bones, rather than just on the surface.'

Jack froze mid-sip, glass halfway to his lips. His eyes fixed on her face with sudden intensity, as if seeing her for the first time. 'What did you just say?'

Guilty heat rushed to her cheeks. 'I just meant the honey might integrate better into—'

'No.' He set his glass down with deliberate care. 'That phrase. "Sweetness into the bones". Where did you hear that?'

Molly's heart hammered against her ribs. She'd slipped again. Aoife often said this when describing anything that needed depth other than surface charm.

'My grandmother again,' she replied, striving for casual truth. 'Used it sometimes when she baked or cooked. Said there was a difference between something sweet on the tongue and sweetness that went deeper.'

Jack's expression shifted, giving way to something more complex – surprise, recognition, and a curious softening around his eyes. 'My own grandmother said the exact same thing,' he said quietly. 'She died before I was born, but Patrick, who knew her well, told me she used to say it when adding honey to an apple tart filling.'

Molly forced a chuckle. 'Must've been a saying for that generation,' she suggested easily.

'Maybe.' But his eyes remained thoughtful, studying her face in the lantern light as if searching for something. The suspicion that had so characterized their early interactions had transformed into something else.

'Those Crest bastards have been circling for years, you know,' he said then, naming the corporation with palpable disdain. His posture changed as he spoke, shoulders squaring defensively. 'Another offer came in this week. Less than what they offered last year, mind you.'

'But you're still not considering it,' Molly said, making it a statement rather than a question. 'Even after everything you just told me about the finances.'

'Would you sell your family's soul for a price?' Jack countered, though without heat. 'That's what Goldenridge is – not just land or trees or some business. It's five generations of Flynns pouring their lives into this soil.'

When he spoke again, his voice had lost its defensive edge, revealing the vulnerability beneath. Jack's gaze met hers, naked fear visible behind the pride. 'Patrick might be from a different line of the family, but he trusted me, mostly because he had no heir of his own. Yet I could be the Flynn who loses it all. The one who couldn't adapt, couldn't find a way through. The one they'll talk about generations from now, if there are any Flynns left to talk, that is.'

The weight of his admission hung between them, heavier than the moisture-laden air.

Molly saw Jack Flynn clearly then; not just the stubborn apple farmer who'd distrusted her almost on sight, but a man carrying a burden passed down through generations, terrified of being the weak link that broke the chain.

'What would happen – honestly?' she asked quietly. 'If Crest Beverages took over?'

Jack's laugh held no humor. 'First, they'd clear most of the heritage tress. Not profitable enough, too labor-intensive. Replace them with five or six commercial types that ship well and look pretty under supermarket lights.' His hand clenched around his glass. 'This press house would become a "quaint attraction" where tourists could take selfies while seasonal workers demonstrated "traditional methods" for show while the real production happened in a sterile factory in Dublin.'

She nodded, well believing it.

'Within a year or two, there'd be nothing left of what makes this place special,' he spat. 'Just another corporate showcase with branded merchandise and manufactured authenticity.'

The bitterness in his voice caught at something deep in Molly's chest. This wasn't just business troubles; this was a man fighting for something he believed in with his whole heart.

'If it helps, I could work up a broadstroke marketing plan for you to take to the bank meeting, based on what I've seen so far?' His back was to her now as he bent to examine a barrel's spigot, but she caught the slight pause in his movements. 'I don't need any financial details or anything like that,' she assured him, in case his suspicions about her being involved with Crest might again be raised. 'Just a standard document illustrating a few expansion suggestions that wouldn't cost the earth, but would generate solid returns. Banks *love* projections.'

'You would do that?' Jack asked, surprised.

She shrugged. 'Of course. Told you I was here to help, remember?'

'Wouldn't something like that take a while though?' he asked doubtfully. 'The meeting's this Friday.'

'Not at all. This is the kind of stuff I do in my sleep,' she assured him. 'A couple of hours on the laptop, and voila.'

Jack turned to face her fully, his expression more vulnerable than she'd yet seen it. The lantern cast shadows beneath his cheekbones, highlighting the weariness etched around his eyes. 'I . . . I'd appreciate that. I think I need all the help I can get.'

The rain's rhythm changed, becoming less frantic but more persistent, a steady drumming. Before she could stop herself, Molly stepped forward, closing the distance between them, and placed her hand lightly on Jack's forearm. His skin was warm beneath the sleeve of his shirt, muscles tensed with the strain of carrying his burden alone.

'You won't lose this place, Jack,' she soothed softly, the words emerging with a conviction that surprised her. 'Not if there's anything I can do to help.' The touch lasted only seconds, but she felt him relax slightly beneath her fingers, the simple connection breaching defenses that financial stress had reinforced.

Then she withdrew her hand, suddenly conscious of the boundary she'd crossed.

Jack's eyes followed the movement, something unreadable flickering in their depths.

Keen to cover her embarrassment, Molly instinctively defaulted to more practical concerns. 'And in the meantime,' she continued, her spine straightening with renewed determination, 'there's the Harvest Festival to look forward to. Let's create enough buzz that even the bank will take notice.'

Jack's smile didn't quite reach his eyes. 'Social media can't fix structural problems, though.'

'No,' she admitted, 'but it can create opportunities. The right exposure could lead to distribution deals beyond the local market.

Premium pricing for heritage varieties positioned correctly.' She paced a small circle on the worn floorboards, energy building as further ideas crystallized. 'To impress the bank and stave off the vultures once and for all, we need to position the cider not just as a beverage, but an experience – a direct connection to centuries of craft and care. The antithesis of mass production.' She turned back to him, hands gesturing with emphatic precision. 'Eva's right, you know. You're not just selling apples; you're selling preservation of heritage, environmental stewardship, resistance against corporate homogenization.'

Jack watched her, cautious hope slowly replacing resignation. 'You sound like you actually believe that,' he said, a question hidden within the statement.

'I do.' And Molly realized with mild surprise that she meant it. She also knew that Aoife would want her to preserve such an important part of Golden Valley's history.

So whatever secrets still lay between her and Jack and despite her original reasons for coming here, Molly's desire to help Goldenridge succeed was genuine.

Chapter 22

Jack studied her face in the amber lantern light, searching for something. 'Why?' he asked finally. 'Why do you care whether a small Irish apple orchard survives?'

The question hung between them, deceptively simple yet dangerously complex. Molly couldn't tell him the full truth – not now when he'd basically just bared his soul.

But she could offer a different truth, one she rarely shared.

'Because this is what marketing *should* be,' she confessed, perching on the edge of an empty crate. 'When I first started – before the corner offices and corporate clients – I believed I'd be helping businesses like yours. Places with soul and substance, products made with care rather than calculation.' She gazed at the rows of barrels, each containing liquid crafted with patience and expertise. 'Instead, I spend most of my time helping tech companies sell gadgets that'll be outdated in eighteen months, or luxury brands convincing people they're inadequate without the latest drop.' A hollow laugh escaped her. 'My last project before coming here was a campaign for artificial sweetener that costs more per ounce than saffron.'

The confession felt both foreign and freeing. In New York, admitting dissatisfaction with success was taboo – a sign of weakness or, worse, ingratitude. Here, surrounded by oak and apple-scented air, such honesty seemed not just possible but necessary.

'You're obviously good at what you do though,' Jack observed, his tone softened by understanding.

'I'm excellent at what I do,' she corrected without arrogance. 'That's part of the problem. Every successful campaign means more clients with deeper pockets and less compelling products.' She traced a finger along the grain of the wooden crate. 'Sometimes I wonder what my younger self would think of the career I've built. Whether she'd recognize me at all.'

Or if Aoife would, she thought troubled, guilty for basically using work as a grief-shield since her beloved grandmother's passing last year.

Jack nodded slowly, recognition dawning in his eyes. 'Like looking in a mirror and seeing a stranger wearing your clothes.'

'Exactly,' Molly breathed, impressed by his perfect articulation of a feeling she'd struggled to name. 'Everyone congratulates you on achievements that feel hollow, while the things that matter the most go unseen.'

The rain's rhythm shifted again, settling into a steady pattern that seemed to emphasize the cocoon-like quality of their shelter. The barn creaked and sighed around them, like a living entity adjusting to their presence.

'This,' she continued, gesturing to encompass the orchard beyond the stone walls, 'feels like coming back to something essential. Marketing in its purest form – highlighting true value, as opposed to manufacturing desire.'

'I'll drink to that.' Jack moved back to the barrel that served as their makeshift table, refilling their glasses with practiced precision. The cider caught the light as it flowed, translucent amber-like liquid sunlight captured and preserved. He handed her glass back, their fingers brushing briefly in the exchange.

The shift between them felt significant, boundaries redrawn by shared vulnerability.

'Is there . . .' Jack paused, clearing his throat. 'Is there someone waiting for you? Back in New York?'

The question caught her off guard, its personal nature a departure from their previous business-focused chat.

'Waiting in what sense?' Molly hedged, studying his face for clues.

'I think you know what sense,' he replied, a hint of challenge in his tone.

She felt heat rise in her cheeks, grateful for the dim lighting. 'No,' she answered honestly. 'There's no one special. My grandfather, my brother. Friends. Colleagues. But no one like . . .' She trailed off, suddenly terrified by the direction of the conversation. 'What about you? Eva tells me you're something of a local heartbreaker.'

Jack's bark of laughter echoed in the cavernous space. 'Did she now?'

'Something about a string of summer romances?' Molly teased, enjoying his discomfort. 'And who was it . . . Maura Delaney chasing you through secondary school.'

'Eva needs to mind her own business,' he grumbled, though without real heat. He took a long sip of cider, then set his glass down with deliberate care. 'No.' He hesitated, then added, 'Not many women understand what it means to be tied to a place like this. Most see limitation where I see roots.'

The simple honesty of his statement struck Molly deeply. She had always valued her freedom, her ability to go anywhere, do anything. Yet watching Jack – witnessing his connection to the land, his commitment to heritage, the depth of his belonging – had awakened something in her.

A recognition that roots needn't be chains; they could be anchors, holding steady against life's storms.

'I . . . think I get it,' she said softly.

Their eyes met across the barrel top and something in the air shifted – an electric awareness that had nothing to do with the distant thunder, and everything to do with the narrowing space between their separate worlds.

Jack's gaze dropped briefly to her mouth, then back to her eyes, a question forming in his expression. 'Molly . . .' he began, his voice hoarse, then leaned forward slightly, the movement so subtle she might have imagined it had her body not responded with sudden, heightened awareness.

The barrel between them felt both obstacle and protection, the few inches of weathered oak holding back a tide of possibilities both were afraid to acknowledge.

Until the barn door creaked open with a sudden gust of wet air, breaking the charged silence.

Patrick entered, hunched slightly against the rain, carrying a tray with three steaming mugs. His silver hair was darkened by moisture, his weathered face brightened by exertion and mischief.

'Thought you two might welcome something hot,' he called, kicking the door shut behind him with surprising vigor for a man his age. 'Weather's turned proper nasty.'

Molly straightened, suddenly conscious of her posture, the heat in her cheeks, the lingering electricity of the interrupted moment. Beside her, Jack cleared his throat and stepped back from the barrel, creating distance with deliberate movements.

'Perfect timing,' she said, her voice overly bright to her own ears. 'We were just discussing a business plan.'

Patrick's eyes, sharp, moved between them with knowing assessment. The steam from the mugs rose in fragrant curls, carrying the scent of tea and something else. His gnarled hands steadied the tray with ease as he approached, the skin spotted with age but the movements sure.

'Were you now?' he asked mildly, setting the tray on a nearby crate.

Jack took a mug with unnecessary focus, avoiding his great-uncle's gaze. 'Just bringing Molly up to speed on some of the challenges we're facing.'

‘Challenges, is it?’ Patrick handed Molly a steaming mug, his eyes twinkling with mischief that belied his innocent tone. ‘And here I thought you two might be finding solutions.’

The double meaning wasn’t lost on either of them.

Molly accepted the tea gratefully, wrapping her fingers around the warm ceramic. The rich scent of the blend rose with the steam, mingled with what she now identified as whiskey. The simple comfort of the drink grounded her, drawing her back from the edge of whatever precipice she and Jack had been approaching.

‘We were just about to taste the Russet batch,’ Jack said, changing the subject with transparent haste. ‘Want to join us, Patrick? Get a second opinion?’

The older man settled onto a crate, his movements measured but not frail. ‘Don’t mind if I do. Though I suspect you’ve already had a valuable second opinion.’ His gaze shifted meaningfully to Molly. ‘Sometimes fresh eyes see what we’ve been looking at for far too long to notice.’

Chapter 23

Friday morning, Molly headed into the village square, where the Harvest Festival market – the unofficial start of the festival weekend – had transformed the cobblestones into a colorful maze of canvas stalls. The older buildings stood sentinel around the temporary stalls, their weathered stone providing a perfect backdrop to the bustling commerce.

Something about the rhythm of this place settled her in a way that truly surprised her. For the first time in forever her shoulders no longer felt knotted with tension.

'Mornin'!' called an elderly woman arranging jars of honey on a wooden table nearby. The amber liquid caught the morning light, glowing like trapped sunshine.

Molly approached, drawn by the golden display. 'It's beautiful,' she said, picking up a small jar. The glass was cool against her palm.

'Taste?' The woman offered a tiny wooden stick drizzled with honey. Molly accepted, touching it to her tongue. The flavor bloomed; sweet certainly, but complex with floral notes and something deeper, almost smoky.

'That's incredible,' she murmured, genuinely impressed.

The woman beamed. 'My bees spend the summer up in the

hills where the heather blooms purple. Makes all the difference.' She tilted her head, studying Molly with curious eyes. 'You're the American staying at the Glen Arms, aren't you? The one helping the Flynns with their marketing?'

Word sure traveled fast in Golden Valley. 'That's me.'

'Well, work your charms on meself if you like; I could always do with the extra business.'

Molly chuckled. 'With stuff this good, I don't think you need any help from me.'

She purchased the honey jar, tucking it carefully into a canvas bag, before moving deeper into the market's heart.

The stalls formed uneven rows that created winding pathways between them. Molly wandered without hurry, pausing to admire hand-thrown pottery glazed in blues and greens that mimicked the lake's changing colors, then lingering over a display of wooden carvings – small animals and Celtic knots polished to a warm glow. A street busker played a tin whistle from a bench at the square's edge, the plaintive melody weaving through the market's ambient sounds.

Farmers arranged their produce in colorful displays – purple and green cabbage heads nestled beside orange carrots and ruby-red beet. Apples too, of course – though few with the character of Goldenridge's heritage varieties. She'd spent enough time with Jack over the last few days to recognize the commercial types, their uniform shape and color pretty but predictable.

The thought of him sent a small flutter through her stomach. Their interactions had improved markedly since that tense moment by the lake boundary.

While he remained guarded as Molly filmed and took notes, especially when Patrick wasn't around, something was shifting between them – moments of genuine connection breaking through his suspicion like sunshine through clouds. Yesterday especially when she'd walked him through the business plan she'd compiled for his bank meeting.

And then there was that moment in the rain-soaked barn . . .

A savory aroma pulled Molly out of her thoughts and, following her nose, she found herself at a butcher's stall where a ruddy-faced man in a striped apron tended a small portable grill. Sausages sizzled on the hot surface, their skin browning as fat rendered with a seductive hiss. The scent was mouth-watering – pork and herbs and something sweet-sharp that she recognized immediately.

'Hello, yourself,' the butcher greeted, noting her interest. With practiced movements, he speared a sausage, sliced it into bite-sized pieces and offered one to Molly on the tip of his knife. 'Goldenridge apples in these. Makes all the difference.'

Molly accepted the sample, the meat still almost too hot to touch. The flavors melded beautifully – savory pork, herbs she couldn't quite identify, and the distinctive sweet-tart note of apple providing the perfect counterpoint.

'Mmm . . . delicious,' she moaned. 'The flavor comes through so clearly. Bloody Butchers?'

He nodded, eyeing her with newfound interest. 'You know your apples, so.'

'I'm learning,' Molly chuckled. 'Hard not to pick up a few tips around here when you're surrounded by them.'

Sunlight had strengthened, burning through the morning mist and illuminating the scene with golden clarity. At a cheese stall, she paused to admire rounds of farmhouse cheddar aged to varying depths of color. The cheesemonger, a woman with strong forearms, offered tastes on small wooden paddles – creamy young cheese, sharp mature cheddar and a crumbly variety washed in local cider that once again, carried echoes of the fruit that had flavored it.

'The cider wash is my husband's invention,' the woman explained, watching Molly's reaction to the complex flavor. 'Goldenridge of course.'

It was as if the orchard was woven into the village, the fruit central to so much of its produce, and its people too. 'Mmm . . . wonderful,' Molly said, the taste tangy and rich on her tongue.

Next came a stall of woolen goods – scarves, hats, and blankets in natural shades and vibrant dyes. Molly ran her fingers over a scarf the color of forest moss, the wool surprisingly soft against her skin.

'Golden Vale sheep,' the vendor told her, an older woman with knitting needles clicking steadily in her hands even as she spoke. 'Not as fancy as merino, but wears far better, I'll tell you that. My mother's blankets lasted forty years or more.'

Molly examined the scarf, immediately thinking of Pops. Her grandfather would appreciate the craftsmanship, and the connection to his wife's homeland. 'I'll take it,' she decided. As the woman wrapped her purchase, Molly caught the tantalizing scent of fresh bread on the breeze.

Following it led her to a stall where loaves in various shapes and sizes covered a rustic wooden table. Behind it, an older man, with arms dusted white to the elbow, shaped dough with practiced movements. The results were works of art that would give Eva a run for her money – crusty baguettes, rustic country loaves, and perfectly formed rounds of soda bread. The baker worked on a fresh batch, his strong hands kneading dough before shaping it into a round and placing it on a floured board. With easy precision, he took a sharp knife and cut a deep cross into the top of the unbaked loaf.

'Deep enough to let the fairies out,' Molly joked with a smile, another well-worn Aoife phrase emerging automatically.

The baker looked up, surprise flickering across his features before his face creased with laughter. 'My mother swore by that too.' He studied her with new interest. 'Not many visitors know it.'

'Irish grandmother,' she repeated, smiling. 'Religious about the bread cross – said it was practical and magical all at once.'

'Wise woman, so.' The baker nodded, flouring another ball

of dough. 'Practical because it helps the dough cook through, magical because it keeps the fairies from spoiling the bread.' His eyes twinkled with humor. 'Though between ourselves, I think it was just to stop the youngsters stealing it.'

Molly chuckled in agreement, immediately recalling how Aoife used to slap Cole's hands away when her brother tried to break into a fresh loaf.

'She made the most incredible soda bread,' she continued, the memory vivid and sweet. 'Dark with caraway seeds and raisins soaked in tea overnight. The place would smell like heaven when it was baking.'

'Ah, tea-soaked raisins! That's an old local trick.' The baker nodded approvingly. 'Your granny must've been a Tipp woman so?'

'Yes.' Molly traced a finger along the rough wooden edge of the stall, suddenly caught between worlds – their Brooklyn apartment where Aoife had baked and told stories, and this village square where those same stories had been born. 'I learned to bake watching her, though sadly I've never been able to match her soda bread.'

'The secret's in the buttermilk,' the baker said, conspiratorially. 'And a light hand with the mixing – too much and you've made yourself a doorstop.' He picked up one of the finished loaves, its crust a perfect deep brown, the cross clearly defined on top. 'Take this one,' he said, wrapping it in brown paper. 'Still warm from the oven. Slather it with good Kerrygold while it's hot – no better taste in the world.'

Their fingers brushed as Molly handed over payment, his hands warm and flour-soft. 'Thank you,' she said, meaning it for more than just the bread.

'Enjoy,' he replied. 'And if herself had any other baking secrets, I'm always keen to learn a new trick.'

Molly hesitated, wondering what Aoife would think of her now, standing in the village square she'd left decades ago, in the midst of the Harvest Festival weekend holding bread made by hands that might even have known hers.

Cradling the warmth against her chest, she continued her market exploration.

The square had filled considerably now, a mix of locals and a handful of festival day-trippers and tourists. She found a bench at the market's edge and sat for a bit, watching the scene with a contentment that felt both new and familiar.

Children chased each other between stalls while their parents browsed. Older men gathered near the fountain, caps on heads, discussing what looked like serious business. The whole village seemed to breathe together as they turned out for the day, connected by the invisible threads of shared history and present community.

Molly broke off a small piece of the still-warm soda bread, the crust crackling pleasantly between her fingers. The interior was tender and buttermilk-tangy, with a familiar homey perfection that made her throat tighten with unexpected emotion. It tasted just like her childhood, like Aoife's kitchen, like . . . belonging.

She chewed slowly, savoring both the taste and the moment. In the week or so since arriving in Golden Valley, she felt not like an intruder or an impostor, but like someone who might, in some small way, have a right to be here?

The feeling was as warm and sustaining as the bread in Molly's hands – complicated, but undeniably satisfying.

Chapter 24

Jack strode into town, each step deliberate despite the hammering in his chest. The manila folder under his arm might as well have been made of lead for all the weight it seemed to carry.

Inside lay spreadsheets, projections and Molly Harris's broad-stroke marketing plan – the sum total of Goldenridge's future balanced on a few sheets of paper.

He'd stayed up half the night revising the numbers, searching for any advantage that might convince the bank that the orchard deserved the finance it desperately needed. His shoulders ached with tension, jaw clenched so tight he could feel a headache building at his temples.

This meeting wasn't just about next season's cash flow; it was about keeping a Flynn on Flynn land for another generation.

The regional office opened at ten, giving him exactly ten minutes to cross the square and prepare his pitch. He'd rehearsed it a dozen times in his bathroom mirror that morning, trying to find the right balance between confident and realistic. Too optimistic and yer man would see through it; too pessimistic and there'd be no reason to approve the loan.

Jack had always hated this part of running Goldenridge – the financial dance, the need to translate generations of passion and commitment into cold figures on balance sheets.

This meeting needed to go well. Without the loan, he'd be forced to sell off something, probably the western parcel – the least profitable section, but home to the oldest Bloody Butcher trees and the wild bee colonies that had pollinated the place for generations. And the old oak.

The folder contained his last hope of avoiding that outcome. Jack's fingers tightened reflexively around the edges, feeling the slight resistance of the papers inside. On top lay Molly's proposed marketing strategy – professionally presented, meticulously researched, and frustratingly brilliant. She'd produced it after mere days of orchard tours and questions, presenting it yesterday with a quiet confidence that had left Jack simultaneously impressed and wrong-footed.

'Traditional doesn't have to mean invisible,' she'd said, walking him through the elegant simplicity of her approach. 'You have to insist that Goldenridge isn't just selling cider; it's selling heritage, craftsmanship, connection to the land. That's what modern consumers are hungry for – authenticity they can trust. And that's exactly what I see here.'

Jack hadn't wanted to be impressed. He'd looked for flaws in her reasoning, holes in her strategy. But the plan was sound – emphasizing Goldenridge's unique strengths without compromising its identity. Patrick had nodded approvingly, his weathered face creasing with enthusiasm as Molly had walked them through projected engagement metrics and conversion rates.

The memory of her face – focused, passionate, her green eyes bright with conviction – triggered a warmth in Jack's chest that he quickly suppressed. Whatever was developing between them was complicated enough without adding financial desperation to the mix.

Besides, despite their growing ease with each other, something about Molly Harris remained elusive, like shadow-play on stone walls. She knew too much about things ordinary tourists shouldn't know, noticed details others overlooked, hummed songs that hadn't been heard for decades.

He hoped he could trust her, he really wanted to, but trust had never come easy to him.

Jack checked his watch and quickened his pace.

The festival weekend had transformed the square into an obstacle course of market stalls and shoppers, the cobblestones barely visible beneath the temporary structures and milling crowds. Normally he'd skirt the whole affair, taking the longer route around the church to avoid the press of bodies. But with time moving on, today he had no choice but to run the gauntlet.

The market's sensory assault hit immediately – the mingled scents of baking bread, sizzling meats and fresh produce; the chatter of vendors calling prices and customers haggling; the visual jumble of colorful stalls against the weathered gray stone of the village buildings.

Despite his hurry, Jack found his steps slowing involuntarily as he passed familiar faces. He nodded to Paudie Molloy who'd been buying his second-grade apples for chutney since they were schoolboys together at St. Brendan's.

He exchanged quick greetings with Kay, the honey seller whose hives pollinated the eastern orchard every spring; then raised a hand to old Des from the neighboring cattle farm, who'd been fighting off the same land-zoning vultures as the orchard had.

Each greeting cost precious seconds, but these were the connections that kept Golden Valley alive – the web of local relationships that sustained the town through hard times and good. The very community Molly was aiming to convey in her grand marketing plan, recognizing instinctively what made Goldenridge special.

'Deep enough to let the fairies out . . .'

The voice stopped Jack mid-stride, his boot hovering above the cobblestones before settling with deliberate quietness. He knew that voice – had heard it all week, listened to it asking intelligent questions about apple varieties, explaining marketing demographics, caught it humming a local ballad it shouldn't have known.

Through a gap between stalls, he saw her standing at the baker's counter, watching as Tommy Clancy scored a cross into a round of soda bread. There was something in Molly's posture – a familiarity, an ease that went beyond typical tourist enthusiasm. She stood with the relaxed confidence of someone who belonged here, her smile genuine as she bantered with the baker.

Tommy laughed at whatever Molly had said, his big shovel hands gesturing animatedly. Jack couldn't hear the full exchange over the market's ambient noise, but he caught fragments, again something about the Irish grandmother. Molly nodded, her face softening with what looked like nostalgia as she traced a finger along the edge of the baker's stall.

A complicated heat spread through Jack's chest. The woman before him bore little resemblance to the drenched, bedraggled woman who'd knocked over his apples in this very square a week or so ago. This Molly – with her casual clothes, easy laughter and evident knowledge of local baking traditions – seemed almost like a different person. But of course that morning, Jack's own suspicions had been clouding his vision.

He should continue on, focus on the meeting that could determine Goldenridge's future. Instead, he found himself rooted to the spot, watching as Molly accepted a wrapped loaf from Tommy, her smile transforming her from pretty to something that made Jack's breath catch in his throat. Even from this distance, Jack could see the warmth in the interaction. Tommy was saying something else now, leaning forward confidentially and Molly laughed again – a genuine sound that carried across the market's bustle to reach Jack's ears like a melody picked out from background noise.

The banker's warning from their last meeting echoed in Jack's mind: 'Sentiment doesn't pay the bills, Flynn.' He should be reviewing his pitch, mentally preparing for the tough questions the regional manager would inevitably ask.

Instead, he found himself cataloging the way sunlight caught in Molly's dark hair, how her face lit up when she smiled, the graceful movement of her hands as she tucked the bread into her canvas bag. It was like she was already woven into the place; far too smoothly for a mere tourist.

The contradiction both rankled and intrigued him.

'Who are you really?' Jack whispered, too quietly for anyone to hear.

The rational part of him still harbored suspicions. Her local knowledge was very specific, her interest in the orchard's heritage varieties too focused, her questions about the ancient oak too pertinent to be casual curiosity. Plus the coincidence of her arrival as Crest Beverages renewed their pressure campaign still nagged at him, despite her denials.

But watching Molly now – sunlight catching her profile as she savored the fresh bread, her expression one of simple contentment – Jack felt his suspicions warring with something stronger, something that tightened his chest and quickened his pulse in a way entirely unrelated to the impending bank meeting.

'Admit it,' Patrick had said only yesterday, his eyes twinkling with mischief, 'you're half in love with the girl already.'

Jack had denied it vehemently, listing all the reasons the American woman remained an enigma they shouldn't really trust.

But Patrick's knowing smile had only widened, his weathered hand patting Jack's shoulder with infuriating condescension. 'Keep telling yourself that, lad. Meanwhile, the rest of us have eyes.'

Now as he strode toward the meeting, Jack found his thoughts dividing like water around a stone – part-focused on the numbers he needed to present, part lingering on the image of Molly's smile.

He straightened his shoulders, adjusted his grip on the folder, and took a deep breath that did little to calm the drumming of his heart. Whatever Molly Harris was hiding, whatever complicated feelings she stirred in him, would have to wait.

This meeting determined whether the trees his great-great-grandfather had planted would continue under Flynn stewardship, be carved up for development, or worse, corporate expansion.

The orchard came first. Always had.

Chapter 25

Later, after the morning market closed, Molly ambled back towards town, where locals now moved with renewed purpose through the square, setting up in advance of the Harvest Festival's official opening night. Hanging colorful bunting between lamp-posts, arranging hay bales around a makeshift wooden stage and raising ladders to hang lights between the trees.

A group of older men carefully positioned a large banner proclaiming 'Golden Valley Harvest Festival' between a pair of ash trees above the central fountain. Their movements were deliberate, practiced – they'd clearly performed this ritual many times before. Teenagers balanced precariously on ladders, stringing fairy lights between the looming chestnut trees whose branches formed a natural canopy over the far corner of the square.

'There you are!' Eva's voice cut through the gentle hubbub. She waved from the café entrance, her auburn curls escaping from beneath a bright-yellow bandana this time.

Molly threaded her way through the activity, returning greetings from villagers who now recognized her with friendly nods or quick smiles. Just a week ago, she'd been the outsider, just another tourist. Now, she was simply Molly – not one of them obviously, but no longer a complete stranger either.

'Sorry I'm late,' she said, reaching Eva's stall. 'They're busy at the hotel, and food service was a bit delayed.'

'And here I thought you were just avoiding more work.' Eva gestured toward a collection of galvanized buckets brimming with wildflowers and greenery. 'The tables need centerpieces and I've volunteered your artistic hands.'

The Cherry Blossom Café's outdoor tables had been rearranged into a winding formation that curved through the cobblestones like a serpentine river. White tablecloths fluttered in the gentle evening breeze, anchored by mismatched vintage crockery that would serve as place settings for tonight's community gathering.

'I've never claimed to be artistic,' Molly protested, though she was already rolling up the sleeves of her sweater.

Eva snorted. 'Your Insta says otherwise. Besides, I still have customers to look after, so someone's got to make these tables look the part.'

Molly settled onto a wooden stool and drew a bucket closer. The mingled scent of the flowers rose to greet her – sweet honeysuckle, peppery marigolds, and something herbal and clean that reminded her of their Brooklyn garden. Without conscious thought, her fingers selected stems, grouping them by height and texture in a natural progression.

'The festival proper always starts with the locals,' Eva explained, watching Molly work while arranging some of her own. 'Everyone contributes something from their harvest – Paudie brings chutney, Maurice does sausages, with Jack's cider as the centerpiece, of course.'

'Of course,' Molly echoed, her tone carefully neutral despite the small flutter in her stomach at the mention of Jack's name. Their almost-moment in the cider barn earlier this week still lingered in her mind.

She was dying to find out how Jack had fared at the bank that morning. Following his confession about the reality of the challenges the business was facing, she felt invested in Goldenridge's success in a way that went beyond a simple media campaign. And had spent far more than 'just an hour or two', crouched over her laptop at the hotel working on suggested plans and projections.

This wasn't just a media campaign, it almost felt like another mission. Which by rights should have made it easier to broach with Jack her true intentions, and the real reason she'd offered to help, but Molly couldn't do it.

Not yet.

She was afraid to risk his and indeed Patrick's disappointment by admitting that her offers of assistance weren't entirely altruistic. In short, she was in too deep.

Still, with work on the business plan helping to focus her efforts, Molly had pretty much all she needed from Goldenridge for a social media campaign, and had already compiled a visual montage incorporating all of the elements she thought pertinent about the orchard. And would of course have plenty more material from this weekend's festival to supplement and highlight Golden Valley itself.

Putting them 'on the map' might be pushing it, but Molly would do her best to honor the promise she'd made and try to convey the essence of this wonderful place that had so quickly captured her own heart.

Now, as Eva popped back in to the café to attend to customers, Molly's hands moved automatically among the flowers, selecting, arranging, adjusting with an intuitive sense of balance and harmony. Purple loosestrife rose from a foundation of feathery greens, complemented by the bold faces of late-season sunflowers and the delicate spikes of wild lavender.

'You've an eye for it all right,' Eva observed, coming back out.

Aoife had taught her to balance colors and textures, to let each bloom speak for itself while contributing to the whole. 'I've always thought store-bought flower arrangements are too perfect to be interesting.'

'Exactly. Nature doesn't work that way.' She winked. 'But maybe don't mention that to Leah the florist tonight if you see her.'

The square grew more animated as evening deepened, shadows lengthening across the cobblestones while the golden light intensified. A young band began setting up by the make-shift stage – a converted truck trailer situated at the bottom of the square.

'This festival's ancient, you know,' Eva chattered, moving to sit beside Molly with a basket of ribbon scraps. 'Pre-Christian even. It was a celebration of harvest, obviously, but also preparation for winter – last chance for trading, marriages to be arranged, or settling debts before the dark months.'

'So not just about the apple harvest?' Molly asked, selecting a sprig of rosemary to add a touch of fragrance to her arrangement.

'The apples came later, when the English introduced their orchards.' Eva cut lengths of burlap ribbon to tie around the completed arrangements. 'But they fit right into the older traditions too. Symbols of abundance, fertility, eternal life when you cut them crosswise.' She demonstrated with her fingers. 'You know how the seeds at the core form a pentagram? Ancient pagans considered that protective magic.'

Molly was intrigued. 'I never knew that.'

'The cider was originally part of the fertility rituals actually,' her friend continued, with a mischievous glint in her eye. 'Young couples would share the special blend on festival night, then disappear into the orchards for privacy. Nine months later, there'd be a crop of festival babies.'

'That's hardly still part of the tradition,' Molly chuckled dubiously.

'Not officially.' Eva winked. 'But the harvest still works its magic. Half the village has birthdays suspiciously close to nine months after the festival.'

As they worked, villagers stopped to chat, each interaction reinforcing Molly's growing sense of belonging. The proprietor of The Glen Remedy asked about her stay, and Tommy the bread baker from earlier, or 'the competition' as Eva jokingly teased him, paused to admire their flower arrangements, after packing up his own stall. Each conversation flowed more easily than the last, references to local landmarks and village personalities no longer requiring explanation.

Molly found herself relaxing into a rhythm that felt both new and familiar – the give and take of small-town life where everyone's business intertwined like the stems in the flower arrangements, separate but connected in ways that created something wonderful in their totality.

'Oh, there's the Flynns now,' Eva said, nodding toward the far side of the square.

Molly's gaze followed. Jack, in his worn leather jacket, stood beside a half-assembled wooden stall, hammer in hand as he secured a panel emblazoned with the Goldenridge logo. The evening light caught in his dark hair and gilded the strong line of his profile as he leaned to check his work. Patrick moved more slowly beside him, passing tools when needed but mostly supervising as he leaned on his walking stick and chatted with neighbors and friends.

As if sensing her gaze, Jack looked up then, his eyes finding Molly's across the busy square with an immediacy that suggested he'd been aware of her presence all along. For a moment, they simply looked at each other, the distance between them filled with unspoken conversations, with the memory of that almost-connection in a rain-surrounded barn.

He nodded once, the beginnings of a hesitant smile softening his features before Patrick said something that drew his attention away. The brief exchange left Molly's heart beating a touch faster, her fingers momentarily stilled among the flower stems.

Did the smile mean things had gone well at the bank? Or had it been meant for her alone?

'Ye two seem to have sorted out your differences anyway,' Eva observed, her tone deliberately casual, though her eyes missed nothing.

Molly resumed her work, focusing intently on balancing a sprig of goldenrod against the deeper purple of wild aster. 'We've reached a . . . professional understanding,' she said, aiming for the same casualness, though not quite achieving it.

'Is that what they're calling it these days?'

'Eva . . .' Molly warned, though she couldn't suppress a small smile.

'I'm just saying, the man's actually brushed his hair for once,' Eva countered, tying a perfect bow around one of the completed arrangements. 'Now if we could just get rid of that manky 'oul jacket we'd be on to a winner.'

Molly laughed, while the heat in her cheeks intensified, betraying her despite her best efforts. 'We've been working hard on the marketing stuff. Stuff that you initiated by the way. That's all.'

'Yeah.' Eva's skepticism was palpable. 'And I'm the Queen of Tara.'

Molly shook her head, unwilling to examine the complicated emotions that Jack Flynn stirred in her – attraction certainly, but also guilt for the secret she still kept, fear of what he might say when she eventually requested access to the oak tree.

The square transformed completely as dusk deepened into evening. Workers had finished hanging strings of lights that now twinkled into life. Oil lanterns were lit and placed on tables, their golden glow creating pools of warmth against the fading darkness.

'Almost done,' Molly said, putting the finishing touches on her final arrangement. The collection of centerpieces stood ready – each unique but harmonious with the others, capturing the essence of autumn in their blending of textures and colors.

'They're beautiful,' Eva said with genuine admiration. 'Definitely in your blood.'

Molly smiled.

'Speaking of blood,' her friend continued, nodding towards the stage, 'the young lads are warming up. I know they look like kids, but they're actually really good. You'll come back for the session later? Mostly just ourselves before the visitor invasion tomorrow.'

'I wouldn't miss it.' Molly smiled. 'Just need to pop back and get changed.'

'Same. I'll meet you back at The Orchard Pub then. Just be sure to put your dancing shoes on, missus! We go all out tonight.'

As if on cue, the first notes of a banjo spiraled into the evening air, melancholy and joyful all at once. A perfect distillation of the feeling in Molly's heart as she stood surrounded by flowers gathered from the same fields where her grandmother had once walked, preparing to celebrate a harvest her ancestors had marked for generations before her.

No longer just a tourist, and obviously not a local – but Molly was finding a space between those extremes where she might eventually belong.

Chapter 26

The Glen Arms Hotel lobby also hummed with festival energy as Molly pushed through the heavy oak door, bringing with her the crisp scent of evening air and the faintest trace of wildflowers from her work in the square.

The antique grandfather clock in the corner had just chimed seven, its sonorous tones reverberating through the wood-paneled walls that had witnessed generations of travelers passing through. Several suitcases were stacked near the reception desk, where Anna sorted through a chaotic pile of registration cards with the efficiency of someone accustomed to managing chaos with limited resources. The proprietor's usually immaculate dark hair had escaped its professional updo in several places, giving her a slightly frazzled appearance that contrasted with her crisp white blouse.

'Everything OK?' Molly asked, and Anna rolled her eyes.

'Siobhan's called in sick – festival flu, I suspect, since her boyfriend's playing in the band tonight.'

Molly unwound her scarf, draping it over the coat stand by the door. 'Need a hand?'

Relief washed over Anna's features. 'You're an angel. The festival rush is well and truly underway, I've got six check-ins waiting already. Haven't even had time to put out the welcome drinks.'

'On it,' Molly said, already moving behind the reception desk as if she belonged there. 'What else do you need me to do?'

Anna quickly explained the check-in process – a blend of traditional hospitality and necessary modernization. Guests would first be welcomed with a small glass of apple cordial, a festival tradition dating back generations. Their details would be entered into the computer system (which was prone to freezing if you typed too quickly, Anna warned), and then they would be escorted to their rooms by staff – or in tonight's case, by Molly.

'Most importantly, make them feel welcome,' she concluded. 'Like yourself, this is the first taste of Golden Valley for most. First impressions matter.'

Molly nodded, remembering her own rain-soaked arrival twelve days ago – how the hotel had seemed both foreign and oddly familiar, how Anna's welcome had contained that curious mix of professional warmth and personal interest that characterized Irish hospitality.

It almost felt like months had passed since then.

The lobby filled gradually with new arrivals – an older couple from Dublin who'd been attending the festival for years; a group of young women from Cork, excited for their first visit; an elderly man who announced he'd been staying in the Ash Room every festival weekend since 1978 and expected the same service his late wife had always enjoyed.

Molly moved between them with growing confidence, pouring cordial into small crystal glasses, explaining festival highlights, answering questions about local attractions. The knowledge she'd absorbed over her stay flowed easily – which paths offered the best lake views, which pub served traditional music, where to find the best soda bread in the village. Information gathered from Eva, from Jack and Patrick, her own explorations – and perhaps, in some small way, from memories passed down through her grandmother's stories.

'You're a natural,' Anna murmured as they passed each other

behind the desk. 'Are you sure you haven't worked in hospitality before?'

'Lots of this stuff in marketing, really,' Molly replied. 'Different industry, same principle – make people feel they've made the right choice.'

Between arrivals, she helped Anna sort welcome baskets containing local products – small jars of honey, lavender sachets for pillows. The routine established itself quickly, a rhythm of welcomes and directions and key handovers that felt surprisingly satisfying in its immediacy. Unlike her work projects that often took months to show results, here the appreciation was instant – visible in the smiles of guests as they stepped into rooms with lake views, in their exclamations over the freshly cut flowers on bedside tables, in their evident delight at the small touches that distinguished the Glen Arms from generic chain hotels.

'You've a good eye for the details,' Anna observed as Molly refreshed a slightly wilted flower arrangement in the lobby. 'Most people wouldn't even notice that.'

She smiled. 'You can tell everything about a place by how they tend to the little things.'

Anna nodded. 'My mother says the very same.'

As if summoned by her daughter's words, Brid herself appeared in the doorway connecting the Ryan family quarters to the hotel proper. Her silver-streaked hair was arranged in its usual elegant coiffure and tonight, she wore a deep burgundy dress. She paused on the threshold, her gaze falling immediately on Molly as she led a newly arrived couple toward the staircase.

'The Rowan Room is on the second floor, third door on your right,' Molly was saying, her posture unconsciously mimicking Anna's professional stance. 'The windows face west, so you'll catch the sunset over the lake. If you need extra pillows or have any questions, just dial zero on the room phone.'

The couple nodded appreciatively, the husband already asking about the best lake scenic spots as they ascended the stairs.

Molly answered with suggestions she'd gleaned from her own explorations.

Brid stood perfectly still, her lined face composed in an expression of puzzled concentration. She hadn't moved from the doorway, her eyes following Molly with the intensity of someone trying to recall an elusive memory.

'Mam,' Anna called, breaking Brid's focus. 'You're blocking the passage. Come in or go out, but don't stand there like an eejit.'

Brid moved forward with the fluid grace that belied her years, her gaze still returning to Molly with distracted frequency. She approached the desk where Anna was entering data into the computer, but her attention remained divided.

'Committee meeting ran late,' she explained, setting her handbag on a small table beside the desk. 'Betty O'Toole wanted to discuss parking, and you know what she's like when she's on her soapbox.'

Anna made a noncommittal sound, her fingers flying over the keyboard with practiced efficiency. 'Was anything actually resolved, or was it just the usual arguments going nowhere?'

'We're using the church grounds for overflow tomorrow,' Brid replied, then paused and looked back toward the stairs. 'That girl really reminds me of someone,' she said, her voice dropping but still audible in the small lobby. 'The American one. But I just can't put my finger on it.'

Anna glanced up from the computer screen. 'Half the tourists remind you of someone, Mam. Remember that Canadian fella you were certain was your cousin Michael's grandson?'

'That was different,' Brid protested. 'This is . . .' She trailed off. 'There's something in the way she moves, the tilt of her head, even. It's just so familiar.'

Anna sighed, smoothly changing the subject. 'Did you bring the festival programs? We should put them on the counter.'

Brid reluctantly turned her attention to her daughter, extracting a stack of colorful brochures from her handbag. 'Fresh off the printer. Added a special mention of Goldenridge sponsors too, thanks to advice from our marketing expert.' She nodded again toward the stairs and a now-absent Molly.

The check-in rush gradually subsided as the grandfather clock struck eight, its resonant chimes filling the lobby with sonorous dignity. Most new arrivals had now settled into their rooms, leaving only the occasional latecomer to disturb the newly established calm. As Molly reappeared downstairs to check if Anna needed anything else, Brid told her she'd gone to check on dinner service in the kitchen.

'You've been a godsend tonight,' she said, studying her. 'Anna doesn't like to admit when she's overwhelmed.'

'Happy to help,' Molly replied. 'It's nice to feel useful.'

Brid's shrewd eyes seemed to be studying her. 'You've settled in well here, haven't you?'

'Yes. It feels . . .' Molly hesitated, searching for a word that wouldn't reveal too much. 'Familiar, somehow. Comfortable.'

'Golden Valley has that effect on a lot of people,' Brid observed. 'Especially those with Tipp blood, no matter how distant. It calls them home, in a way.'

The comment struck far closer to truth than Brid could know. Molly nodded noncommittally and headed back toward the stairs.

The movement brought her face-to-face with one of the old photographs she hadn't noticed before. Mounted a few steps from the bottom in a simple wooden frame, it showed a woman she now recognized as a much younger Brid – perhaps twenty? – standing arm-in-arm with another young woman beneath a Harvest Festival banner.

Both wore bright dresses adorned with autumn leaves, flower chains on their heads, their faces alight with laughter and youth. The other girl was slender and dark-haired, her features blurred slightly by the photograph's age but beautiful in a delicate, serious way that contrasted with her joyful expression.

Molly's heart stilled in her chest. She knew that face – had seen it in family albums, in the framed portrait that had stood on her grandmother's bedside table until the day she died. Younger than in any photograph she had ever seen, but unmistakably Aoife Brennan, before she became Aoife Harris.

'I was Harvest Queen,' Brid's voice said close behind her, making her start a little. 'What year it was I couldn't tell you, but a long time ago now, that's for sure.'

Molly swallowed hard, forcing herself to maintain a neutral expression as she turned to face Brid. 'Looks like you were having fun,' she managed, her voice surprisingly steady despite the tumult inside her.

'And that's my old friend, my best friend,' the older woman continued, her eyes fixed on the photograph with the dewy-eyed focus of someone looking into the past. 'We were inseparable in those days.'

'What happened to her?' Molly asked, the question emerging before she could consider its wisdom. 'Your friend?'

Brid's expression clouded slightly. 'She left Golden Valley not long after that picture was taken. Went to America, we heard eventually. We lost touch over the years – 'course, this was well before the internet or cheaper international calls.' She sighed, the sound heavy with old regrets. 'Life takes people in different directions.'

Molly nodded, unable to trust her voice. The photograph seemed to pulse with significance, a visual confirmation of the very connection she'd come here to honor. Her grandmother had stood in this very building, had even laughed with the woman beside her, had been part of the festival Molly herself was now helping to prepare. The realization made her feel simultaneously more authentic and more fraudulent – her presence here both a homecoming and a deception.

Should she say something to Brid? Maybe tell her . . .

'There you are.' Anna's voice broke the moment as she returned to the reception area. She smiled at Molly. 'I can't thank you enough for your help. Go on away now and enjoy yourself after all your hard work.'

Molly nodded. 'A pleasure.'

Anna turned to Brid. 'Your friend, Mrs Donnelly, is looking for more towels in the Hawthorn Room, Mam.'

Brid turned away from the photograph. 'I'll sort it,' she said, looking conspiratorially at Molly. 'She likes to reminisce about the days when towels were proper towels, not these modern thin yokes.'

As Brid moved away, Anna gave Molly another smile. 'Honestly. Thanks again for stepping in tonight. You've been a tremendous help.'

'Not a problem,' she replied, her mind still half-captured by the photograph. 'I should probably go get ready for tonight.'

Anna nodded. 'You'll enjoy it I'd say. The band's brilliant and the craic is mighty.' Her smile turned conspiratorial. 'Jack Flynn might even be persuaded to play a tune or two in the pub after-hours. He's quite talented on the guitar, though he'd die before admitting it.'

The mention of Jack added another layer of complexity to Molly's already tumultuous thoughts. Jack, a musician? The man had hidden depths she'd barely uncovered.

As Molly ascended the steps, the weight of the photograph's revelation followed her. Her grandmother had been here in the Glen Arms Hotel, had breathed this same air, had been young and full of dreams in this place before life took her in unexpected directions.

The thought was both comforting and unsettling.

Especially since unlike Brid it seemed, Molly knew exactly the direction Aoife's life beyond Golden Valley had taken.

Chapter 27

In her room, Molly perched on the armchair by the window, her phone almost incongruous against the traditional backdrop.

Outside, Golden Valley was still transforming for the festival, windows lighting up across the village square, the distant sound of music drifting up from below as the band started up. The screen brightened as Cole's call connected, his familiar face appearing with a wide grin that immediately eased something tight in Molly's chest.

Her mind still hummed with the implications of the photograph – tangible proof of her grandmother's life here, of her friendship with Brid. She hadn't expected to find such direct evidence of Aoife's past so casually displayed on the hotel wall and wondered how on earth she'd spent all this time here without noticing it. But then again, Molly only ever knew her as Nan, not as a young Irish woman full of her own hopes and dreams.

'Hey,' her brother greeted, his voice slightly tinny through the phone's speakers. He was freshly showered, hair still damp, wearing a team-branded hoodie that suggested he was on his way to hockey practice. 'How's life in the land of shamrocks and leprechauns?'

'Ha! Neither of which I've encountered yet,' Molly replied with a smile, settling more comfortably against the windowsill.

'*Please* tell me you're not holed up in your room working,' Cole said, severity creasing his brow as, behind her on the desk, he caught sight of her open laptop and notes from her work on the Goldenridge campaign yesterday. 'This was supposed to be a relaxing retreat, Mol.'

'I'll have you know I'm actually headed out to the harvest festival in exactly—' she glanced at the clock on the mantelpiece '—five minutes. So make it quick.'

Cole leaned closer to the camera, his expression growing more serious. 'Pops and I were both just wondering . . . have you made it to the magic tree yet?'

The question sobered Molly afresh. 'Not yet,' she admitted, absently twisting a strand of hair around her finger – a nervous habit she thought she'd outgrown years ago. 'Like I said, it's . . . complicated. The oak is on private property and the owner . . .' She shifted, adjusting the phone so Cole couldn't see the flush she felt rising to her cheeks. 'He's . . . warming up to me.'

Cole's eyebrows shot up, a knowing grin spreading across his face. 'The angry hot farmer?'

'And don't kill me –' Molly winced, ignoring the remark – 'but I'm actually helping him with some marketing stuff.'

'I knew it!' Her brother harrumphed, the sound echoing slightly in his minimalist apartment. 'Seriously, you just can't help yourself, can you? Workaholic doesn't even begin to describe it.'

'It's nothing, honestly; just a few projections for a bank loan and a social media thing. I'll send it to you when it's done, actually; maybe you could give it a share.'

It was impossible to explain to Cole about the true task she'd undertaken for Goldenridge, about the hours spent with Jack learning the orchard's history, about the moment in the cider barn that had almost tipped into something more. Her brother knew her too well – would see immediately how entangled

Molly's heart was becoming with what should have been a simple mission.

'And this is all part of your charm offensive? Mol, haven't you considered just telling the guy the truth?' Cole suggested, his tone gentler now. 'That we're just trying to fulfill Nan's last wish?'

She sighed, turning to gaze out the window at the village square below, where the last light of day had given way to the soft blue of evening. 'Of course I have. But like I said, he's suspicious of outsiders, and now it seems wrong to suddenly reveal that I'm not just a tourist like I told him. Besides,' she added, 'there's more to it now. I've sort of . . . gotten entangled with the locals too.'

'Entangled how?' Cole pressed, clearly sensing her evasiveness.

'Just helping out. Making friends even.' Molly kept her tone deliberately casual, brushing past specifics, like her fondness for Patrick and her growing feelings for Jack. 'There's a woman who runs the local café – Eva, same age as us. She's funny, direct, no patience for nonsense. Makes *incredible* baked goods. I've put on about ten pounds since I got here.'

Cole guffawed. 'She single by any chance?'

'Famously so, according to herself.' Molly grinned, relieved at the change of subject. 'Used to go out with some famous hurler apparently, but is now looking for, and I quote, "a good strong man who doesn't need someone to mammy him".'

'Good strong man – check,' her brother quipped, his interest clearly piqued. 'What else does this Eva do besides baking and setting high standards?'

'She's addicted to real-estate renovation TV shows, coaches her niece's camogie team, knows the entire village. Has a laugh that makes everyone in range smile automatically.' Molly found herself warming to the topic.

'Got a picture?'

'I'm not showing you creeper shots of my new friend!' Molly laughed. 'But if you like, I'll casually mention my charming, pro athlete brother to her sometime. Test the waters.'

He grinned. 'You do that. Though I don't know what good it'll do, since you're coming home next week,' he pointed out, and the thought of leaving Golden Valley sent an unexpected pang through Molly's chest. 'Aren't you?' Cole's expression turned more serious. 'From the way you're talking about the place, it almost sounds like you're putting down roots.'

The observation struck uncomfortably close to truth. Molly glanced around the cozy room with its handcrafted furniture and views across the lake, thinking of the connections she'd formed in such a short space of time – Eva's cheery friendship, Anna's quiet warmth, Patrick's gentle wisdom, Jack's complicated pull on her heart.

Even Brid's scrutiny had begun to feel like a form of belonging.

'I'm here to do what Nan asked,' she said firmly, as much to remind herself as to answer Cole. 'Everything else is just temporary.'

He studied her through the screen, his expression softening with understanding. 'But you are enjoying it,' he observed. 'This village, these people. I can see it in your face, Mol. You look . . . lighter somehow. More you.'

Molly didn't know how to respond to that – to the truth of it, to the implications for her carefully constructed life back home. She'd come to Ireland with a singular mission, expecting to complete it efficiently and return to her normal routine. Instead, she found herself caught up in village life, in helping a small family business, in feelings for a man who still didn't know her true purpose for being here.

'I should . . . go,' she said instead, glancing at the clock. 'I'm meeting Eva at the pub soon.'

Cole nodded, understanding her deflection but not pushing further. 'Enjoy. But, Molls?' His expression grew more serious. 'Remember why you went there, OK. Nan's wish is important.'

'I know,' Molly said softly. 'I haven't forgotten. I'll find a way to the oak tree, I promise.'

His smile returned. 'Call me after you've completed the mission. And once you've properly won over your brooding orchard owner.'

'Goodbye, Cole!' Molly sang firmly, though she couldn't help returning his smile.

'Send me pictures of baker girl, 'k?' he blurted out just before she ended the call.

The screen went dark, leaving Molly alone with her thoughts in the quiet room. Outside, darkness had fully settled over Golden Valley, the square now illuminated by streetlamps and the glow from shop windows. The opening notes of a song floated up through the air, as if sirening villagers and visitors alike.

Molly stood and moved to the wooden wardrobe, selecting a floral wrap dress and a pair of black knee-high leather boots. As she changed, her thoughts circled back to Cole's observations – about roots, about the change he'd noticed in her, about the need to remember her true purpose here. The oak tree remained her goal, the reason she'd traveled here in the first place. Her grandmother's final wish still waited to be fulfilled.

Yet in pursuing that mission, Molly had somehow found herself threaded into the fabric of Golden Valley in ways she hadn't anticipated. The business advice for Goldenridge. Fondness for Patrick, friendship with Eva and fun with the locals.

And above all, the complex, growing connection with Jack Flynn that trembled on the edge of something far deeper than landowner permission.

Molly applied a touch of mascara and a hint of red lipstick, studying her reflection in the antique mirror above the dresser. The woman who looked back at her seemed both familiar and strange – still Molly Harris, Manhattan marketing exec, but somehow softened around the edges, changed subtly by the Tipperary air and the connections she'd formed here.

The small midnight-blue pouch remained tucked into the wardrobe, a constant reminder of her purpose. Molly reached in and touched it gently, feeling the velvet softness beneath her fingertips.

'Soon, Nan,' she whispered. 'I'll get there. I promise.'

Chapter 28

The Orchard Pub embraced Molly with a wave of warmth as she stepped through its doorway, leaving the cooler evening air behind. Light spilled from copper lanterns, illuminating low-beamed ceilings stained amber from decades of hearth smoke. The by-now familiar scent of fermenting apples mingled with the earthy perfume of peat burning in the massive stone hearth created an atmosphere that felt new, yet oddly like coming home.

Her eyes adjusted to the dim light, scanning the crowded room until she spotted Eva's bright-yellow bandana bobbing enthusiastically amidst a crowd gathered near the far corner. Laughter rose and fell above the hum of conversation, punctuated by the occasional clink of glasses and the creak of worn floorboards beneath shifting feet.

Molly navigated through the packed bar area, brushing past worn wooden chairs and mismatched tables. Behind the bar, rows of bottles reflected jewel-toned light – amber whiskeys, ruby-red liqueurs and, of course, the golden array of ciders that served as the region's liquid ambassadors. In pride of place above the cash register was a framed blue and gold Tipperary hurling jersey, and alongside it an autographed headshot of a broad-chested, deeply handsome jersey-clad player – county team captain perhaps, Molly mused.

The crowd parted slightly as she approached, friendly nods and smiles greeting her arrival. Eva stood at the center of a group of visitors and locals, flour still dusting one eyebrow despite her evening attire of leopard print dress and cowboy ankle boots, her hands moving expressively as always.

'Ah!' she called, waving Molly close and holding out a glass of cider. 'You're just in time for the barmbrack cutting. Come on, squeeze in here now.'

Molly edged into the crowd beside a silver-haired woman she recognized as the honey seller from the market, and an older man whose weathered face suggested decades spent beneath Tipperary skies.

'As I was saying,' Eva continued, brandishing a bread knife with theatrical flair, 'barmbrack isn't just fruit bread. Each loaf hides different charms and what you find in your slice tells your fortune for the year ahead.' Her eyes sparkled with mischief as she surveyed the captive audience of tourists. 'A ring means romance is coming your way. A coin promises wealth. A thimble means you'll remain single, and the little pea means you won't settle down this year. The ring . . . well, we all know what *that* means.' She lowered her voice dramatically, leaning forward. 'But watch out for the cloth, now – that's a warning of hard times ahead.'

'My mother found the cloth the year before the big frost killed half the spud crop,' offered the older man.

'There you have it,' Eva said, nodding at the tourists.

Molly's fingers traced the rim of the glass, the cool smooth edge grounding her as another long-forgotten childhood memory surfaced; Aoife in their Brooklyn kitchen, soaking dried fruit in tea overnight, explaining this special bread that revealed what lay ahead. She'd never mentioned it was called barmbrack, though. That detail must have been lost in translation or Molly's own memory.

The first slice revealed bread studded with plump raisins and candied citrus peel, the warm scent of cinnamon and nutmeg rising with the steam from the freshly cut loaf. Eva placed various pieces on a small plate and passed them around.

'Guests first,' she insisted. 'Careful now, feel around before you bite.'

The bread was still warm, dense with fruit and moist. Molly pressed it gently between her fingers, searching for the hidden charm. Something hard met her touch near the crust, and she carefully extracted a small silver coin.

'Coin!' Eva announced triumphantly. 'Prosperity coming your way, my friend. Though considering what you marketing types charge, that's hardly surprising.'

Laughter rippled through the group as Eva continued slicing, each piece finding eager hands. A tourist discovered a tiny ceramic thimble and sighed dramatically, declaring her continued independence from 'men who'd only make a mess of my house.' The weather-faced local found nothing at all and seemed relieved, muttering something about 'enough surprises in farming without adding more.'

A thin young man with ink-stained fingers bit into his slice and winced, extracting a small metal ring. The group erupted in cheers and good-natured teasing.

'Poor Liam hasn't had a date since school,' Eva stage-whispered to Molly. 'This'll give the village matchmakers something to focus on besides Jack and yourself.'

Molly nearly choked on her barmbrack. 'There's no . . . we're not—'

'Save your protests for someone who hasn't seen you two making eyes at each other all week,' Eva dismissed with a wink.

The brack continued its journey around the circle, fortunes received with varying degrees of seriousness and laughter. Until Molly felt a prickling awareness at the back of her neck and turned slightly to find the source.

Jack stood at the bar, his dark eyes fixed unmistakably on her. Unlike his usual wary observation, his gaze held something softer tonight– curiosity perhaps, or appreciation even. When their eyes met, he didn't look away but offered a small nod of acknowledgment.

The overhead light caught the strong angles of his face, softening the usual serious set of his mouth. His ever-present worn leather jacket hung open over a navy shirt that looked freshly ironed, and his hair, usually tousled by orchard winds, appeared to have indeed been – as Eva mentioned earlier – deliberately brushed. The overall effect was striking enough that Molly felt heat rise to her cheeks as she returned his nod with a small smile.

'What did I tell you?' Eva murmured beside her, having tracked Molly's gaze. 'He's even wearing his good shirt. Patrick must have forced him into it at gunpoint.'

Through the open windows and doors, music filtered in from the square – the sweet, mournful notes of a fiddle rising above the deeper rhythm of guitar and banjo. It wasn't purely traditional music – Molly could detect contemporary guitar influences in the arrangement – but it carried the soul of it.

She took a sip of the harvest special cider, savoring the complex notes that she now recognized as distinctive to Goldenridge's heritage varieties. Thanks to Jack's impromptu tasting session in the barn, she could identify the sharp brightness of Cavan Russet balanced against the mellower sweetness of Cox's Orange Pippin. Each sip connected her to the orchard, to the trees whose branches she'd walked beneath, to the barrels she'd seen aging in amber-lit stillness.

As Eva distributed the last of the barmbrack, a collective gasp rose from the far end of the circle. A dignified woman in her sixties held up a small piece of cloth between trembling fingers.

'The cloth,' she whispered, her face paling slightly beneath her practical makeup.

A momentary hush fell over the group, the weight of superstition temporarily silencing even the most skeptical among them. Eva reached out, placing a reassuring hand on the woman's arm.

'It's just fun, Maura,' she said gently. 'And sure, we all face hard times now and then. Nothing we can't handle together.'

Molly noticed Jack watching the interaction with interest from the bar, his expression thoughtful. When he caught her looking, he raised his glass slightly in her direction – a silent toast across the crowded room, and she nodded a greeting in return.

The music outside shifted to a livelier tune, the tempo quickening as more instruments joined in. The notes danced through the open door, tugging at the pub's patrons like an invisible tide. Small groups began to drift outside, drawn by the irresistible rhythm and the promise of dancing under the lights.

'Shall we?' Eva suggested, gathering up empty plates with practiced efficiency. 'Real fun's just starting.'

Molly nodded, finishing her drink in one final sip. As they prepared to join the migration outdoors, her gaze once again found Jack. He had moved from his position by the bar and now stood closer, his path clearly intended to intercept theirs.

'Enjoying yourself?' he asked, his voice pitched just loud enough to be heard over the ambient noise.

'Very much,' Molly replied, suddenly aware of how near he stood, close enough that she could detect the faint scent of cedar and apples that seemed to cling to him regardless of setting. 'Eva's been telling fortunes with barmbrack. Apparently, I'm coming into money.'

'Is that right?' His mouth curved into a half-smile. 'Hopefully some of that will rub off on Goldenridge.'

A subtle shift had occurred between them since their rain-soaked conversation in the cider barn – a lowering of defenses, a tentative trust emerging from mutual vulnerability. It revealed itself in small ways – the ease with which they now stood together, the absence of the wariness that had characterized their early interactions, the way his eyes lingered on her face as they spoke.

'How did the meeting go?' she asked, keen to find out if her attempts might have helped at all.

'Come on, you two!' Before he could reply, Eva called from the doorway, her figure silhouetted against the twinkling lights outside. 'They're playing a jig, and I need witnesses to my legendary spinning skills.' She smiled mischievously at Jack. 'And a partner.'

He gestured toward the door with a slight incline of his head.

'Will we?' he asked Molly, his tone light but his eyes holding a question that seemed to extend far beyond the immediate invitation. She nodded, strangely nervous and excited all at once.

Jack's gaze rested on her face. 'And no work tonight – only play.'

Chapter 29

The square was now a wonderland of light and sound. Fairy lights strung between the lampposts twinkled against the deepening blue of the evening sky, while flickering candles in copper holders cast golden pools across the café tables that edged the impromptu cobblestone dance area in front of the fountain.

At the far end, the band occupied the makeshift stage – a handsome lead singer of about twenty with a guitar, and three other young men playing more traditional instruments with the tight synchronicity that obviously came from years of shared playing.

Molly breathed in the crisp evening air, laden with the mingled scents of woodsmoke and the ever-present sweet tang of apples that seemed to permeate every corner of this village. The temperature had dropped enough that her breath formed small clouds, yet the press of bodies and the warmth of excitement kept the chill at bay. The lively music washed over her in waves – the banjo soaring above the deeper throb of the bodhran, the guitar and fiddle weaving intricate patterns beneath.

Eva had already plunged into the thick of the dancers, her yellow bandana visible as she spun between partners with practiced ease. Her laugh carried across the square, infectious enough to draw smiles from onlookers. Around her, locals and visitors of all ages moved in the organized chaos – some with perfect precision born of decades of practice, others with the enthusiastic approximation of occasional participants.

'The same jigs for hundreds of years,' a voice observed beside her, and Molly turned to find Josie from the newsagents watching the scene with evident satisfaction. 'The moves don't change, just the people moving through them.'

'It's beautiful,' Molly replied, watching as an elderly couple executed a spin with the grace of long partnership, their movements slower than the younger dancers but perfectly synchronized.

'You should give it a go yourself,' Josie encouraged before being pulled away by another local.

Molly remained at the edge of the swirling activity, fingers tapping against her thigh in time with the music. Despite her enjoyment, she hesitated to join in. In New York, her dancing was limited to occasional club outings with friends or the formality of corporate event mingling.

The music shifted, the tempo increasing even more as the band launched into a particularly energetic jig. The dancers responded immediately with a cheer, their movements quickening to match the pace. Eva's face glowed with exertion and joy as she linked arms with the pharmacist from the Glen Remedy, both laughing as they spun in perfect rhythm.

'"The Siege of Ennis" not fast enough for you?'

The voice behind her sent a shiver down Molly's spine that had nothing to do with the evening chill. She turned to find Jack standing closer than she'd expected, his expression transformed by a half-smile that softened the usual seriousness of his features. The festival lights caught in his dark eyes, reflecting golden pinpoints that made them appear unusually warm.

'It looks . . . scary, actually,' she replied, strangely flustered by his sudden proximity. 'So fast. Yet everyone seems to know exactly what to do.'

'Basic steps are simple enough,' he said, his gaze moving from the dancers back to her face. 'But the craic is in the more . . . creative interpretations.'

There was something different about him tonight – a true relaxation of the guardedness that typically surrounded him like invisible armor. Whether it was the festival atmosphere, a positive meeting at the bank, or perhaps the cider she'd seen him drinking earlier, Jack Flynn seemed more approachable now than at any time since she'd been here.

The current tune ended with a flourish, dancers laughing and catching their breath as they awaited the next. After a brief consultation among themselves, the band struck up a slower melody – still traditional in its lilting rhythm, but more forgiving in its pace.

'Better,' Jack observed, and to Molly's astonishment, he extended his hand toward her. 'Easier to learn with this one.'

The callouses on his palm revealed all those years of physical work, yet there was nothing rough about the gesture itself, which held a surprising gentleness.

'I'm really not a very good dancer,' Molly warned, even as her hand seemed to move of its own volition toward his.

'Neither am I,' he replied with unexpected humor. 'We can be terrible together.'

Their hands met, his fingers closing around hers with careful warmth. The simple contact sent a current of awareness through Molly's arm, heightening her senses until she could feel each point where their skin touched. His palm was warm despite the cool evening, the callouses creating a textured landscape against her smoother skin.

Jack led her toward the edge of the crowd, positioning them where they would have room to move without colliding with the more exuberant dancers. With a confidence that belied his earlier disclaimer, he placed his free hand lightly at her waist, creating a frame for the traditional waltz position.

'Just follow my lead,' he said, his voice dropping slightly as he leaned closer to be heard over the music. 'It's all in the rhythm.'

The melody pulled them forward and to Molly's surprise, Jack moved with unexpected grace. His frame provided clear guidance, the subtle pressure of his hand at her waist telegraphing each turn before it happened. Despite his size and the physical strength she knew he possessed from orchard work, there was nothing heavy-handed in his lead – just gentle suggestion that made following him feel natural.

'Side, back, forward, and turn,' he instructed as they moved, his breath warm against her ear. 'Then repeat.'

Molly concentrated on the pattern, her logical mind analytically breaking down the sequence even as her body attempted to execute it. The first few measures went smoothly enough, building her confidence. Then came a more complex turn, and her foot landed squarely on Jack's boot.

'Sorry!' she gasped, mortification heating her cheeks.

To her relief, he didn't wince or pull away. Instead, a genuine smile transformed his face, crinkling the corners of his eyes in a way she'd rarely witnessed.

'Could've been worse,' he assured her. 'At least you're wearing delicate city boots tonight instead of those thick hikers.'

His easy response dissolved her embarrassment, allowing her to laugh at herself as they resumed the pattern. The square had grown more crowded now, residents and visitors alike joining the festivities. They navigated through the throng, Jack subtly guiding them away from the more enthusiastic dancers whose movements required considerable clearance.

Molly gradually relaxed into it, allowing her natural rhythm to surface. The steps pattern became easier as they moved, though occasional variations introduced by the more traditional dancers still caught her by surprise. Jack's steady presence anchored her through these moments of uncertainty, his hand warm and secure at her waist.

As the tempo swelled, the dancers increased their pace slightly. Caught up in the joy of the moment, Molly attempted a more ambitious turn than she'd managed previously. Her foot caught on an uneven cobblestone, sending her stumbling directly toward a white-haired man dancing nearby.

Before disaster could strike, Jack's arm tightened around her waist, smoothly pulling her back against his chest and away from collision. For a breathless moment, they stood pressed together, her back to his front, his arm a solid band around her middle. The older man continued dancing, blissfully unaware of the near miss.

'That was close,' Jack murmured, his voice near enough that she felt the rumble of it against her back. 'Old Gerry might have had heart failure.'

The absurdity of it; her clumsiness, his rescue, the oblivious Gerry, bubbled up into unexpected laughter. Still connected, they turned to face each other, their shared mirth creating an intimacy that transcended physical proximity. Molly couldn't remember when she had last laughed so freely.

'I warned you I was terrible,' she reminded him, smiling.

'You did,' he agreed, his eyes still bright with amusement. 'But you neglected to mention you were dangerous too.'

They resumed their dance, now more comfortable with each other's movements. As they turned, Molly caught sight of Eva watching them with undisguised delight as she moved through the crowd with her own dancing partner, a man Molly didn't recognize. When their eyes met, Eva raised her eyebrows significantly, before turning away with a satisfied smile.

Across the square, she saw Patrick sitting at a small table near the pub entrance, a mug of something steaming cradled between his weathered hands. Despite the chill that had driven many older residents indoors, he remained outside, wrapped in a thick wool sweater, his cane hooked over the back of his chair. His gaze rested on his nephew with quiet satisfaction, a smile softening his lined face as he observed proceedings.

When Jack turned them again, following the circular pattern

of the dance, Molly noticed several other locals watching with varying degrees of subtlety.

Tommy the baker nudged his wife and nodded in their direction, while another woman Molly recognized from the café smiled as she and her husband whirled by. The attention wasn't unfriendly – if anything, it felt approving – but it underscored for Molly how quickly she had become entwined in the village's collective awareness.

'Everyone's watching us, I think,' she murmured, uncertain whether to be amused or self-conscious.

'Let them.' Jack's expression shifted to resignation tinged with humor. 'Small village. Entertainment options are limited.'

'Is that all we are? Entertainment?' she challenged lightly.

His eyes met hers, suddenly serious despite his light tone. 'I think we both know we're far more interesting than that.'

Chapter 30

Molly's body tingled but, before she could respond, the lead singer's voice called out across the square: 'We'll slow things down a bit now, folks. Next one's an original – a tribute to our little corner of the world.'

The first notes of a gentler, more contemporary melody rose into the night air, the guitar introducing a theme that the fiddle soon echoed with gorgeous melancholy.

Around them, some dancers departed while others moved closer together, adjusting their pace to the more intimate rhythm.

Jack's eyes found hers, a question in their depths as the music invited a different kind of dance. The space between them suddenly felt charged with possibility, the next moment balanced on the edge of decision.

'Another?' he asked simply, his hand still holding hers.

'Yes,' Molly replied simply, the word carrying more significance than its brevity suggested.

The crowd around them had thinned as dancers rejected the more modern number for refreshments or conversation, leaving a lot more space on the cobblestones.

Jack's hand shifted at her waist, drawing her slightly closer as the tempo of the song established itself. Unlike the structured pattern of the traditional ballads, this one required no special steps or memorized sequences. His touch was light but certain, guiding without commanding, and Molly found herself relaxing into the gentle sway that carried them in small circles beneath the canopy of twinkling lights. The band settled further into the melody, their instruments finding a harmonious balance that allowed the lead singer's voice to emerge – strong and slightly husky, with that distinctive Tipperary lilt in every phrase.

Jack adjusted their position, his hand sliding from her waist to the small of her back in a subtle shift that brought them closer together. The space between them narrowed until Molly could feel the warmth emanating from his chest.

'OK?' he asked quietly, his voice low enough that only she could hear.

Molly nodded, not trusting her voice as she cautiously allowed her cheek to rest against his shoulder. The cotton of his shirt was soft against her skin, and beneath it, she could feel the solid presence of him – steady and substantial in a way that made New York seem impossibly distant, as if it existed in another lifetime.

The vocalist's gravelly voice carried across the square with poignant clarity:

'Stone walls and green fields . . . morning light breaks through the branches,

And whispers of secrets long held in thrall . . .'

'It's a beautiful song,' Molly murmured, genuinely moved by both the melody and lyrics that painted such a vivid picture of the landscape. 'They're very talented.'

'They wrote it a few years back,' he explained. 'Played it first during a particularly good lock-in at the pub.'

As they turned slowly, Jack nodded toward the stage where the band played with evident passion. 'The lead singer, Conor, is Maeve's youngest. Been playing since he could hold an instrument. And the one on the fiddle is Maurice the butcher's kid – trained as an accountant in Dublin.'

Molly watched the musicians – Hearthland, they were called – with renewed interest, seeing beyond their immediate talent to the web of community connections that had nurtured it.

'But they're so good,' she observed, amazed they weren't already better known. 'Professional quality.'

'As good as some of the best by my reckoning,' Jack agreed. 'But breaking into the music industry here is another story. They've been sending demos to labels in Dublin for years now. Plenty of interest but nothing doing.'

The song continued, the chorus rising with harmonies that sent shivers across Molly's skin:

'Where time moves slow as the river's flow, the land remembers every story,

Of those who stay and those who go . . .'

'Reminds me of someone else I know,' Jack continued, his voice dropping lower with mirth. 'Exceptional quality, under-appreciated by the wider world. At least until this Yank marketing expert shows up with her big plans.'

The teasing note in his voice surprised her. 'Are you actually admitting my ideas might be worthwhile, Jack Flynn?' she asked, leaning back slightly to see his face.

The corner of his mouth curved upward. 'Don't let it go to your head. But yes, as it happens, your plan did come in handy for my bank plea today.'

She stared at him, delighted. 'They approved the finance?'

His expression sobered slightly, though the tension that had characterized their previous discussions of Goldenridge's finances was less pronounced now.

'Not yet, but they didn't turn me down outright for once,' he told her.

'I'm sure all's good,' Molly assured him, wishing she felt as confident as she sounded. But it was encouraging that he'd used her presentation all the same.

'Like I said, let's not worry about these things tonight . . .'

he murmured, his mouth so close to her neck it made her skin tingle.

They continued to sway together as the song moved into a bridge, the fiddle now taking center stage with a haunting solo that seemed to escalate what was unfolding between them.

Molly felt Jack's chest rise and fall with a deep breath, his hand unconsciously drawing her closer as the music intensified and the chorus returned, the vocalist putting his whole heart into the lyrics now, his husky voice rising with passion that resonated across the square.

Jack's eyes found hers as they moved together, something unspoken passing between them that made Molly's breath catch in her throat. His hand tightened almost imperceptibly at her waist, drawing her fractionally closer until the space between them seemed charged with possibility.

Time seemed to slow, the world beyond their small circle of movement fading into indistinct background noise.

The music continued, but Molly heard it now as if from a distance, her awareness narrowed to the points where Jack's body touched hers - his hand at her back, his other hand holding hers, the occasional brush of his chest against her own as they swayed to the rhythm. She noticed details with heightened clarity - the slight roughness of stubble along his jaw, the small scar near his left eyebrow, the way his lips parted slightly as his gaze dropped to her mouth.

His head dipped slightly toward hers, his intention unmistakable in the gentle pressure of his hand drawing her closer. Molly found herself rising subtly to meet him, her body responding without conscious decision. The space between them narrowed until she could feel his breath against her cheek, warm and slightly uneven.

The band's melody built toward its crescendo as the vocalist sang with increasing emotion:

'Beneath the ancient oak's protection, where lovers carve their names with care,

The secrets of our hearts lie waiting,
For those with courage to meet them there . . .'

The mention of the oak tree in the lyric registered with sudden clarity, and Molly stiffened a little in Jack's arms.

He drew back, confusion replacing the warmth in his expression. 'What?'

'The song,' she explained. 'The oak tree . . . that's your oak, isn't it?' The melody continued around them, building toward its final chorus, but the intimate spell had been broken. They still moved together in the gentle rhythm of the dance, but the charged moment of potential had passed, replaced by a different kind of energy.

'And here I thought t'was my devastating charm that made you gasp,' Jack replied dryly, though the humor in his eyes softened the words. 'And it's not my tree,' he continued. 'It's been around for generations, long before my time, Patrick's too.' The song reached its conclusion, the final notes hanging in the air. Around them, the crowd applauded appreciatively, their enthusiasm causing the band to bow with evident pleasure. 'Uh . . . speaking of which, I should check on him,' Jack mumbled, though he made no immediate move to step away.

Molly nodded, understanding, but also disappointed. 'Of course.'

Jack hesitated, then added with careful casualness. 'Since you're so interested, I could take you out to the oak tomorrow, if you'd like. Make up for hounding you off that first day. Meet you there after my deliveries, say, around midday?'

The offer sent a surge of emotion through her – excitement at finally gaining access to her grandmother's beloved oak, mixed with guilt for not telling him the whole truth.

'I'd like that,' she replied, hoping her voice didn't betray the complexity of her feelings.

Then Jack hesitated and added, 'Whatever happens next, with the loan I mean, I wanted to thank you. For your help with that, yes, but also for . . .' He paused, searching for words. 'For seeing Goldenridge the way I do. For understanding what makes it worth fighting for.'

'It is worth fighting for,' Molly assured him. 'And we're not done fighting yet.'

Hearthland announced that they would take a short break, and Jack finally stepped back, his hands releasing her. 'See you tomorrow, then,' he confirmed.

Molly nodded, already anticipating the moment when she would finally stand beneath The Wishing Oak.

The tree that, for reasons still mysterious even to her, was so central to Aoife's last wish.

Chapter 31

Mid-morning mist clung to the valley as Molly picked her way through the dew-soaked orchard rows, her boots leaving dark imprints in the silvered grass.

She'd risen early, unable to sleep through the anticipation that hummed beneath her skin. Light filtered through the eastern hills, casting long shadows across Goldenridge.

Today was the day.

Jack had said midday, but Molly couldn't wait that long. The need to see the tree alone first, to experience it herself and all it represented, had pulled her from sleep and out into the morning.

The orchard appeared transformed in this nascent light – rows of apple trees standing straight, their fruit gleaming with dew. As she walked deeper, the trees seemed to watch her passing. The air smelled of earth and apples and something greener, more primal – the scent of growth and decay entwined in perfect balance. Her pace quickened as she rounded the final bend, anticipation tightening her chest. And then, suddenly, it stood before her.

The Wishing Oak.

Molly stopped. Nothing could have prepared her for the reality of it up close – this ancient giant rising from the earth like something born of myth rather than nature. Its massive trunk twisted upward in gnarled majesty, splitting into enormous limbs that reached toward the sky. The canopy of leaves spread outward in all directions, creating a cathedral that filtered the morning light into dappled patterns on the grass below.

'Oh,' she whispered, the sound escaping without conscious thought.

She approached slowly, almost reverently, as if drawing near to something sacred. The tree commanded such respect by its mere presence; a silent witness to centuries of human drama played out beneath its branches. How many generations of Golden Valley locals had sheltered in its shade? How many lovers had whispered promises against its bark?

Closer now, she could see the countless markings etched into its trunk – initials, dates, hearts, and symbols carved by lovers, and friends. Some were fresh enough, the wood still pale around the edges; others had been smoothed by time until they were barely visible, just ghosts of past connections. Names and dates spanning decades, a physical record of human connection in this place.

Molly ran her fingers over the carvings, feeling the indentations against her skin. The bark was rough and cool beneath her touch, deeply furrowed with age.

She circled the massive trunk slowly, taking in the full circumference with wonder. On the far side, where mid-morning sun now illuminated the bark more fully, she found older carvings, their edges softened by decades of growth. Her fingers traced these more tentative etchings from another era, wondering about the hands that had created them, the hearts that had felt compelled to leave their mark.

Had her grandmother carved her initials here too, she wondered. And if so, with whom?

Not her grandfather; Eddie barely left Brooklyn, let alone America and she knew for sure he'd never spent a second in Ireland. Perhaps whoever it was, was the reason for all the mystery?

The song from last night echoed in her mind – '*Beneath*

the ancient oak's protection, where lovers carve their names with care . . .' The lyrics seemed to hang in the air around her, as if the tree itself had written it.

Then suddenly Molly saw it. She leaned closer, feeling her heart rate accelerate as she studied the carving. A little different from the casual etchings of passing lovers, and something done with care, the letters perfectly formed despite the decades of growth that had distorted them.

PF + AB

The initials were enclosed in a carefully carved heart, with a date beneath, that time had rendered almost illegible. Molly's fingers trembled slightly as they traced the letters, a strange vertigo sweeping through her. AB. Could it be Aoife Brennan? Had her grandmother stood in this exact spot, watching as her beau carved their initials into the living wood? Had this been their special place, the refuge mentioned in so many of her stories?

'Golden Valley is where I first knew what love meant, *mo chroí*,' Aoife had told her on her deathbed. 'Under a tree so old it seemed to breathe with its own life. Where the roots went deep into Irish soil and the branches reached for heaven itself.'

Molly had always assumed it was just another of her grandmother's famously poetic reminiscings. But standing here now, feeling the solid presence of the oak, she understood the truth in those words. This tree did seem to breathe with its own life, its roots anchored deep in the soil of Golden Valley, its branches creating a sanctuary from the ordinary world.

A sudden urge to share the moment overwhelmed her. Molly pulled her phone from her pocket. She tapped her brother's contact, the phone connecting with soft electronic burbles. Seconds later, his voice came through; groggily given the time difference, yet alert.

'Mols, everything okay?' he asked, sounding worried.

'It's perfect.' She smiled through tears, turning slowly to take in the full majesty of the oak. 'Sorry to wake you but I'm here, Cole. I'm standing under Nan's tree. Right now.'

'You got there, amazing! What's it like?'

'It's . . .' She searched for words adequate to the reality before her. 'It's even more beautiful than she described. Massive, ancient. You can feel the history in it.' Her voice dropped to an awed whisper. 'There are initials carved everywhere – generations of them. I think I even found . . . well, you can guess.'

'No way,' Cole breathed. 'Nan's initials. Are you serious?'

'I think so,' Molly confirmed, her fingers returning to trace the carving.

'Holy shit!' He laughed softly. 'All those stories, but seeing actual evidence . . .'

'I know.' She couldn't stop smiling, imagining her grandmother here as a young woman, perhaps standing exactly where she stood now. It made everything so much more poignant somehow.

And better explained her dying wish.

Molly walked around the tree again, phone pressed to her ear, describing details to Cole as she moved – the way morning light filtered through the leaves, how the ground beneath felt different, softer somehow, as if centuries of fallen leaves had created a special soil. She told him about the song last night, the lyrics written specifically about this very tree.

'So,' Cole said finally, his voice shifting to a more pragmatic tone, 'are you doing it right now – what she asked?'

Molly looked up, studying the branches overhead, then surveying the surrounding area. 'No, I wanted to see it first.' Plus she wanted to tell Jack, take him into her confidence before carrying out such a deeply personal and ceremonious task on his land.

'I can't remember, did she give any specific instructions?' Cole asked. 'I mean, besides the tree?'

'Not really,' Molly sighed, moving to examine another angle. 'Just that it was where she felt most at peace, where she was happiest.' She gazed at the carved heart again. 'I guess it has to be here, on this side, where the initials are.' She walked the wide perimeter of the trunk again, studying the ground, the way light fell, the view outward from different positions. 'I just can't quite figure out the best vantage point,' she mumbled, uncertain. 'Far superior views of the lake on the north side, but the light is better where the initials are.'

'What about—?' Cole began, but Molly suddenly stiffened, a prickling awareness creeping up her spine. Had she imagined it? But no – a twig snapped in the distance, followed by the soft crush of footsteps on dewy grass.

'Better go,' she said softly. 'Call you back later?'

Molly ended the call quickly, slipping the phone into her pocket as she turned in the direction of the orchard. The quiet of the morning seemed different now, charged with unseen presence. She straightened her shoulders, composing her features into a casual smile. She would say she couldn't wait, that she'd been too excited after the festival to sleep properly. Molly felt the weight of eyes on her back, an assessing silence that stretched several seconds too long. When she finally turned, the smile froze on her lips.

Jack stood at the edge of the clearing, his face a mask of rigid control that did nothing to hide the storm brewing beneath. His jaw was clenched, shoulders tight with tension, eyes narrowed in a gaze that cut straight through her practiced composure.

'Jack,' she began, her voice unnaturally bright to her own ears. 'I was a bit early so I—'

But his expression stopped the words in her throat.

'I knew it,' he said, his voice dangerously quiet. 'I should have known better than to trust you.'

And Molly realized, with sinking clarity, that whatever Jack Flynn thought he knew was far worse than the truth she'd been hiding.

Chapter 32

Jack's stomach twisted into a knot of rage and humiliation as he stood at the edge of the clearing, watching her face drain of color. After yesterday's promising meeting at the bank, and last night's 'moment' while dancing, he'd been only too happy to show Molly the oak she'd seemed so bloody curious about and share some of its history.

Only to find her here already, speaking furtively about lake views and vantage points like some scout preparing for an invasion.

'I knew it,' he repeated, his voice hardening with each word. 'I should have known better than to trust you.'

She took a step toward him, one hand extended as if to bridge the chasm. 'Jack—'

'Don't.' The word came out sharper than he'd intended, slicing through the morning air. Behind her, the oak's leaves rustled in a gentle breeze, the sound nearly drowned by the rushing of blood in his ears. 'I heard you. Did they send you to actually get the lay of the land? Or just figure out the best way to carve up the place?'

Confusion flickered across her face, quickly replaced by something else. 'No! That's not—'

'So you didn't lie when you said you weren't working with Crest Beverages, but instead you're one of those developer leeches, aren't you?' Jack advanced into the clearing, each step deliberate, controlled despite the rage burning in his chest. 'Wheedled your way into our business and finances, knowing all our weak spots before you made your move.'

The sun caught in her dark hair as she shook her head vehemently. 'No! Jack, I swear I'm not working for any developer. That's not at all why I'm here.'

'Then explain what I just heard.' He gestured toward the phone still clutched in her hand. 'Explain why you've been so interested in our business, in our operations, in this oak specifically. Pretending to be interested in . . . everything.'

Her face had gone completely white now, freckles standing out starkly against her pallor. Her eyes darted briefly toward the carved initials on the trunk before returning to his face, something almost like panic in their green depths.

'I promise you, I'm not here to hurt Goldenridge or to spy for any developers. This is . . . personal.'

Jack laughed bitterly, running a hand through his hair. The gesture felt foreign, disconnected from his body. 'You've got an answer for everything, don't you? But somehow never the whole truth.'

Around them, the orchard was vibrant – birds calling from the apple trees, autumn light strengthening as it poured across the hills. The beauty of it all felt like a mockery now, too perfect a backdrop for this ugly scene.

'I was speaking to my brother,' Molly blurted suddenly. 'Cole. He's not a developer; he's a hockey player, plays professionally.'

Jack stared at her, momentarily thrown by this random detail.

'Believe me, I'm not who you think I am.' Her voice cracked slightly, eyes pleading with him to understand. 'My interest in the oak is purely personal. It has nothing to do with hurting the orchard or buying the land.'

‘Then why all the bloody secrecy?’ Jack demanded, taking another step toward her. ‘Why lie about why you’re really here?’

‘I didn’t lie,’ she insisted, though her gaze slid away from his. ‘I just . . . didn’t tell you everything.’

‘A lie of omission is still a lie.’ The words tasted bitter on his tongue. He thought of that afternoon in the cider barn, the rain drumming overhead as they’d shared drinks and confidences. How she’d touched his arm with such apparent sincerity, promised to help with the bank. How he’d begun to trust her, to see beyond the polished New York exterior to something that felt genuine. Her upturned face beneath the lights in the square last night, their bodies close. And that almost-kiss.

What an idiot he’d been.

‘And the social media stuff, your big marketing plan.’ Jack almost winced at how wounded his voice sounded. ‘Was that all part of it too? Reel us eejit locals in enough to learn all our vulnerabilities? Eva doesn’t deserve that, none of us do.’ He stepped back, needing physical distance from her, from the earnest expression that had once seemed so authentic. Was enough to lower his defenses. Now he understood it was just another tool in her professional arsenal, another way to manipulate situations to her advantage.

‘No, of course not! Eva’s my friend, she’s . . .’

‘Save it,’ he spat, fury rising up within him as he realized just how stupid he’d been. ‘I trusted you,’ he said quietly, the admission hanging in the air between them. ‘Despite every instinct screaming at me not to, I let you in.’

‘Jack—’ Her voice broke on his name, and for a moment, the raw emotion in it nearly shook his resolve.

‘I showed you everything,’ he continued, unable to stop now that the words had started flowing. ‘Told you about our financial struggles. Hell, I even danced with you at the festival last night in front of the whole town. When all the while you were faking an interest in me, me and Patrick, trying to get us on side.’

She flinched at that, as if he'd struck her. 'That wasn't fake,' she whispered. 'None of it was. Last night definitely wasn't—'

'Forget it.' He cut her off, unwilling to hear whatever justification she'd crafted. 'Whatever game you're playing, I'm finished being a pawn in it.'

His boots crushed the dewy grass as he strode away, heading back toward the main orchard path. The sunlit glow that had seemed so optimistic minutes ago now felt harsh, exposing, as if it illuminated every foolish choice he'd made since that woman had arrived in Golden Valley.

The worst part was the hollow ache in his chest, the space where something had begun to grow over the past week – something he hadn't allowed himself to name but had felt nonetheless. That tentative connection now withered, poisoned by distrust.

As always, he'd been right not to trust outsiders and his initial suspicion of her had been justified after all. He should feel vindicated, not devastated.

Despite his resolve not to look back, Jack found himself turning slightly at the edge of the clearing, just enough to see her in his peripheral vision.

Molly stood exactly where he'd left her, one hand pressed against the oak's massive trunk as if needing its support. Her face was lifted toward him, the light catching the unmistakable gleam of tears on her cheeks. For a moment – just a heartbeat – doubt flickered through him. The pain in her expression looked genuine, too raw to be feigned.

Then Jack remembered how skillfully she navigated professional situations, how effortlessly she'd integrated herself into village life, winning over the locals. Of course she'd be good at this too – at appearing wounded when confronted.

That was their playbook, these types.

He squared his shoulders and continued walking, each step carrying him farther from the oak and the woman who'd breached defenses he hadn't realized were so vulnerable. His jaw ached from clenching it, tension radiating through his neck and shoulders like steel cables pulled too tight.

Jack returned to the orchard, seeking solace from the surrounding trees. Goldenridge had survived for generations; he would survive this too.

Chapter 33

On the low stone boundary wall between the land and the lake, Patrick sat motionless, his weathered hands resting on knees that protested his usual morning walk.

A perfect harvest morning – crisp enough to sharpen the senses without the bitter edge that would come with winter's approach. Above him, swallows still darted across the pale-blue canvas of sky, their swift movements a counterpoint to his own stillness.

From his position near the lake path, the ancient oak stood in perfect silhouette against the brightening sky, its massive form dwarfing the two figures beneath its branches. He'd witnessed it all – not close enough to hear every word, but near enough to read their body language, to see Jack's rigid anger and Molly's placating gestures.

His great-nephew had stormed away, his long stride eating up the distance between the oak and the main path back to the orchard, shoulders hunched forward like a man walking into gale-force winds.

Patrick had seen that posture before – after his parents' funeral, during the worst drought seasons, and all too frequently lately when Jack felt the weight of the orchard's legacy pressing down most heavily.

Molly remained by the oak, one hand pressed against its bark as if drawing strength from the ancient wood. Even from this distance, Patrick could see how she seemed to fold in on herself, her typical animation replaced by a defeated stillness that tugged at something in his chest.

He'd seen her circling the tree before Jack's arrival, watched her fingers trace the carved initials with what looked like reverence.

Patrick shifted slightly, easing the stiffness in his hip. The solid stone beneath him held the morning's chill, a reminder of his own mortality that he generally found more amusing than frightening. Time was a currency he spent more carefully these days, weighing each expenditure against diminishing reserves.

The sequence played out again in Patrick's mind, details shifting as he considered alternative interpretations. Jack had seemed defeated beneath his anger – yesterday's bank meeting must have gone poorly, so. His great-nephew's pride would never allow him to admit how much the rejection hurt, how personally he took each financial setback. Instead, that pain had evidently found another target in Molly Harris.

But was Jack right after all? Was this polished American just another vulture circling their struggling orchard?

Patrick had observed Molly carefully since her arrival in Golden Valley. He'd seen her genuine interest in the orchard, her thoughtful questions that went beyond surface curiosity, the way she'd looked at Jack for approval when producing projections for the bank.

More telling were the unguarded moments – how her eyes softened when she hummed that old song, the one Patrick hadn't heard in decades. How she sometimes seemed to lose herself in thought when looking out over the valley, as if seeing ghosts in the landscape.

And then there was her interest in the oak itself.

Patrick's gaze returned to the massive tree, its sprawling canopy creating patterns of light and shadow on the ground beneath.

He himself knew most of the names carved into its bark - had watched many of those markings being made over the decades, had even carved a set himself in the flush of first love.

Those who lived in Golden Valley understood the oak's significance beyond its obvious beauty or age. It stood as silent witness to generations of promises, some kept and some broken, its roots reaching deep into soil that held the village's collective memory.

Patrick rose slowly from the wall, his joints protesting the movement after sitting in the morning chill. He needed perspective beyond his own observations, wisdom from someone whose memory reached as far back as his, whose insight might help illuminate what his was missing.

With practiced movements, he settled his walking stick against the ground, testing his balance before starting toward the village. Beyond the boundary, the lake path narrowed as it wound between meadows dotted with late wildflowers - purple clover and yellow ragwort creating bursts of color against the green. His pace was deliberate but steady, each step placed with the careful attention of a man who knew his body's limitations but refused to be defined by them.

Generations of Flynns had weathered challenges before - late frosts, yield crashes, changing tastes. Each time, the orchard had adapted and survived.

But this felt different somehow. The world moved faster these days, with less patience for tradition or craftsmanship. The varied business interests that sought to acquire Goldenridge weren't interested in its history or the quality of its fruit - only in the commercial potential of its acreage.

Jack carried that burden, albeit by his own choice. The lad had always been stubborn about accepting help, seeing it as an admission of weakness rather than the shared strength Patrick knew it to be. And now his great-nephew's pride had potentially driven away someone who might well have been an unexpected ally.

The village beckoned ahead, its stone buildings golden in

the morning light. Smoke rose from chimneys in thin vertical columns, signs of life stirring as Golden Valley prepared for the next day of the festival. Patrick continued his journey, his destination clear in his mind, though he hadn't spoken it aloud.

His pace quickened slightly, purpose lending strength to his steps as he headed for the square and then onwards to the Glen Arms Hotel.

Behind him, the oak stood ancient and patient, guardian of secrets both old and new. Ahead, the promise of clarity, of puzzle pieces falling into place.

Chapter 34

Molly traced her steps back through the orchard, each footfall heavier than the last. The morning sun that had seemed so promising now felt harsh against her skin, exposing every vulnerability she'd tried to keep hidden.

Jack's words still echoed in her mind, sharp-edged and cutting. 'I trusted you.' Past tense.

The finality in his voice had left no room for explanation. Her chest ached with a hollowness that surprised her with its intensity; they'd known each other such a short time, yet his rejection carved a wound far deeper than it had any right to.

The dampened grass clung to her boots as she walked, leaving prints that would vanish with the sun's ascent, ephemeral marks of her passage through Goldenridge. How fitting that even the evidence of her presence here would soon disappear, as if she'd never walked these paths at all.

She brushed away tears with an impatient hand, angry at herself for the display of emotion. This wasn't who she was – Molly Harris didn't cry over misunderstandings, over men who jumped to conclusions without giving her a chance to explain. She compartmentalized, and strategized, moved forward.

Always forward.

Yet something about Jack Flynn had bypassed all her carefully constructed defenses. The same stubbornness that now condemned her had also drawn her in – his fierce protection of Goldenridge, his reluctant smile when she said something that amused him despite himself, the surprising gentleness in his calloused hands when they'd danced last night beneath the festival lights.

'I'm not who you think I am,' she whispered to the empty path, words that had fallen on deaf ears when she'd spoken them to Jack. She hadn't come to Golden Valley to help developers acquire Goldenridge, true enough. But neither had she been entirely forthright about her reasons for her interest in the land.

As she crested the small rise that overlooked Golden Valley, Molly paused. The village spread below her, stone buildings nestled against the backdrop of hills and lake. Festival decor fluttered between lampposts, bright triangles of color against the weathered facades.

So much planning on her grandmother's part had gone into her trip here, yet in less than two weeks, this place had become more than just the setting for a promise fulfilled. It had become something Molly looked forward to waking up to each morning, its rhythm somehow familiar despite its novelty.

And now she would leave it, mission incomplete in more ways than one, for Jack surely wouldn't allow her to return to the oak to carry out Aoife's task. Nor allow the orchard to benefit from her efforts, as he'd surely discard all of her ideas for the business, bank loan be damned.

The very thought settled like a stone in her stomach.

No, Molly decided then. She'd failed at many things in her life, but never at a professional commitment. Whatever Jack thought of her personally, she had promised that she would help with Goldenridge's marketing.

And that, at least, was a promise she could still keep.

With renewed purpose, Molly continued down the path into the village, an idea already taking shape.

Day two of the festival was now well underway, locals back at their market stalls while visitors wandered the square. She skirted the central activity, not ready to face Eva's perceptive gaze, or worse, teasing about Jack.

Instead, she headed for Wildflower Books, its distinctive hand-painted sign swinging gently in the morning breeze.

The shop enveloped her immediately; the scent of paper and ink mingled with plants and flowers arranged haphazardly throughout the space. Worn wooden shelves lined walls of exposed stone, their contents organized not by standard categories but by intriguingly named sections: 'For Rainy Afternoons', 'When You Need Courage', 'Books That Feel Like Coming Home'.

Most striking was the ceiling that Molly hadn't noticed on her first day – a painted mural of native Irish wildflowers spreading across the entire surface, each bloom labeled in elegant script with both English and Irish names. She found herself looking up, momentarily distracted from her purpose by the beauty of the artistic rendering.

'They say if you stare at it long enough, you'll find the flower that matches your soul.'

The voice startled Molly from her contemplation. She lowered her gaze to find the friendly proprietor watching her from behind the counter, intelligent eyes set in a face lined with what appeared to be equal measures of laughter and concentration.

Maeve Gleeson, mother of Conor, the lead singer of last night's band, Jack had told her.

'It's just so beautiful,' Molly replied, gesturing toward the ceiling. 'I've never seen anything quite like it.'

'My late husband's work,' Maeve explained, pride evident in her voice. 'He painted one flower each year on our anniversary. Took seventeen years to complete.' Her gaze sharpened as she studied Molly's face. 'You look like you've had a difficult morning, pet. Late one last night?'

The gentle observation, delivered without prying, nearly undid

Molly's composure. She swallowed hard, forcing a smile. 'No, I didn't drink much. But yes, this morning's been . . . challenging. Is it that obvious?'

'Only to someone who's spent a lifetime watching people find comfort in books,' Maeve replied, her tone matter-of-fact as opposed to pitying. 'Were you looking for something specific, or just a quiet corner?'

'Actually,' Molly began, gathering herself, 'I wanted to ask about Hearthland. Their song from last night.'

Maeve's expression brightened with maternal pride. '"Beneath the Oak"? That one's special – Conor wrote it during his final year in Dublin when homesickness was eating him alive. What's your interest, if you don't mind my asking?'

As Molly explained, something flickered in Maeve's expression – curiosity, perhaps, or recognition. 'I thought Jack wasn't interested in all that stuff. He was pretty clear about that in the café that day.'

'He wasn't. Isn't,' Molly corrected herself, the shift to present tense a painful acknowledgment of their morning confrontation. 'But circumstances change. The business situation is . . . challenging. And he's too stubborn to admit it.'

Understanding dawned in Maeve's eyes. She nodded slowly, hands clasped in her lap. 'Jack Flynn, stubborn? There's a surprise. But I still don't know where the song comes in.'

But when Molly told her what she had in mind, Maeve smiled. 'Oh, the boys would only be thrilled. Conor especially – that song means the world to him,' she continued, clearly proud of her son's music. 'He was studying sound engineering in Dublin – the first in our family to leave Golden Valley for university. Hated every minute of city life, though he loved the course itself.' Her fingers tapped gently against the countertop, finding rhythm in the memory. 'Called home every Sunday evening in tears for the first month. Not that he'd admit to it now, mind you.'

Molly smiled despite herself, thinking of Cole's similar stubborn pride as a youngster whenever he lost a hockey game.

'He'd visit the oak whenever he came home,' Maeve continued. 'Said it was the one constant in a changing world. That tree's seen generations of locals grow up, watched young lovers become parents, then grandparents.' A wistful quality entered her voice. 'So he wrote "Beneath the Oak" during finals week, after he'd been too busy to come home for nearly three months. Said the melody came to him fully formed, like the tree itself was sending it across the country to remind him where he belonged.'

The idea resonated with something deep in Molly's chest – that same sense of belonging, of connection to place, that had eluded her for so long. Had Golden Valley begun to fill that void? Was that why Jack's rejection hurt with such unexpected intensity?

'The lyrics about carving names,' she ventured carefully. 'It's based on actual tradition then?'

'Oh yes,' Maeve confirmed, eyes crinkling at the corners. 'Some say when you carve your initials with your beloved on The Wishing Oak, the love lasts forever. Others claim it's magical – that wishes made beneath its branches always come true, though sometimes in unexpected ways.'

The hairs on Molly's arms stood up, a physical reaction to words that seemed to speak directly to her unspoken purpose. Her grandmother's own stories echoed in the song itself – tales of wishes granted and promises kept, of a tree that remembered what people forgot.

Exactly why the song had captured her attention last night.

'More than that,' Maeve went on, 'I've always considered it a keeper of stories – surprise, surprise.' She laughed. 'A Golden Valley archive in living wood. My own parents' initials are there somewhere, though the bark has surely grown over them by now. Most of the couples in the village have marks on that tree, going back generations.'

'It's a beautiful tradition,' Molly said, now keen to get to work. 'And thank you for permission to use the song. I'll make sure Hearthland gets proper credit.'

Maeve moved back toward the counter. 'Maybe give me your email and I'll get Conor to ping you the master, save you having to find it?'

'That would be amazing,' Molly agreed, grateful for the practical focus. They exchanged contact information, Maeve promising to have her son reach out asap.

As Molly prepared to leave, the older woman selected a small book from behind the counter and handed it to her. 'A little gift,' she said with a warm smile.

The volume was slim, bound in soft green cloth with a simple title embossed in gold: *Coming Home to Yourself.* Inside, the pages contained poems about belonging and finding peace, the margins decorated with delicate illustrations of native Irish wildflowers.

'I couldn't possibly—' Molly began, but Maeve shook her head firmly.

'Books always find their rightful owners at just the right time,' she insisted, smiling.

Something about the simple kindness – offered without expectation or agenda – broke through the fragile composure Molly had maintained since her confrontation with Jack. She clutched the book to her chest, blinking rapidly against unexpected tears.

'Thank you,' she whispered.

Maeve patted her arm gently. 'Whatever's troubling you, pet, always remember that stones still remain after storms pass.'

The phrase nearly undid Molly completely. She nodded, unable to speak further, and made her way to the door.

Outside, the festival sounds created a cheerful backdrop that felt discordant against Molly's internal landscape. Yet alongside the ache in her chest, a quiet determination had taken root.

Jack might never trust her again, might never know the truth about why she'd come to Golden Valley. But she could still keep her promise to help Goldenridge, could still create something that might make a difference to the orchard's future.

And perhaps, find a way to let him know how much she truly cared.

Chapter 35

By the afternoon, Molly's room at the Glen Arms had transformed into an impromptu studio, her laptop perched on a writing desk beneath the window. Onscreen, thumbnails of captured footage lined up in the editing software. Hundreds of moments from her time here – each frame holding pieces of the place she'd come to love in ways she hadn't anticipated.

She'd left New York as Molly Harris, marketing executive, but somehow, in less than two weeks, Golden Valley had unearthed something else – a version of herself she barely recognized, yet felt more authentic than the polished professional persona she'd perfected over so many years.

Outside, traditional busker music drifted up from the square, a cheerful counterpoint to the quiet intensity with which she'd worked all day.

Now, Molly pulled her hair back into a messy bun, securing it with the pencil she'd been using to jot notes as her fingers moved across the trackpad, finalizing the first sequence of footage.

Establishing shots of Lake Corrin and Goldenridge from the hill overlooking the orchard – morning mist rising from rows of apple trees, sunlight catching on dewy leaves, the ancient stone walls defining boundaries that had remained unchanged for centuries.

Her marketing eye had captured the perfect angles to convey both the heritage and beauty of the land, framing shots that emphasized depth and history rather than mere picturesque charm.

Molly adjusted the color temperature slightly, enhancing the golden morning light without making it artificially vibrant. The footage needed to feel authentic, not manufactured – the real Goldenridge, not a glossy approximation. It was what Jack wanted.

What he deserved, regardless of what he thought of her now.

The next sequence began with Jack himself silhouetted against the morning sky, the shimmering lake waters as backdrop, walking between orchard rows with the measured pace of a man intimately familiar with his terrain. She'd captured him unawares earlier that week, the lens following his movements from a respectful distance. There was something almost poetic in his gait – purpose without hurry, confidence without swagger. He paused to examine a branch, his profile sharp against the water and Molly's breath hitched, just as it had when she'd first recorded the moment.

She hesitated, finger hovering over the delete key. Would using footage of Jack feel like further betrayal? But removing him would be removing the soul of Goldenridge. The orchard and the man were inseparable – his passion for the land evident in every gesture, every careful movement among the trees.

The laptop software hummed softly as Molly continued working, selecting a clip of his calloused hands as they gently pruned a small branch. His fingers moved with surprising delicacy for their size, palms cradling apple blossoms with the tenderness one might show a newborn. The contrast between his rough-hewn strength and the fragile flowers created a visual metaphor more powerful than any scripted narrative.

She paired this with footage from the cider barn – the copper press gleaming in lantern light, wooden barrels lined against stone walls, Jack drawing amber liquid into glasses with easy precision, the cider catching light as it flowed, transformed into liquid gold.

'This isn't just about him though,' Molly murmured to herself, though the lie tasted bitter. Of course it was – his dedication, his struggle, his fierce protection of something precious and endangered.

But it was also about Patrick, Goldenridge and Golden Valley itself, about heritage and tradition worth preserving.

The technical aspects of the task grounded her, providing structure when emotion threatened to overwhelm. She adjusted transitions between scenes – cross-dissolves for pastoral moments, straight cuts for the more dynamic processing sequences. The pacing needed to feel natural, the narrative building organically rather than rushing toward a predetermined conclusion.

Molly moved to footage of the village next, weaving it into the orchard sequences to establish context. The Cherry Blossom Café, morning light streaming through windows as Eva arranged fresh pastries, her infectious laugh captured as she bantered with customers. Her friend turning suddenly toward the lens, flour dusting one cheek, her smile widening in recognition as she noticed Molly filming.

The moment held such genuine warmth that it made the perfect transition to clips of village life – her careful eye had documented the easy camaraderie of locals, the rhythm of a community where everyone's role was both individual and interconnected. The cobblestone square on market day – children darting between stalls while locals chatted with customers and wrapped up fresh produce.

Molly's stomach growled, reminding her that breakfast had been a long time ago, but she ignored it. The work demanded completion – not just as professional obligation but as emotional necessity. Creating this piece had become her way of processing everything that had happened on this trip, everything she felt about this place and its people.

She returned to more intimate orchard footage then; close-ups of various apple varieties that highlighted their distinctive characteristics. She'd captured the fruit in morning dew, in midday sun, in the golden hour before sunset, each lighting condition revealing different qualities. The cider-making process followed – a brief shot of Patrick demonstrating the traditional methods for her, his weathered hands moving with the confidence of decades of practice. His lined face was animated with pleasure as he shared knowledge accumulated over a lifetime.

Further time passed without Molly noticing, the festival sounds outside shifting as afternoon advanced into evening. She paused only to accept an email from Conor Gleeson with an enthusiastic note about Hearthland's song being part of her project.

The tune downloaded, its gentle introduction playing through her laptop speakers – gentle guitar notes at first, fiddle rising with plaintive beauty beneath Conor's own rich baritone.

The haunting melody wrapped around Molly once again, the vocalist's graveled singing about roots and belonging, of a tree that remembered what people forgot. Tears pricked at her eyes, but she blinked them away.

Later, she could fall apart. Now, she needed to finish what she'd started.

Chapter 36

The light outside had begun to soften toward dusk when Molly finally addressed the footage of the oak tree. That morning, she'd filmed it from multiple angles in an attempt to capture its essence for Cole and Pops.

She selected a sweeping shot that began at the tree's base and slowly tilted upward, revealing the full majesty of its spread against the sky. The movement felt almost like a gesture of respect, the visual acknowledging the oak's significance to both landscape and community.

This would serve as the ultimate coda to her piece, the final image before the call to action directing viewers to Goldenridge's website.

As the song reached its crescendo, Molly synchronized the music with her most evocative footage – the moments that captured not just the visual beauty of Goldenridge, but its very essence. The harmonies in 'Beneath the Oak' swelled as she layered in the final elements – subtle text identifying heritage varieties, brief facts about Goldenridge's history, and generations of Flynn stewardship.

Nothing heavy-handed or overtly commercial – just enough information to provide context without distracting from the visual narrative. Her marketing expertise guided these choices, years of professional experience informing each decision. But something else guided Molly too – a personal connection she'd never experienced with a client project before.

Finally, as shadows lengthened across her hotel room floor, Molly watched the completed piece from beginning to end. Two minutes and thirty-seven seconds of visual poetry that captured the orchard by the lake in all its complex beauty – traditional yet vulnerable, enduring yet endangered.

What she hadn't anticipated was seeing her own heart so clearly displayed in the work. Every editing choice, every lingering shot of Jack's profile against the sunset, every careful pairing of image and lyric . . . revealed feelings she'd barely acknowledged to herself. The reel had become more than marketing material; it was a visual love letter to Golden Valley, to Goldenridge and, in truth, to Jack Flynn himself.

'Well,' she whispered to the empty room, 'at least you're consistent. Go big or go home, Molly.'

Which was sadly what she'd be doing next.

Her shoulders ached from hours hunched over the laptop, and her eyes burned with fatigue. But alongside the physical discomfort was the quiet satisfaction of having created something worthy of its subject. Whatever happened now – whether Jack ever saw the piece, whether it made any difference to Golden Valley or Goldenridge's future – she'd captured the essence of this place as she'd experienced it.

Conor Gleeson's voice sang the final lines as the oak tree filled the screen, sun setting behind its massive form, creating a silhouette that seemed both protective and eternal:

'*Where time moves slow as the river's flow, the land remembers every story,*

Of those who stay and those who go . . .'

The lyrics faded, leaving only instrumental notes that seemed to linger in the air. Perfect timing for the simple text that appeared on screen: 'Goldenridge Orchard – Roots that run deep. Tradition worth preserving.'

She sat back, emotionally drained yet strangely peaceful. The piece wouldn't save the business or anything – no small social media campaign could solve structural financial issues or modernize aging equipment. But it might open doors, might bring attention from the right quarters, appease the bank, or even gently guide Jack in ways he'd never acknowledge.

Without allowing herself to reconsider, Molly uploaded the file and prepared it for sharing across platforms. The professional part of her mind worked automatically – optimizing file size, selecting appropriate hashtags, scheduling posts for maximum visibility. But beneath these practical considerations ran a current of emotion she couldn't fully contain.

This place had changed her. These people – Eva with her unashamed warmth and friendship, Patrick with his gentle wisdom, Maeve with her kindness, Anna with her undemanding welcome, even Brid with her gossip and nosiness.

But of course, most of all, Jack with his complicated mix of gruffness and surprising tenderness – they'd all become more than subjects for Molly's campaign.

They'd become people who mattered, whose lives she wanted to see continue and undisturbed by corporate interests that might destroy everything unique about the place.

She added a simple caption to accompany the video: *Some places hold magic in their very soil. Some traditions deserve to continue. Goldenridge Orchard – keeping heritage alive for over two hundred years. #TheOrchardbyTheLake*

Her finger hovered over the 'share' button for just a moment – a final hesitation before committing. Then Molly pressed it firmly, sending her work out into the world.

Done. Whatever happened next was out of her hands. As the upload completed, exhaustion settled into her bones, a physical manifestation of emotional depletion.

Then, also forwarding the piece to Cole like she'd promised, Molly closed her laptop and moved to the window.

The song's lyrics replayed in her mind as she watched the village below, its melody becoming the soundtrack to this moment of quiet accomplishment:

'The secrets of our hearts lie waiting,
For those with courage to meet them there . . .'

Chapter 37

Exhaustion settled deep into Molly's bones then, the kind that sleep alone couldn't cure. She sat on the edge of the bed, her body heavy with fatigue while her mind continued to spin much like the loading circle on a buffering video.

The reel had posted, beginning its journey through the algorithms, finding its audience – or not. She'd done her professional best for Goldenridge, for Jack. But the other half of her purpose in coming to Golden Valley remained unfulfilled – the promise that had brought her here in the first place, her grandmother's final wish still waiting in the velvet pouch she'd carried across an ocean.

Her phone buzzed with a notification. Cole's response to the reel was a string of fire emojis and a simple message: Holy shit, sis. This isn't a marketing video. This is a declaration. You in love with the orchard? Or the guy running it?

Molly set the phone down without responding. Her brother's jokey perceptiveness, usually endearing, felt too raw right now. She'd poured everything into that campaign – not just her professional skills, but all the complicated emotions she'd developed for Golden Valley and its stubborn, principled orchard keeper.

The evidence was there for anyone to see, especially someone who knew her as well as Cole did.

The room felt suddenly confining, its cozy charm transformed into a space too full of unresolved intentions. Molly moved to the window, pushing it open to let in the cool evening air. Traditional music from a different band drifted up from the square, the jaunty tune at odds with the heaviness in her chest.

She should be down there, enjoying it with the locals who'd welcomed her so readily. Instead, she was hiding in her room, nursing wounds both professional and personal.

She needed to call Pop. The thought settled with certainty, though her stomach knotted at the prospect of admitting failure. Her grandfather had been so confident in her ability to fulfill his beloved wife's final wish, had buoyed Molly before she left with assurances that Aoife would be 'so proud, so proud of their girl.'

She picked up her phone again, her finger hovering over Eddie's contact for several seconds before she finally pressed it. Three rings, then the familiar booming voice that had narrated so much of her childhood.

'There's my girl! I was wondering when you'd call. How's Tipp treating you?'

The warmth in his voice nearly undid her. Molly swallowed hard, fighting for composure. 'It's beautiful here, Pop. Everything she said it would be.'

'I never doubted that for a minute,' he replied. There was a slight pause, then: 'So did you do it? Did you find the spot?'

The directness of the question left no room for evasion. Molly sank back onto the edge of the bed, suddenly grateful for its support. 'I found the tree, yes,' she said quietly. 'It's exactly as she described – ancient, massive. Covered in carved initials going back decades.'

'That's amazing.' Eddie's enthusiasm faltered when she didn't immediately continue. 'Isn't it?'

'The tree is on private property,' Molly explained, her voice catching slightly. 'The landowner, he . . .' She sniffed, despite herself, eyes filling with tears. 'I think I've made a mess of things, Pop.'

'Tell me,' he encouraged gently.

The story spilled out then – how she'd met Jack Flynn the first morning, his initial suspicion, their gradual warming to each other, her decision to help with a business plan for the orchard. How this morning had shattered everything when Jack overheard her conversation with Cole and jumped to the wrong conclusion.

'He thinks I'm working for developers trying to buy his land,' she concluded, embarrassed to hear her voice crack with emotion. 'He won't listen to me. Won't let me explain. And without his permission, I can't . . .' She trailed off, unable to voice the failure explicitly.

There was silence on the other end for a moment, just the soft sound of Eddie's breathing. When he spoke, his voice carried the measured wisdom that had guided her through every crisis since childhood. 'That's a pickle, all right. Guy sounds like he's got a helluva stubborn streak.'

'Titanium,' Molly confirmed, with a watery laugh.

'Reminds me of someone else I know,' Eddie observed, the smile evident in his voice even across an ocean. 'Someone who doesn't give up easily when something matters.'

'This is different,' she protested. 'He won't even talk to me.'

'Maybe,' Eddie allowed. 'But, honey, I've never known you to accept a first no as final, especially from someone who matters to you.' He paused again, and she could picture him running a hand over his closely cropped white hair, a habit when he was choosing his words carefully. 'That's not like you, giving up before all options are exhausted.'

'What options?' Frustration edged Molly's voice. 'He won't let me near the tree again. I can't exactly sneak onto his property.'

'Couldn't you?' he challenged mildly.

'Pop! That would be trespassing.'

'Just checking your ethical boundaries.' He chuckled. 'Your

grandmother would have had no such compunction, believe me. Woman could justify nearly anything when her heart was set on it.'

The observation drew a reluctant smile from Molly. Aoife's moral flexibility had been legendary within the family – not dishonesty, but a certain . . . creative interpretation of any rules that stood between her and her objectives. And that she blithely insisted was 'a Tipperary thing'.

'Sweetheart,' Eddie continued, his tone softening, 'don't make any snap decisions. Give yourself time to think, to explore all possible routes.' He paused, then added, 'Like Nan always said, the right path only reveals itself to those who start walking.'

The familiar saying settled over Molly like a warm blanket. How many times had she heard those words from Aoife throughout her childhood? When she'd struggled with which college to choose, or a job offer, when she'd debated ending a relationship that no longer served her.

Heck, even last week when she'd first arrived here and was trying to locate the hotel, that very phrase had popped into her head. Always the same gentle guidance – start moving, and clarity will follow.

'I miss her so much, Pop,' Molly whispered, the admission raw with longing. 'Being here, seeing the places from her stories . . . sometimes it feels like she could be just around the next corner.'

'I know, honey.' Eddie's voice roughened with his own grief. 'I feel that way every morning I wake up, expecting to hear her clattering around in the kitchen. A whole year on and I still reach for her in the night.'

The shared loss hovered between them, acknowledged without need for further words.

Eddie cleared his throat, pulling them both back to practical matters. 'Whatever you decide about staying or going, about this orchard guy or the oak, just remember that Nan believed in you. Trusted you with this for a reason.'

They spoke for a few minutes more – Eddie updating her on

neighborhood gossip. The familiar rhythm of his stories grounded Molly, reminding her of the bedrock beneath the shifting sands of her current situation.

The call ended, leaving her with the whisper of accordion music below the window, and her own thoughts for company. She moved to the closet, opening the creaking door. Hidden beneath a sweater was the velvet pouch, its navy fabric soft against her fingers as she drew it out.

The weight of it was familiar in her palm – not heavy by any measure, but substantial with meaning. The contents were seared into her memory, as was the promise she'd made while holding her grandmother's fragile hand in those final days.

'I'll see it done, Nan. I promise,' she'd whispered as Aoife's breathing had grown more labored, her once-vivid eyes cloudy with approaching demise. Her grandmother's fingers had tightened briefly around hers, a fleeting pressure that had conveyed more than words could have.

The trust in that gesture had been absolute – Aoife Brennan, who had crossed an ocean and built a new life from nothing, placing her final wish in the hands of the granddaughter who had inherited her stubborn spirit, if not her accent.

Now, sitting in an Irish hotel room less than a mile from the exact oak tree that was the very center of that promise, Molly felt the weight of that trust transform into the leaden reality of failure.

'I'm sorry,' she whispered to the pouch cradled in her hands. 'I tried. But I can't finish what you asked of me.'

She traced the pouch's embroidered edge, following the pattern of Celtic knotwork that had so fascinated her as a child. Her grandmother had used it to store various keepsakes over the years – a lock of baby hair from Molly's first haircut, a pressed flower from Cole's high school graduation, the small smooth stone from Coney Island that Eddie had given her on their fiftieth anniversary.

Now it held something far more significant, the physical embodiment of a final journey home.

Chapter 38

A sharp knock at the door startled Molly from her thoughts, the sound echoing through the quiet hotel room like an unexpected reprieve.

She hastily tucked the pouch back into the closet and crossed to the door, expecting perhaps Anna wondering if she was coming down for dinner.

Instead, Brid Ryan stood in the corridor, her silver-streaked hair arranged in its usual elegant coiffure. The older woman wore a fuchsia cardigan over a floral dress, a thin gold chain glinting at her neck in the warm hallway light.

'There you are,' Brid said, her voice dropping to her usual near-whisper, even though no one else occupied the corridor. Her eyes gleamed with a conspiratorial light that immediately put Molly on alert. 'Patrick Flynn's downstairs in the garden. Says he'd like a word.'

Molly's heart stuttered. 'Patrick? Is he – is everything alright?'

'Wouldn't tell me what it's about,' Brid replied, her tone suggesting this personal affront would not soon be forgotten. She glanced over her shoulder as if checking for eavesdroppers, then leaned closer. 'Though between ourselves, he's not looked this serious since the frost of '86 took half the orchard.'

The statement did nothing to calm Molly's nerves. Had Jack told his great-uncle about their confrontation? About her so-called betrayal?

'I'll come down right away,' she said, smoothing her hair self-consciously.

'Good girl,' Brid said, nodding approvingly. 'He's waiting in the walled garden. I've just lit the heat lamps. The 'oul fool's not as young as he thinks he is to be out in this evening chill.'

Molly followed Brid downstairs and through the hotel's narrow corridors, their footsteps muffled by the worn runner that stretched the length of the hallway.

'Mind the step there, pet,' she cautioned, misinterpreting Molly's hesitation as she paused at the photograph of her grandmother that had previously caught her eye. 'That third one from the bottom has a mind of its own.'

They continued through the reception area, now quiet, as most guests were out enjoying festival activities in the square. Wooden floorboards creaked beneath the antique carpet, announcing their passage through the old building.

Brid led Molly through a door behind the check-in counter, down a short passage lined with service carts, and through another door that opened unexpectedly onto the hotel's walled garden. The transition from interior to exterior space was so abrupt that Molly blinked in momentary disorientation.

The outdoor space existed in a world apart from the festival's jubilant chaos. Stone walls, softened by climbing roses and ivy, created a sanctuary of stillness. Copper heat lamps had been positioned strategically throughout the space, their gentle glow creating pools of warmth against the evening's growing chill.

'There you go,' Brid said, gesturing toward a stooped figure seated on a weathered iron chair and table set alongside some rose bushes. 'I'll bring some tea out in a bit, unless you'd prefer something stronger?'

'Tea would be great,' Molly replied automatically, her attention already fixed on Patrick's silhouette against the gathering dusk. He looked up, his lined face catching the copper light from the nearest lamp and his eyes studied her with quiet intensity.

'Tea be grand, thanks, Brid,' he replied, dismissing her. 'Hello, Molly.'

He sat with the patient stillness of a man accustomed to nature's rhythms. His walking stick rested against his chair, his weathered hands placed carefully on his knees. He wore a thick wool sweater the color of heather, and a tweed flat cap that had seen decades of Irish weather. The set of his shoulders suggested contemplation rather than the accusation Molly had feared.

'Mr Flynn,' she greeted softly as she approached. 'Brid said you wanted to see me.'

He gestured to the seat opposite his. 'Thank you for coming. And it's Patrick, please.'

Molly settled onto the chair, its cast-iron scrolled back cold through her sweater. Between them, a small table held a copper lantern, its flame dancing behind glass panels.

'Is everything alright?' she asked, tension threading through her voice despite her efforts to sound casual.

Patrick's mouth curved in a slight smile. 'That depends entirely on your perspective, I suppose.' He looked past her toward the stone wall where late roses still bloomed, their petals pale in the fading light. 'I wanted to tell you a story, if you don't mind listening to an old man's ramblings.'

The request surprised her. 'Of course,' Molly said, curiosity displacing some of her anxiety.

He nodded once, as if confirming a decision already made. 'I was eighteen when I first saw her,' Patrick began without preamble, his voice dropping to a more intimate register. 'She was standing in the square with a book clutched to her chest, looking at the fountain as if it might hold all the answers she sought.'

Molly nodded cautiously, wondering where this unexpected tale was going.

'She had the darkest hair,' he continued. 'And eyes that changed color with her moods; green in laughter, gray in thought. The first time I heard her laugh, I knew I was in trouble.' His expression softened with the memory, years falling away from his weathered face. 'She was like no one I'd ever met. Read poetry and collected folk tales. Could name every wildflower in the valley and knew the old beliefs about each one.'

Suddenly, a shiver ran through Molly that had nothing to do with the evening air.

'We were inseparable that summer,' Patrick continued, his gaze now fixed on some middle distance where the past played out before him. 'She'd help at the orchard when her father didn't need her at their shop. We'd talk for hours under the old oak tree. I told her everything – my dreams, my fears about not measuring up to family expectations.' His voice caught slightly. 'She listened in a way that made you feel truly heard, truly seen.'

In the distance, music continued to drift over the garden walls, the cheerful melody incongruous against Patrick's wistful remembrance.

'I carved our initials in the oak that autumn,' he said, his fingers moving as if tracing invisible letters. 'Took my time with it, made sure the letters were perfect. She teased me for being so careful, said love wasn't meant to be tidy.' His smile turned sad at the edges. 'But I wanted it to last, you see. Wanted something permanent to mark what we'd found together.'

The revelation struck Molly like a physical blow. The carved heart she'd traced that morning – her grandmother's initials intertwined with the very man sitting before her now. *PF + AB* inside a heart.

Patrick Flynn and . . . her grandmother?

She gripped the edges of her chair, steadying herself against sudden vertigo.

'Yet a few months later, she was gone.' Patrick's voice hardened slightly. 'No goodbye, no explanation. Just disappeared from the village overnight. Her parents said she'd gone to stay with relatives in Dublin, but something in their manner . . .' He shook his head. 'I knew there was more to it. I wrote letters. They were returned unopened. I tried phoning the number she'd given me for her cousins, but they claimed not to know where she was.'

Molly's throat tightened with emotion.

'I was . . . heartbroken,' Patrick admitted, the word seemingly difficult to voice even after so many decades. 'Kept expecting her to return, to explain. Each morning I'd wake thinking "today might be the day". Then months became years.' He looked down at his hands, the skin mottled with age spots, veins prominent beneath the surface. 'Eventually, I stopped expecting. Started living again, though not quite the same way.'

A painful tenderness filled Molly's chest, imagining this lovely man waiting for a woman who would never return, who would instead build a life across an ocean with someone else.

'It was Brid who finally told me the truth,' Patrick continued. 'Aoife had emigrated to New York. Started a new life there.' His voice grew thick with emotion. 'I'd worried, you see, if something had happened to her. If that was why she never came back. Learning she was alive and well – it should have been a comfort.'

'Was it?' Molly asked, already guessing the answer.

Patrick met her gaze directly, his eyes sharp despite the gathering darkness. 'No,' he said simply. 'It was harder somehow, knowing she'd chosen to leave. Chosen not to say goodbye.' He paused, his breath visible in the cooling air. 'I've often wondered what I missed, what signs I failed to see. Whether she was unhappy or didn't feel what I felt but I was too wrapped up in my own feelings to notice.'

The garden had darkened further, the heat lamps now creating warm light in the deepening blue of evening. Above them, the first stars punctured the twilight sky, bright pinpricks against the encroaching night. Festival bustle continued beyond the garden walls, but it seemed to belong to another world entirely – one separate from this quiet space of confession and memory.

'And you never married?' Molly ventured gently, though she already knew the answer from her conversations with Jack.

He shook his head. 'Came close once or twice. But something always held me back.' His smile turned self-deprecating. 'Jack thinks I'm a romantic 'oul fool. But he's a lot more like me than he thinks.'

Brid appeared at the garden door then, a tray balanced in her hands. She approached with calm efficiency, setting out cups and saucers on the small table between them. 'Something to warm you both,' she said, pouring steaming tea from a blue willow teapot. Her sharp eyes moved between them, clearly burning with curiosity, but she retreated without comment after ensuring they were supplied with sugar and milk.

Patrick waited until she'd disappeared back into the hotel before speaking again. 'I don't tell you this story for pity, mind,' he said, wrapping his hands around his teacup as if drawing strength from its warmth. 'I've had a good life, a fortunate one in many ways. Goldenridge has been my constant companion through it all.'

'Then why tell me now?' Molly asked, though a suspicion was forming in her mind, a sense that Patrick knew more than he was letting on.

'Because,' he said, his eyes finding hers with startling directness, 'when I see you standing by the lake, or hear you humming that old song, or watch you arrange wildflowers with such familiar care—' he paused, his gaze steady and knowing '—I see it. I see *her*.'

The implication hung in the air between them, unspoken yet unmistakable. Molly's heart hammered against her ribs, her hands suddenly unsteady around her teacup. The garden seemed to close around them, the stone walls holding this moment of truth separate from the festival revelry beyond.

Her hands trembled slightly, rattling the fine china against its saucer. The secret she'd carried across an ocean pressed against her lips, demanding release after all these years of silence.

'You know who I am,' she said softly, not a question but a realization.

Patrick's expression remained gentle, his eyes never leaving her face. 'I've had my suspicions for a while. Harris . . . that was her married name?'

She nodded, her throat tight with emotion. 'Yes.'

'And when you hummed that song, and were so keen to see the oak . . .' His voice trailed off, years of wonder condensed into that unfinished thought.

Molly set her teacup on the table, afraid her unsteady hands might drop it. The moment of decision had arrived – whether to confirm what Patrick already suspected, or to maintain the fiction of being just another American tourist with Irish roots. But sitting across from this man who had loved her grandmother, who had carved their initials into a tree that still stood, truth felt like the only possible choice.

'Aoife Brennan . . . was my grandmother, yes,' she said, her voice stronger now with certainty. 'She died last year.'

Though Patrick had clearly suspected this, the confirmation still registered on his face with a physical impact. His eyes closed briefly, a small flinch betraying the emotion beneath his composed exterior. When he opened them again, they glistened in the lamplight.

'I knew it,' he said, his voice rougher than before. 'I knew it from the very first time I saw you at the farm shop. There's something in the way you tilt your head when you're thinking, the very same gesture she had.' His gaze traveled over Molly's features as if cataloging resemblances.

'I had no idea,' she said, leaning forward slightly. 'About you, I mean. She told stories about Ireland, about Golden Valley and the oak tree, and why she left, but she never mentioned anyone specific . . .' She hesitated, searching for the right words.

Patrick's weathered hands tightened slightly against his knees. 'I suppose that's not surprising. If she wanted a clean break, a fresh start.'

'It wasn't that simple though,' Molly said, the words tumbling out now that she'd begun. 'Aoife left Golden Valley because she had to. Because she was pregnant.'

The garden fell utterly silent, suspended in the wake of this revelation.

Patrick's face went completely still, his expression frozen between one heartbeat and the next as the implications registered. 'Pregnant,' he repeated, the word barely audible.

Molly nodded, her eyes never leaving his face. 'With my mother, Tara. Your daughter.'

Patrick's breathing changed, becoming shallow and rapid. One hand moved unconsciously to his chest, pressing against his sweater as if to contain the emotions surging beneath. 'My . . . daughter,' he echoed, the words seeming foreign on his tongue.

'In those days, as you know . . .' Molly continued gently, 'Nan said her father would have disowned her. That the shame would have destroyed the family. So she ran. To New York, where she had a distant cousin willing to take her in.'

The copper lantern between them flickered, sending shadows dancing across Patrick's face as he absorbed this information.

'I guess she never knew how to reach out afterward,' Molly reckoned. 'Didn't know how to bridge that gap once it had formed. Then years passed and she met my grandfather, Eddie, in Brooklyn. He adopted my mom when they married. They built a good life together.' Molly paused, watching Patrick carefully. 'But she never forgot Ireland. Never forgot Golden Valley or the oak tree. Or you, it seemed.'

Patrick's hand moved from his chest to cover his mouth, as if physically containing the words that threatened to spill out. When he finally spoke, his voice emerged thick with emotion. 'I have a child,' he said, wonder and grief mingled in the statement. 'A daughter I never knew existed.'

'Had,' Molly confirmed gently, her voice cracking a little. How awful to have to snatch this away from him so quickly. 'My mother died when I was very young.'

'I'm very sorry to hear it,' Patrick said automatically, genuine sympathy cutting through his own shock. Then something shifted in his expression as a new realization dawned. 'So that makes you my . . .'

'Granddaughter,' Molly finished, her voice barely above a whisper as the realization struck her too. 'Yes.'

Patrick's eyes widened, his gaze traveling over her features with new intensity, as if seeing her properly for the first time – not just as a reminder of Aoife, but as part of himself, his own blood.

'Granddaughter,' he repeated, the word soft with wonder. Then his hand reached across the table, trembling slightly, fingers outstretched.

Molly met him halfway, her smaller hand enveloped in his weathered palm. Much like Jack's, his skin was warm and calloused, bearing the marks of decades working the orchard – an entire life lived, all the while unknown to her.

'Is that why you came to Golden Valley?' he asked, his voice uneven. 'To find me?'

Molly shook her head apologetically. 'Like I said, I didn't know about you specifically. Nan just spoke of her first love, and the reason she had to leave Ireland.' She squeezed his hand. 'No. I came because she asked me to do something for her. In her final days.'

Something in her tone made Patrick tilt his head, a question in his eyes. 'Asked you to do what, exactly?'

Molly took a deep breath. 'Maybe I should show you,' she said, reluctantly withdrawing her hand from his. 'Wait here a moment?'

At Patrick's nod, Molly rose and hurried back through the garden door into the hotel.

Chapter 39

Jack stood frozen in the shadows of the Glen Arms courtyard archway, his body rigid as Molly and Patrick sat facing each other across a small table, copper lantern light casting their profiles against the darkness. The garden's stone walls trapped their voices, carrying every word to where he stood.

Granddaughter.

The realization hit him like a physical blow, stealing his breath and rooting his feet to the flagstone path. He'd come to collect Patrick at Brid's request, the older woman insisting with unusual urgency that his great-uncle needed a lift home 'right this minute'. Now he understood her cryptic smile, her insistence that Jack enter through the garden side entrance rather than through the hotel. Brid had orchestrated this – ensuring he would witness a truth that changed everything.

Now Jack watched his great-uncle reach for Molly with trembling fingers, the older man's face transformed by wonder and grief intermingled.

'Granddaughter,' Patrick repeated, the word seeming to reshape the very air of the garden.

Jack's mind raced, stumbling over this confusing revelation. Granddaughter? But that would mean . . .

A sudden wave of realization washed through him. That woman his great-uncle once talked about, who he had loved and lost half a century ago. The one who'd disappeared without explanation – she had been pregnant when she left Golden Valley.

Pregnant with Patrick's child. And that child had given birth to Molly, apparently.

He pressed himself deeper into the shadows as Molly suddenly rose and disappeared into the hotel building while Patrick remained seated, his worn face visible in profile, moisture tracking unchecked down his cheeks.

Jack had never seen his great-uncle cry – not at funerals, not during the worst drought years, not even when they'd nearly lost the orchard to frost damage. The sight sent a jolt of discomfort through him, as if he were witnessing something too private for any eyes.

He should leave. This moment wasn't meant for him. Yet his feet remained planted, unable to tear himself away from what was unfolding before him.

When Molly returned minutes later, she carried something in her hands – a small dark pouch that she placed carefully on the table between them.

'This is why I came,' she said simply.

No, Jack couldn't leave. Not yet.

Chapter 40

When Molly returned to the garden, Patrick hadn't moved, though his expression betrayed the tumult of emotions he'd experienced in her absence.

The garden had grown darker, the lanterns creating an intimate circle of warmth against the night. She resumed her seat, carefully placing the velvet pouch on the table between them.

'This is why I came.'

Patrick looked at the pouch, then back to her face, confusion evident in his expression.

'To bring Nan home,' Molly explained, her voice soft with reverence for the wish she carried. 'She wanted her ashes scattered beneath the tree where you carved your initials, The Wishing Oak. Where she was happiest, she said.'

Patrick's intake of breath was audible in the quiet garden. He stared at the small pouch, understanding transforming his features into a mask of profound emotion. 'Aoife,' he whispered, the name a prayer on his lips after decades of silence.

'She made me promise,' Molly continued, 'in her final days. Said there was nowhere else she'd rather rest for eternity than beneath that oak, watching over the orchard, the lake and the place she loved so much.'

A tear escaped from the corner of Patrick's eye, tracking slowly down his weathered cheek before disappearing into the collar of his sweater. He made no move to wipe it away, his dignity in grief somehow more moving than any attempt to conceal it.

'That was why I was so interested in getting to it,' she said, finally explaining the mystery that had caused such friction with Jack. 'I didn't know how to ask Jack for permission without telling the whole story, to say nothing of the fact that I didn't know . . .' She hesitated. 'About you.'

Patrick reached out, his hand hovering above the velvet pouch without quite touching it. 'I've spent a lifetime wondering about her. Wondering what became of the only woman I ever truly loved. To think she remembered too. That she wanted to come home to us after all these years.'

'She never stopped loving here,' Molly said, swallowing against the tightness in her throat. 'Our house in Brooklyn was filled with Irish music, stories and legends. She taught me how to bake soda bread and apple tart. To recognize wildflowers from a country I'd never visited. When she spoke of Golden Valley, her whole face would transform.' Molly smiled through threatening tears. 'She'd say, "*mo chroí*, it's where *my* heart first opened".'

Patrick's breath caught at the endearment. '*Mo chroí*,' he echoed. 'She called you that?'

Molly nodded. 'Cole too – my brother.'

'A grandson as well,' Patrick murmured, as if testing the reality of all this new knowledge. His fingers finally made contact with the velvet pouch, tracing the embroidered Celtic knotwork with reverent care. 'And she remembered our oak.' His voice broke slightly on the word 'our', the simple pronoun containing decades of loss and connection.

'She described it so perfectly that I recognized it immediately that first day at the lake,' Molly said. 'The massive trunk, the way the branches spread like protective arms. She said it was ancient even then, that it had witnessed countless lovers' promises.' She paused, gathering courage for her next words. 'She told me that's where she first discovered what love was.'

Patrick closed his eyes briefly, the statement clearly piercing some deep place within him. When he opened them again, they shone with a mixture of grief and gratitude. 'Did she . . .' He hesitated, vulnerability naked on his face. 'Did she ever regret leaving, do you know? Not telling me?'

The question hung in the cool evening air, laden with decades of wondering. Molly chose her words carefully, honoring both the man before her and her grandmother's memory.

'I think she regretted not saying goodbye,' she said gently. 'She told me once that running away was both the hardest and the easiest thing she'd ever done – hardest because she was leaving her heart behind, easiest because she couldn't bear the disappointment.'

'Disappointment?' Patrick's voice cracked on the word. 'I would have married her that very day. Would have cherished both her and the child.'

'I think she knew that,' Molly assured him gently. 'But she was young and scared. She feared bringing shame to both families in such a small community.' She reached across the table, placing her hand on his. 'She didn't regret the life she built, the family she raised. But here remained her heart's first home.'

Patrick nodded slowly, his gaze returning to the velvet pouch that contained the earthly remains of his first love. 'And now you've brought her home,' he said, his voice steadying with each word. 'Back to where she belonged.'

'I've tried,' Molly admitted. 'But without permission . . .' She let the sentence hang unfinished between them.

'Permission?' Patrick straightened, sudden determination replacing his emotional vulnerability. 'Pet, you need no permission. That oak has stood on Flynn land for centuries, bearing witness to generations of love stories, including mine and Aoife's.' His hand closed gently around hers. 'Of course you must fulfill her wish. And I—' his voice caught briefly before he continued '—I would be honored to help you if you'd let me.'

The simple statement, offered with such dignity and grace, broke something inside Molly that had been held taut since her confrontation with Jack that morning. Tears spilled over, tracking silently down her cheeks as relief and gratitude washed through her.

'Thank you,' she whispered. 'I would love that.'

Patrick reached toward her with trembling fingers, his weathered hand gently brushing away a tear from her cheek – a grandfather's tender gesture toward a granddaughter he hadn't known existed until minutes before. The touch was tentative, almost reverent, as if Molly was something precious and fragile.

'No,' he said, his voice steady despite the emotion evident in his eyes. 'It is I who should be thanking you. For bringing her home. And for bringing yourself back to me as well.'

Chapter 41

The oak tree.

Still in the shadows, understanding crashed through Jack with the force of a winter storm. This was why she'd been so interested in the tree. Why Molly had been there this very morning, talking about the 'best spot'.

Not for developers or sales brochures – but to fulfill a final wish for her grandmother.

For Patrick's lost love.

Shame burned through him now, hot and caustic. He'd accused her of the worst possible motives, had practically thrown her off the property. Had refused to listen when she tried to explain. When all the while she'd been carrying out a mission of profound personal importance, a promise made to a dying relative.

'That was why I was so interested in getting to it,' Molly continued. 'I didn't know how to ask Jack for permission without telling the whole story, to say nothing of the fact that I didn't know . . .'

Jack's hands clenched and unclenched at his sides, his nails digging half-moons into his palms.

Everything Molly had done since arriving in Golden Valley shifted in his perception, reframing itself from suspicious, to poignant. She hadn't been using or manipulating them. She'd been trying to connect – to her heritage, to her grandmother's homeland, to the place that had shaped her family history.

And Jack had met her efforts with suspicion and barely concealed hostility.

His gaze fixed on Molly's profile as she spoke about her grandmother's regrets, about her fears of bringing shame to both families. The gentle way she explained complex emotions, honoring both her grandmother's choices and Patrick's decades of wondering, revealed a compassion that Jack had completely misjudged. He'd viewed that empathy as manipulation, her interest in the orchard as ulterior motive. When in reality, she'd been navigating a delicate situation with a grace he'd refused to recognize.

'And now you've brought her home,' Patrick was saying, his voice steadying with resolve. 'Back to where she belonged.'

'I've tried,' Molly admitted. 'But without permission . . .'

'Permission?' The strength in Patrick's voice carried clearly to Jack's hiding place.

He watched as his great-uncle reached toward Molly with trembling fingers. The gesture; so tender, so unlike Patrick's usual reserved manner, struck Jack with unexpected force. This was a lonely bachelor claiming family, claiming connection after decades of solitude. The significance of the moment pressed against Jack's chest, making it difficult to breathe.

Movement at the garden door to the hotel caught his attention then. Brid appeared, her silhouette unmistakable against the light from the hallway. She would surely spot him if she looked toward the archway.

Jack stepped backward, retreating deeper into the shadows of the path that led around the garden. The flagstones were cool and damp beneath his boots as he moved silently away, his mind still reeling with everything he'd witnessed.

He paused at the far corner, partially concealed by a large holly bush. From this vantage point, he could see Molly helping Patrick to his feet, the older man leaning slightly on his cane while still clutching the velvet pouch in his free hand. Their heads were bent close together, the physical resemblance between them suddenly striking now that Jack knew to look for it – something in the set of their shoulders, their side profile.

Then his phone buzzed in his pocket, the vibration so unexpected that he nearly dropped it in his haste to silence it. The screen glowed brightly in the darkness, forcing him to cup his hand around it to contain the light.

Notifications cascaded across the display:

The Orchard Pub tagged you in a post
Eva O'Sullivan and 147 others liked your post
Maeve Gleeson reshared your post
79 new comments on your post
New message from Declan O'Shea: 'Unreal!'

Jack stared at the screen in confusion. He hadn't posted anything on social media. Hadn't shared any content online since the basic orchard updates Molly had suggested for the festival.

Yet his phone continued to buzz with increasing frequency, notifications stacking atop each other faster than he could process them.

With one eye still on the garden to ensure he wouldn't be spotted, Jack tapped on the most recent notification.

His screen filled immediately with moving images – Goldenridge at dawn, mist rising between apple trees, the ancient stone walls catching first light. The camera moved with graceful precision, capturing the orchard from angles that made it appear both familiar and somehow magical, as if seeing it through new eyes.

The music began – Conor Gleeson's distinctive voice singing 'Beneath the Oak', the local band's haunting tribute to Golden Valley. The sound was low through his phone's speakers, but Jack recognized it instantly – the very song he and Molly had danced to last night in the square.

As the melody built, the video continued; close-up shots of heritage apples in morning dew, the cider press gleaming in lantern light, Patrick's hands demonstrating traditional methods with practiced grace.

And then, unexpectedly, Jack himself appeared on screen – silhouetted against the morning sky, walking between orchard rows with measured steps. The camera followed him with respectful distance as he paused to examine a branch, his profile sharp against the light.

His throat tightened with emotion as he recognized the footage – moments from a few days ago when he'd been too hyperaware of Molly's presence to even notice her filming.

The video continued – village scenes interwoven with orchard footage, creating context that explained Goldenridge's significance to the area. Eva laughing in her café, flour dusting one cheek. Market stalls in the square. The heritage apple varieties displayed with their distinctive characteristics highlighted. Each segment flowed seamlessly into the next, telling a story of tradition and community that transcended mere marketing.

As the song reached its crescendo, the final sequence began – the ancient oak filmed from multiple angles, its massive trunk and spreading branches captured with the same reverence afforded to a living character rather than mere scenery. The camera tilted slowly upward from the oak's base, revealing its full majesty against the sky as Conor sang the final lines:

'Where time moves slow as the river's flow, the land remembers every story,

Of those who stay and those who go . . .'

Jack lowered the phone, his vision blurring slightly as he noticed the timestamp. Molly had done this – created this beautiful tribute to Goldenridge and sent it out into the world – despite their confrontation that morning. Despite knowing she might never be welcome on his land again.

Despite believing Jack thought the worst of her.

Yet she'd captured something essential about the orchard and his connection to it – the care in his movements among the trees, the reverence with which he approached even the most routine tasks. She'd seen him, really seen him, in ways no one else ever had.

Jack scrolled quickly through the comments, stunned by the response. Locals expressing pride. Visitors asking about tours and tastings. Several food bloggers inquiring about featuring Goldenridge in upcoming reviews. Even a comment from a respected craft beverage distributor expressing interest in their heritage ciders.

And inexplicably, a load of American hockey players.

The realization of what Molly had accomplished washed over him. She'd managed what he'd thought impossible – presenting Goldenridge not as a quaint relic of the past, but as a living tradition worth preserving. Worth visiting. Worth supporting. She'd seen the essence of what made the orchard special and translated it for others to appreciate.

And she'd done it all while carrying the weight of her grandmother's final wish – a mission he'd nearly prevented her from completing with his suspicion and stubbornness.

'Thank you,' Molly was saying to Patrick now, her voice thick with emotion. 'It would mean everything to her, knowing you were there too.'

Jack remained motionless against the wall, letting the cool evening air fill his lungs as his thoughts raced. He needed to make things right. The connection he'd felt from the beginning, that immediate sense of recognition he had fought against so stubbornly, suddenly made perfect sense.

Molly Harris belonged here – in Golden Valley – in ways neither of them had truly fully understood.

Chapter 42

Jack's boots whispered against the path as he stepped out of the shadows and into the walled space. The air felt different somehow – intimate and enclosed, yet vast with possibility.

Overhead, stars emerged in the deepening blue of evening, each pinprick of light sharp and clear in the autumn air. The copper lamps scattered throughout created islands of warmth against the gathering chill, their glow catching on the dew-dampened rose petals and turning them to jewels.

Molly hadn't noticed him yet, her gaze fixed somewhere beyond the garden walls, and he took the moment to simply watch her – the woman he'd misjudged so completely, the woman who had somehow become essential to him in ways he was only beginning to understand.

When Jack had appeared through the archway, Brid moved to lead Patrick inside with a knowing glance that confirmed to Jack that she'd orchestrated the moment perfectly.

'I'll keep him warm with a wee drop of whiskey,' she'd murmured, patting Jack's arm as she guided Patrick through the hotel door.

His great-uncle paused, studying Jack's face with eyes that saw too much. 'She's something special, our Molly,' he said softly, gripping his shoulder with surprising strength before allowing Brid to usher him inside.

Our Molly. The simple phrase carried weight that settled into Jack's chest like stone – faintly connecting them all through ties of blood and history he still couldn't quite comprehend.

Jack moved then, and something in his step alerted Molly to his presence. She turned, her face registering surprise that quickly shifted to wariness. The expression struck him like a physical blow, a reminder of how thoroughly he'd destroyed her trust with his accusations that morning.

'Jack,' she said, her voice carefully neutral despite the emotion that flickered in her eyes. 'Didn't expect to see you here.'

'I came to find Patrick,' he mumbled, moving closer but stopping with enough distance between them that she wouldn't feel crowded. 'Brid said he needed a lift home.'

'He's just gone inside.' Molly gestured toward the hotel.

The silence between them stretched, laden with unspoken words.

He took a deep breath, letting the garden's scents fill his lungs – roses and damp earth, the faint sweetness of lavender from the border plants. Somewhere a night bird called, its voice carrying over the stone walls, a single perfect note that hung in the air between them.

'I heard everything,' he said finally, his voice low and steady despite the hammering of his heart against his ribs. 'About your grandmother. About Patrick. About why you really came to Golden Valley.'

Her eyes narrowed. 'You were eavesdropping?'

'Not intentionally.' He held her gaze, refusing to look away despite the shame that heated his neck. 'I came through the side entrance to collect Patrick and . . . overheard your conversation.'

Her shoulders stiffened, arms crossing protectively over her chest. 'So now you know.'

'Now I know,' he agreed quietly, taking another step closer.

The copper lamp nearest them caught the gold flecks in her eyes, turning them luminous in the soft light. 'And I need to apologize, Molly. I've been wrong about everything since the day you arrived.'

'You don't have to—'

'I do.' He interrupted gently but firmly. 'I accused you of the worst possible motives at every turn. Refused to listen this morning when you tried to explain.' His voice roughened with emotion. 'You were carrying out a promise to your grandmother, and I treated you like a corporate spy.'

The wariness in her expression began to soften, something cautious but hopeful taking its place. 'You couldn't have known.'

'I could have trusted you,' he countered. 'Could have given you the benefit of doubt instead of assuming the worst.' His hands unclenched at his sides, a conscious effort to release the tension that had gripped him since he'd arrived. 'I've spent so long defending Goldenridge against outside interests that I stopped seeing people clearly. Started categorizing everyone as either threat or ally, with nothing in between.'

Molly's arms slowly uncrossed, her posture relaxing slightly. 'It's understandable. Your livelihood is at stake.'

'That's no excuse for how I treated you.' Jack moved closer still, close enough now that he could detect the subtle scent of her perfume beneath the garden's heavier fragrances. 'Especially when the truth is, I've been falling for you since that first morning in the rain.'

Her breath caught audibly, eyes widening at his confession.

'Even when I was being my most stubborn, most suspicious self,' he continued, the words coming easier now that he'd begun, 'something about you kept breaking through. The way you looked at the orchard – really looked at it, seeing what makes it special. The questions you asked that went beyond the surface. How you cared about the old ways, the traditions.'

'I did care,' she said softly. 'I do.'

'I know that now.' Jack's voice dropped lower, meant only for her despite there being no one else in the garden. 'I've seen the video, Molly.'

'You've – what?' Confusion flickered across her face.

'The online video. With Hearthland's song. My phone hasn't stopped buzzing all evening.'

Understanding dawned in her expression. 'Oh, I – I wasn't sure whether you would.'

'It's . . . beautiful,' he said simply. 'What you captured about the orchard, about Golden Valley . . . it's everything I've never been able to put into words. You cut straight to the heart of it all.'

A flush of pleasure colored her cheeks. 'I just shared what I saw.'

'That's just it,' he said, taking the final step that brought them face to face, close enough that he could see the subtle constellation of freckles across her nose. 'You saw what matters. You get me, Molly Harris, in ways no one else ever has. But now, by God, I need to get you too.'

Jack reached for her, one hand gently cradling her cheek while the other found the small of her back. Her skin was cool beneath his palm, but her eyes held a warmth that drew him in, permission and invitation clear in their depths.

The first touch of his lips against hers was tentative, a question rather than a declaration. Molly's hands came up to rest against his chest, neither pushing away nor pulling closer, simply anchoring herself as they navigated this new territory together.

Then her mouth softened beneath his, answering his unspoken question with absolute certainty.

What began as careful exploration quickly deepened, mutual restraint giving way to something far more urgent. Her hands slid upward, fingers threading through his hair as she pulled him closer. Jack's arm tightened around her waist, erasing the remaining space between them until he could feel the rapid beating of her heart against his own. She tasted of apples and cinnamon, of afternoon tea and something uniquely herself. The air around them seemed to crackle with energy as their kiss continued, neither wanting to be the first to pull away.

When they finally parted, both were breathing unevenly, their foreheads resting together as they steadied themselves.

'I've wanted to do that since . . . forever,' Jack admitted, his voice rough with emotion.

Molly laughed softly, the sound warming him more effectively than any lantern. 'That makes two of us.'

He brushed a strand of hair from her face, still amazed that she was here in his arms, that they'd somehow found their way to this moment despite all the misunderstandings. Then he pressed a gentle kiss to her forehead.

The buzz of a phone interrupted the moment, vibrating insistently from Molly's pocket. She made a small sound of frustration that drew a laugh from Jack.

'You should probably get it,' he said, though he made no move to release her.

With obvious reluctance, Molly extracted her phone, glancing at the screen. 'It's . . . my grandfather in Brooklyn,' she said, panic and uncertainty coloring her voice. She accepted the call, keeping one arm loosely around Jack's waist. 'Pop? Is everything OK?'

He could hear the tinny voice on the other end, words indistinct but the tone unmistakably determined.

'What?' Molly's eyes widened. 'Where are you?' A pause, then, 'JFK? As in the airport?' Jack raised an eyebrow, watching as disbelief transformed her expression. Her voice rose slightly. 'Here, to Ireland? Now?'

Another pause as the voice on the other end continued speaking, gruffer now.

'Pop, you didn't have to—' Molly stopped mid-sentence, apparently interrupted. Her free hand found Jack's, fingers interlacing as if seeking an anchor in the face of whatever was happening. 'Yes, I get it. Of course.' She glanced up at Jack as she listened a moment longer, her expression softening. 'I know, Pop. She would have. I guess I'll see you tomorrow, then. Text me your flight details, OK?' A final pause. 'Love you too. Safe travels.'

Molly ended the call and looked up at Jack, something between amusement and astonishment in her eyes.

'He's getting on a plane here, landing in the morning. Says he's coming to – and I quote – "get the job done once and for all".' She shook her head slightly, wonder replacing the initial shock. 'He's never even left America before. Hates flying. But he says some things are worth facing your fears for.'

Jack's arms tightened around her. 'I like him already.'

Her expression grew thoughtful. 'He and Patrick – do you think they'll . . .?'

'Come to blows?' Jack chuckled. 'Two strong-willed fellas in love with the same woman, meeting for the first time? It'll certainly be interesting, anyway.' He tucked a loose strand of hair behind Molly's ear, his touch lingering against her cheek. 'But since they both adored your grandmother, I'm sure they'll find common ground.'

Molly leaned into his touch, her eyes closing briefly.

The garden settled around the two of them, night sounds creating a gentle backdrop to their quiet conversation.

Tomorrow would bring its own challenges – the meeting of two grandfathers, the final fulfillment of Molly's quest.

But tonight, in this walled garden with its copper lamps and climbing roses, Jack held the future in his arms and found it far brighter than he'd ever dared to dream.

Chapter 43

Molly shielded her eyes against the morning sun, scanning the empty road that led into the square. The airport bus was due any minute, bringing her grandfather to Irish soil for the first time in his seventy-seven years. She shifted her weight from one foot to the other, stomach fluttering with a mixture of excitement and apprehension.

Eddie Harris, former Brooklyn firefighter, stubborn as granite and soft-hearted as fresh bread, was about to meet Patrick Flynn – the man who had carved his initials alongside his late wife's in an oak tree decades before.

Golden Valley looked different this morning. The festival bunting still hung between lampposts, but the frenetic energy of yesterday had subsided. Locals moved at a more measured pace, nodding to each other as they went about their business.

A few curious glances came Molly's way from passing villagers – word of her connection to Patrick had already spread, she suspected, traveling through Golden Valley's intricate social networks with the efficiency that only small communities can manage.

The memory of what else had happened last night unfurled, vivid and immediate.

Jack.

The hotel garden, its old stone walls holding the day's warmth long after dusk had settled. The way the lantern light had caught in his eyes when he'd revealed that he knew the truth – about Aoife, about why Molly was really there, about the burden she carried with her like a secret she'd been holding her breath around.

And the kiss.

Molly closed her eyes and let herself return to it.

He had smelled like the orchard itself – clean and grounded, apples and damp earth, the faintest hint of rain. Not cologne, not anything manufactured. Just Jack, as if the land itself had marked him. That scent had drawn her in before she'd even realized she was moving.

The first touch of his mouth had been tentative, almost questioning, giving her space to step away. Molly hadn't. She'd stepped closer instead, her fingers catching in the fabric of his jacket, the solid warmth of him beneath her hands anchoring her in place. The taste of him had surprised her; sweet with a sharp edge, like cider not yet finished fermenting. When the kiss deepened, when his hand settled at her waist as though it belonged there, the thought had come to her, sudden and terrifying in its clarity.

She wanted it to last forever.

Not just the kiss. The promise of what came next. The quiet certainty of more.

What if she stayed? The thought rose unbidden.

Mornings by the lake instead of crowded subway platforms. Work that smelled of apples and rain rather than burnt coffee and gridlock. Days shaped by walks by the lake, café conversation and music drifting through open doors in the evenings. Jack, steady and rooted, looking at her as if she were something worth choosing.

And Patrick, her grandfather.

Yet New York waited. Her career. The responsibilities she'd

spent years shouldering without question. The life she'd built through discipline and sacrifice.

The distant rumble of an engine drew Molly's attention back to the road. A white coach appeared around the bend, sunlight glinting off its windows as it made its steady approach and her heart rate quickened.

The bus slowed as it approached the village square, hydraulics hissing as it came to a stop beside the stone shelter. The doors swished open, and a few travelers descended – a teenager, an elderly couple clutching a guidebook and finally, a tall figure with military-straight posture despite his years.

Eddie Harris stepped onto the square with the careful deliberation that characterized everything he did. His white hair was neatly trimmed, his blue eyes sharp beneath bushy eyebrows that had retained their original dark color. He wore a pressed button-down shirt beneath his old bomber jacket; and carried a weathered duffel bag that had seen him through decades of weekend fishing trips.

'Pop!' Molly called, emotion thickening her voice as she rushed toward him.

His face broke into a smile that erased years from his features. 'There's my girl,' he said, setting down his bag to engulf her in a bear hug that smelled of Old Spice and coffee. His arms were still strong, a testament to his old firefighting days and now the carpentry work that kept him busy in retirement.

'I can't believe you're actually here,' she gasped, pulling back to study his face. 'How was the flight?'

'Better than I expected, far scarier than I hoped,' Eddie replied with characteristic dry humor. He glanced around, taking in the surrounds with keen assessment. 'So this is it, then. The place she never stopped talking about.'

The bus driver – the same one who had brought Molly to Golden Valley what felt like a lifetime ago – handed Eddie his suitcase from the luggage compartment. 'Welcome to Tipperary, it's not that long a way after all,' he quipped, giving Molly a knowing smile before climbing back aboard.

The doors closed with a pneumatic sigh, and the bus continued its journey, leaving them standing in the quiet square.

Eddie turned slowly in place, absorbing his surroundings with deliberate care. His gaze lingered on the stone buildings, the narrow lanes leading away from the square, the distant hills that embraced the village like protective arms.

'Exactly like she described,' he said softly.

Molly slipped her arm through his, steadying him as much as herself. They walked slowly through the square, Eddie's worn boots falling into rhythm beside Molly's. She pointed out landmarks that had become familiar to her over the past two weeks – the stone fountain where local children still tossed coins for wishes, the church whose bells Aoife had described so accurately that he nodded in recognition before Molly even mentioned it.

'That's Wildflower Books,' she said, gesturing toward the shop with its painted sign and bay window display. 'Maeve, the owner, supplied the song for my video. Her son wrote it about the oak tree.'

Eddie nodded, his attention caught by each detail as if cataloging them against memories of Aoife's stories. 'And there,' he said, pointing to The Orchard Pub before Molly could, 'is where she worked summers. Said the barman back then had hands like hams and a laugh that shook dust from the rafters.'

'You remember everything she told you,' Molly said, surprised by his recall.

Eddie's expression softened. 'Fifty-seven years together, sweetheart. You learn to listen when something matters to someone you love.' He paused, squinting toward the hills where apple trees were visible in neat rows. 'That the orchard, then? Where that guy tends his trees?'

'Goldenridge,' Molly confirmed. 'It's beautiful, Pop.'

They continued their walk, Eddie's pace unhurried as he

absorbed the village that had shaped his wife's early years. As they passed The Cherry Blossom Café, the door swung open, releasing the scent of fresh baking and coffee into the cool morning air.

'Molly!' Eva called, wiping her hands on her apron as she stepped onto the cobblestones. Her curly auburn hair was secured in a messy bun this time, and her cheeks were flushed from the kitchen's heat. 'Is this himself, then?'

Molly made the introductions, watching as Eddie shook Eva's hand with the courteous firmness that was his hallmark.

'Patrick's been at the Glen Arms since dawn, pacing like a man half his age.'

'We're headed there now,' Molly said, her own stomach tightening with renewed anxiety.

Eva reached out, briefly squeezing Molly's arm. 'All will be well,' she said with quiet certainty.

They continued toward the hotel, their pace slowing as it came into view. The Georgian facade gleamed pale gold in the morning light, ivy climbing its walls in intricate patterns. Jack's truck was parked nearby – he'd offered to drive Patrick into the village, understanding the older man's need for support during this momentous meeting.

'Nice joint,' Eddie commented, his voice betraying none of the nervousness Molly knew he must be feeling.

The Glen Arms lobby welcomed them with the scent of beeswax polish and fresh flowers. Anna nodded from behind the reception desk, her usual professional reserve softened by a genuine smile. She'd been among the first to congratulate Molly after the video went viral, her quiet pride in Golden Valley's sudden online fame evident beneath her practical concerns about increased bookings.

'They're in the lounge,' Anna said, gesturing toward a doorway to their right.

Molly thanked her, then turned to Eddie. 'Ready?'

He took a deep breath, adjusting his collar with fingers that betrayed the slightest tremor. 'As I'll ever be.'

Patrick stood immediately as they entered, his posture straight. He wore a deep-green sweater over a collared shirt, his silver hair neatly combed, his walking stick leaning against the chair beside him. Jack rose too, positioning himself slightly behind his great-uncle, a solid presence offering silent support and Molly's heart melted afresh at the sight of them both.

The room crackled with unspoken emotion as Eddie and Patrick faced each other for the first time – two men who had loved the same woman across different continents and decades. They studied each other with careful assessment.

Molly held her breath, aware of Jack watching with equal intensity. This moment could unfold in countless ways – awkward formality, territorial hostility, or worse painful silence. The seconds stretched, tension building until it seemed the room itself might crack under its weight.

Then Eddie stepped forward, hand extended, his blue eyes direct and clear. 'She spoke very fondly of you, buddy,' he said simply.

Patrick's weathered face softened, relief flickering briefly across his features as he wholeheartedly accepted the handshake. His grip was firm, his gaze steady as he measured the man who had shared Aoife Brennan's life in his stead.

'I'm glad to hear it,' he replied, his voice rough with emotion. 'She deserved nothing but happiness.'

'Yes,' Eddie agreed. 'And she found it with both of us in different ways, I guess.'

Something in the simple acknowledgment broke the remaining tension. Patrick gestured toward the chairs arranged near the fireplace. 'Will you join me? I've asked for tea, but if you'd prefer something stronger . . .'

'Tea's fine,' Eddie said, settling into one of the leather chairs with the careful movements of a man aware of aging joints. 'Though I wouldn't turn down a whiskey later, if you're offering.'

Patrick's mouth curved in a slight smile as he lowered himself into his own chair. 'I enjoy a drop or two myself.'

Jack caught Molly's eye, a silent question in his gaze. She nodded, and he moved toward a small table near the window, pulling out chairs for both of them – close enough to be present, far enough to give the older men some privacy.

The hotel staff appeared with a tea tray, setting it on the low table between Patrick and Eddie before discreetly withdrawing. Patrick poured with precision, his hands steady as he passed a cup to Eddie.

The conversation began tentatively – short observations, careful questions, each man offering small pieces of Aoife like gifts to the other. Patrick described her as a young woman, collecting wildflowers and reciting poetry beneath the oak tree. Eddie spoke of her fierce independence in Brooklyn, how she'd worked double shifts at the diner until she could afford night classes at the community college.

'She never lost her accent though,' Eddie said, his own American cadence a stark contrast to Patrick's soft Irish lilt. 'Not entirely. It would come back strong when she was tired or angry or telling those old stories to the grandkids.'

Patrick nodded, his eyes distant with memory. 'She had that lilt in her voice, even as a girl. Could charm the angels with it.'

They fell into a natural rhythm, their initial awkwardness gradually giving way to shared laughter and occasional misty eyes as they recognized pieces of the woman they both loved in each other's memories. The tea grew cool in their cups, forgotten as the two men leaned forward in their chairs, bridging decades of separation through their common love for Aoife.

'She kept this,' Eddie said then, reaching into his jacket pocket to extract a small, worn photograph. He handed it carefully to Patrick. 'Never displayed it, but I'd find her looking at it sometimes.'

Patrick's hands trembled slightly as he took the photo. It showed a much younger version of himself standing beside Aoife beneath the oak tree, both smiling widely at the camera, her dark hair blowing across her face in the breeze.

'I remember that day,' he gasped softly. 'My cousin had just got a new camera, was practicing on anyone who'd stand still long enough.' He traced the edge of the photo with one finger. 'But I never knew she had this.'

From her vantage point nearby, Molly watched the two men with a sense of wonder, tears pricking at her eyes.

Jack's hand found hers beneath the table, his fingers warm and reassuring as they interlaced with her own. She turned to find him watching her, his dark eyes soft with understanding.

'They're finding their way,' he murmured, low enough that only she could hear.

'They are,' she agreed, squeezing his hand gratefully. 'Just like you and me.'

Chapter 44

The following evening, Goldenridge glowed in the fading sunlight, each tree haloed in a golden hue that turned ordinary leaves into fragments of stained glass.

Molly walked beside Jack, his steady presence a welcome comfort as they followed Patrick and Eddie along the narrow path between the rows.

None of them spoke as the four moved deeper into the orchard, their silence a reverence that seemed appropriate. In Molly's jacket pocket, the velvet pouch rested against her heart, a physical reminder of the promise that had brought her across an ocean to this exact moment.

The day had drifted toward evening, the harsh edges of sunlight mellowing into the golden hour that photographers chase and poets attempt to capture in words. It bathed the orchard in a light so rich it seemed tangible – as if Molly could reach out and let it pour through her fingers like honey. The air hung still and cool, carrying the sweet-sharp scent of ripening apples and the earthier notes of autumn soil.

Patrick led their small procession, his walking stick finding secure purchase in the soft ground between apple trees. Eddie followed a few paces behind, his typically stiff posture softened by wonder as he absorbed the surroundings that had shaped his wife's early years. Jack remained close by Molly's side.

The velvet pouch seemed to grow heavier against her chest with each step closer to the oak. Not physical weight, but the gravity of meaning – a final wish, a journey home six decades delayed. Jack's hand found hers, his calloused palm warm against her suddenly cold fingers.

'Alright?' he asked softly.

She nodded, grateful for the simple question and the complex understanding behind it. 'Just thinking about how circular life can be,' she replied. 'Nan left here never expecting to return, and now I've brought her back. Found a grandfather I never knew existed.'

Jack squeezed her hand gently, his thumb tracing a small arc across her skin. 'Found more than that, I hope.'

The warmth in his voice drew her eyes to his face, where she found a question and an affirmation in equal measure. 'Much more,' she confirmed, the words simple but laden with promise.

Ahead of them, Patrick had stopped at a junction in the path, waiting for them to catch up. 'Just through here,' he said, indicating the smaller trail that wound between older trees.

'We should call your brother now,' Eddie said.

Molly took her phone from her pocket, unlocking it with slightly trembling fingers. 'He's waiting.' She handed the phone to Jack. 'Would you set it up? I'm not sure my hands are steady enough right now.'

Jack nodded, navigating to the video call app. Moments later, Cole's face appeared on the screen, her brother's features resolving from digital pixelation into familiar lines. He was in his apartment in New York, the city lights visible through a window behind him.

Jack held the phone at an angle that included Molly in the frame. 'We're almost there,' she said to Cole. 'Just wanted to make sure you're with us.'

His face softened. 'Just wish I could be there in person.'

'You will be,' Jack stated, speaking directly to Molly's brother for the first time. 'I'll make sure of it.'

Cole nodded, his expression shifting as he registered Jack's presence. 'You must be the apple guy,' he said, a hint of protective brother in his tone.

Jack met his gaze without flinching. 'And you must be the hockey player.'

A moment of assessment passed between them, man to man across an ocean, before Cole's face relaxed into a smile. 'Thanks for looking out for my sister,' he said simply.

'My pleasure,' Jack replied, the sincerity in his voice drawing a flush to Molly's cheeks.

They continued along the narrowing path, Jack now holding the phone so Cole could experience the journey alongside them. Patrick and Eddie had fallen into step together, their earlier silence replaced by quiet conversation as Patrick pointed out specific trees or views that held significance.

'Your grandfather's doing well,' Jack murmured to Cole, keeping his voice low enough that the older men wouldn't hear. 'He and Patrick have found common ground quick enough.'

'Pop's good at reading people,' Cole replied, his voice slightly tinny through the speaker. 'Always says you can tell a man's character by how he treats what he values most.'

Molly was pretty certain Jack didn't miss the gentle warning, but his face gave nothing away.

The path curved once more, then opened into the clearing where the ancient oak stood sentinel. Molly's breath caught afresh at the sight of it bathed in the evening light.

The massive trunk glowed like burnished bronze, its deeply furrowed bark catching shadows that emphasized every groove and hollow carved by centuries of growth. Above, the spreading branches created a canopy that filtered the low-angled sun into dappled patterns on the grass below. Leaves rustled in a gentle breeze that seemed to exist only in this one spot, as if the tree generated its own weather, its own atmosphere.

The four of them – five, including Cole's digital presence – approached slowly, instinctively falling into a reverent hush. Patrick paused at the edge of the clearing, emotion visible in the set of his shoulders, the slight tremor in the hand that gripped his walking stick. Eddie moved to stand beside him, their shared history with Aoife transcending the brevity of their own acquaintance.

They formed a small semicircle facing west, positioning themselves where the sunlight streamed directly through the oak's branches. Jack stood slightly behind Molly, holding the phone so Cole remained part of their circle. The significance of their orientation wasn't lost on her – west, where Aoife had traveled to build her new life, now receiving her remains as the day began its own journey into darkness.

Molly's hand trembled slightly as she reached into her pocket for the velvet pouch. The fabric felt warm against her fingers, as if it had absorbed her body heat during their walk or perhaps carried some inherent warmth of its own – the last physical connection to the grandmother who had shaped so much of who she was.

She withdrew it carefully, cradling it in both hands as she turned to face the oak tree.

On the phone screen, Cole's face was solemn, his eyes bright with unshed tears. 'I really wish I was there,' he said again, his voice rougher than before.

'You are,' Molly assured him.

Eddie moved to stand on one side of Molly, Patrick taking position on her other side. Without discussion, each placed a supportive hand on her shoulder – two men who had loved her grandmother in different times and ways, now united in this moment of final farewell.

She took a deep breath, her eyes traveling over the ancient oak that had featured in so many of Aoife's stories. The carved initials were visible on the trunk at eye level – PF + AB within a heart, the letters weathered but still distinct after half a century.

With careful fingers, Molly untied the drawstring that sealed the pouch. Inside, the ashes looked nothing like the vibrant woman they had once been – just a fine, gray powder that contained no hint of Aoife's bright eyes or lilting laugh, her stubborn determination or fierce love for those she claimed as her own. Yet they were her, or what remained of her physical presence in the world. Everything else – her stories, her wisdom, her particular way of seeing beauty in ordinary moments – lived on in those who had loved her.

'Ready?' Eddie asked softly, his hand warm and steady on Molly's shoulder.

She nodded, unable to speak past the thickness in her throat. The moment stretched, suspended in the golden evening light – three generations connected across time and space, gathered to fulfill a promise made in a Brooklyn hospice room as September rain tapped against the window.

Molly raised the pouch, took one final breath to steady herself, and with a gentle, sweeping motion, scattered Aoife's ashes in an arc beneath the oak's spreading branches. The fine gray powder caught the breeze, creating a momentary cloud that seemed to dance in the sunset light. Particles glittered as they drifted, golden specks suspended in air before settling gently onto grass and tree roots, earth and fallen leaves.

For a heartbeat, it seemed as if the pieces hung motionless, caught in a moment outside of time. Then the breeze strengthened slightly, carrying them in a widening spiral that encompassed the entire clearing. Some rose higher, catching on air currents that lifted them into the oak's lower branches. Others drifted toward the carved initials, a few particles settling into the grooves of the heart that Patrick had carved so carefully more than half a century before.

No one spoke. No words seemed adequate for the moment – this final return, this completion of a journey that had begun decades ago when a young woman left her home carrying heartbreak and an unborn child. The only sounds were the rustle of leaves overhead, the distant call of a bird heading to roost, and Cole's barely audible breathing through the phone's speaker.

The light continued to change as they stood in silence, the golden hour across the vale deepening toward the richer amber of approaching sunset. It caught in Patrick's silver hair, and cast long shadows behind them all. Eddie's face was turned upward, a single tear tracked down his weathered cheek, but his expression held peace rather than grief – the bittersweet acceptance of a journey finally completed.

Jack's free hand found Molly's, his fingers gently enfolding hers. On the screen, Cole wiped at his eyes with the back of his hand, the big strong hockey player unafraid to hide his emotion.

'Goodbye, Nan,' he whispered, the words carrying clearly despite the distance.

Molly stood between her two grandfathers – one by blood, another by choice – their hands warm on her shoulders as the last of Aoife Brennan Harris returned to the place where she had first discovered love. The ancient oak seemed to embrace the addition, accepting the ashes as it had countless promises and secrets over centuries.

'She's home,' Patrick said finally, his voice rough with emotion but steady with certainty.

Eddie nodded, squeezing Molly's shoulder gently. 'She is,' he echoed, the words both acknowledgment and release.

The four of them remained beneath the tree as twilight began to gather around them, none wanting to be the first to break the spell.

The orchard settled into evening, shadows lengthening between trees, even the first stars appearing in the deepening blue of the eastern sky. On the western horizon, the sun's final rays painted low clouds in shades of pink and gold.

A fitting farewell, Molly mused, to this day that had brought both Aoife's and her own journey, full circle.

Chapter 45

Later, the Glen Arms restaurant glowed with soft amber light, candles on each table creating islands of warmth in the wood-paneled room.

Molly sat beside Jack at a quiet corner table while Patrick and Eddie sat across, their shared grief completely dissolved into the easy companionship of similar-aged men discovering unexpected common ground.

Outside, darkness had fully claimed Golden Valley, transforming the glass into mirrors that reflected their small gathering.

The table in front of them bore evidence of the community's collective embrace: alongside the hotel's offerings sat contributions that had arrived throughout the day. Eva's apple tart took pride of place, its golden crust draped perfectly above slices of Goldenridge apples, the edges crimped in the way Aoife had pressed into countless crusts in their Brooklyn kitchen.

A wheel of local cheese wrapped in waxed cloth bore a note from the woman whose stand Molly had visited at the market. Maurice from Carved Oak Butchers had insisted on the hotel using his signature oak-smoked bacon for tomorrow's breakfast, 'so the New York fireman can taste proper rashers.'

Brid supervised the supper arrangement herself, adding sprigs of late-blooming heather in small crystal vases on the table, her previous interference giving way to genuine warmth as she'd squeezed Molly's hand before retreating again to the kitchen.

'To Aoife,' Eddie boomed, raising his glass of cider. The amber liquid caught the light as the others lifted their glasses to join the toast.

'She would have been pleased, I think,' Patrick said after a moment, his wizened fingers tracing the rim of his glass. 'The oak looking its best in that light, the breeze carrying her across the golden vale.'

Eddie nodded. 'That woman always had a sense for just the right moment, the right place.' His gaze moved to Molly with evident pride. 'Kinda like our girl here, making sure her wishes were honored, no matter how many stubborn obstacles stood in her way.' He looked pointedly at Jack, whose chuckle broke the solemnity, his shoulder bumping gently against Molly's.

'I've already apologized for that, haven't I?'

'Three times today alone,' she confirmed, warmth spreading through Molly's chest at the easy affection they'd already established.

'Make it four so,' he said, turning slightly to face her. 'I'm sorry for being the most suspicious, stubborn eejit in the country.'

'That fella apologizing? News to me,' Patrick quipped, his eyes twinkling.

'Speaking of news . . .' Jack's expression shone bright as he addressed the table. 'The bank has officially approved our loan.'

Molly's eyebrows rose in delight. 'That's amazing! When did you hear?'

'I got a text Saturday morning,' Jack admitted, his hand finding hers beneath the table. 'Right before I . . .' He hesitated, a flush coloring his neck. 'Right before I jumped to all the wrong conclusions. I was about to tell you the good news, but then I just wouldn't please you.'

Molly smiled at the phrase, a classic she'd heard Eva utter a few times, summing up the almost comical obstinateness that was inherent among Tipp people.

'The full amount and everything?' Patrick pressed, his eyes filled with cautious hope.

Jack nodded, smile widening. 'Every penny. They were delighted with the projections. We can repair the north barn, upgrade the pressing equipment, and still have enough for those new heritage saplings we talked about.' He inclined his head toward Molly and winked. 'Though after this one's viral video, we might need to consider a visitors' center next.'

'It's really made that much of an impact?' Eddie asked, glancing between them.

'Let's just say the village committee, led by Brid, Eva from the café, and the boys from Hearthland of course, are already planning a bronze statue in the square to honor Molly's heartfelt tribute to Golden Valley,' Jack joked, though his eyes conveyed sincere gratitude. 'You really did put us all on the map.'

Molly felt her cheeks warm at the praise. 'I just showed what was already there,' she demurred. 'Everything that makes this place special.'

Patrick patted her hand and looked proudly at his great-nephew. 'Like I always told Jack, sometimes it takes an outsider's eyes to help see the value in what we've always taken for granted.'

The hotel staff appeared with their main courses; venison for Patrick and Jack, salmon for Molly, and traditional Irish stew for Eddie, who had insisted on experiencing 'the real thing, not that watered-down crap they serve in the Irish pubs back home.'

The rich aromas mingled with the scent of fresh bread and Kerrygold, creating a sensory celebration just as satisfying as the gathering.

'Oh man,' Eddie groaned as he tasted his first bite of stew. 'Mols, how can we ever go back to New York food after this?'

'Actually . . .' Grasping at the opening, Molly gathered her courage to raise something she'd been considering for the past few days, but had decided for certain earlier at the oak tree, when everything had suddenly aligned with crystalline clarity. 'I've made a decision,' she said, setting down her fork and straightening slightly in her chair. 'I'm going to take some extended leave from my job.'

Three pairs of eyes fixed on her with varying degrees of surprise. Eddie recovered first, his expression shifting to understanding as he nodded encouragingly.

'I've accumulated months of vacation time anyway,' she continued, her gaze moving between them. 'And can easily sublet my apartment for income. It's just . . . after today . . . well, there are important connections here I'm not quite ready to walk away from.' Her eyes lingered on Patrick, whose lined face had softened with evident emotion. 'I've just found a grandfather I never knew existed. There's history here I've barely even begun to uncover.'

'You're welcome to stay as long as you like, pet,' Patrick said, his voice gruff with feeling. 'The old holiday cottage on the western edge of the orchard has stood empty too long.'

'Oh, I wouldn't dream of . . .' Molly began, but Patrick waved away her response.

'It's yours by right,' he insisted. 'Would have been your mother's someday anyway. Now it can be yours whenever you want it. A home away from home as it were. I'm sure Jack won't mind helping clean it up for you.'

The offer – so casually made but so profound in its implications – momentarily robbed Molly of words.

A home . . . here in Golden Valley.

Jack's hand tightened around hers beneath the table, a silent affirmation.

'And there's *this* guy, of course,' Eddie piped up with the direct pragmatism that had always characterized his approach to life. His blue eyes twinkled as they shifted between his granddaughter and the orchard keeper. 'Don't think any of us have missed those looks you two have been exchanging all day.'

'Pop!' Molly protested, though she couldn't help the smile that tugged at her lips.

'What?' Eddie spread his hands innocently. 'I'm old, sweetheart, not blind. And I've seen that expression before – on your nan's face when she first looked at me across a room.' He turned to Jack, his gaze sharpening slightly in assessment. 'You'll take care of her, buddy.' It was a statement not a question.

Jack met the older man's eyes without hesitation. 'With everything I have,' he promised, the simple words carrying the weight of absolute sincerity.

'Jaysus,' Patrick's soft chuckle broke the moment of intensity. 'Look at us,' he said, gesturing around the table. 'Four strangers a month ago, family now.' He raised his glass again. 'To unexpected blessings.'

'And family,' Eddie amended, lifting his own glass to meet Patrick's.

'And new beginnings,' Jack added, his voice low and meant primarily for Molly.

She raised her glass, meeting each of their gazes in turn – Pops with his lifetime of steady support, Patrick with his newfound place in her heart, Jack with his promise of something wonderful and unexpected.

'To Nan,' she said simply, her voice steady despite the emotion swelling in her chest. 'For making it all possible.'

Through the windows, Golden Valley spread in nighttime splendor; the lake a black mirror reflecting scattered stars, barley fields swaying in gentle rhythms against the evening breeze, the distant silhouette of the oak above the orchard a darker shadow against the night sky.

Molly felt Jack's thumb trace a gentle pattern against her palm, the small gesture communicating more than words could express.

'When will you tell your boss?' he asked quietly, his dark eyes serious in the candlelight.

'I actually called him this afternoon,' Molly admitted. 'He wasn't thrilled, but believe it or not, the Goldenridge video reached them too, so they're viewing it more as a sabbatical to "explore alternate creative approaches".'

Jack's smile was slow and warm. 'And is that what you'll be doing? Exploring alternate approaches?'

'You could call it that,' she replied, holding his gaze with newfound certainty. The past two weeks had transformed her in ways she was only beginning to understand – not just in finding family and roots, but in rediscovering parts of herself that New York's pace and pressure had gradually buried.

'I'm glad,' Jack said simply. 'I really wasn't looking forward to saying goodbye.'

'Neither was I,' she admitted. 'Even before our . . . misunderstanding, I was reluctant to leave Golden Valley.' Her fingers tightened around his. 'Leave you.'

The admission – honest and unconditional – hung between them. Jack's eyes softened, the usual guardedness now completely absent as he looked at her. 'The orchard has always been my anchor,' he said quietly. 'But you've helped me see it doesn't have to be my boundary.'

Brid reappeared at their table then, her silver-streaked hair elegantly coiffed, her manner brisk yet warmly familiar. 'Will ye be having dessert?' she asked, her gaze lingering significantly on their linked hands beneath the table.

'Definitely,' Eddie replied, his appreciation for food undiminished by the day's emotional intensity. 'Some of that apple tart please. And coffee, if you have it.'

'Of course, pet,' Brid assured him with a fondness that made Molly suspect her grandfather had already thoroughly charmed the hotel proprietor during the short time they'd known each other. 'I'll bring it with some custard.'

As Brid departed, Patrick leaned back in his chair, his expression more relaxed than Molly had yet seen it. The lines of his face seemed less pronounced, as if some long-carried tension had finally eased.

'It's mad,' he said, his gaze moving between them. 'I've spent decades wondering what became of Aoife, imagining all the paths her life might have taken.' He nodded toward Molly and Jack. 'I'm only delighted those paths led to good places.'

'Full circle,' Eddie agreed, his face softening as he winked at Molly. 'She'd appreciate that, too. Aoife always did like to finish things properly.'

Epilogue

Molly paused outside The Cherry Blossom Café, her breath forming small clouds in the crisp March air as she studied a poster in the window. *Golden Valley Blossom Festival*, it proclaimed in swirling pink letters above a watercolor illustration of apple trees in full bloom.

She pushed open the door, and the café's familiar interior enveloped her immediately, carrying the mingled scents of cinnamon, coffee and freshly baked goods. The wooden floors creaked beneath her boots as she unwound her scarf, still necessary despite the warming spring temperatures.

Each small detail here had become precious to her over the last six months – the worn leather bench in the corner where Patrick often joined her for a chat, the antique mirror behind the counter that reflected the village square.

But most of all . . .

'Helloooo,' Eva sang from behind the counter, her hands busy with a steaming teapot as she poured for the morning regulars. Her curly hair was piled into its usual messy bun, held together today by what appeared to be a wooden spoon. 'Just in time, I've a fresh batch of those fruit scones you're so fond of.'

'You're a mind reader,' Molly replied, settling onto her usual stool at the counter. The familiarity of the routine – this daily morning treat in town before heading up to the orchard – still struck her with occasional wonder. How quickly the extraordinary could become habit.

Eva placed a steaming mug before her, strong with just a splash of milk, no sugar. 'Sleep well in that drafty cottage of yours? I warned you those west-facing windows needed new seals before you moved in.' Due to all those property shows she watched, Eva was a self-proclaimed renovations expert.

'They're fine,' Molly assured her, wrapping her hands around the warm mug. 'Jack helped me weather-strip them in January.' She smiled at the memory; the two of them working side by side in comfortable silence, gentle rain falling beyond the windows as they sealed out the bitter cold.

Eva winked with a knowing smile. 'Not all he stripped, I'd say.'

'Stop it,' Molly replied, blushing traitorously. 'Besides, the sunset view over the lake is worth a bit of a draft.'

The cottage at the western edge of the orchard had become Molly's passion project throughout the winter months. What began as a temporary stay had gradually transformed into something more permanent; shelves filling up with interesting recommendations from Maeve at the bookshop, the kitchen updated with new countertops that Patrick himself helped install and a front garden area cleared and ready for the native planting and wildflower seeds she'd ordered.

Eva glanced around to ensure other customers were attended to before leaning forward. 'Cranky Jack not with you this morning?'

A flush of warmth that had nothing to do with the tea spread across Molly's cheeks. 'Probably covered in dust and arguing with Patrick about the best way to herd the tourists.' The affection in her voice was impossible to disguise, even had she wanted to.

Before Eva could respond, the café door swung open with authority, admitting Brid Ryan in a gust of cool morning air. The older woman wore her silver-streaked hair in its usual elegant coif, a sunflower yellow coat belted tightly at her waist and her signature all-business expression.

'Morning, all,' she announced briskly to the café at large before zeroing in on Eva. 'I've the final approval from the council for the market layout. We're cleared for twenty stalls this time, and they've granted permission for the bandstand to be set up for three nights instead of two.' Brid settled beside Molly at the counter, nodding a greeting 'The Tidy Towns committee had another meeting about your video. They're projecting triple the usual visitors for the Blossom Festival – all wanting to see the famous oak tree and the good-looking farmer. Mostly the good-looking farmer, I'd say, so better be on your toes,' she added, and Molly wasn't sure whether the warning was intended as a joke or for real. With Brid, you could never tell.

'It's still so surreal,' she admitted. What had begun as such a personal tribute to Jack had transformed into a viral sensation that continued to draw attention to Golden Valley months later. 'I just hope the village is OK with that kind of influx.'

'Oh, we'll manage,' Brid assured her with characteristic confidence. 'Anna's already fully booked at the Glen Arms, and your grandfather's offered to help out with any Yank tour groups if all comes to all.'

The mention of Eddie brought a smile to Molly's face. Her grandfather had returned to Brooklyn immediately after his impromptu visit in October, but the connection he'd formed with Patrick – and with Ireland itself – had drawn him back for a longer upcoming visit next month for the spring festival. And to see her, obviously.

'So we'll need your input on the marketing materials, Molly. And speaking of which—' Brid extracted a folder from her handbag, flipping it open to reveal printed mockups of festival brochures '—the designer sent these over for approval. No better woman to give them a final review.'

Before Molly could examine the materials, the café door opened once more.

Jack stood in the doorway, his tall frame silhouetted against the morning light. His dark hair was disheveled as always, and traces of debris dusted the shoulders of his work jacket – evidence of his morning in the dusty cider barn where he'd been in the thick of the clean-up for some of the brand-new tour offerings. His eyes found Molly immediately, his face breaking into the smile that still made her heart flutter after all these months.

Months of slow, careful building, from tentative trust to outright passion and then something much deeper, had changed them both in ways neither had anticipated.

'There you are,' he said, crossing to the counter. One hand came to rest lightly on her shoulder. 'Morning, Eva. Brid.' He nodded to each in turn.

'Tell us about these new saplings,' Eva prompted, passing him a warm scone. 'Patrick said you ordered enough trees to practically double the orchard size.'

'Not quite,' Jack corrected, pulling up a stool on the other side of Molly. Their knees brushed beneath the counter, a small point of contact that anchored them both. 'But we're expanding the heritage section a fair bit.' Pride shone in his eyes as he detailed their plans, his previous reticence about sharing Goldenridge's business now completely absent. 'We've sourced twenty Kerry Pippin saplings – they're an eighteenth-century variety that's nearly extinct. And fifteen Cavan Russets from a conservation orchard in Donegal. Patrick's over the moon about those; apparently his grandfather had a few trees that died out in the frost of '63.'

'The northwest field is already ready for planting,' Molly added, pulling up photos on her phone to show Eva. 'We spent most of February clearing it. The soil tests came back perfect – just the right mineral balance.'

Jack's hand moved to rest at the small of her back, a gesture both protective and proud. 'The trees will be planted in a spiral pattern that maximizes sunlight exposure while creating natural windbreaks. Nothing like the traditional grid system.'

'Innovation with respect for tradition,' Brid observed with approval. 'Seems to be your trademark combination.'

'Fascinating . . .' Eva drolled, rolling her eyes, but her smile was good-natured. She refilled their mugs as Jack described the spring pruning schedule, his enthusiasm evident in the animated gestures that accompanied his explanation.

Molly watched him with undisguised affection, still occasionally struck by the transformation in the man who had once regarded her, and indeed all outsiders, with such suspicion.

While her leave of absence had initially been for another month, as winter had deepened, so had her roots in Golden Valley. The request to extend her sabbatical to a full year had been met with reluctant approval from her New York bosses, particularly after her viral Goldenridge video had showcased her talents so effectively.

While she missed Pop and Cole, Molly still couldn't quite believe how easily she had become embedded in Irish life, a world apart from her old one. Her relationship with her newly discovered grandfather had also deepened through the winter months, through chatty cups of tea here at the café, evenings spent poring over old photographs at his cottage, walks in the orchard where Patrick shared stories of the land's history, and quiet moments by the fire when words weren't necessary at all.

Jack squeezed Molly's hand again before releasing it, their attention turning back to Brid's festival plans.

As always, the café hummed with morning conversation, the clatter of teacups against saucers providing percussion to the background radio.

At a corner table, a local gestured animatedly, his voice carrying above the general murmur. 'There they are again,' he announced. 'Our lads on the radio.' He nodded toward Molly, approval mingling with outright pride.

Her heartfelt tribute to the orchard had also sparked something else far beyond her intentions when Hearthland's 'Beneath the Oak' had captured imaginations well beyond county borders. The band's success, while certainly earned through years of hard graft, accelerated with startling speed after the reel went viral.

Spotify plays had jumped from mere hundreds, to hundreds of thousands within days of the video's release. Music blogs had featured the band in glowing write-ups, praising their 'authentic trad roots' and 'connection to the land.' Last she'd heard, the lads were recording an album in a Dublin studio, with even talk of a small European tour in the summer.

'They've signed with some fancy London record label now though,' piped up another customer nearby, before adding with some derision. 'Hopefully they won't get too high and mighty.'

Along with everything else, Molly had also become familiar with the classic Irish small-town pastime that was begrudgery.

'Not a chance,' Jack refuted quickly. 'Those lads won't forget their roots.'

'Still though – will they come back for the Blossom Festival now they're proper famous? Can't imagine them wanting to play again in the square when they could be at some big concert venue.'

The question hung in the air, voiced for the first time but clearly on many minds.

'I feel a bit guilty sometimes,' Molly admitted, her voice low enough that only Jack and Brid could hear.

The viral video's success had brought significant attention not just to the band, but to Golden Valley itself. Tourism had increased immediately afterwards, even through the quieter winter months, with visitors making pilgrimages to see the famous oak tree featured in the video.

The Glen Arms Hotel had remained fully booked over Christmas and lots of local businesses welcomed a steady stream of visitors eager to experience the picturesque golden vale they'd glimpsed online.

For the orchard, the impact had been particularly significant. Goldenridge's heritage cider, once sold primarily within the region, was now shipped to specialty shops across Ireland and the UK.

'Course they'll be back,' Eva declared with certainty, wiping her hands on her apron as she rejoined the conversation. 'The lads wouldn't miss the Blossom if they were playing for the Pope himself.' The pride in her voice echoed what Molly had come to recognize as a defining characteristic of Tipperary – this fierce protection of their own, combined with (mostly) genuine pleasure in seeing them succeed. Like another celebrated Golden Valley native, Declan O'Shea – the sports star Eva used to date. The hurler had apparently moved away to the city at the height of his fame, and some of the locals had never forgiven him for it.

Her phone vibrated against the counter then, screen lighting up with an incoming text. Cole's name appeared above a thumbnail image too small to make out clearly.

The image expanded as she opened the message, revealing her brother in his hockey gear, helmet tucked under one arm, his trademark grin slightly lopsided. But what immediately caught Molly's attention was the hospital crutch and plaster cast clearly visible in the frame.

The accompanying text read: Shattered knee. Loooong hiatus incoming. Good timing for Irish jaunt with Pop, maybe? Miss you.

'Everything OK?' Jack asked, noticing her expression shift.

'Cole damaged his knee,' Molly explained, turning the phone so he could see the image.

'Who damaged what?' Eva appeared beside them, teapot forgotten in her hand as her gaze fixed on the phone screen, and her voice brightened noticeably. 'OK now, who is THAT?' Her eyes widened as she leaned closer to better examine the shot of Cole in his hockey gear, dark hair tousled from his helmet, his athletic build obvious despite the bulky equipment.

'My brother,' Molly replied distractedly. 'Cole. Remember I told you he plays ice hockey? When he's not breaking bones, apparently.'

'Poor pet. Will he be alright?'

'Not sure, but he needs to stay off the ice for a while . . .' Molly turned the phone back toward herself, typing a quick response. 'He might come visit, he says. Cole is *not* one for sitting around.'

Eva wiped her hands deliberately on her apron as if preparing for a serious conversation. Her tone aimed for casual interest but landed somewhere much closer to eager anticipation. 'And when might that be? Just thinking about accommodation options . . . since everywhere's so busy, like.'

Jack's shoulders shook with silent laughter that he unsuccessfully attempted to disguise as a cough when Molly shot him a glance. 'Plenty of room at the cottage once we finish the guest bedroom,' he told Eva solemnly. 'So no panic.'

She nodded, then launched into a supposedly casual line of questioning that was hilariously transparent. 'And how long would he be staying, do you think?' she asked Molly. 'Any dietary restrictions I should know about for here? Or a girlfriend . . . who might be allergic to flowers or anything?'

'No idea,' Molly answered blithely, trying not to meet Jack's eye. 'But I'll let you know if he decides to come,' she promised, unable to suppress her smile. 'And introduce you properly when he gets here.'

'Come on,' Jack said then, rescuing her from Eva's inquisition. 'We'd better get going.'

As Molly and Jack stepped outside into the spring morning, his arm slipped around her waist, pulling her close against the March chill. 'Playing matchmaker now – is there no end to your talents?' He harrumphed good-naturedly. 'Just don't ask me to play wingman, if your brother does visit. Sure, I'm no good at all that romantic stuff.'

Then he paused on the street mid-stride and Molly glanced

back surprised when from his coat pocket, Jack drew out a square velvet box – deep green, the color of moss after rain. He looked a little uncertain as he placed the box in her hands, and his fingers lingered for a second before he stepped back to give her space.

'What . . . what's this?' She stared at him bewildered, and he shrugged, his expression shifting into something more thoughtful, almost shy.

'Six months,' he murmured, with a small shrug. 'Felt like it deserved marking somehow.'

Inside the box lay a fine gold chain, delicate but strong, the links catching the pale spring light. Suspended from it was a small charm – an oak tree, intricately detailed, its roots and branches curling in quiet symmetry.

For a moment, Molly couldn't speak.

'Got it made by a jeweler in town,' Jack stammered. 'Thought it . . . was fitting.'

Molly lifted the necklace carefully from the velvet lining. The oak was tiny, but unmistakable. Steady. Enduring.

'The roots . . .' he added, stepping closer again. 'That's the part I liked most. Not just what you see above ground, but what holds everything in place.'

Her throat tightened. She thought of Aoife. Of the promise she'd made to her grandmother without understanding it. Of the day she'd stood beneath the oak, scattering ashes into the wind while Jack stood beside her, silent and steady.

And everything that had grown since.

'It's . . . perfect,' she said, her voice barely above a whisper, tears brimming in her eyes.

Jack reached for it. 'May I?'

She nodded, turning as he fastened the chain at the back of her neck. His fingers brushed her skin, sending a familiar warmth through her. The charm settled just below her collarbone, light but present. She turned back to him, her hand instinctively rising to touch it.

‘I wanted you to have something that belonged here,’ he continued. ‘Like . . . you do now.’

Molly felt the words land deep, anchoring somewhere steady inside her.

Six months ago, she’d stood in this place as a visitor – carrying grief, promises, and a return ticket she didn’t know she wouldn’t use. Now Goldenridge Orchard was as familiar to her as her own reflection. The village knew her name. The lake marked her mornings. And Jack . . .

‘I think,’ she said softly, her fingers still curled around the tiny oak, a lump forming in her throat, ‘this might be the nicest gift I’ve ever received.’

He smiled that slow, sure smile she’d come to love as he leaned down for a kiss, and all Molly could think was – despite what he’d said earlier – Jack Flynn was very good at all that romantic stuff indeed.

Return to Golden Valley with . . .

The Cherry Blossom Cafe

He makes trouble. She makes headlines.
Discover *Only in New York* . . .

'The perfect escapist romance' ***THAT'S LIFE***

Experience the magic of the Big Apple with this irresistible, charming, and funny romance from Melissa Hill.